Praise for StarCrossed Hearts

"Ms. Carter expertly builds the relationships between Jessica, Dane and Mac. Both the story and rich characters keep the pages turning..."
--*Michelle McBride, Ivy Quill Reviews*

"...the complexity of the story makes for an interesting read that will hold audience attention to the end." Four Stars!
--*Donna Bolk, Affaire de Coeur Magazine*

"StarCrossed Hearts begins with a terrific hook and never lets go. The emotions run deep and the tangles of the heart complex with this talented author's pen. Highly recommended."
--*Cindy Penn, Midwest Book Review*

"I found myself so caught up in the romantic triangle and Jessica's mixed feelings for both the men in her life that I couldn't put the book down."
--*Kate Douglas, Award winning author of*
WOLF TALES, ON WINGS OF LOVE and HONEYSUCKLE ROSE

Preview

StarCrossed Hearts

"**Y**ou're sweet."

"Don't pass it around. Teddy says being 'sweet' could ruin my career."

"You can be sweet and still be...erotic." The green eyes were coaxing, challenging; then they looked away. Dane paused, gathering his thoughts. "Look, Jessica...if you and I are going to have...a relationship, there's something you should know. I'm not at least anymore, I've discovered—a good risk. I'm not a particularly reliable person. I can't seem to make or keep promises like I should." He checked her reaction before continuing. "I'm my own person, Jessie. I've hurt too many people, including myself, so all bets are off on what I'll do next. Major disclaimer, take it or leave it."

His eyes were back with hers, delving, seeking her compliance. "You understand what I'm saying, right? I could really, really piss you off."

Jessica's eyes were wide with open amazement. No man had ever spoken this frankly to her before. No presumptions, no surprises. And no commitments. But he *was* offering her *something*. Something she wanted.

She nodded in silent understanding. She didn't care about getting hurt, or unkept promises, and even if she did, right now she would gladly forsake all for even one kiss.

Dane sighed. Uncomfortable on the coffee table, he moved to sit next to Jessica on the sectional. He ran his fingers through his hair, something, she noticed, he did unconsciously when he felt stressed.

"This divorce is killing me. I keep asking myself, is what I've done so wrong?" He leaned forward, looking down at the floor. He was such a picture of despair Jessica couldn't help but delicately place her hand on his shoulder in sympathy.

Dane turned slightly and stared at her for a long moment. A sublime moment. An overwhelming, heated madness spread throughout her, born of her simple contact with his body. Dane exuded maleness like no man she'd encountered, filling her at once with both desire and trepidation. Jessica sat captured by his gaze, the emerald eyes stripping away layer after layer of her carefully built defenses...seeking her vulnerabilities, her sensitivities.

Slowly he turned and took both of her hands in his, pulling them around his neck, then slid his hands down her arms and around her in one smooth movement. She barely had time to moisten her lips before his were on her, exploring her cheek, her ear, her neck, her mouth...but slow. Slow, and hot, and sensual.

Any shyness she had anticipated on her own part evaporated and she returned each kiss with fervor. Abruptly, he stopped and again stared into her face.

"You really want this, right?"

Star Crossed Hearts

A CONTEMPORARY ROMANCE

ANNE CARTER

BEACON STREET BOOKS

StarCrossed Hearts

By Anne Carter

Copyright © 2001-2022 by Pamela Ripling

Edited by J. R. Turner

Cover Art by Tell Tale Book Covers

ISBN 978-0615536590

Previously Published ISBN 1-59088-999-1

February, 2022

Beacon Street Books

Santa Clarita, CA 91355-2026

http://www.beaconstreetbooks.com

Published In the United States Of America

To my sister Tina
for sticking by this project,
for the tireless readings and collaboration,
and for believing that
Reel Heroes do exist;

to my husband Michael
for being a real hero
and making this all possible;

and to the late Lorraine Stephens,
for believing in me
and for giving my heroes life.
I miss you, LOLly.

ONE

The Dali Capitan

"*And what have we here?*" the pirate asked. He walked slowly around the two young wenches brought to his cabin by the first mate, appraising them as they stood trembling in wide-eyed terror.

"A bit o' female cargo from the St. Vincent, Cap'n. What shall we do with 'em?"

"I'll decide their fate when I'm ready."

The evaluation continued as the buccaneer came close to the first woman, an aristocratic young woman with an expensive gown and dainty slippers.

"And what might be your name, miss?" The pirate's sinister tone belied his polite words. Handsome and virile, the rogue captain towered over her in both size and presence.

"I am Marlena D'Medici," she said bravely, as if the sea dog should recognize her name. "And you are the 'dread' pirate, Simon the Dancer. I have heard the good people of the Barbary Coast call you the Dali Capitan."

"The Devil Captain! Yes. You are well informed, my lovely."

"We were bound for Portugal. How, now, are we to arrive there?"

The pirate chuckled.

"Arrive indeed," he murmured, taking the liberty of caressing the woman's powdered cheek. "And this sweet package, what name be hers?" He moved to peer into the eyes of the second woman, who turned her face away in trepidation and disgust.

"Ah! She is feisty, this little one." He grasped the servant's chin and forced her to look at him. For a moment, his gaze softened in what might have been sympathy for the girl, so recently torn from the St. Vincent and her would-be protectors.

"She is my handmaiden, Lucida. Sir, I must insist—"

"You must insist what!?" Like emerald fire, the pirate's green eyes flashed at her words. Any sentiment dissolved as quickly as it had appeared.

"I do not understand your intentions. This ship is not even underway, the waters are so calm. Will we drift for an eternity?" the Medici woman asked, finding strength in words but not in spirit.

"*Little faith have ye in the winds of Hades, dear lady.*" The pirate peered out the porthole at the sea, a mirror of jade ice. "*Why, the fetid breath of Satan himself moves this vessel through these waters*...Fetid breath? What the *hell* is that?"

"Cut! Dane, what's the problem now?" The Assistant Director slammed his script to the floor.

"I want this *fixed*. What's with this 'fetid breath' crap? Who authorized this carnage?"

The cast began to move around uneasily as the tall, rugged Dane Pierce, leading man and executive producer of *Bellerive*, stormed past them and off the set. His third such outburst of the morning on a film that was already behind schedule.

Jessica had been waiting since yesterday to utter her first and only line in the film. And they'd almost reached it! As Lucida, the young lady-in-waiting to the main character, the hopeful starlet would soon be finished with the role and off-camera; but today she'd had enough of the pompous, arrogant Dane Pierce.

Merrily Mitchell, the leading lady, swept past Jessica, her taffeta gown rustling with her brisk pace. "I've gotta have a smoke. Wanna come?"

"I don't smoke, but I wouldn't mind a break from this circus." Jessica hurried to match Merrily's stride as the two headed for the soundstage door.

Soon they stood in the bright sunlight outside Studio B, where all the interior scenes of *Bellerive* were shot on an elaborate soundstage built to recreate the interior of a three-masted pirate schooner. Merrily lit her cigarette and leaned against the stucco wall.

"Dane's got a hair up his ass about something. I wish he'd just get off it." Merrily looked into the distance across the studio lot.

"I don't really know him," Jessica murmured.

"Maybe you don't want to. He's a killer. God, I could just about fall into those deep green eyes of his! A killer."

"I don't know. He's no Errol Flynn," Jessica replied candidly. "He seems pretty full of himself."

Merrily squinted at Jessica with a bemused smile.

"Don't ever let *him* hear you say that," she advised. "Oops—too late."

Dane sauntered from the open doorway and joined them. He perused Merrily's face quickly before turning to gaze upon Jessica, who looked away.

"We're not on camera, *little one*," he said, sarcasm coloring his words and Jessica's face. "So, you think I've been miscast? Possibly?"

"I wouldn't know," Jessica replied, taking care to give him a wide berth as she went back inside.

Dane shook his head.

"This is turning out to be one shitty day." He stared after Jessica, a frown creasing his already tense face.

"Wanna smoke?" Merrily offered, holding out her pack.

"Naw. I'm off 'em right now. Let me ask you something. Who the hell is that girl?"

"She's my handmaiden, of course," Merrily replied dryly.

"No, I mean, who *is* she? She been around?"

"She's a rookie. Her name is Jess Taylor. Jessica. Why?"

"She's...cold."

"You mean, she hasn't thrown her panties at you yet." Merrily tossed her cigarette to the ground and snuffed it out, unmindful of the satin on her slipper. "I'm sure she'll come around."

Dane broke into a grin and followed Merrily back inside.

The afternoon didn't improve, with more than the usual interruptions plaguing the production. Jessica did finally utter her one line and gratefully leave the stage. And while weary of the sluggish progress of the day, she decided to hang around until the crew called it quits. She sat on the floor amid empty boxes and discarded props in an adjacent storage area, her script open in her lap and an apple poised in her hand. In the adjoining sound stage, she could hear a commotion and realized that filming had once again hit a snag.

Alert, she tensed as footsteps approached, a thunderous echo preceding them. Angry footsteps, accompanied by equally angry mutterings of foul words, cursing some unknown devil. She froze where she sat, hoping to remain unseen to this oncoming presence.

Jessica held her breath as Dane Pierce stormed past her and out the side door, the auto-closer slamming it behind him. She relaxed with a sigh and had no sooner looked back down at the script than the raging star reappeared in the doorway, looking around in frustration for something to punch. His fist eventually met with a pile of Styrofoam boulders, the toppling of which forced a small cry from Jessica's lips. His eyes immediately searched for the source of the sound and found Jessica hastily getting to her feet, dropping her script from the tangled folds of her floor-length costume. She knelt to retrieve the script; he knelt also and reached it first with an implied apology.

"I didn't know anyone was here," he muttered, handing her the now-curling, bradded manuscript. He put his anger on hold as he waited expectantly for her response.

"Obviously." Jessica clenched the uneaten apple behind her back and hoped her annoyance was clear. "You're not having a very good day, are you?" Not sounding nearly as sarcastic as she'd intended, Jessica forced a bold smile and peered into the actor's face. "What's wrong now?"

He turned toward the closed door. "Everything. Nothing." He paused, then looked at her again.

Jessica wished for an end to the awkwardness. "Is there something I can do... to help?" Her offer was half-hearted and sounded it. Anticipatory, she gathered her belongings for a hasty escape to her car.

"I just wanted to get out of here for a while...you know, sometimes you just need to get away from a problem to see the upside of it...but I remembered when I got out here that I have no wheels." He pushed open the heavy door and scanned the parking lot. Jessica waited while he ran his fingers through his ashen hair, combed back and grown long for his role as the pirate captain of the *Bellerive*. He leaned against the doorframe and sighed in apparent despair.

Jessica found herself staring; the breeze coming through the door rippled the voluminous sleeves of his pirate shirt. She shook her head briefly.

"If...If you need a lift somewhere, I was just leaving." *Not that I want to spend any measurable amount of time with you.* She cleared her throat and waited. He looked back at her, the lowered green eyes intense, as though memorizing her face for a later review. A slow smile spread across his famous lips, and Jessica could see "up close and personal" what made this man a top box office draw among women around the world. Other women, of course.

Oh God, he's not really going to take me up on it? Heat filled her cheeks and she hoped it wasn't too obvious.

"Yeah, if you don't mind, there *is* someplace I'd like to go, Miss—?" He held out his hand. Reluctantly, she completed the handshake.

"Jessica. Jessica Taylor."

"Jessica." His enunciation made her name sound special, as though he'd bestowed some great, coveted award, and yet she resented the feeling. She wouldn't fall prey to his manipulation and forced herself to move toward the door. Her rough cotton gown felt leaden as she encountered the June sun.

Jessica led Dane to her car, parked beneath the "KEEP CLEAR" sign alongside the building. "I like your parking place," he told her, "and I love your car."

"It's okay." After she started the bright blue two-seater, she casually unlatched and threw back the "ragtop" convertible while the engine warmed. "Do you mind?" She gestured to the open top on the sports car.

"Absolutely not," he responded, adjusting the small bucket seat to accommodate his long legs. "Miata?"

Her confidence building, Jessica turned the car around and headed up the hill from Studio B. "Mazda Miata. Yeah."

Dane directed her to a picnic area on one of the hilly back lots. They got out and viewed the studios from above. "Not in a hurry, are you?" he asked, sitting down on the grass beneath one of the studio's two-hundred-year-old oak trees.

"No, nothing much is happening back there anyway," she quipped, watching for his reaction to her sarcasm. He rewarded her with a friendly chuckle.

The breeze was warm but comfortable, the sun expending its late afternoon rays before it would dip into the horizon of the Pacific. Jessica felt conspicuous and began re-tying the laces on the bodice of her costume as he watched; she hated the shapeless dress and the fact that her light brown hair, which normally fell in soft curls to her mid-back, was a matted mess from the ride with the top down. At least she was still made up from this morning's shoot, and the artist had highlighted her features to bring out the gold flecks in her brown eyes. Soft color accented her slightly high cheekbones. Her lips had been made to look a little fuller and peach colored. So much trouble for such a brief scene, but others had remarked that Pierce was a perfectionist; every detail had to be just right. Perfectionism *and* egotism; a great combination!

She absently brushed aside her few, thinly layered bangs.

"Too bad about the haze. The view is usually better. You from around here?" he questioned.

"I was born and raised in that valley."

"Yeah? So was I. Thought you looked like a 'Valley Girl.'" Pierce offered her a grin.

"I didn't know there was a look to it."

"You don't like me, do you?" he asked, still smiling, more to himself than to Jessica.

Momentarily stunned by the bluntness of his question, Jessica looked at her hands. "What makes you think that?"

Dane threw back his head and laughed. "Would it help if I admit up front that I'm a conceited hunk of bull crap who's so full of himself that most *real* people can't stand me, and millions of fans have been duped into thinking I can act?"

Jessica looked at him now, his eyes capturing her stare and holding it. She saw no conceit, no egotism, no real immodesty. She swallowed her embarrassment. "I'm sorry if you got the wrong impression."

Pierce chuckled at her discomfort. "Forget it. You just don't know me yet."

Maybe you don't want to know him. Why had Merrily said that?

"So, what do you think of the film?" he asked suddenly.

She turned to face him, relieved at the simple question. "It's magnificent," she said simply. "It's sure to be a smash. I can only guess at how the filming is going, but I've read the script over several times, the cast is terrific...I just love Merrily as the pirate's lady, and..." she paused, mortified by her childish enthusiasm.

"Don't stop!" He motioned for her to continue. When she didn't, he did. "You know, the only thing wrong with my being so involved with the film is that I can never get a fresh outlook on it. I have to just stick to my original, first impression, and not get too balled up in the analysis of it all." He looked to the distance again, his fingers randomly pulling at blades of grass and tossing them down.

Jessica sat across from him, wrapping her arms around her knees and tucking her feet under the long gown. With his eyes diverted, she was able to gaze freely upon him. She guessed him to be in his mid-thirties. The breeze lifted his hair and he repeatedly pushed it back from hanging over his ever-changing eyes. His face was thin but not drawn, with a prominent nose and lips that some women would term "promising;" a whimsical smile seemed almost permanent. Overshadowing the look, however, there remained an aura of self-importance.

Despite her negative assessment, his remark about the film impressed her. "I can't even imagine what it must be like for you," she offered softly. Dane broke from his faraway gaze and looked back to her, the ready smile crinkling his eyes.

"So tell me, Jessica Taylor, are you going to be a big star someday?"

"Perhaps."

"What would you like to do?"

"Like what? You mean, what roles would I play if given a choice?"

"Yeah."

"Never thought about it," she said coyly, her eyes down.

"Bullshit," he drawled, narrowing his.

Jessica chuckled involuntarily. On the set, she'd been rather awed by this larger-than-life hero, but here on the shady hillside she began to see him as just a guy, human and casual like everyone else.

"I guess I sometimes imagine myself in a remake of *From Here to Eternity.* I would love to have been in *Gone With the Wind.*"

"Scarlett O'Hara?"

"Of course."

"Good for you. And your leading man?"

"Dangerous question, my dali capitan," she replied, "but of course you are the public's choice for today's Rhett Butler."

"But not yours."

Jessica shrugged with a small smile. "There are a number of leading men in my wish book. I would invite you to compete."

"Your generosity is touching." Dane leaned back against the oak, a blade of grass held loosely in his teeth. After a moment of regarding her, he continued. "So, you like the old movies. What's your background? What else have you done?"

"My favorite question." Jessica rolled her eyes. "Nothing. A few plays...a couple of walk-ons...I think I'm a *career extra.*"

"Commercials?"

"No. I hate them."

He laughed. "Good. Don't ever do them. How did you get into *Bellerive*?"

"Fate. My friend, Jackie, was signed, but she broke her leg last weekend and... here I am." He didn't need to know her agent had performed some quick footwork. "It's not like I had a lot of lines to learn, you know, and I would have given almost anything to be in it anyway."

Damn, why is he listening so close just when I'm rambling on? He's too nosy.

"You have an agent?"

"Well, sort of...he's a friend; he's new in the business."

"I see." Dane's gaze lingered on her for several more moments, then he looked at his watch. "Well, I think the boss must be on his way back." He stood and brushed the grass from his trousers.

Relieved, Jessica stood also.

Dane walked around the little car with appraising eyes. "Four cylinder?"

"Yeah, but it's got plenty of power."

"I could tell by the way you tore up this hill. Get many tickets?"

"A few," she lied. She'd never even been stopped. "And what do you drive?"

"Right now, a Porsche 911 Targa. It's in the shop. I just bought a monster SUV for Rita, my wife, and I have a Mercedes 9...million or something. I love cars, although I'm afraid I don't spend much time taking care of mine. Would you mind?" He opened the driver's door.

Jessica hesitated, then handed him the keys to the Miata. "It's nothing like a 911."

"We'll see about that." Gingerly he threaded his legs under the steering wheel, and again adjusted the seat. "You must be a midget."

"Five-four, thank you," she replied, fastening her seat belt and wondering if her insurance was paid up as Dane raced the little car around the grassy hillside, war-whooping as they went.

Back at Studio B, Jessica moved into the driver's seat as her companion shook out his legs. "Great car just needs to be a foot longer," he complained, and turned toward the door.

Jessica started the car but paused. "Mr. Pierce? Whatever was bothering you before, did it go away?" She allowed herself one flirtatious smile.

"The only thing bothering me right now is your calling me *Mr.* Pierce.*" He tugged on a lock of her hair. "See you around, Miz Scahlett."

The following day, Jessica received a package of papers from Pierce Productions. She ripped it open in anticipation and found it to be the forms and agreement substituting her into Jackie's role. As always, there was the requisite employment application, union forms, waivers and limits of liability. Hastily she sat down to complete them, because she had no hope of getting paid until they were returned.

Jessica Lynne Taylor; 28; Divorced.

Four years, was it? She looked down, twisting the wedding ring now worn on her right hand. She wondered what Wesley would think of her finally getting a speaking part; so what if it was a one-liner?

"References" was the easy part. Roxanne Boudreau had been her confidante and partner-in-crime for more than half their lives, and although she already held an MBA degree, Roxanne's biggest ambition was to design women's formal attire. She heartily supported Jessica's efforts to become a successful actress and had already created several lovely gowns for her.

Putting down her pen, Jessica picked up her open copy of *Variety*, reached for the phone and dialed.

"Hey, Rox. There's an open audition on Friday. Want to come?"

"You know I have to work. The boss has already warned us about taking off too much time. The rainy season is our busiest period. People wreck their cars, they call us." Roxanne laughed. "Insurance is so glamorous! But thanks for asking."

"You could have a part in a minute. I keep telling you—"

"You keep telling me, but I'm not into acting. I'm gutless, Jess. I'd fall apart."

"You are so beautiful; all you'd have to do is stand there."

"Yeah. Me 'n Angelina. Good luck, though. I hope you get it. Call me?"

She had only read for television once before. A depressing experience, she remembered, a cattle call for young heifers like herself hoping to get a break as somebody's next door neighbor's girlfriend on a mindless sit-com. It was such a downer she had shied away from TV until Teddy, her agent, had pleaded with her to try just once more.

The show was as yet untitled but tentatively called *Countdown*, a sci-fi episodic already in production for a September premiere. She wasn't sure of the role, only that she should look space-age, whatever that meant.

Friday morning found Jessica up at dawn, painstakingly twisting her hair into Princess Leia braids and winding them into mounds over her ears. She grimaced at her reflection but stuck a couple of extra hairpins in before cementing the whole creation with hair lacquer.

Castle Studios was in Burbank, not far from NBC. She parked in the lot and got out, taking a moment to straighten the white, rectangular tunic she wore over black leggings and boots. A wide, black, elastic belt finished what she hoped would seem a "futuristic" look.

Once inside, she was surprised to find an empty waiting room. A woman sat behind a reception counter, and she looked up with a warm, if amused, smile. The clock on the wall behind her chimed nine-thirty; maybe she was just early for the ten o'clock call.

"I'm here for the audition," Jessica said softly.

"I'm sorry?"

"Audition?" she repeated, her voice cracking. Jessica attempted to clear her throat, now feeling horribly awkward.

"Well, let's see..."

The woman looked confused and began rummaging through the papers on her desk. A door opening from a side office interrupted her search, and a man strode briskly into the area behind the receptionist, pausing to retrieve a small stack of messages from the corner of the counter. Quickly he perused them, crumpling some and pocketing others. He raised his eyes, briefly meeting Jessica's before turning his attention back to the pink slips.

"Mac, this young lady says we have an open audition for today. You know anything about it?" the receptionist asked, still pawing through her desk.

The man again looked at Jessica, this time taking in the braids, the unusual attire and her growing discomfort. He walked around the counter and into the waiting area to meet her.

"We do have a couple of women coming in to read for a part this afternoon, but...something tells me that's not the role you came in here looking for."

Jessica felt herself blush; she looked up at the tall stranger who so graciously tried not to laugh.

"Is it the braids? I can lose the braids really fast." Quickly her fingers found and began pulling out the hairpins on one side, dropping the braid to her shoulder where she then unbound and shook it free.

Now the man called Mac did laugh.

"No, no, it's not that at all." Self-conscious, he ran his fingers through his own summer-streaked hair, which was cut collar-length and layered in the back. "The role we're filling is for a more...mature lady."

"I can do mature. I've done forty, forty-five..." Jessica said hastily, still trying to unravel the braid.

Mac shook his head, still chuckling.

"Seventy. Can you 'do' seventy?"

"Oh." Despite her disappointment, Jessica took only a moment to compose herself before smiling shyly. "I guess there was some kind of mix up. I apologize for taking your time."

"No problem at all. I wish we *could* use you." His smile was genuine, as was the sincerity in his brown eyes.

"Well, thanks." Jessica took her time putting away the hairpins, shifting her portfolio and handbag in her grasp, wondering what to do next. Behind her, she could hear him comment to the receptionist.

"I've just gotta get cleaned up and grab a bite in case anyone's looking for me. Be back in about an hour."

He followed only a few yards behind Jessica as she got into her car and snatched the scrap of paper from the console of the Miata.

"Castle. It says Castle! Damn!"

The top was down, and the sudden shadow crossing her lap startled her.

"Can I help you somehow?"

He looked even taller standing beside her miniature car. Perhaps sensing the distance, he squatted down beside her door and grasped the top of it with his hands.

"Oh, I just...is there another Castle, by any chance?" She looked back at the note in her hand, and he leaned closer to read it also.

"That says Castle Productions. This is Castle Studios...wait. I'll bet that's Cassel - C-A-S-S-E-L, Richard Cassel Productions, and they're over on Alameda. They do space flicks, Star Trek type stuff."

Could this get any *worse?* Jessica thought fleetingly. She couldn't think of what to say, so complete was her embarrassment.

Mac looked at his watch. "If it's at ten, you can still make it. It's just left at the corner, down a block and over on the right."

She looked at him now in gratitude. He wore a dark blue T-shirt and jeans, and was covered with dust, she noticed. Yet the fingers grasping the black vinyl of her door were slender and well-manicured, and for a moment she found it hard to tear her eyes away.

"Sorry for the dirt," he said. "I've been out there since 7 a.m. mending fences and chasing sheep."

Jessica nodded, still tongue-tied. She pushed her key into the ignition and smiled.

"You should have your agent send over your stills. Maybe we could use you someday," he said, standing up and backing away.

"Thanks," Jessica finally managed before fleeing the parking lot, tires squealing.

"It was, undoubtedly, the most mortifying thing that has ever happened to me!" Jessica spun around in her bedroom, falling back onto the bed with the phone still against her ear. "How could you do that to me?" Her tone was more comical than accusing as she lambasted her agent that afternoon.

"Jessie, pumpkin, I'm sorry! I *said* Cassel. You wrote C-A-S-T-L-E. What can I say? Sheesh. But you think you have a chance?"

"Oh Teddy, it was so weird. They loved my hair half-done, and there were girls there with silver spiked hair, girls with no hair, girls who were really boys..."

"Oooh, why didn't you call me?"

"Teddy...How can I get you dates when I can't even get me dates?" Jessica laughed. "Anyway, I made the first cut. We'll see. They want me back next Friday. But God I was embarrassed at Castle. The guy there was soooo cute, too. Figures."

"Castle makes *Doctor Jim*. It wasn't Cory MacKendall you met, by any chance?"

"Cory? No, that wasn't his name. It was...Bud, or, Rex, or something like that. Jack? Anyway, he was so nice to me. I think he might be a grip, or something. He mentioned something about working on fences or tending sheep, could that be? What's *Doctor Jim*?"

"Only NBC's number three show. Don't you *ever* watch the tube?"

"Not if I can help it."

"It's about a country doctor who solves crimes. Kind of a *Murder She Wrote* meets *James Herriot*, on Friday nights. You'd like it. The guy's a real stud muffin."

"James who? I quit watching TV when they cancelled *F.R.I.E.N.D.S.*"

One week to the day later, the production crew of *Bellerive* began some of the miscellaneous outdoor scenes on an empty, grassy back lot, where a small forest had been constructed overnight to represent the entrance to a pirate's lair. Except for the half day she'd taken for the audition, Jessica had not missed a minute of filming and tried to find ways she could melt into the many clutches of professionals allowed on the set. This day found her quietly tagging along in jeans and T-shirt, her hair haphazardly tied at the top of her head in ribbons and a pair of sunglasses perched on her nose. She carried a clipboard and a script and tried to look like she belonged, her expired set pass dangling from her neck.

Today's segment was especially exciting, although she knew she wouldn't be seeing Dane Pierce perform. Certainly, his stunt double was highly visible as the scene involved a great deal of skilled horsemanship. She wished she had brought a small set of binoculars so she could get a better view of the action.

At around noon, a grip tapped her on the shoulder. Startled, she turned quickly, and the glasses flew from her face. The crew member picked them up. "You Jessica Taylor?"

Now I'm busted for sure. She'd heard about the tight security on this, a "closed" set.

"Yes." She couldn't very well lie at this point. In the distance she could see the blue Miata and she wished she'd parked closer. How humiliating to be kicked off the set.

"Boss wants to see you," the man said, handing her the glasses.

"The boss? Mr. Pierce?" Oh God, she thought, this is worse than I thought. "Where do I find him?"

"That trailer over there." He pointed to a large motor home parked several yards away.

Jessica straightened up, put the glasses in her purse and walked purposefully toward the trailer. She tapped lightly on the door and entered at his acknowledgment.

"You wanted to see me?"

He sat at a small desk, studying set designs and scratching changes on them with a pencil. Looking up, he focused on her through gold rimmed glasses, then removed them and smiled. "Why Miz Scahlett...how nice of you to drop by."

There was no hiding her blush this time, and the relief that he wasn't angry was so great she let out a sigh that almost turned into a giggle.

"You know, I make it a point not to eat during the first half of the filming. My angst is just too great eating makes me sick. I know things are winding down when I begin to get hungry. And this morning, tearing around out there on that damned horse, I saw a vision—a vision of this little blue car away in the distance—and I took that vision to be my meal ticket to lunch."

She stared at him in surprise and confusion. "Are you asking...to borrow my car?" This man's ego never quit. *How dare he?*

At this, he roared, his laughter filling the small trailer. "I'm asking you to lunch, lady." Dane grinned at her, a warm, personal smile that caused her to tremble slightly inside. Hiding her embarrassment, she feigned a boldness she didn't feel.

"I thought you'd never ask."

They drove to a nearby cafe in the Valley where Dane lately dined unnoticed. They entered through the kitchen.

"I have to change haunts every few days. People find out. God, I hate losing my privacy."

"I have to ask you—what did you mean earlier about the horse?"

"On this morning's shoot. Didn't you see me?" He leaned forward in mock chagrin.

"That was *you*?" she asked, clearly astonished.

"I love horses. I ride better than my double, anyway." There remained no trace of pomposity in his voice, only conviction. Jessica was once again taken by surprise.

They talked at length about the film, his satisfactions and disappointments, and ultimately, plans for his next film. "It's called *Lost Season*, about two aristocrats shipwrecked in the early 1800's on a desert island. I know, I know...it's been done, but not by me."

"You'll star, of course," she responded.

"Yes. I'm seeking the rest of the cast right now."

"Don't you have casting people?" she wondered aloud.

"Yes—but with certain roles, I need to be involved in the decision." His words revealed his perfectionism. "I have to have the right sense about my leads —even supporting cast members are extremely, critically important," he said levelly. She nodded, wondering if she dared to ask a question lurking in her mind for some time.

"Dane," she began, the formation of his first name on her tongue tickling her somehow, "I've heard you often work with unknowns. Women, that is...they say you hate being upstaged. How can any woman upstage someone of your talent, your popularity..."

"Talent? Moi?" His eyes reflected his whimsical smile. "*They* say that, do they? Hmmm..." Then, more seriously, "I usually have nothing to say about it. But when I do, I just look for the *best* person for each role. I do try to find people who aren't spoiled by previous roles, haven't been stereotyped, you know. People I can work with. Shit—what was it W.C. Fields used to say, 'never work with animals or babies'? I've done both." Now he laughed. "Actually, it doesn't take much to upstage me."

"I find *that* rather hard to believe," Jessica said, wondering if there might be a humble bone or two in his body. She also wondered if she'd missed her chance to get an audition.

At day's end, Jessica drove to the modest yellow clapboard house she rented, not far from the studios. It was an odd, custom-built flat on a hilly residential street. Pulling the Miata into the garage, she wished she could afford to buy the house, for although it was small, she had come to love its coziness and charm. Entering through a door from the garage, she stepped into the small, apartment-style kitchen. A brief dinette area, living room, two bedrooms and baths completed the home. French doors from the master bedroom led down a wooded path to a large pool and Jacuzzi, shared by two adjacent homes on the hillside. An unusual arrangement, she had thought originally, but efficient and convenient. Especially attractive was the view from a small balcony, accessed through sliding doors off the kitchen's dining area.

She checked her voicemail before going to her room but found no new messages. Lying back on her bed, Jessica stared at the white ceiling and replayed her incredible lunch with Dane Pierce. Every word was repeated, each gesture and movement relived in her mind. She giggled like a child, her arms wrapped tightly around her waist. "I can't believe it!" she whispered.

Her smile faded as she reminded herself of whom she was thinking. Despite his apparent charm, charisma, and the magnetism he exuded, Dane Pierce was still the sexist womanizer she'd always believed him to be. Her fangirl mentality was silly. The watchman in her heart flashed the yellow light: proceed with caution.

Jessica began to see her cellphone in a new light: either no one called, or the wrong people called. There was no word yet on *Countdown*, not a good sign. The bank would be calling because her car payment was late. She reluctantly considered going back to Costello Insurance to work with Roxanne.

She hated giving up, having promised herself a year, but it didn't look like her finances would hold out that long. The money she had scrimped and saved the last two years, living and working with Roxanne, was nearly gone. She knew it was her own fault, she shouldn't have rented the house *and* bought the car.

But today the "new message" icon appeared, and Jessica tapped. She listened sullenly to Teddy's sing-songy baby talk telling her they had been paid for *Bellerive*. Well, at least she could keep the bank at bay for another month or two. The message went on to say that he might have a commercial lined up for her if Richard Cassel didn't come through. She wrinkled her nose.

Jessica's thoughts were interrupted by the doorbell. She was suspicious, not expecting anyone, and solicitors were uncommon in the hilly neighborhood.

"Yes? Who is it?"

"A courier, miss. I've a package for you." A man's voice, colored with a decidedly British slant, called to her from behind the locked door. Peeking through the viewer, she saw he indeed carried a large envelope, and opened the door.

Jessica was taken by the man's striking features. He was not particularly tall, his brown hair nearly gone on top but long on the sides and back, tied into a neat ponytail. Clear blue eyes that smacked of sincerity and interest peered at her from over small, oval glasses, and he handed her a perfect red rose bud and the envelope. Speechless at first, she finally found her voice.

"Is there a card or letter?"

"'magine so, miss, in the envelope. He's not much on writing these days, but I'm sure he's wrote something, as I'm supposed to wait for a reply."

"Oh, then...come in, please." Although uneasy at admitting a stranger, she somehow trusted this Englishman and asked him to sit down while she opened the package.

The script surprised her, the words *Lost Season* printed across its cover. Immediately her heart began to pound. A *Pierce Productions* note paper-clipped to the inside read:

Please tell Peter you'll join me for dinner Friday
night —Dane.

Speechless, Jessica stared at the man called Peter, who politely looked around the room while waiting. The script seemed to grow hot in her hands, and she read the note again. She cleared her throat, gaining Peter's attention.

"You're a friend of Dane's?" she asked, her voice sounding squeaky to her ears. She cleared her throat again.

"I'm what you might call his man Friday, right arm, unofficial business manager, you name it; I pick up his laundry as well."

"Well, please tell him, Dane, I mean, that I would be happy to join him."

"Great! He'll be pleased about that, I'm sure. Be ready at seven then."

"Thank you, uh, Peter?"

"Sorry, Peter Welles, and you're Jessica, *I hope*?" He held out his hand, and when she offered hers, he squeezed it warmly. She was touched by this funny little Brit and watched with interest as he drove away in an older, metallic gold 911 Porsche.

Of course, she stayed up all night reading the script, bonding immediately with the female lead, a rebellious businesswoman in 1800's Boston named Maria. Early in the story she is renamed "Mariah" by the hero, which, he tells her, means "like the wind."

Exhausted by her imaginary adventure, Jessica fell asleep with the script on her chest and dreamed of being shipwrecked with a mysterious, green-eyed pirate.

TWO

Lost Season

Friday afternoon was like another dream to Jessica as she prepared for her big date. Even a call from her bank did not dampen her spirits. After finishing the script two nights before, she fantasized that Dane would offer her the role of Bettina, the distraught sister of the missing Maria. She knew it was far-fetched since the admission of her meager experience had probably killed any faith Dane might have had in her abilities. Nonetheless, she would go out with him and nothing else mattered.

She chose a simple black dress and shawl and worked her hair into a French braid. She stared into the mirror, critically appraising her appearance, her thoughts alternating between the script and Dane Pierce himself.

It's just business, she warned herself. *Maybe he'll offer me a job.* Despite what the tabloids said, everyone knew that Dane Pierce was happily married, with three children to boot. Those grocery store check stand rags were notorious for printing outrageous lies. The bigger the star, the more outlandish the story. What was it he'd said about having just bought his wife...a car? No, a Jeep or something.

Still...the green eyes flirted with her memory. She was nearly breathless with anticipation.

Seven o'clock arrived simultaneously with Peter's knock on her door, and she was surprised that she was being "sent for." Peter complimented her appearance and helped her into the same Porsche she had seen him in earlier that week.

"Is this *your* car?" she inquired, taking in the details of the interior.

"Oh no, miss, this belongs to Dane. He sends his regrets that he can't pick you up himself, but he's under such time constraints these days. Hopefully, he'll be ready by the time we return."

He drove courteously and in twenty minutes or so they passed through the gated entry of a private driveway. The house was large and modern, set on a hilltop with, Jessica imagined, never-ending views from every room. The circle drive put them in front of double-wide front doors, through which Jessica found a foyer the size of her entire living room. Polished marble floors spread from huge white columns, accented with indirect lighting at the ceiling, which had to be twenty feet high. The living room beyond the entry was a large yet inviting circle, with off-white leather, casual furniture, soft light, and a number of plants.

Here she waited for Dane, who soon appeared looking quite dapper in a black suit and white shirt, casually unbuttoned at the neck with no tie. She marveled at the change from his past "pirate" attire, but the roguish good looks were still most apparent as his lowered, appraising eyes checked out her dress, her legs.

"Hi." He reached for her hand. His eyes never left hers as he pressed his lips to the back of her hand with a most deliberate kiss. The lips were warm, and Jessica smiled at her own thoughts. *Of course they're warm; this man is very much alive.*

"Nice place," she commented.

"I'd show you around, but I'm not really fond of it. I want to move to the beach, but I haven't had time to even think about it. I'm not used to this stuff," he said, perusing the lofty ceilings and articles of affluence around him. "I'm just a simple guy. When the kids come down here, they say, 'ooh, Daddy, are we rich?' I try to tell them it's just *stuff*. They don't get it." Dane shook his head comically.

They walked back to the driveway where a sleek, black Mercedes Benz had replaced the Porsche.

A simple guy, thought Jessica, driving a ninety-thousand-dollar car. "Where are they living? Your family, that is?"

"Sausalito, up by San Francisco. My wife's folks live there. Since I'm gone so much, she likes to have, you know, some help. They show up every couple of weeks and disrupt the disruption of my life."

In the car, he talked about the editing of *Bellerive* and the continual setbacks and frustrations. It seemed no time before they were ushered into the private dining room of an elegant downtown restaurant. The waiters called him by name and Jessica felt as if she moved through a dream, or perhaps this was her role, maybe *this* was a movie.

They were immediately served an excellent wine, and Dane turned to Jessica. "Well. I suppose you're wondering why I've gathered you here tonight." A lazy grin moved onto his lips. She felt her gaze fighting to rest on both his eyes and mouth at once, and she had to force herself to straighten up and listen to his words. "Did you read it?"

She nearly asked, 'Read what?' when she remembered the incredible script. "Of course, I did," she replied, sipping the wine and leaning back in the booth. In doing so, her back pressed against his arm resting there, and she quickly sat forward at the touch. Her shy gesture was not lost on him, and his face reflected a mild amusement.

"And?" he continued.

"And...it's tremendous. It's different, not your usual desert island story. I couldn't put it down."

"Good! I'm glad you liked it. Truthfully, are the characters believable to you?"

"Well, as your average movie-goer not well-versed in 19th century Boston, I'd say you have some room for creativity. I found the characters to be the way they should be, bigger-than-life, but credible."

He seemed satisfied, possibly impressed, with her estimation, and delivered his next words pointedly.

"Tell me, as you were reading, did you envision...did you find faces you knew playing the roles?"

"You mean did I cast the film for you?"

"With every script I read, I always see what the character should or could look like. Of course, using 'unknowns' like I do, that can be difficult," he teased.

"Don't worry, the part of Roger was written for you, Dane," she answered with a smile.

"And the part of Mariah, for whom was that written?"

Jessica's face grew warm. Again, the struggle with the eyes and lips...*Why does he affect me this way?* Clearing her throat, she tried to respond intelligently.

"Gosh...That could be a tough call. She runs from confident and coy to terrified and small, then on to strong...she's seductive, yet sensitive..." Momentarily distracted, Jessica tried to form a picture of the main character in her mind.

"What would you say if I said you were my Mariah?"

Someone had surely pressed 'pause.' Jessica froze in mid-breath and her eyes fixed openly on his. Nothing seemed to work, her mouth wouldn't move, her eyes wouldn't blink. Dane reached over and touched her chin with his fingers, gently shaking her head.

"Jessica? Hello?"

She quickly came around and swallowed. "You're either joking or crazy, Dane."

"I'm dead serious. I want you for the part."

"No."

"What?"

"I said no. No, I can't do it. Uh-uh."

Dane laughed out loud, then stopped and took her right hand in his, delicately playing with her diamond ring and speaking softly.

"I've thought a great deal about the decision. I've already set an appointment with Ted Langley."

Jessica's eyes widened. He'd done his homework.

"This is important to me, Jess."

"Of course it is, and that's why you should choose someone...someone with experience, someone like Julia Rothchild, or Maryann Larkin...God, Dane, a million girls would give their eye teeth, *would pay you* to be in one of your films."

The gentle finger playing stopped. He squeezed her hand insistently. "I want *you.*"

Hot and cold. Eyes and lips. She shook her head gently to clear it, but he *was* holding her hand. He was a perfect gentleman, right? Just trying to make an impression. To convince her to take the role. But perfect gentlemen did not usually turn her insides to jelly She pulled her hand away.

"I think you're out of your mind. But I'd be out of mine not to respond to your outrageous offer. I'll test for the part, but only if you test others as well."

"A screen test? It's not necessary." Real or imagined flirtations abandoned, Dane picked up his wine and drank it down.

"Please?" she asked meekly, giving him her most appealing look. "I couldn't in good conscience begin such an important project without first reading for the part."

Dane was thoughtful, his expression reflecting amusement mixed with mild irritation. "Okay. Monday morning, I'll have Peter take you down for a reading."

"Great! What scene should I study?"

"Any one you want."

"You'll test other actresses, too?"

"If that's what it takes."

After dinner, he drove her home and she thanked him on the porch for the evening. Awkwardly, she invited him in and was relieved when he declined, blaming an early morning meeting with film editors and a thousand minor details that would last an eternity. Inside, she screamed into her pillow, and once more fell asleep with *Lost Season* spread open on the bed beside her.

The screen test was easier than she thought it would be. She knew the scene like she had already lived the role, and Peter applauded her performance afterward. She was disappointed that Dane had not attended, but realized it was probably for the best.

She tried to put aside her anticipation in the week that followed, busying herself with plans to find less expensive housing and trying to invent ways to further cut her expenses. Living alone could be solitary, and with Roxanne on vacation, Jessica felt isolated and alone. She warmed a mug of milk in her small microwave oven and took it to her room. It was 11:00 p.m. and sleep evaded her for the seventh night in a row. The house was cold; heat was expensive. She pulled on a pair of sweats to sleep in before turning on the TV to some late movie show.

The milk made her drowsy, but she sat bolt upright at the sound of someone tapping on her front door. *Perhaps it's Roxie,* she thought, tiptoeing to the door and peeking out. In the darkness, she could just make out Dane's tall figure on the porch, and she immediately opened the door.

"I just realized, it's really late, isn't it?" he asked.

"I guess that's a relative question." She laughed nervously. "Welcome to my little hole in the wall."

He glanced around the small living room, then back to her.

"Please—sit down. Can I get you a drink or something?"

"That would be nice. I didn't wake you, did I?"

"No, not at all." She poured him a glass of wine and they sat down.

"I wanted to get by here earlier today, but Jesus! You wouldn't believe the stuff I'm into, trying to wrap up this picture. It's incredible."

"I have a phone..." she said, smiling.

"I hate phones." He smiled back. "Besides, this can't be done on the phone." They sat looking at each other for several seconds. His stare warmed her, and she boldly surveyed his appearance, deciding that he had already been drinking before appearing at her door. He was in jeans and T-shirt, a leather bomber jacket and his hair was disheveled. She liked the look.

"Well," she began.

"Well," he echoed, standing up and walking to the middle of the room before turning to face her.

He's directing his own moves, she thought with a smile. *So dramatic.*

"*You*...got the part. And," he continued before she could protest, "you got it without me. We tested ten ladies, and I turned the whole project over to my most trusted casting director. It was a blind audition. You still got it."

His words sank in quickly and she was on her feet, rushing him with a bear hug and kissing his cheek. Then suddenly, the "eyes and lips" became "eyes, lips and body," and as Dane embraced her, she felt heat; feverish heat in every place they touched. She pulled away, fleetingly embarrassed – he was married, after all -- and yet so excited, she danced around the room like a child before collapsing on the couch. He grinned at her.

"See why I couldn't do that over the phone?"

Jessica dumped out the unfinished milk and poured herself a glass of wine as she refilled Dane's. They discussed *Lost Season*, which was to begin pre-production in just weeks. Most of it would be filmed on location, he told her, sharing her excitement and enthusiasm.

"Ever been to the Caribbean?" he ventured.

"Never. Sounds exciting."

"It will be. You can count on it." Dane's smile held a touch of mischief.

A small clock on a shelf in the dining area chimed midnight. The wine was gone, and the rush Jessica had experienced had left her senses lulled into a contented, delicious warmth that would soon culminate in sleep. Dane, however, seemed reluctant to go and instead, grew more agitated as time passed. It was obvious to Jessica that something was wrong.

"You're stressed about something, aren't you?"

He stared at her for several moments, his eyes belying some inner torment.

From his pocket, Dane threw down a packet of crumpled, rolled up documents. Picking them up, her vision slightly blurred by the wine and the dim light, she saw the words "Petitioner," "Respondent" and "Dissolution." It did not take long to realize that these were instruments of a divorce, Dane's divorce, and Jessica uttered a soft groan. The papers had been right, after all. "Oh, God—Dane—I'm sorry."

His back to her, he stood staring out at the midnight sky.

"She can't do it. She can't take my kids away," he muttered. He turned back to Jessica. He spoke to her as if she *knew*, as if she was his confidant. "She's mad, she's hurt, and I understand that. I'm not there. It's hard to raise three kids without a dad. I understand that. I'm an asshole. I understand *that*. But she is not taking my kids away from me!" He was yelling now, and Jessica was reminded of the day they'd met, and Dane's fiery disposition. Her first instinct was to go to him, to comfort him, to quiet him down. But instead, she sensed his need to vent and sat back, listening while he cursed, ranted, and raved on about his wife.

"And the worst part, Jess, the worst part is, the bitch is pregnant." He went to her refrigerator seeking more to drink and helped himself to a beer. His voice had taken on a quieter, more lethal tone, and Jessica marveled at his character. "She's accusing *me* of being a bad influence, and she's sleeping with her God-damned tennis instructor."

"Are you sure? I mean, are you sure it's not y—"

"Damned right I'm sure...sure as hell it isn't mine. I took care of that when Zoe was born." He sat down finally, his anger spent and the alcohol taking hold. "I have a 9 a.m. flight to San Francisco. Our attorneys are...talking."

Silently, Jessica went to him and tugged off his jacket. She left the room and returned with a pillow and a blanket which she placed on the couch next to him, then took the beer from his hand and put it on the coffee table. She knelt in front of him and softly told him to lie down, which he did, and she covered him with the blanket. As she started to rise, he grasped her arm and pulled her back.

"I'm drunk, but not too drunk to say thank you for your kindness."

Jessica's mind was tangled by her own exhausted emotions. She threaded her arms around his neck and gently lay her head down on his chest, closing her eyes, relishing the feel of his arms slowly encircling her back as he squeezed her tightly to him. The sound of his heart beating was a comforting, rhythmic drum inside her head. Soon, his breathing told her he was asleep, and she reluctantly pulled away, retreating to her own bed.

Dane was gone when she rose the next morning, and a cryptic note seemed to promise a call when he returned from San Francisco.

·❤·❤·❤·❤·❤·

"Maybe he really *is* a wicked, arrogant pirate," Roxanne joked as she and Jessica shared lunch in a cafe near her office.

"I can't believe he hasn't called. It's been two weeks, Roxie. Surely he's home by now. What if he's changed his mind about my role?"

"Jess, he's a big, *big* star. He probably can't even go to the bathroom alone, much less worry about you, worrying about him. I wouldn't concern myself if I were you. I think you're falling for the lug."

"I'm not. He's just a nice guy, really. I just feel bad about what's happening to him." Jessica dragged a fork through her salad.

"Yeah, but there are two sides to every divorce, Jess. You, of all people, know that," Roxanne reminded her. "You know what they're saying."

"*They* don't hold any weight with me."

"Nobody in Hollywood stays faithful. That's just the nature of the business. And I'll bet you any amount of money that he cheated first. Women throw themselves at men like Dane Pierce. It's all about egos and hormones and entitlement."

Jessica withdrew her defense and pushed away her plate. Roxanne sighed and then brightened.

"Doing anything fun over the Fourth? Wanna check out the fireworks down at the beach?"

"Is it the Fourth already?" Jessica answered vaguely.

Roxanne only shook her head. Her attempt to change the subject failing, she took her leave with a promise to check back later.

Jessica's feeling of malaise continued into the evening, however. She was running out of hope that there was anything to her friendship with Dane. He *had* been drunk, she reminded herself. The ringing phone jolted her out of her daydream, and she was delighted to hear Peter's distinctive voice on the line.

"Jess, there's a wrap party for *Bellerive* Friday night, you'll be there, eh?"

"Where, Peter?"

"Studio B. We're havin' it right on the set, before they trash it."

"Is...is Dane back? He'll be there?" she asked cautiously.

"Of course...yeah, back about a week now. He'll be there, with bells on, I'm sure."

"Roxie, please come with me," Jessica later begged into the phone. "I just have to go, and I can't go by myself. Please?"

"What are friends for?" Roxanne sighed dramatically. "Besides, maybe I'll meet some hot guy myself, what do you think?" Then, her tone became serious. "Friday did you say? We've only got three days! And you've got to look absolutely sensational."

That Friday afternoon found them dressing for the party at Roxanne's townhouse. Roxanne's sewing machine was still smoking as she held up a short, royal blue strapless taffeta party dress for Jessica's approval.

"You brought the shoes?" she asked, watching Jessica open a box containing dainty, royal blue satin pumps. "Perfect. Now, this—" Roxanne went to her dressing table and located a blue satin choker with a single teardrop pearl pendant.

Jessica sighed. "What would I do without you?" Looking in the mirror, Jessica turned her head from side to side, her long, loose curls brushing her shoulders perfectly.

Roxanne frowned. "You look *too* good. Here, help me with my earrings." Roxanne had chosen a white suit-dress, with a short, cropped jacket adorned with white bows; matching bows were sewn above the skirt's back slit.

"Very classy," Jessica admired. "You're sure to attract a hot guy with that."

Unlike Jessica's light brown hair, Roxanne's was rich chestnut, complimenting her striking blue eyes and fair complexion. The suit enhanced her already ample figure, and Jessica was openly envious of Roxanne's shape.

They joked and laughed all the way to the party, Roxanne attempting to alleviate some of Jessica's anxiety. They had to park some distance from the building, Jessica ruefully noting the gold Porsche parked against the wall where she used to leave her car.

Studio B was alive with three hundred or more people, several hosted bars and a plethora of hors d'oeuvres. A live band blared from one corner; each band member dressed as a pirate. It was easy to lose themselves in the crowd, mingling as they made their way to a bar where Jessica discovered a small pocket of people she knew from the film. She introduced Roxanne to everyone she met, including Zachary Slade, the hot young actor playing the supporting male lead in the movie. Jessica noticed Roxanne was quite taken with Slade's sharp looks and wit, and she inconspicuously sauntered away to let them talk.

Perusing the crowd, she made conversation with anyone she could engage, casually working the room. She started as someone grabbed her arm and she turned to Peter's smiling face. The long hair was carefully drawn into a neat queue, and he wore a T-shirt bearing bright, horizontal "first mate" stripes.

"Hello, Jessica! Glad you could make it!"

"Great party," she offered, looking cautiously around for Peter's employer.

"Would you care to dance?"

Jessica considered his offer and smiled warmly. "Sure."

Peter, it turned out, was an excellent dancer, and she laughed and giggled on the dance floor as he taught her the latest steps. It felt good to let go; it had been ages since she'd danced, and she needed some relief from the tension of the past weeks.

Breathless as the song ended, Jessica started to leave the dance floor as the band turned to a slow number; Peter held out his hand. She took it and he led her again onto the portable oak floor.

Their dance was soon interrupted by the Devil Captain himself.

"May I?"

Peter dutifully handed Jessica over, much to her discomfort.

She avoided his eyes at first, hotly peering over his shoulder as Dane took her into his arms. The heat began again as their bodies came together like warm clay.

She felt her pulse quicken and she wondered if he could feel the heat, too, if he noticed her chest heaving against his. His hand warmed her skin as he slid his fingers across her back. Forgetting her anger, Jessica slipped into a euphoric wonder at the feel of his body moving against hers; a feeling she had fantasized about for weeks.

"Enjoying the party?" he asked, his lips close, much too close to her ear. A current ran down her spine, causing her to shiver. He felt her flinch and he turned to lean his face closer and study her eyes.

Despite the fever of his closeness and the overpowering attraction she felt, Jessica looked at him coldly. The tiny angel on her shoulder begged her to stop, but instead she spoke.

"Enjoying it? Not really. But I'm sure you are."

He looked puzzled at her jab. They continued to dance in silence. As the song ended, she murmured a quick "thank you," then darted away, fighting her way through throngs of people still lingering on the dance floor. Glancing over her shoulder, she saw Dane attempting to follow.

Jessica paused just long enough to shoot Roxanne a text. "I'm ready to go." She hurried on until she found a door to the outside. Without looking back, she sensed Dane was still pursuing her and heard him call out. She quickened her pace. He overtook her just as she reached her car, demanding that she stop. She turned toward him, breathlessly bracing herself against the car door.

"Why didn't you stop?" he asked, a frown creasing his tanned face.

"Why didn't you call?" As she tried to catch her breath, Jessica hated herself for having voiced her question. Things seemed different now, with Dane standing before her; his life was none of her business. "I'm sorry. I guess I was just concerned."

The phone in her hand buzzed. "I'm not," was Roxanne's simple answer.

Dane stuffed his hands into his front pockets. "I wanted to call you, but...I couldn't. I didn't want to involve you with all the shit that's going on. I've..." He looked away, reluctant but obviously determined to be honest with her. "I've been ripped on and off for four days. Mostly on."

He went on to tell her that things had not been easy in San Francisco, that it would get nasty in court, and he wasn't taking it very well.

"I've thought about calling you. I have. But I hate phones, and I was in no condition to see you." He boldly took her face between his hands. "I need to talk to you, Jessica...would you...could we...get together later?"

Dane's eyes were penetrating, his touch searing. Without a thought she nodded her head as if in a trance.

"Do you remember how to get to my house?"

Again, she nodded. From her face he moved his fingers to her hair, absently arranging it around her bare shoulders.

"Good."

Jessica closed her eyes when Dane's fingers left her hair. What had just happened? Did she really agree to go home with him? Before she could question her decision, Dane began walking back toward the studio. He stopped and waited for her, and they rejoined the party together.

Jessica immediately sought out her friend and whispered her plans. Roxanne happily advised her that she was leaving with Zachary and wouldn't need a ride home anyway. With Jessica's mouth still gaping, Roxanne winked and followed Zachary out onto the dance floor.

It was near one in the morning when Jessica parked the Miata on the circle drive behind Dane's Porsche. It looked strangely out of place, but she ignored the feeling and walked decisively up the steps to the massive entry.

Expecting Peter, she was surprised when Dane met her at the door and showed her past the living room to a large, comfortable den. A wide-screen television was centrally located across from the sectional where she sat down. Bookcases lined the walls filled not only with books, but awards, gold statuettes and trophies as well.

The room was normally lit by hanging billiard-style lights, but these were now off, and soft table lamps cast a dim glow. She waited while he paced the floor, a drink in his hand, obviously at a loss for words.

"My kids call it fizzy water," he said with a chuckle, holding up his glass. He sat down on the coffee table in front of her. In his white, oversized cotton shirt and tight black trousers, he was once again the dread pirate Simon.

"Tell me about them."

"The kids? Last I looked, there were three of the little gremlins. Alex, my boy, he's around six. Mimi, well, Melissa, she's the oldest, she must be seven. And my little princess, Zoe, she's all of three. Ish." Dane paused, clearly thinking about the children and the uncertainty of their futures. "I can't really talk about it," he began, a frustrated sigh escaping his lungs. "I get too upset. Basically, we go to court for a preliminary hearing next month."

"I see," she murmured.

"I owe you a drink or...several, actually," he offered, smiling sheepishly, remembering the night he'd spent on her couch. "What are you drinking?"

"Nothing, thank you. I had enough at the party." She tugged at the top edge of her dress to conceal her cleavage. "Dane, I'm sorry about running away tonight. I was mad at you, I guess. I feel awful about what's happening to you, and I've been thinking that maybe I could...help somehow." This was awkward, but she felt she had to explain her behavior.

"You're sweet."

"Don't pass it around. Teddy says being 'sweet' could ruin my career."

"You can be sweet and still be...erotic." The green eyes were coaxing, challenging; then they looked away. He paused, appearing to gather his thoughts. "Look, Jessica...if you and I are going to have...a relationship, there's something you should know. I'm not, at least anymore, I've discovered, a good risk. I'm not a particularly reliable...dependable...person. I can't seem to make or keep promises like I should." He checked her reaction before continuing. "I'm my own person, Jessie. I've hurt too many people, including myself, so all bets are off on what I'll do next. Major disclaimer, take it or leave it." His hands gestured an ultimatum; his eyes were back with hers, delving, seeking her compliance. "You understand what I'm saying, right? I could really, really piss you off."

Jessica's own eyes were wide with open amazement. No man had ever spoken this frankly to her before. No presumptions, no surprises. And no commitments. But he *was* offering her *something*. Something she wanted.

She nodded in silent understanding. She didn't care about getting hurt, or unkept promises, and even if she had, right now she would gladly forsake all for even one kiss.

Dane sighed. Uncomfortable on the coffee table, he moved to sit next to Jessica on the sectional. He ran his fingers through his hair, something, she noticed, he did unconsciously when he was feeling stressed. "This divorce is killing me. I keep asking myself, is what I've done so wrong?" He leaned forward, looking down at the floor. He was such a picture of despair that Jessica couldn't help but delicately place her hand on his shoulder in sympathy.

Dane turned slightly and stared at her for a long moment. A sublime moment. An overwhelming, heated madness spread throughout her, born of her simple contact with his body. Dane exuded maleness like no man she'd encountered, filling her at once with both desire and trepidation. Jessica sat captured by his gaze, the emerald eyes stripping away layer after layer of her carefully built defenses...seeking her vulnerabilities, her sensitivities.

Slowly he turned and took both of her hands in his, pulling them around his neck, then slid his hands down her arms and around her in one smooth movement. She barely had time to moisten her lips before his were on her, exploring her cheek, her ear, her neck, her mouth...but slow. Slow, and hot, and sensual. Any shyness she had anticipated on her own part evaporated and she returned each kiss with fervor. Abruptly, he stopped and again stared into her face.

"You really want this, right?"

Her response was silent but clear, and he stood, lifted her off the couch and carried her to his bedroom.

Jessica's heart pounded as they undressed, the room lit only by the garden lights glowing outside his glass bedroom wall. She repeatedly told herself not to think, just to act; thinking about this would just confuse her, and all she wanted now was to have Dane Pierce belong to her.

She stole appraising glances at his physique while he tore the comforter and blankets from the bed. He was neither muscleman nor athlete, but he gave new meaning to her understanding of "sexy." She blushed unwillingly at her own embarrassment; it had been a long time since she had been this intimate. She crept hesitantly onto the bed, awaiting his initiating touch.

He didn't speak, and although his experience and discipline were obviously greater than hers, there was nothing routine about his actions. He kissed her again and again, a sense of urgency and searching building as their passion grew. His hands seemed to be everywhere at once, expertly exploring places he already knew would bring her pleasure. So complete was his control over her, she was only remotely aware of the intensity of his own arousal.

Jessica, her mind in turmoil and filled with dreamlike pictures and wine-induced dizziness, abandoned all conscious thought and allowed herself to melt into him, until she could no longer sense they were more than one. The urgency became a demand, and together they merged into a dimension of feeling without time or space, filled with electric sensuality, clinging to each other in a desperate, passionate fever.

"This isn't the first time you've been unfaithful to your wife." She said it as a statement of fact, pulling his shirt around her later as they relaxed in his bed. Realization that Roxanne had been right didn't sit well, diminishing her euphoria.

"Have I been? Now that she's been unfaithful to me, what are my responsibilities to her? We're divorcing, for Christ's sake."

"It isn't, right?" Jessica asked again. "The first time?"

"No, not in a technical sense..."

"What's that supposed to mean?"

"Are you upset, Jess?" he asked quietly, caressing her hair from her face. "I meant, there have been a couple of others, you know, studio girls, little better than prostitutes, really, nobody I knew or cared about. These girls are, like, provided. So, technically, I didn't count it as cheating – it was just sex."

"Provided by whom? It's like finding a fifth of Scotch and a fruit basket in your hotel room?"

He smiled at her shocked expression, then leaned over to kiss her. "What's the matter?" he whispered. "You can't be this preciously naïve. You must realize...we spent six months making *Sioux Nation*, most of it in Wyoming, in the winter to boot. I didn't see Rita for months. She refused to come."

Jessica thought of her own brief marriage, five years ago. If Wesley had even slept with a *robot*, she would have killed him. "Did Rita know about these... these *provided* girls?" she asked, unable to use the word he'd chosen.

"I don't know." He eyed her thoughtfully.

"I find that hard to believe," she murmured. "I can't help but wonder, Dane, if this is really a...a casting couch," she said quietly, pulling his hands away from her. The startled look on his face made her wish she had kept her mouth shut.

"No, Jessica, this is *my* bed." His voice was tight with disappointment. "Is your experience so lacking that you can't tell the difference between screwing and making love?"

Her face burned at his suggestion. "I'm sorry, Dane. I just...I just don't usually do things like this, and I never thought I'd get involved with...someone like you." she rushed the words out, her naiveté obvious even to herself. "I knew you were married, and yet I still... I still..."

"It's okay." He smiled softly and gently pulled open the shirt she'd wrapped around her, dragging his fingertips lightly down her chest and stomach. Her passion spent, she now felt modest under his gaze. "It was a...reasonable question, I guess. And if I'm to be honest, and I really try to be, I think our marriage was already toast. Once my career took off..." He sighed and shook his head slowly, considering her.

"Hollywood ruins relationships. I guess you're right; I'm as naïve as they come."

"You *are* luscious, my dear, and so vulnerable. You enticed me that first morning at the studio. You're standing in the doorway of a whole new life, and you have so much to learn. I hope you're not as generous with others as you've been with me." He stroked her hair. "And there will be others. As much as I'd like to, there is no way I could protect you from those who would sample your favors—in the manner of which you've accused me."

A pain went through Jessica's heart as she absorbed his words. She couldn't tell him that there would be no others, not now. Her "favors" were, quite possibly, entirely his. Despite his precarious morals.

She laid her head on his shoulder, molding her petite form to his long, lean one. She smiled to herself; one thing was for sure, Dane's sexual prowess was no disappointment. There were many sexy stars, made so by makeup, seductive clothing and provocative roles. But this man's passion and skill were for real, and no one could ever take tonight away from her.

She fell asleep on his shoulder, and the next morning, it was her turn to leave a note. She couldn't see waking him, and she knew Peter would be around to shake him up for whatever appointments he might have. Her note would be brief: "Dane, thanks for a great time..." She giggled. *No, how about,* "Dane, sorry I couldn't stay..." *No.* Finally, she jotted, *"See you in the movies"* and signed her name with a small heart.

THREE

"Happy New Year"

"I can't believe it's only three weeks 'til Christmas," Roxanne observed, as she and they carried groceries into Jessica's kitchen. "By the way, since the film's been finished for a while now, are you getting more money?"

"No. It was a one-time pay." Jessica winced at Roxanne's reference to *Bellerive*, reminding her of the night spent with Dane and the fact that she hadn't heard from him since. Roxanne had been dating Zachary Slade steadily since the party—nearly five months—so *something*, perhaps, had come of it all.

Jessica tried to analyze her feelings about Dane but was thwarted each time by the sheer pain of remembering his touch. He had left a bookmark in her life story that he hadn't bothered to retrieve. Alone and grief stricken, she recalled the warning he'd voiced before taking her to his bed. Was he, then, relieved of all responsibility? Was it her fault? She saw his face before her nightly, sometimes through tear-swollen eyes that searched for solace and found only sorrow.

She was making a major motion picture with this man and dreaded the day when she'd be forced to face him again, for a meeting, a rehearsal, an on-camera scene. And yet she ached, ached for his touch, his intimate, teasing eyes that could caress her sensually from across a room.

Jessica felt anger, too; anger at Dane and at herself. Despite his "major disclaimer," he knew she didn't believe him; had to have known that she cared deeply and that such disclaimers were worthless against her dangerous heart.

"Let's have a party," Roxanne announced one evening after the two had eaten dinner together. "Come on, it'll do us good. We'll have it here; it'll be great fun."

Jessica wrinkled her nose.

"Look Jess, you can't mourn this guy forever. It was fun, wasn't it? But these days, you have to move on. I know that, Dane knows that, and you should know it, too. It doesn't mean he doesn't like you, I'm sure he does. But the man has commitments up the wazoo. So knock it off, and let's do this party, okay?" Roxanne put her arm around her friend.

"I'm not up to it, Rox you'd do all the work, and it wouldn't be fair." Her face burned at the reminder of her pain.

"So what? We need to have some fun. I'm sure Zach has some friends who could liven things up."

Jessica wouldn't admit it, but she didn't care for Zachary Slade, and suspected Roxanne wasn't truly enamored with him either but loved the excitement of dating a star.

After significant prodding, Jessica finally conceded. They would get a tree and trim it at the party, heat the spa and make merry. It sounded okay, just as long as she didn't have to act happy or talk to anyone, *especially any men.*

The afternoon before the party, Jessica bemoaned the fact that she had nothing to wear, and the house wasn't clean enough.

Roxanne sighed. "I wish you would cheer up. I almost hope that piece of rancid meat shows up so I can give him what for. You look great, by the way. You only need a little...of this!" Tossing a pinch of glitter into Jessica's hair, Roxanne gave chase as the two ran through the house, laughing and throwing tinsel and ribbons at each other until they were out of breath.

At around eight o'clock, Zachary arrived with three or four people, toting in cases of eggnog and champagne. Jessica busied herself with a recipe for wassail while Roxanne organized the guests, the drinks, the music and answered the door every few minutes. It seemed to Jessica that there were a hundred people in her small house, spilling out onto the balcony, the bedroom, the pool area. It also seemed to be taking hours for the wassail to heat up. Roxanne kept asking her help in mixing drinks, and she sampled here and there to make sure she wasn't killing anyone. The alcohol warmed her, even if the kitchen seemed to stay cold.

Frustrated with being stuck at the stove, Jessica gingerly touched the side of the large pot filled with cider, and finding it cold, leaned down to check the flame, which had gone out.

"Damn," she murmured.

"Probably would help to light a fire under it," a male voice suggested from just behind her. Exasperated, she whirled around, ready to punch out the face behind the voice. Instead, she stopped short and stared into warm, brown eyes that were sincerely offering to help.

He was standing close, too close for a stranger, but with six people in a kitchen designed for two, there wasn't much choice. Jessica backed closer to the stove to put some room between them and to give herself a better look at him. He was tall, maybe even taller than Dane, and wearing jeans, Nikes, and a ski sweater; he had her box of kitchen matches in his hand. Without further ado, he leaned across and lit the errant stove burner, starting the wassail back on its way.

"Thanks! I don't know what made it go out," Jessica offered shyly.

"Probably that frigid blast every time they open the door. Should I put this in here?" He showed her a bag and motioned to the refrigerator.

"Sure if there's room." She helped him force more cans into the already full refrigerator, then turned to face him. "I'm Jessica. Have we met?" Her question was lost, however, as rock music suddenly exploded from the speakers in the living room. She motioned to the balcony, currently unoccupied, and he followed. Once outside, she closed the sliding door most of the way. Braving the cold was better than competing with the noise inside.

"Much better," he commented, leaning slightly over the rail to take in the view. "I like this. Lived here long?"

"No, in fact, I'm renting it. My lease is up in February, and I don't know if I'll be staying." He nodded, and Jessica reviewed his profile; he had a strong jaw, and firm, expressive lips.

She continued to stare, knowing she knew this handsome guy from somewhere. His hair was light brown, not unlike her own, with blonde highlights picked up by the glow of the patio bulbs. He had kind eyes and an easy smile.

"We've met, haven't we?" she asked again, frowning at her failure to remember as he nodded. "You aren't insured by Costello, are you?"

He chuckled. "No, all my insurance is through *SAG*."

"You're in the business then?"

"Yeah," he said, still smiling at her. "Could it have been...an audition?"

Jessica puzzled. She'd been on so few.

"You had your hair..." he began, pointing to his ear and making a swirling motion.

"Oh my God, you're the guy from Castle!" She covered her mouth for a moment in surprise, then held out her hand. "I'm Jessica Taylor. I'm sorry, I have a terrible memory for names."

"Cory MacKendall." He shook her hand warmly.

Jessica was again astonished. This was a name she did remember. Cory MacKendall, the television star. Teddy had been right.

"*You're Doctor Jim...*"

"And you're Mariah Sinclair."

Jessica felt herself blushing. "You're well informed."

"Oh, I pick up *Variety* once in a while." He turned and looked back toward the party, and Jessica wondered if she was keeping him from a date inside.

"You probably want to get back to your friends," she said, motioning to the crowded house.

"Actually, I was just walking down the street and this crowd of people swept up behind me and here I am," he quipped. "No offense, but big parties intimidate me. I prefer more intimate groups, limited to maybe fifty or sixty?"

This comment made her laugh, which in turn caused him to smile, now revealing two long dimples that perfectly framed his sensitive lips.

"But *you* certainly have friends in there...?"

"A handful at the most," Jessica replied. "Tell you what, let's check on that cider, then I'll show you the grounds."

"Sounds good."

She walked him through the bedroom and French doors to the path leading down to the pool and spa, which was one ground lower than the house and around a hundred feet away. Halfway down, an old garden glider sat to one side of the path, and they paused to sit and watch the revelers stewing in the Jacuzzi below.

"This your pool?"

"Well, the landlord owns all this land. They live across the arroyo. Do you live around here, Cory?"

"Please, call me Mac. Not far, in Laurel Canyon. I bought what you might call a 'time-honored' estate last year, and I'm just getting around to having it renovated. What a job. So much has to be replaced; I'm beginning to wonder if I shouldn't just start over with raw land."

"You...live alone?"

"Yeah. You?" he returned, and she nodded. His eyes reflected the pool lights as he turned his gaze back to the partiers. "You hang around with Slade's crowd much?"

"No. Not at all. They're...not my type."

He smiled. "They're not my type either. I actually came with Bill Campbell." His eyes were now busy looking at her hair, and she became immediately self-conscious. "Did you know you've been decorated?" His fingers picked a thin piece of silver tinsel from her hair.

Jessica giggled, then pressed her lips together tightly. She wasn't supposed to be having fun.

"How do you know Bill? He was 'Slackjaw' in *Bellerive*."

"He's 'Chance' in *Doctor Jim*. He's a good friend."

Jessica was about to expound on that happy coincidence when Roxanne appeared, chastising her for delaying the tree-trimming. With an apologetic smile, Jessica reluctantly led Mac to follow Roxanne up the hill to join the others in the living room.

"All things considered, it was a pretty good party," Jessica admitted, smiling at Roxanne as they sat down, exhausted, before their beautifully decorated tree.

"You didn't talk to any *men*, did you Jess?"

Jessica smiled again. "Actually, everyone was quite nice. I had a fun time. Thanks for doing this."

"I'm glad you finally got the chance to remember that all men are not as stuck on themselves as Mr. Dane Pierce." The words stung, but Roxanne's point was well taken, and Jessica loved her friend all the more for saying it.

A week passed and Jessica was all at once busy with pre-production costume fittings and early rehearsals. She was assigned a coach and she met with him daily to polish what she considered to be her meager skills.

But today was set-aside for Christmas shopping, and having so little time, she walked the mall until her legs were useless. Once home, she collapsed amid her packages on the bed and realized she hadn't checked her voicemail all day. She dreaded another fitting or meeting or some such time gobbler. With a sigh, she reached for her phone.

"Hi, it's Jackie; are you sure you can't get me a part in *Lost Season?*" *Beep.*

"This is your mother; why *can't* you come to Seattle for Christmas?" *Beep.*

Nodding to herself, Jessica made a mental note to call her mother and her sister and bring them up to speed. She'd been woefully remiss about keeping in touch.

"Hi Jessie, it's Mac MacKendall...I hope you don't mind, I got your number from Bill..." Jessica sat up and listened closely. "There's this premiere tomorrow night for Hemsworth's new film, with a party afterward, and I thought you might like to go, unless of course you're having a few hundred people over or something..." Jessica giggled at his reference to her party, then sat with the phone in her lap, suddenly struggling with her emotions. Maybe she shouldn't call him. Maybe she was just getting herself into another situation. She sighed, remembering Mac's soft brown eyes and easy, non-threatening manner; *maybe* she was just being hysterical. She tapped the "call" icon.

Chris Hemsworth's new film turned out to be a winner.

Watching it in the darkened theater with Mac, Jessica relaxed and played back, in her mind, the luscious scene that took place upon their arrival at the theater; the fans, the flashes, the reporters, and she on the arm of Cory MacKendall.

"I loved the film!" she exclaimed as they drove to the party, held at the prestigious Oaks Country Club. Mac agreed as he parked the black BMW 850i himself and helped her out.

"Sorry, I have this thing about other people parking my car," he apologized. "I worked too hard for it."

"I'm with you," she smiled. Photographers swarmed around them at the door.

"You don't have to talk to them, you know," he told her as they entered, and reporters seemed everywhere.

"Okay." She was grateful for the advice; she was not quite ready to give up her privacy yet. It hadn't, in fact, even occurred to her that anyone would want to talk to her at all.

The room was filled with glitzy, beautiful people, and Jessica's head swam with the ambiance. It was easy, comfortable, being with Mac. He was warm, witty and unpretentious. They walked freely among other stars and celebrities, and the impact of her new career overwhelmed her. It was obvious that Mac, too, enjoyed himself, finding Jessica's fresh outlook entertaining and her enthusiasm amusing. She whispered and giggled, sharing her abstract thoughts and impressions of everyone they encountered.

Unconsciously, her grip on his arm tightened as her eyes lit on Dane Pierce, standing not ten feet in front of them. Although the possibility of his appearance had crossed her mind, she wasn't prepared for the intensity of her own reaction to seeing him again, especially in the company of another woman. If Mac noticed her tension, he didn't show it, boldly marching her right up to Dane, who had attended the party with Merrily Mitchell. With a slight nod to Jessica, Merrily wandered away.

"Jessica, how nice to see you again," Dane said cordially, reaching for her hand. Jessica nodded, but she kept both hands wrapped securely around Mac's arm. Mac, however, extended his hand.

"Pierce, I hear you're turning out some awesome stuff these days. How do you keep it up?"

"I'd say six seasons on the network is keeping it up fairly well yourself, MacKendall."

"Well, I think the trick is that you have to reserve time for R & R, you know what I mean?"

Oh, he knows what you mean, Mac, thought Jessica, now staring boldly at Dane.

"I guess you must be doing something right, you have my leading lady welded to your arm there, pal." Dane's eyes flashed a brief, knowing look at Jessica. "So, what do *you* do for R & R?" Dane asked.

"I run, I ski, I fly. In fact, Jess and I are flying to Santa Barbara tomorrow for lunch," Mac said coolly, then quickly turned to Jessica. "What did you say you wanted to drink?"

"Uh...Sprite, please," she managed, her thoughts a terrified jumble of *Who's-flying-where?* and *Don't-you-dare-leave-me-alone-with-him!* Her eyes pleaded, but Mac did leave, and Dane smiled down at her.

"Not welded, after all," he mused. Then, "MacKendall seems like a nice guy. I was going to ask you to attend the *Bellerive* premiere with me, but now I guess you're already spoken for."

Jessica nodded, burning inside. "Do we have a premiere date?" she asked icily.

"A couple of weeks; New Year's Eve, as a matter of fact." His eyes became serious for the first time, and he lowered his voice. "Jess—I'm going through hell. I really want to see you."

Jessica held up her hand. "Save it, Dane. Give me a call...or better yet just send Peter around," she said, in a voice that could have frozen boiling water. She kept her gaze steady, watching his eyes for some sign of remorse...and saw it. Her rebuff had hurt him. Oh no...*the eyes and the lips again*...She felt the heat, her heart beginning to hammer in her ears...

"Here you are, babe...Sprite—*with a twist*." It was Mac, dear, smooth, Mac, gently pressing the cold glass into her hand and bringing her back to the here and now. She turned to him and caught a barely perceptible wink as he slipped his hand around her waist. "Come on, I want to introduce you to Chris. See ya 'round, Pierce."

She didn't hesitate to invite him in. Still high from the evening, she wasn't ready to say good-night.

"Well...okay," he consented, clearly hesitant.

"It was a great party, wasn't it? All those incredible people! The atmosphere was so...electric." She moved around the living room in an excited, animated fashion, switching on lights and removing her coat. Mac sat down and watched her in amusement.

"Get used to it, Jessica. It'll soon become a way of life. And you probably won't always love it."

She smiled at him appreciatively. He was rock-solid, genuine, and she felt enormous comfort in his presence.

"I'm sorry, would you like a glass of wine or something?" she asked.

"No booze tonight but thank you. I'm flying tomorrow." Mac paused, wetted his lips, then smiled indulgently. "About which, by the way, I meant to ask you; *would* you like to go with me to Santa Barbara?"

"You meant that, then? You're a pilot?"

"I have a small Cessna. It would be just for lunch."

"Yes! I'd *love* to."

"Wonderful. I'll pick you up at...8 a.m. okay?"

"You've got it." She walked him back to the porch, where he took both her hands and squeezed them.

"You're a nice person, Jessie, I like knowing you. Now go inside so I'll know you're in safe."

Her head was in a good place as she dressed for bed. Despite her encounter with Dane, she felt a new confidence growing from her friendship with Mac. She looked forward to seeing him in the morning.

The flight exhilarated her, and consequently, him as well. Mac spent time describing the various instruments, giving Jessica an opportunity to fly the plane herself. They touched down in Santa Barbara in thirty minutes. Near the airfield, he opened a small storage space and rolled out a Kawasaki motorcycle, equipped with two helmets.

Jessica laughed. "You are one prepared guy!"

He drove her to the mountain neighborhood of Montecito where they stopped at a small deli and took a picnic lunch to a grassy bluff nearby. Jessica felt she'd stepped into someone else's charmed life; the weather was perfect, the food great, and the company exceptional. She came back to reality when he explained his ex-wife and daughter lived in a small, upscale Los Angeles suburb and that his mother had emphysema and lived in a minimum care senior community nearby.

She felt surprised that this peaceful man could have an *ex*-wife. Was Wesley somewhere right now with a girl who wondered the same?

"It's the business that breaks people up. Sad but true." He stared out at the sea. Jessica thought about Dane and his awful situation.

"Is it even possible to stay married?" she wondered out loud. She told Mac about her own failure at wedded life. "We were the proverbial high school sweethearts. He wanted to be a film editor, but couldn't seem to break in. I was doing 'little theater' and typing scripts. He became...very depressed. One day he just decided to move to Canada, and I...I didn't go." Jessica paused, unable to meet her companion's eyes. She didn't want to dredge up more than was necessary to satisfy Mac's natural curiosity. "I guess it was for the best. He'd never fit in with the life I have now."

"Is he remarried?"

"No, I hear he's with someone, but I think he's probably afraid to get married again."

"What about you?"

"Am I afraid? No. But my ideas about marriage and relationships in general have changed, are still changing." The pain of her encounter with Dane Pierce was still fresh and she had vowed privately to never give herself to another man until she was sure she truly loved and was loved. Old-fashioned, she admitted, but right for her, nonetheless. "People are too fast these days. Things happen too fast; people race through life without finding out first if they're enjoying it." She paused again, choosing her words carefully. "My brother and my sister are both happily married, and I'm happy for them. But right now, I'm not in the mind frame of being serious."

Mac smiled. The look on his face told her he agreed, but she felt uncomfortable and opted to change the subject.

"So, how old is your daughter?"

"Megan is five going on fifteen."

Jessica saw the love in his eyes as he spoke fondly of his little girl, whom, she discovered, he visited every other weekend without fail. Divorced, but devoted.

Mac again turned his face into the breeze. "We have to start back. Fog's coming in."

·♥·♥·♥·♥·♥·

"Another costume fitting? I've already had more costume changes than there are scenes in this film." Jessica hung up the phone and made the now-familiar drive to the wardrobe department. Once there, she complained to the tailor. "I've already tried this on."

"There's uh, been some changes, miss." Some more pins, some more tucks. Impatiently she accommodated the embarrassed seamstress, finally escaping out the door and down the steps toward her car. Deep in thought, she nearly collided with Dane as he approached the shop himself.

"Jessica!" He grabbed her arms to steady her. Chills immediately rippled over her back, and she caught her breath. Pausing to gain her composure, she took a step backward.

"Hello, Dane. Don't tell me they haven't got your costumes right yet either?" She tried to sound light, cool, aloof.

"No...do you have a few minutes? Can you wait—I'll only be a moment; we could get some coffee..." Jessica didn't answer. Instead, she looked down. "Please?" Dane caressed her forearms affectionately; his touch was effective.

"Dane, I don't think..." she began.

"Just ten minutes."

She sighed and nodded reluctantly. She sat on the hood of her car and waited while he raced into the shop. He was back in moments. They walked to the cafe on the corner, where he put on tinted glasses hoping to deter gawkers. With coffee before them, she asked what he wanted to talk about.

"First, business. Your contract's been signed. Your agent drove a hard bargain."

Jessica winced to think of young, gay Teddy facing Dane's tough negotiators and demanding some outrageous price.

"He asked us for...a significant sum," Dane sipped his steaming coffee. "But I held out for twice what he wanted."

Jessica stared at Dane. "You're joking, of course." Her eyes widened as he shook his head. She grabbed his arm. "Oh, Dane, I don't know what to say!"

"Say...you're not angry with me anymore."

Jessica lowered her eyes. "You can't buy forgiveness, darling." *I hope I looked like Garbo saying that.*

Despite the rebuff, Dane pulled off the dark glasses and his eyes sparkled from his tired, unshaven face. "I know you can't understand why I haven't been in touch. Please believe my intentions were not what they seemed; I did warn you, you know," he said heavily.

"I know. Okay." Her agreement sounded half-hearted, too easy, and it was. Truthfully, she didn't think she would ever allow herself to trust Dane again, but that didn't change the tremendous attraction she felt or the unbidden sympathy that rose every time she thought about his life and his problems. Maybe they could be friends of a sort. If she kept him at arm's length.

He walked her back to the car.

"I'm glad I ran into you. I've called you a few times, Jess, but—I refuse to talk to machines. I guess the tailor is as good a place to meet as any." It was small talk, but something in his voice tipped her off; he had arranged the redundant fitting to create a convenient coincidence. She started to accuse, to let the anger surface, but her heart couldn't help feeling just a little flattered, touched by the fact that he'd made the effort to force an encounter.

The overcast sky and brisk breeze chilled her momentary warmth. For the first time since their night together, she allowed herself to really look at him closely.

"I still have a landline and a voicemail for a reason," she began. "Look at you. Dane, you're too thin." In response, he looked down the street, running his fingers through his hair. Driven by some unseen force, Jessica reached out and gently placed her hand on his chest, slightly inside the leather jacket. Still avoiding her eyes, he quietly responded.

"You know I don't eat when I'm working a film." He placed his hands on her shoulders, then slowly slid one across her back while the other gently pressed her head to his chest. His heart beat in rhythm with hers, and she closed her eyes as his fingers massaged her head. He lowered his chin near her ear and his voice was tight with emotion. "I'm spending Christmas Eve with my kids."

Tears sprang to her eyes, and she wrapped her arms tightly around his waist. "Oh Dane, that's wonderful," she managed to whisper, then turned her face up to his. She kissed him briefly on the cheek and offered a quick "Merry Christmas," then hurried into her car and drove away. With tears streaming down her cheeks, Jessica watched him in her rear-view mirror as he walked slowly back to his car. *So much for keeping him at arm's length.*

Christmas came and went with a minimum of revelry. Jessica spent the holiday with Roxanne and her family, who lived in nearby Pasadena. A couple of tearful phone calls put her in touch with her sister, mother and brother, and she only briefly mourned days past when holidays were spent as a family.

She was a live wire the day of the premiere. Despite her bit part in *Bellerive*, she was already known in Hollywood as the starlet who had landed the plum role in *Lost Season*. During the week, she'd received offers from both Ralph Lauren and Christian Dior to wear their gowns. She jokingly told Teddy she was holding out for a Versace, but everyone knew Roxanne was hard at work on a fabulous dress.

Mac had graciously accepted the invitation to escort her but had complained about having to wear a tuxedo twice in one month.

"But you looked so *dashing!*" she teased him from the kitchen, where she was putting away clean dishes. She could see him across the living room, standing in the bathroom shaving. He leaned close to the mirror, shirtless and in cut-off jeans, and Jessica quietly admired his well-toned form. He's built like a lifeguard, she thought fleetingly.

"Dashing is not a description I strive for," Mac hollered back, patting his face with a towel and emerging from the bathroom. She leaned on the counter and sighed.

"You *could* go just like that," she suggested, smiling.

"Only if you dress accordingly." He sat on the couch and picked up the remote for the TV. "Do I have time to watch the bike races from Paris?"

"That depends. How long are they on?"

"All weekend?" He smiled his sweetest, revealing his normally hidden dimples, and she threw a dishtowel at him.

"You have one hour before we have to leave."

They were comfortable with the easy friendship that had developed between them, each looking for no more or less. She assumed he saw other women, and he had never asked her about the incident with Dane Pierce.

The premiere was glamorous, the party even more so. Most of Hollywood's "A" list attended, and Jessica was having a grand time. She and Mac made quite a handsome couple, and the room virtually buzzed with speculation about them. Jessica's dress alone was worth a cover story, a lacy, white evening gown resplendent with hanging, sparkling, miniature beads; a choker-style satin collar met with a sheer voile, modestly (but not too effectively) covering a plunging bodice, sewn with hanging, iridescent bugle beads and discreetly cut away to expose her shoulders. The back was the same, filmy material, and twenty tiny buttons made a trail from the nape of her neck to her waist. Mac had sighed deeply as she had emerged from the bedroom, which Jessica felt was far more satisfying than a whistle.

Dane Pierce was in rare form. Animated, in control, he exhibited none of the vulnerability of their last meeting. The "man of the hour," he escorted Merrily to the premiere and the party, pausing for numerous photo opportunities; many of these featured the two of them kissing. Ever the promoter, thought Jessica with disdain. The feelings of rejection resurfaced. *That should be me.*

Her defense was to drink something strong, something that would take the edge off the pain. She did, and did again, and Roxanne exchanged a concerned look with Mac as they stood in a small group at the bar. The timing couldn't have been worse for Dane to approach them.

"Well, I've been upstaged again," he said with a smile. "You are sheer dynamite in that dress, Jessica."

"On the contrary Dane, you look dazzling, wearing Merrily."

Nearby, Zachary laughed aloud, and Roxanne elbowed him in the ribs. Dane stared at Jessica for what seemed to the others an uncomfortable eternity. Mac moved in close behind her and slipped his hands around her waist, holding her steady. Feeling his presence, she subtly leaned back against him, and he discreetly supported her without so much as a sigh.

Dane ultimately chose to ignore her comment, instead taking her hand warmly. "I'm looking forward to beginning *Lost Season*. It will be a...wonderful experience working with you again." He smiled and a strobe flash fixed them eternally on film for some bold photographer. Both Dane and Mac shot looks of displeasure at the photog, who was immediately hustled away by a bouncer in black tie.

"I'll just bet you are," Jessica replied bitterly, as Merrily rejoined her escort and wrapped her arms around him affectionately.

As they turned away, Jessica found the floor was moving under her feet. "Mac take me home, please," she whispered, turning and drawing her arms around his neck. "I can't stay here."

"I can see that," he replied. He quickly scanned the room for a side exit and found one. "Roxie, stay with Jess while I bring the car to that door."

Roxanne nodded and placed her arm around her friend. "Jessie, hang on to this one, honey," she advised. But Jessica could see only Dane's face before her, sharing his lips with someone else.

Mac was soon at her side and carefully directed her to the car.

"I'm not so very drunk, Mac. Just hurting." She spoke quietly and did indeed sound pained.

"I know babe, just hang in there 'til we get home."

Before long, he was lifting her from the car and carrying her to the bedroom, where he sat her down on the bed. She started to lie down, but he stopped her. "No, not yet you don't. Stand up. Jessica, *stand up*." She obeyed but swayed dizzily against him. Gently, painstakingly, he unbuttoned the spangled gown and slid it down past her slender hips, where she dutifully stepped out of it. He spied her dressing gown on the bed and patiently threaded her arms into it, leaving her strapless bra and panties in place. She flopped back onto the bed while he carefully hung up the expensive dress. Then he left the room.

Jessica's head was spinning, and she could hear the clatter of kitchen cabinet doors and pans; what in the world was he doing, eating while she was *dying?* He soon returned with a steaming cup of herb tea.

"Here, drink this." Sliding his arm around her, he helped her to sit up.

"No. I'll get sick."

"Jess, drink it. It'll make you feel better, honest."

"It smells like poison. If it *is* poison, I'll drink it."

"Drink it."

She sipped the liquid, and her eyes flew open. "This is horrible!"

"Good, then I made it right. Drink it all, Jessie." Mac's voice was gentle, but firm.

Sure enough, she soon felt better. Her head was hurting, but the nausea and dizziness had subsided.

She leaned over her lap, covering her face with her hands. "Mac, I'm so sorry. I'm so ashamed. It was a rotten thing to do. And stupid, and..." She began to weep quietly.

He stood in front of her and began tugging at his tie, removing it.

"So, Pierce's got your number. Big deal. You'll get over it." He tossed the tie onto the dresser and began working on the tiny, jeweled tuxedo buttons.

"How do you know?" she moaned.

"Because I know. I know he's a womanizer and you're a baby, and it happens all the time in this business. It'll pass." There was no sympathy in his voice. If anything, it was thinly veiled anger she was hearing.

"Mac, I really cared about him." New tears slid down her cheeks.

The shirt was off, but she was too miserable to wonder or care if he was going to continue with the pants. He hung up the shirt, and responded, his tone guarded and tight. "I would hope you care something about someone you're sleeping with."

His comment made her stop crying and sit up. "How did you know? Did you read *that* in *Variety* too?" she asked bitterly.

Mac parted his lips and then closed them, sitting down on the bed before responding. "How could I not know?" He looked at his hands and spoke slowly. "Look, Jessie, I know this sounds trite, but where you're at...I've been there myself, and not long ago. I hate to see you hurting like this. But I can't tell you what to do, or how to feel. Only you can control your life."

Jessica's anger melted as quickly as it had formed. Mac was right, but she could hardly imagine him going through the turmoil she was experiencing. She stared at him questioningly.

"Her name is Lauren Winter," he began, standing up and stepping into her bathroom to change out of his tuxedo trousers. "She's twenty-four and gorgeous." He returned, now back in the cut-offs. "But she's a user. She wants me to be available all the time, but she can't be available to me. One minute she's all over me, then she'll disappear for days." He shrugged. "I told her I'm not looking for any big commitments, and that's a fact. I can barely handle the ones I have." Mac paused, pulling a clean T-shirt out of his bag and over his head. "But I expect a reasonable level of fidelity..."

"Is she an actress?" Jessica asked, rounding out an impression in her mind.

"She's a wanna-be. I think she'd do just about anything to get in."

"Do you love her?"

Mac didn't answer, instead going to the window and pulling open the louvered blinds. In the distance, fireworks lit the night sky.

"Happy New Year," he muttered, and left the room, closing her door behind him.

Four

Roommates

Jessica awoke with the sun in her eyes and reached up in vain for the wand on the window blind. She rolled out of bed and stumbled into the bathroom.

"Oh God," she exclaimed at the mirror, her image a mess of tear-streaked make-up and matted hair. She looked down at her robe and remembered the night before. With a groan, she stepped into the shower and took a long, hot rinse, hoping to purge the depression of the previous night.

After several minutes of half-hearted primping, she was reasonably satisfied, and went to the kitchen to start some coffee. She was filling the pot with water when the front door opened, startling her so badly she dropped the pot into the sink. Mac, breathing hard, was returning from a run, his shirt wet and his hair curling around his face.

"Good morning," he said, leaning against the doorjamb while catching his breath. "What's for breakfast?"

Jessica stared at him in stunned silence.

"Well...just decaf would be fine," he said, noticing the pot in her hand, which had miraculously remained intact. He turned and trotted into the bathroom where she heard the shower start and the remote, off-key hum of his voice as he sang.

She went to the refrigerator. No eggs. No bacon. No ham. None of the things men liked for breakfast. She sighed, suddenly annoyed and tired. "Well, he'll just have to eat what I eat if he doesn't warn me he's staying the night," she said to herself in exasperation. She threw out an expired pear but found two passable apples and a nearly ripe imported peach which she sliced into a large salad bowl, adding some diced pineapple from a can, then threw some store-bought blueberry muffins into the toaster oven.

Moments later, Mac stuck his head out the bathroom door. "Jessie, I don't eat bacon or sausage and such," he hollered across the room. "Please don't go to a lot of trouble." And as an afterthought, "but I could use some hot coffee after this *cold* shower."

Jessica smiled, her earlier irritation evaporating. Mac was a funny guy, and despite her glimpse of his dark mood the night before, it was somehow comforting to know that this new friend was not always so perfect, happy, and content.

They dined on the patio balcony. "This is great," he remarked. "I love fruit for breakfast."

Jessica was surprised. "I figured you for steak and eggs."

Mac grimaced. "Too much cholesterol. I want to live to tell stories to my grandchildren."

No mention was made of the night before. Neither seemed interested in recalling the pain each had suffered for different reasons.

Soon, Mac gathered his gear and she walked him to his car. "I really appreciate you letting me dress here last night. My bathroom is currently under blue sky, and the roofers haven't even shown up yet."

"No problem. It must be rough living there right now."

"Truth is, I've been sleeping on Bill's couch for a week." He twisted and rubbed his neck. "And now I'm told it might be another month."

"That's awful," Jessica sympathized.

"I've got to get some lodging arranged. I'll probably end up taking a room at the Hilton," he said, throwing his bag into the trunk of the BMW.

"You're welcome anytime, Mac."

"Appreciate that." He paused before getting into the car and glanced back toward the house. "It's a comfortable place."

Jessica followed his gaze and nodded, a thought forming. A crazy thought, but worth mentioning. "Mac, I have an idea. Come back inside."

He followed her back in and she led him to the closed door adjacent to the bathroom. She opened it and they entered the second bedroom of Jessica's small home.

It was two rooms, really, a smaller one intersecting a larger one. The door opened into the smaller room, which held a roll-top desk, a highboy dresser and mirrored wardrobe closet. A second access door to the main bathroom completed the room's features. Through the corner, a step down led to the larger room, housing a queen-sized bed and a wicker chair. The room was long and there was a single French door at the opposite end that opened to a path that turned to the street.

Currently, the bed was piled with odds and ends, "Goodwill" clothing, books and scripts. Jessica turned to Mac. "This is Roxie's room, but since she doesn't often stay here, I'm sure she wouldn't mind sharing it with you for a while." She laughed, clasping her hands together over her brilliant idea.

Mac looked around the room, then back at Jessica. "I don't believe this. You're offering this room to me?"

"Sure, until your roof's done, and your house is livable."

"Are you sure?" He looked at her incredulously, then hesitantly. "It's perfect."

"Well, far from that, but it has a private door, so you can come and go as you please; I'll clear out this closet and get rid of all this junk," she offered, sweeping her hand toward the bed, "and you can stop sleeping on couches."

Mac pressed his fingers to his lips in indecision. He opened the closet again, not really looking inside, his expression unreadable. Finally, he turned back to Jessica. "I'll pay you, of course," he began. She held up her hand.

"Don't offend me, please. Just stock the pantry with whatever you like to eat."

"I keep really bad hours, Jess, I'd be showering at four in the morning and dragging in at ten at night..."

"No problem."

"...and bringing in strange women..."

"That's what the side door is for," she smiled warmly, and he tousled her hair.

"It's a deal. How much of a security deposit do you want?"

For Jessica, it was a vastly different kind of New Year's Day. They hadn't even turned on the TV to see the Rose Parade, which had always been a big deal to her while growing up. Nonetheless, there was still the sense of a new beginning in the air.

By that evening, a Sunday night, Mac had moved a few items and clothing into Jessica's spare room, and he went to bed early. He explained that most of his calls were at five in the morning, and that he might not see her much except on weekends, if then. Not used to having a roommate, this was fine with Jessica, and life went pretty much back to normal. She did hear him showering the first couple of mornings but drifted back to sleep each time. There was something comforting about having him around.

Lost Season rehearsals began in earnest and Jessica's own hours became erratic. One evening she returned home late to find Mac already retired and a note on the refrigerator door.

Jess—Pierce stopped by. 7:30 p.m. —Mac

Her face grew warm, and she looked at the clock. 10:30. Thinking it could be about the film, she decided to call him back.

"How about dinner Saturday night? I'd like to go over some of the scenes and get your ideas about the location shoot."

Jessica took a deep breath. "I guess...sure. Can I meet you somewhere?"

"No, I'll pick you up." He paused. "So, you have a *roommate*?" he asked casually. "If I'd known you were taking in boarders, I would have applied."

Jessica didn't take the bait. "See you Saturday."

Despite her efforts to remain calm, Jessica's angst returned at the prospect of seeing Dane. In the kitchen, Mac stood over his own stir-fry chicken dinner on the stove, chiding her as she flitted around the house.

"Hey, Jess, he's just a guy, right? Just a guy."

"No, Mac, *you're* just a guy. *He's* Dane Pierce, and he's got my number, remember?"

Mac feigned hurt feelings at her comment, and Jessica smiled, then rearranged her hair for the fifth time. "Where are my keys?"

"Don't worry, you probably won't need them."

She stopped and gave him a frown, then went back to the mirror. Finally, she confronted Mac across the breakfast counter. "I'm nervous."

"Well, you don't have a very strong track record against this guy. Just keep up your guard, and if he gets fresh, throw him a right hook—between the legs." Making a fist, he demonstrated a low punch for her. She pouted at his failure to be serious, and he leaned across the counter, his face close to hers. "Look, if it weren't for this film coming up, I'd tell you to just blow him off. I wouldn't even *let* you go. But you are about to have a very intimate encounter with him —as Mariah Sinclair—and for that to come off okay, you have got to get past this obsession. Get it?"

Jessica nodded.

"And," he added, "I'm not going to wait up for you." He pointed his finger and touched her nose.

The doorbell made her jump; Mac rolled his eyes and went back to the stove. She let Dane in and went for her coat.

"MacKendall. What's cookin'?"

"Dinner. I offered to share, but Jessie said you'd rather go out." Mac offered Pierce a sliced carrot, which he took good-naturedly but stopped short of putting in his mouth.

"Wouldn't try to poison me, would you Mac?" His eyes glittered, and Jessica hastened to get him out the door.

But Mac was not to be outdone. "Have her in by midnight or don't bring her back." Jessica frowned at him behind Dane's back, and he grinned indulgently, then blew her a kiss as they went out.

Dane was quiet during dinner, and Jessica still felt nervous. She stole an appraising look at him while he was talking to the waiter. Still thin, but still immensely attractive. *Just a guy*, she reminded herself. Finally, she spoke up. "Dane, why did you ask me out?"

"I had to see you again."

Jessica paused, carefully nursing her drink. She would never allow herself to drink to excess again. A New Year's resolution she intended to keep.

"Jessie, are you sleeping with MacKendall?" Dane's question was aimed right between the eyes and was so unexpected that she nearly upset her glass.

"Dane, that's absurd! What a thing to ask!" She colored with surprise, then regained her composure. "As if it's any of *your* business."

"You're absolutely right, it *is* none of my business," he conceded, but was obviously quite satisfied with her denial.

"Besides, he's not interested in having a relationship with anyone right now." Jessica detected a look of surprise but went on to change the subject. "How is your family?"

"Okay, I guess...They seemed fine at Christmas, the kids I mean, except that Zoe doesn't remember me. I guess I don't remember her too well either...Hey, it turns out Rita's tennis guy is a law student. A fucking law student! Hey, that's funny." His sarcasm was bitter, and out of reflex she put her hand over his. Seeming to take her gesture as a positive sign, he threw down a wad of bills. "Let's get out of here, Jess."

They walked back to the Porsche, and, instead of starting the car, Dane reached for her. She resisted his advance, and he spoke softly. "Jessica, come home with me."

Jessica's spine turned to jelly. She sat silent, searching his eyes, his face, his lips...and back to the green eyes, sensually asking her for another night of lovemaking and intimacy.

"No."

There. She said it. She felt her eyes burning and prayed that she wouldn't start crying.

"Ah, Jess...I know I'm a complete jerk. I know I blew it with you. Please, let me make it up to you..."

"Stop. Just...look." She took a breath and went on. "I think the world of you, Dane, please believe me. But we're out of sync, you and I." The tears were going to come anyway, and she touched his face affectionately. "The timing's not right. I can't be what you want, and you can't be what I want. There's a lot at stake here, not just the film. I want to help you, but what I have isn't what you need. Maybe someday, when things settle down for you...but for now, it's best if you just take me home."

"Things will never settle down for me, Jess. We're good together, and you know it. No one sets me off like you do...and I know you feel something for me...we can come up with some arrangement that would work for us, I know it." When she didn't respond, he continued. "I hate this cat and mouse game we play. And I hate it that you're shacking up with MacKendall. I want you, Jessie..." His parted lips met hers, now wet with tears. She let him kiss her, then held her cheek against his.

"Take me home, Dane. I'm sorry, really," she sobbed. "You've got to...to understand...why...this won't work...for me. Please?"

He sighed and lowered his chin to his chest, then started the car.

"Looks like your roommate is out," Dane mused, as they stopped at the curb before the darkened house. Jessica looked down, feeling for her purse on the floor of the car. Instead of a handbag, her fingers closed on a small book, which she retrieved. Black, with a soft leather cover, she almost expected it to say "Holy Bible" across the cover. Instead, the gold embossed letters in the lower right corner spelled "DANE T. PIERCE." Instantly he snatched it from her hand and tossed it into the black abyss of the back seat.

Jessica looked at him in surprise, but Dane ignored her look and glanced again at the house. "By the way, Jessie, regardless of what he tells you, he *is* involved with someone."

Now grasping her purse, she frowned. Dane seemed to delight in stirring her up, and she decided not to encourage more conversation about Mac. She shrugged, then hastily got out of the car. She leaned down to look back in, keeping her swollen eyes guarded.

"Goodnight, Dane. I...had a nice time. See you at rehearsals."

Quietly Jessica crept across the living room. Indeed, the house was dark, and she turned on the small television in her bedroom, the volume low. On auto-pilot she prepared for bed, then laid down and grasped a pillow to her stomach. Silent tears wet the pillow as she tried to put the evening behind her. It had been hard to say good-bye to Dane, hard to deny herself one more night of owning him, of being treated, if only briefly, like she belonged to him.

A movement caught her eye and she looked up to see Mac standing at the foot of her bed, rubbing his eyes and squinting at her.

"You okay?" he asked softly, shutting off the television.

"Yeah," she whispered, but he came to her anyway and sat on the edge of the bed. In the dim glow afforded by the back porch light, Jessica took in Mac's appearance. Despite the chill in the house, he was wearing a tank shirt and running shorts, and looked ready for a marathon at a moment's notice.

"I didn't really expect you home. What happened, didn't he ask you to stay?" Although seemingly calm, his voice was edged with a touch of disdain.

"Yes," she whispered between sobs.

"So? Why are you here?"

"I told him no."

"What?" Mac's eyebrows went up. "I don't understand. He invited you home for fun and games and you turned him down?" Jessica nodded, sniffing. "But I thought that's what you *wanted!*" Mac jumped up and paced to the French doors and back to the bed, his arms outstretched in demonstration of his surprise. "I don't get it." He sat down again, his back to her in exasperation.

"I couldn't do it, Mac. I told him that we weren't compatible, that it wouldn't work and that maybe things would change, after he gets his life together."

Mac turned to look at her, and with a sigh, stretched out on his side next to her. "I can't believe you did it. I'm proud of you."

Despite his encouraging words, the tears continued, and Jessica grasped his shirt in her fist and pressed her face against his chest. Her gesture touched him, and he gently lifted her chin to reveal her eyes to him.

"It's just so sad, Mac," she explained miserably.

"I know," he murmured, pulling the covers up to tuck her in, "but you did the right thing, and these will be the last tears you shed over that guy." He began brushing her hair from her face with his fingers, repeating the motion until she fell asleep.

Somewhere, a phone was ringing. Jessica thought she was dreaming because the ring seemed far away. Still, she stirred in the direction of the noise, and in doing so, found she was not alone. Bound by an arm tucked comfortably around her waist, she could feel slow, even breathing at the back of her neck.

Alarmed at first, she turned her head quickly toward the source and looked onto her roommate's sleeping face, apparently undisturbed by the ringing telephone. Her little-used, landline phone was on the opposite nightstand, and as Jessica turned to reach it, the arm maintained its grip on her. Finally retrieving the phone, she fell back on the pillow, Mac's protective hold still embracing her.

Her eyes wide, she lifted the receiver. "Hello?"

The voice on the line was a young child's, identifying herself and asking to speak to her daddy.

"Your *daddy?*" Jessica said groggily.

"Yes, his name is Cory Lee MacKendall and he's late. Is he there?" The little girl was assertive, there was no doubt.

"Um...I think so," Jessica stared in awe at Mac's sleeping form next to her, "I'll go see; hold on, honey." She put her hand across the mouthpiece and struggled to turn herself to face him. In doing so, she discovered that her legs, bare beneath her short nightgown, were comfortably nested against his—long, warm and also bare. She loathed waking him.

"Mac!" she whispered loudly, "Wake up! It's Megan!" Gently she shook his shoulder.

Mac lifted his head up and took everything in at once. "Am I in your bed?"

Jessica nodded, amused at his reaction to finding himself with her; gingerly he pulled his arm free of her waist.

"Mac, it's Meggie! On the *phone*!" She tried to make him comprehend.

"Megan? What time is it?"

"Nine-thirty."

"Damn!" Mac took the phone, and his agitated state went under wraps. "Hi sweetheart. Yeah, it's Daddy. Yeah, I'm still coming, you know how I sometimes get busy..." At this Jessica couldn't contain her giggles and pressed her face into a pillow. "One hour, Meggie, I'll be there, sugar. Let me talk to Mommy." Jessica heard his voice change. "Yes, I am coming. Yeah, yeah, yeah. Gimme a break. As if you never made a mistake. Yeah? Well, I guess I made that one, too." Although the words seemed unkind, he laughed in good humor before handing her back the phone, then plopped back into his pillow with a groan.

He lay there only a moment before bounding out of the bed, slapping her on the behind and commanding, "Get up. We've got to be in Camarillo in an hour."

Jessica propped herself up. "What do you mean, 'we'?"

He hollered at her from his bedroom as he began gathering his clothes. "You're going with me," then, as he peeked back around the corner of her door, he added, "if you want...I could use the company...please?" with a most beguiling smile.

Having nothing better to do, she nodded and raced to get ready.

It was an hour drive to Camarillo. They took Mac's ancient Ford pick-up and headed across the south Valley, chatting about the city, the weather, and local politics. It seemed refreshing to talk about *normal* things, and Jessica began to relax for the first time in weeks. After a few moments of quiet, Mac spoke of the night before.

"Sorry about falling asleep in your bed," he began. "One minute I was staring at the moon through your window, trying to figure out the meaning of my life, and the next, well, you know the rest."

"Your life can't be that boring," she said with a laugh, taking the edge off his apology and letting him know she wasn't annoyed. It had been a long time since she had awakened to the feel of a warm, masculine body wrapped comfortably around hers...no, she certainly wasn't annoyed.

"It's getting better," he said softly, stealing a sideways look at her as he drove.

Megan was a bright, articulate child, still a baby and yet quite a young lady in many ways. With curly brown hair and her father's sensitive brown eyes, she was petite but a tornado of energy, full of questions and opinions about worldly things. Jessica loved her immediately, and they enjoyed a splendid day shopping in Ventura Beach. It was obvious to Jessica that Megan was the single most important person in Mac's life. Once, she and Wesley had planned a baby, and Meggie seemed just like the child she had always envisioned.

While waiting for Mac to purchase carousel tickets, Megan crawled onto Jessica's lap.

"Daddy says you're his special friend. Are you going to marry him?"

Jessica stroked the little girl's hair. "Do you want your daddy to get married?"

"No. Mom says he wouldn't come for me anymore if he gets married."

"Well, you should never worry about that. Your daddy loves you more than anything in the entire world. He'll never stop coming."

"I wish he lived with us." Megan's face puckered.

"You know your dad works very hard at his job, and he can't always be there, but he wishes he could be with you, I know. He told me. And when his house is all finished, he wants you to come and stay with him for a while."

"I don't think my mom will let me. She says I won't like it there."

"She just might change her mind, Meggie. It's a beautiful place, with a special room, just for you."

Mac returned with tickets and ice cream cones. Megan scrambled off Jessica's lap and threw her arms around Mac's legs in a rush of affection for her father, who quickly handed the ice cream to Jessica. He lifted Megan and tossed her into the air, catching her in a bear hug and kissing her neck playfully. Jessica watched with unabashed envy.

Jessica found Linda MacKendall to be a complex person, someone still not comfortable with being divorced and trying to protect her daughter from the negative influences of separation. Although she was cordial, almost friendly to Jessica, Linda seemed to resent Mac and his chosen lifestyle, and therein lay the conflict in raising their mutual child. Jessica found herself thankful that she and Wesley had been childless. She couldn't fathom going through Mac's struggle to keep his daughter close, nor Dane's heartbreak at losing touch with his youngest.

With promises to return in two weeks, they left Megan waving good-bye in Linda MacKendall's driveway, loudly reminding Daddy not to be late next time.

They spoke little on the drive back, and at last Mac broke the silence.

"Penny for your thoughts?"

"Just remembering Meggie asking about how seagulls kiss."

Mac smiled. "She's pretty precocious. I dread her becoming a teenager." He shook his head in mock panic. "She's very fond of you."

Jessica grinned. "I'm certainly not much of a role model."

"Don't sell yourself short."

"By the way, what does Linda do? Is she a career person?"

"Yes. She teaches at the University."

"Oh." Jessica was again quiet. Something was on her mind, and it would not go away. "Mac, Dane said the strangest thing last night."

"Yeah? What pearls of wisdom did he impart now?"

"You really hate him, don't you?"

"No. I just don't *like* him. There's a difference. Now, what amazing thing did he say?"

Jessica swallowed. "He said...you were...involved with someone."

Mac narrowed his eyes. "What? Was he talking about Lauren? I knew the tabloids picked that up, but Pierce doesn't seem the type to—"

"No. I don't think so."

Mildly annoyed, Mac shrugged it off. "I don't know what he's talking about. I haven't enough room in my life to get a haircut, much less entertain a lady." He unconsciously ran his fingers through his long, shagged hair. "With Mom sick, and Megan, and the show, and that damned house..." He shook his head as his voice trailed off. "You know, it took me a long time to get used to being single. And I'm comfortable with it. I wasn't expecting to get tangled up with Lauren, and it taught me the value of being in control of my life. Pierce's life is so screwed up, he expects everyone else's is, too."

Jessica reached across the cab and squeezed his arm. "Hey, relax. You certainly don't have to explain your life to *me*. He's mistaken, that's all." She smiled warmly and wouldn't let go of his arm until he glanced her way.

"He's not mistaken, he's lying. He's pulling your chain, Jessica."

Oddly, she rather liked his defensive demeanor, and decided to tell him the rest. "He also thought we were sleeping together."

Instead of getting angry, Mac threw back his head and laughed.

"What's so funny?" she asked, confused. Mac shut the engine off. They were home.

"Well, I guess we have, haven't we?" A smile spread across Jessica's lips, and they laughed together as they entered the house.

It was eight days before the roommates saw each other again. Other than the presence of a few personal items and an occasional bump in the night, each hardly knew the other existed. The demands on Jessica's time increased steadily as Pierce Productions began preliminary filming in the studio; Mac's season would be winding up in a few weeks and the pressure was on to finish a quota of episodes. Jessica nailed up a small corkboard in the kitchen, and it was here that they left communication for one another, pinned up their schedules and tacked up reminders. Jessica began to miss talking with Mac, and one evening decided she'd do something about it.

She was up at 4:30 the next morning, baking croissants and brewing coffee. Brewed coffee was a luxury, she was coming to find out, and the smell of it and the rolls were not lost on Mac. He emerged from his room dressed warmly for an early morning's location shoot.

"Jessica? Is that you?" He laughed, shaking her hand in mock surprise that they did, in fact, still live under the same roof. "Oh, Jess, this is wonderful."

They chatted brightly while devouring the rolls and coffee.

"What are you up to today? Rehearsals?" he asked.

"No. I've demanded a day off. Rox and I are going to the beach."

"Lucky. Watch that you don't get fried." He stuffed the last of a croissant into his mouth, then stood up. "I've got to tell you, this is working out so well, I'm selling my house and buying this one."

Jessica narrowed her eyes. "That's ironic. The owner called last week, he's sold the house and it's in escrow."

Mac frowned. "No," he moaned. "Will you have to move?"

"Don't know yet. They may keep it as a rental, and if so, they may keep me as a tenant."

Mac sighed and carried plates to the sink. "Gotta go, dear, I'm late for the office."

"Don't forget your coat," she grabbed his jacket and followed him to the door to the garage. "Bye, *dear*." On her way back to her room to fall back into bed, she turned as he stuck his head back inside.

"Hey, thanks for breakfast." She waved him off and he was gone.

She was surprised upon entering the house that evening to find Mac again sitting at the kitchen table, script pages spread out in front of him.

"A little late for you to be up, isn't it?"

"I've got a problem with this scene, and we're shooting it tomorrow. I'm not sure I should have opted to direct this one...How's Roxie?"

"Okay." She put down her things and went to look over his shoulder. He described the problem as she absently began massaging his neck. "Have the girl wait on the roof while Doctor Jim goes down the chimney. That way she'll be able to warn him when the bad guy comes, instead of being stuck in the chimney with him. And," she added, "your camera can then stay on the roof, looking down at you."

He thought it over. "You're brilliant, and I'm brain dead, and don't stop what you're doing to my neck." He made a note, then put down his pencil and closed his eyes as her fingers pushed the tension from his muscles.

"I'm not surprised, after twenty hours. At least *I* went back to bed." She turned away and he sighed his disappointment comically.

Mac considered her as she took off her black leather jacket. "You're sunburned. So what's wrong with Roxie?"

"How did you know something was wrong?"

"Because you always say 'great' when I ask how she is. You didn't this time." Mac opened the refrigerator. "Hungry?"

Jessica sighed and sat down. "No! I'm stuffed. Popcorn, candy, soda...ugh." She crossed her arms on the table and lay her head down.

"Ah, you went to the movies. You'll be dead by morning." He poured them each a glass of sparkling water instead.

"Roxie's breaking up with Zachary. It's all about drugs and sex with this guy."

"Sounds about right."

"I feel awful for her, Mac. She's so sweet, and worthy of someone nice. Why does the world have to be so messed up? There's just too much pressure. She shouldn't have done it."

"Done what?"

"Slept with him." Jessica looked at her hands.

"Aren't you being a bit harsh? What did you expect her to do, play Scrabble with him instead?"

Jessica looked up, exasperated. "It shouldn't be like that, Mac. Women shouldn't feel like they must have sex to get a second date from a guy! It's disgusting."

"I agree. But I also believe women, and men, have choices."

Jessica stared at him in question but refrained from prodding. His eyes told her his statement was not just an idle comment.

After a thoughtful pause, she calmed down. "She's just had an AIDS test."

Mac looked alarmed. "You don't think—"

But before he could finish, she raised her hand. "It was negative."

He accepted her response. They sat in silence for several moments, each reflecting on their discussion.

Finally, Mac reached to the counter. "Here's your mail."

She shuffled through the envelopes, then selected one with a groan. Sure enough, it was a letter from the landlord with the news she dreaded. It was more than she could handle tonight. Tossing the envelope down on the table, she stood.

"Good night, Mac," she said softly as she started for her room. "You should go to bed."

FIVE

Departures

Rehearsals and filming continued in sporadic, make-shift spurts. Jessica believed she saw some improvement in her skills, but she also knew that location shootings and time itself would change her perspective. She carefully put aside any thoughts and fears she had about facing Dane, hoping that time would also help her reorganize her feelings about him. She purposely avoided opportunities that might lead to an encounter.

At home, five weeks had passed since Mac moved in, and things had settled into a comfortable, if haphazard, routine. They continued to leave notes for each other, and it became a game to leave something whimsical or witty for the other once or twice a week.

Jessica stared at today's note in wonderment.

> *Jessie - Any chance you could come down to the*
> *set tomorrow at lunch? If so, leave me a note &*
> *I'll leave instructions. I'm going on location—we*
> *have to talk — Mac*

She picked up the pack of sticky notes and carefully penned a reply.

> *Mac—Can do, should I bring food? —Jess*

Late that night she found a reply:

Jess—No food, take this card to the front gate,
they'll direct you to where I am. 12:00 or ? —
Mac

Wednesday morning, Jessica put the top down on the Mazda and drove to Castle Studios where *Doctor Jim* was filmed. She smiled to herself, remembering her first visit to the studio, her first encounter with the man she had mistaken for a production assistant. The gate guard pointed the way and she nodded.

"Wait until the red light is off, miss," he advised.

Jessica mentally rolled her eyes. Was there anyone left in this city who didn't know that a red light meant filming was in progress?

The light went off. She crept inside and silently joined the group of people on the dark side of the room. Her stomach tightened involuntarily when she caught sight of Mac, who was discussing the scene in progress with two others. Highly animated, in make-up, she had never witnessed him at work before, and found it exciting.

Soon, the cameras were rolling. Jessica's heartbeat picked up; she was thrilled to watch Mac in action. The scene took place in a living room, and Doctor Jim was confronting two rough looking characters with obviously sinister motives. A scuffle ensued, and a bag of jewels was accidentally emptied on the floor. Jessica watched the action closely as they stopped and repeated the take several times. Near twelve, the director called lunch, and people began cleaning up and wandering away. Mac was still engrossed in conversation with a technician but broke it off abruptly when he caught sight of Jessica waiting.

"Good to see you. C'mon." He led her quickly out of the soundstage and across an alley to another building, where Mac maintained a small apartment-style dressing room.

"Mac! This is cute!"

"My home away from home, away from home. I'd be staying here full time if it was permitted."

Jessica looked around and noted all the amenities: small refrigerator, sink, microwave, daybed, bathroom, dining and dressing tables; lots of photos of Megan. Fitness gear.

"You lift weights *too?*"

"When I'm bored. Let's eat, I'm starved." He brought out a delectable salad from the fridge, a bag of rolls and sparkling cider.

"This looks great!" She walked around while he dished out the lunch. "So. You're leaving me?" she asked in mock humility.

"'fraid so, darlin'," he responded in kind. She sat down and they consumed the lunch together, bringing each other up to date on their individual plans.

"I'm leaving on Tuesday. We're off to Berlin."

Jessica's eyes widened. "Really? Gosh..." She hadn't thought that he would be going so far. "How long?"

"A couple of weeks. And you're off to the Caribbean?"

"Yes. Amande." She closed her eyes briefly. "It's a tiny island, in the Grenadines. We're leaving...the 26th, I think. In a couple of weeks." At her response Mac reached to his dressing table for a piece of paper.

"Let's see...my return trip is...the 27th." They stared at each other for a moment, then he folded the paper and tossed it back to the table. "How long will *you* be gone?" he asked.

"A month, at least." Her voice was rough, and she cleared her throat. "A good part of the film happens on the island."

Mac said nothing at first, slowly chewing his food. He seemed to be working something over in his mind. Finally, he spoke. "When do we have to be out of the house?"

"Two weeks. Today's the..." she looked around for a calendar.

"Seventh. We have six days." Soon his face cleared, and he spoke decisively. "Okay. Here's what we're going to do." Mac outlined a plan to move Jessica into his newly finished home over the weekend.

Jessica's eyes grew wide, and she tilted her head. "Huh?"

"Just until you leave. It's only two weeks, and anyway, I need you to inspect the roof and test the faucets." He grinned at her, but Mac was adamant. "It's crazy to drive to North Hills and back every day, when I live so close to the studio."

"Are you sure?"

"Don't be silly. Of course, I am. We'll just move your stuff back with mine, and it can stay there while you're on location. When you get back, if you come back, you can look for a place at your leisure. You'll be making tons of money by then, and you'll probably buy a big fancy mansion and two or three more Miatas."

This made her relax, and she laughed. "What do you mean, 'if' I come back?"

Mac glanced at the clock. Just then a heavy-set woman burst into the room with several garments on hangers.

"Oh! So sorry Mr. Mac, I didn't know you had company." She put her hand over her mouth.

"Ruby, no problem. This is my roommate, Jessica." Jessica marveled at the way he introduced her. Was he really that casual with others about their arrangement?

"Oh, how do you do, Miss Jesseeca. Here's your wardrobe changes for today and tomorrow, Mr. Mac. Anything you need?" she asked while hanging the clothing in the closet.

"Naw, everything's under control, Ruby. Thanks." With his dismissal, Ruby left the bungalow as quickly as she had arrived. Mac picked up their plates and put them into the sink. "You're welcome to stay as long as you want. I have to get back early and make a change or two before we roll this afternoon."

They walked back to the set, and before anyone else could command his time, he turned to her and placed his hands on her shoulders.

"So, this will work out fine, right? Are you okay with the plan?"

Jessica nodded slowly.

"Good. I'm trying like hell to get Saturday off so I can take a closer look at the house." He motioned with his head toward the set. "But if things don't straighten out with this scene..." He squeezed her shoulders then released her. "See you...sometime." She smiled as he rushed off toward the set, calling out to several technicians for an impromptu meeting. Her time becoming more precious daily, Jess decided to go home and start cleaning out her closets.

Mac's house was an authentic, "old Hollywood estate," and at first glance, it seemed right out of Sherwood Forest. Indeed, there was a veritable woodland of trees and shrubs, mature but well maintained, cradling the storybook abode, which was resplendent with fieldstone fireplace chimneys and ancient ivy tendrils claiming ownership of its exterior walls. Jessica's breath stopped short at the sight of the home as they drove Mac's pickup over a deep carpet of leaves, twigs and gravel that Saturday evening.

The rambling, single story California ranch style frame had been painstakingly crafted to resemble an English country home, complete with cobblestone walks, exposed wooden beams, and a formal English garden near the entry, overgrown with weeds and untended perennials. Jessica sighed, taking it all in. Off to the side and angled to the house was a garage, large enough for four vehicles and designed to look like an old carriage house; it was connected to the dwelling by a breezeway, through which one could walk to a small orchard, adjoining the backyard.

Diamond-paned, beveled glass windows that cranked open adorned the front, many without screens. Wooden French doors opened into the little garden, and Jessica wondered if Mac planned to restore the grounds to their original splendor or if they would fall prey to a more convenient design.

Mac snapped his fingers, and she turned her head quickly to find his hand outstretched, waiting to help her down from the truck's elevated cab. "Sorry," she murmured, "I'm dazzled."

Inside, they toured the "modest" 5,000 square foot residence, she in awe and he in critical search of the most current changes effected by his hired craftsmen.

"This is beautiful!"

"This is a mess..."

"I love these windows!"

"They'll have to fix this sill."

"The kitchen is huge!"

"I'm hungry."

She stopped expounding and turned to Mac. "Hungry?" she asked, not able to comprehend his being hungry in the middle of their incredible home tour. "Starved. Missed lunch."

Jessica huffed in mock disdain and went to the refrigerator. The open-plan kitchen was large and updated, with an island work area in the center and counter space all around. A long breakfast bar behind the sink counter overlooked a tremendous family room, darkened now by heavy draperies and poor lighting.

The refrigerator was, of course, empty but at least cold and running. She turned to Mac and shrugged. "Chinese?"

"Yeah, let's go," he offered, but Jessica was not yet satisfied and demanded he show her the rest of the home. The house was "U" shaped; the kitchen, living and family rooms central and a wing on either side. The south wing included a bedroom identified as Meggie's, drab and undecorated, but with an appealing layout that would lend itself to an attractive decor; Megan's bath, adjoining; a maid's room, another bath, a utility and laundry room.

The north wing had been completed with the recent upgrade. A study came first, a small, cozy, office-style room, rich with mahogany paneling and built-in bookcases. Next down the hall was a small bedroom, freshly painted white but undecorated. Mac's bedroom was a huge suite that also included a bath and dressing room, finished decidedly masculine with antiques and Scottish details. And finally, another large bedroom.

"This would belong to the mistress of the house, if there was one," Mac explained as he threw the door open wide. Inside, Jessica's heart stopped as she surveyed this last bedroom. Another full-sized suite, this spacious L-shaped room provided a dressing area, large walk-in closet, and a bathroom nearly the size of the study. The bath contained both a stall shower and a jetted tub, and everything appeared to be brand new.

"Oh, Mac..." she whispered, looking around. French doors with lace panels opened into what she supposed was the backyard, and through the fading light she could see a vast, rectangular pool just steps away. Antique furniture adorned the room, a queen-sized, four-poster mahogany wood bed was central, with a large matching mirrored vanity and chair adjacent. A feminine patchwork and eyelet comforter draped the bed, with matching window panels and valances. "This is...just..." She sought words but could find none fitting.

"The bath's just been added. You'll have to let me know if the tub works," he said, winking at Jessica, as she emerged from the closet. He then unlocked and pulled open the French doors. She followed him out.

"You want *me* to try out the *tub*?"

"The pool isn't finished, but hopefully by summer...they're adding a solar heater, new filters, new decking...it's horribly cracked from earthquakes."

Jessica was still thinking about the splendid bedroom, the Jacuzzi tub and the wink Mac had given her. *He means for me to stay in that gorgeous room.* Mesmerized, she gazed at the pool.

Mac crossed his arms and sighed. "Can we go eat, now?"

His feigned annoyance caused her to look up. Back on her stride, she ignored his question. "What's that building?" She pointed to a structure that matched the house, about the size of the garage, just beyond the pool.

"The guest house, of course. But there's nothing to see in there right now. It's a mess. It's last on my list." With this comment, he took Jessica by the wrist and pulled her back toward the French doors. "I am *starved*."

They rose early on Sunday. Roxanne joined them for coffee at 8:30, after which the three began their task. The truck was filled and ready to go by two o'clock, just in time for the cleaning crew Mac hired to commence with the tedious chore of cleaning and vacuuming.

Jessica threw herself vigorously into the move, but when it was time to go, sadness overtook her and she became quiet, repeatedly checking the closets and cupboards.

"Well, I'll see you at Mac's. I have the address," Roxanne announced, waving a slip of paper on which Jessica had scribbled directions. Jessica only nodded and turned back toward the bedroom. After a sympathetic look to Mac, Roxanne took her leave.

"Tough, huh?" Mac asked softly, moving to stand close behind Jessica as she stared out the window toward the pool.

"Yeah...I guess I'm being overly dramatic. I've only lived here a year, but it's been an especially important one for me. A lot has happened. It's scary to move." She gazed out the bedroom window once more. "I guess we'd better go." Her eyes burned with restrained tears. She turned toward Mac and without another thought, pressed her face against his chest. His arms were around her in an instant, holding her tightly for several moments while she sought the strength to leave.

"Don't be scared. You're going to be too busy to even think about it for a long time. And when you come home, we'll take care of everything."

Mac's words embraced her heart, and she felt his lips press against the top of her head.

"Okay, I'm all right." She pulled away from him and wiped her eyes on her sleeve. She sniffed, then smiled. "Let's go."

"Well, it works!" Jessica announced as she joined Mac in the kitchen late the following evening, wrapped in a voluminous terry robe, her hair tied up. She had worked all day; Mac, however, had taken the day off to prepare for his trip, and was still tying up loose ends. To his puzzled expression, she explained her joy. "The tub! It's mah-volous!"

"Sounds wonderful. Next time, invite me." Before she could protest his impropriety, he opened the freezer door. "How about some Cookies 'N Cream?"

Her response was now a decided nod, an "Mmm" escaping her throat. He dished out a bowlful for each of them, and they sat together at an old-fashioned oak kitchen table. "You went shopping," she commented. "Thank you."

"Just a few things. Can't live without ice cream, can we?" Despite his animated conversation, Jessica could tell Mac was preoccupied and she anticipated some weighty conversation. Soon, he reached for a large envelope on the counter, and carefully slid its contents onto the table.

"Okay." He paused to taste the ice cream in between statements. "Keys: front door, garage, guest; alarm key; and garage door opener." Each item was displayed in turn, then pushed aside as she nodded. "Phone numbers: Mom's, Megan's, Gretchen's—she's the housekeeper who will be coming weekly; and this is a number where I can be reached in an emergency. I'll get you a better number after I arrive in Berlin." Again, Jessica nodded, her mood growing somber as she realized Mac was truly leaving in the morning.

Next Mac picked up a checkbook. "This account has some money for household expenses and emergencies. I also pay Gretchen from it. I've signed a few checks, so keep these tucked away. And there's some cash in here, for small stuff, you know, just in case the plumbing blows up tomorrow or something." He lifted another spoonful, but playfully stuck it into her gaping mouth as she stared at the cash and checkbook. "There's supposed to be a massive storm moving in tonight. I'm hoping this roof holds."

Jessica's throat felt tight, despite the delicious cold of the dessert. Things were happening too fast. She'd lost her home and now she was losing Mac, who was whimsically feeding her another spoonful. She couldn't speak, so opened her mouth dutifully. Soon, she, too, would be leaving L.A. and leaving Roxanne behind. *Can I handle this?* A sense of disquiet fell over her.

Mac's voice brought her back. "I need you to do a couple of things before *you* leave, okay?" When Jessica nodded, he continued. "Start up the cars a couple of times while I'm gone, especially the truck. I meant to get it tuned up this week, but I just ran out of time. It gets pretty sluggish if I don't drive it once a week or so."

"Sure," she finally managed to croak. "What else?"

"Call Megan when you can, tell her that I'm fine and will be home soon."

"I think I can handle that," Jessica replied, clearing her throat. "What...what time do you leave in the morning?"

"I have to be out of here by five-thirty."

"Can I drive you to the airport?"

"No, there's a limo coming. Besides, if it *is* raining, you won't want to be driving to LAX. Here, last bite." He scraped up the last of her ice cream and gently put the spoon into her mouth. "You aren't going to get all maudlin on me, are you?" he asked, watching her eyes thoughtfully.

"Too late for that," she smiled, finally forcing herself to appear confident and strong. She stood and took their bowls to the sink. Her back to him, she fought to keep her voice casual. "And when do you get back, exactly?"

"The day *after* you leave. Can't change it, I tried...there's some sort of festival occurring over there that we need to film. This is our finale, you know."

"Oh," she managed, absently rinsing the bowls and putting them into the dishwasher.

"So! You must be pretty excited about going to...where is it?"

"Amande, yes, I'm really looking forward to it," she said woodenly.

"Boy, was that convincing! Sounds like you'd rather face prison." When she didn't respond, he tugged on the back of her robe and motioned for her to sit back down. She complied and forced a smile. He took her hand in both of his and sighed. "Talk to me."

The warmth of his hands was comforting, too comforting for him to be leaving tomorrow.

"I'm just a little nervous, that's all."

"About what?"

"Everything. The trip, being gone so long, the filming, my performance, and I won't know *anyone*. God, Mac, it's this tiny little island, they probably don't speak English...and you can't even drink the water." Her words, slow at first, rushed out as she opened the flood gate holding her fears.

His fingers slowly massaging her hand, Mac spoke with firm but gentle conviction. "Hold on, Jessie...give yourself a little credit here. Don't wimp out. I know it's hard to believe right now, with everything happening at once, but you'll be fine. More than fine, you'll be brilliant." He stopped rubbing her hand and squeezed it warmly between his.

His eyes were serious and delving; she felt the strength he was offering her. She brought her other hand to join his. And with his tone slightly altered, he ventured his real concern. "Are you afraid of Pierce?"

Her eyes immediately flashed to his. His perception was uncanny when it came to her feelings about Dane, and right now there was no place to hide.

"No," she responded, boldly lying to his face, and they both knew it. Mac seemed torn between chastising and applauding her. He chose to accept the lie as fact.

"Good. You know, vampires can't come in unless you invite them."

"I'll be sure to pack silver bullets," she assured him, smiling. Inside, the terror remained, but it was now covered with the gentle blanket of his words. As usual, he had her laughing again and she could be strong in the presence of his comforting aura, but she dreaded the morning and his departure like death.

Five o'clock came much too soon for either of them. Mac was irritable and complained of a headache. Jessica ignored his crankiness and helped him gather his luggage at the door.

"Where's my jacket?" he demanded, then smiled sheepishly as he spied Jessica holding it to her chest. He took it from her just as the limo driver honked, signaling his arrival at the porch.

The rains had indeed come, pouring buckets instead of drops, and Mac looked at the ceiling warily. "Would you check around?" he asked, donning the jacket and opening the door. "Hello, Henry." He shook the driver's hand. "Bit wet?"

Henry was extremely large, Jessica noted, but equally friendly. "A bit, Mr. MacKendall. I dare say we'd best get on down to LAX. It's going to be living hell down there. I'll load your luggage."

"Thanks."

Jessica became suddenly animated.

"Passport?"

"Yup."

"Directions? Wallet? American Express?" Mac checked off each item she questioned, finally breaking the tension with a laugh. They moved outside to the porch as Henry loaded the last of Mac's bags. Mac stepped down one step and turned to Jessica, now eye to eye with her. The stormy gray dawn darkened his brown eyes as they searched hers for some note on which they could say good-bye.

"Well, this is it." He took her hands but dropped them in favor of placing his on her cheeks. A tear had escaped, and he brushed it away with his thumb. "Ah, ah, none of that," he scolded. "Promise me you'll be careful?"

She nodded slowly. "And you," she managed in a tight whisper. She felt an eternity was passing in seconds, her eyes taking in the entire scene, almost as if she could see the two of them from some remote angle. I need to remember this morning, she thought fiercely, it will be two months before I see him again.

"I'll call you in a few days," he said softly into her ear as they embraced quickly. He kissed her cheek, then dashed through the sheeting rain to the waiting car.

She did not stand and wave but returned to the house and numbly closed and locked the front door.

Dear Mac,

It is unbelievable that I am finally leaving. As I write this, I know you are packing to come home just as I am packing to go. I am moving around like a zombie, and I hope I've remembered my toothbrush when I get there.

It was wonderful talking with you the other night. I called Meggie this morning and she is excited that you will be there on Saturday. She said the sweetest thing, wishing I could be with the two of you. Glad to hear your film is good and your trip successful. I am trying not to think about what is ahead for me, you know I'm apprehensive – no, petrified – that I will be awful or freeze up. A car is coming for me at seven, and I guess I'm ready.

I had the truck tuned up, I hope you don't mind, it's running great. By the way, the plumber said the kitchen sink will now perform for another 70 years after he replaced the pipes last week. Also we need to have the roofers replace some cracked tiles over the study. No leaks, thankfully.

Jessica stopped typing and looked at the last two sentences. She deleted the "we" and inserted "you."

Thought you might like to know, Amande is one of the "Windward Islands," part of the Grenadines, near Barbados. They grow almonds there, hence the French name for them. We are staying in a remote beach location where there is only a hotel, a little market, a few houses and a primitive airstrip. We're bringing in our own food and water, and a doctor. We'll be shooting just up the beach from the hotel. A replica ship is already moored there. The nearest big town is on another island. BTW, cell service is poor. Unreal!

Mac, the most incredible thing has happened! Roxie is doing a dress for Jennifer Lawrence! She has been getting calls ever since People Weekly did an article on the Bellerive premiere, and she finally answered one. I just know she'll make it big, she has so much talent and creativity. Since I can't be there, will you please call her and ask her how it goes? She'd love to hear from you, in any case.

There is a large fruit salad and some leftover lasagna Rox and I
couldn't finish last night, so you're set for now...and of course,
there's ice cream."

She smiled at the thought of Mac teasing her with a spoonful.

Well, I will call you Saturday night and confirm that I am still
alive. Dane has promised that no time will be wasted and that
we will be home the minute the film is in the can. (He has also
offered to taste every glass of water for me, such is my obvious and
insane paranoia.) I was so glad to hear that you have the next
several weeks off, and really hope you will take the opportunity to
zone out for a while. (Or maybe you could have the pool done by
the time I come home?) Please take care of yourself. I miss you.
Love, Jessica

Mac read the letter thoughtfully, sitting at the kitchen table after returning home the following evening. He alternately smiled and frowned at all her news, then read the letter once again before popping the tray of lasagna into the microwave. Her casual mention of Pierce's "promises" caused him an inordinate level of annoyance, but he passed it off as Jessica's way of letting him know she was "okay" with Dane's attitude.

After a brief dinner, Mac went to the phone to call Roxanne. He wanted to hear her news, and to be prepared for Jessica's questions when she called on Saturday.

Roxanne was thrilled to hear Mac's voice, and hers indicated success to Mac's ears. He smiled broadly as she recounted, blow by blow, her exciting interview with Jennifer Lawrence and her hysteria upon getting the order.

"And what's more, she'll be wearing it to the Oscars! Can you believe it? Oh Mac, she's really, really nice in person, and she invited me to have lunch next week when I bring the sketches!" Roxanne's voice had taken on a feverish pitch, and Mac could not contain his laughter. She laughed with him, though, and they chatted about her future for several minutes.

Soon Mac asked about Jessica, and Roxanne sighed. "She was...okay, Mac. I spent a couple of nights there, while you were gone. She was nervous, of course, but she was up to it." Mac's silence indicated he wanted more, and Roxanne gave it up. "She missed you."

Mac responded with a deep breath and a sigh of his own. "Well, I missed her, too. The girls over there are all rather...uninteresting." He laughed. They agreed to keep in touch.

The big house seemed too quiet somehow, too large and impersonal. He roamed throughout the rooms, taking note of Jessica's touch here and there, finally collapsing onto the family room couch. He turned on the television, something he rarely did. Staring blankly at the screen, he changed the channels aimlessly, unable to follow any program for more than a few seconds. The commercials seemed particularly inane, and he wondered ruefully if the sponsors of his own series were as obnoxious as some of these. He stiffened as Dane Pierce's face flashed in a promotional teaser for *Bellerive*, now streaming online or playing at a theater near everyone watching.

Mac groaned in disgust and pressed the "off" button. Maybe a run would do him good.

Six

Stormy Weather and Island Chicken

Jessica found Amande an enigma of paradise and fear. At least in the area where they were to stay, she felt "archaic" was being generous. The Marquis Hotel was not exactly the Hilton, nor was it particularly well built or bug-free, but it was basically clean and had electricity and plumbing. The main building consisted of several small rooms, a restaurant and "cantina." surrounded by twenty or so small beach bungalows. Jessica's room was one of the latter and she estimated that it sat on only about a hundred square feet of sand.

She unpacked her bags, dashed out a quick postcard to her sister, Christine, and then laid down for a nap. Filming would commence the following morning as soon as the crew had rigged storm machines and readied the boat with cameras and lights. After three consecutive flights, she needed some rest badly, and instantly passed out.

A loud knock on her door brought her around some five or six hours later. Still fully dressed, she called out to inquire but Dane's voice barely preceded his entry into the tiny room. He closed the louvered door quickly to prevent a torrent of wind from tearing through the small bungalow. A ceiling fan turned lazily above them, picking up wobbly speed as the gust hit it.

"How are you doing?" he asked. She sat back on the bed as he dropped into a wicker chair that was wedged between the bed and wall. He looked as if he, too, had been sleeping, and he pushed his hair back from his eyes to no avail.

"Better," she admitted, yawning. "Is it morning already?"

"I'm afraid so. But it's dark because of the storm. Looks like we might not need the storm machines." Jessica remembered their last, terrible flight of the day before, and the tropical storm that had caused the turbulence.

"Oh, really? That will be interesting."

"It makes for great effects, but it's murder on our crew, trying to keep the equipment from getting trashed." Again, the hand in the hair.

"Dane, you're stressing," she observed. "You need a drink." She surprised herself by saying it, and he nodded.

"You're probably right, and when I see what direction we're going to go, you can treat me, in the cantina."

Jessica made no reply to his offer, but instead stood to look out the window. The sea looked angry and scary. High winds were pitching their ship, the *Pacifica*, mightily to one side, and the giant palms were leaning landward a sporadic forty-five degrees.

"What do you want me to do?" she inquired.

His expression turned intimate, eyes reviewing her appearance. Her hair, carefully curled for the trip, a mass of tangles around her face; her white lacy blouse was carelessly lopsided off one shoulder, her faded blue jeans partially covering her small, bare feet.

He was tired, for sure; but he lowered his eyes and smiled, that same, lazy smile she had fallen for on the grassy hillside near Studio B. Jessica saw him in a new light. An incredibly attractive man, for whom she knew she would always have a weakness. A talented man, for whom she held the deepest professional respect and trust. A sensitive man, whom she knew understood her desires like no one else, and who would unintentionally ignore his own sensitivity and hurt her with his callous ways. And, a lonely man, whom despite all else, loved her somehow, and somehow, she knew that this love hurt him, too.

Yes, the weakness was in her, and a powerful weakness it was, especially when he sat silently conveying his desire for her. Yet Jessica felt an odd sense of control for the first time in months. Standing before him, she smiled sweetly but spoke aggressively. "Dane, you are out of your lecherous, disgusting, *filthy* mind if you think for one minute these jeans are coming off for you, either now or later." To enhance her point, she leaned down toward his face while speaking, her arms akimbo.

Without anger, Dane's smiled deepened as did the heated look in his eyes, and before she could move away, he stood, grabbing her by the shoulders. He pulled her closer, his lips barely touching hers. "I love it when you talk dirty," he whispered, then kissed her lustily.

Stunned, Jessica did not struggle at first, her entire body suddenly aflame at his touch. Then, breathless, she pulled away. She fleetingly thought of slapping him, but immediately realized she had invited the attack. Her pulse racing, she turned away, hoping to disguise the intensity of her response to the kiss.

"It's okay to like it." Dane's voice taunted her; she heard the bed springs squeak in response to his weight as he moved from the chair. Desperately she searched for a way to reason with him.

"Look, Dane..." she began, turning back to face him. As if to further incite her, he stretched his long legs out on her bed. She refused to get angry. "We have to work together here. We have to face a few obvious problems..." This statement caused him to laugh out loud.

His slow, characteristically sexy drawl tantalized her. "A few *obvious problems*, Jess?" He laced his hands behind his neck and waited for her next move. She stared at him, unconsciously wringing her hands, and he grinned at her. "You're stressing Jess, you need a drink." He patted the bed next to him, leaning back against the wall. "Sit down, at least, will you? I won't do it again. I promise."

He's incredible. He just doesn't give up. And despite the fear and confusion he'd stirred up in her chaotic mind, Jessica wanted to be near him and sat tentatively on the edge of the bed. She tried to formulate what she wanted to say, but he moved first. He reached his hand to her cheek and brushed it with his fingertips, dragging them down her neck to her shoulder where he corrected the errant blouse. Jessica felt a trail of fire as his fingers stroked her skin, and she could not begin to control the molten heat pumping throughout her body.

"Obvious problems," he repeated quietly to himself, his tone changing to a more serious one. "Do me a favor, Jessica. Remember that I'm a man, a man who could spend a month in this room with you and not get enough. Remember that I am not a god, and that I have no magic power to stop how I feel. This will be difficult for both of us. I can't hide behind the big brother role with you like MacKendall does, understand?"

His words smacked of an honesty that shook her.

"I can deal with a lot when I have to. But I need your help. If you don't want me, the way I want you, then don't...do...*this*." He grasped her blouse and pulled it roughly back off her shoulder, becoming more agitated as he spoke. "The audience will benefit, surely, by the passion they'll see on the screen. But I want no casualties." With these words, he stood up and stepped to the door. She looked after him in awe and confusion. Grasping the doorknob, he stared back at her.

"I guess I need you to know that I struggle with my own demons, and that despite how things look, I care about you and want success for you without the pain I've known. You are both a delight and...an *obvious problem* for me." His eyes demanded her understanding. She stared back, hers becoming soft and liquid.

"We'll meet in thirty minutes to firm up the schedule. In the cantina." With that he was gone into the wind. Jessica shook her head in wonderment over the complexity of this tempestuous man. She crossed her arms tightly across her chest, her head bowed and her eyes closed, waiting for the trembling to subside.

By the time the cast of *Lost Season* arrived on Wednesday, the special effects wizards had already worked their magic by creating the extraordinary setting called for in the script. By Friday most of the stormy shipwreck had been shot from fifty different angles. Dane was tremendously pleased with the footage and had been wearing a permanent smile for two days. An impromptu party commenced Saturday night in the cantina, where much of the cast and crew spent their evenings drinking, dancing, and trading fish stories. An old jukebox blasted out scratchy, decades old rock music, and ceiling fans did their best to confuse the continual flight of a million insects who apparently liked the company of the American troupe.

Claustrophobic in her nine-by-nine-foot bungalow, Jessica knew it was too early to call Mac and decided to join the cantina group for a short time.

Outside, the storm raged on, and she had to fight to get to the main building where the bar was located. Surprised faces looked up as she entered, and she made her way across the crowded room to a corner where her double, Melinda, and a few other cast members and extras sat around a large round table. She was offered a Daiquiri and she accepted it, after being jokingly assured it contained no tainted water. She looked anxiously around for Dane, to no avail.

The drink liquefied her unnourished body, and she ordered a second. Melinda patted her on the back. "Glad to see you're really one of us, Jess," she said, and laughed. If only they knew, thought Jessica, how much more experienced they were than she. They seemed like such seasoned players, it didn't feel fair that she was suddenly a big star, with such little history of struggle.

Cigarette smoke fogged the hot, muggy room; the windows were all battened down against the violent wind. Jessica wore a knit tank top and walking shorts, and still the heat was nearly unbearable. Braless, she felt sweat trickle down her chest and paint a dark streak on her shirt. The drinks made the cantina into a scene from an old movie, and she dreamily imagined Gary Cooper or Humphrey Bogart walking into the dim, smoky room.

She caught her breath as she noticed a familiar figure approaching her from the jukebox across the room; but her chest sank in an odd combination of relief and disappointment when she recognized the young man as Kyle Wagner, Dane's stand-in and stunt double. He leaned down before her and smiled.

"Hello, Miss Jessie, nice of you to join us." Kyle was probably five or six years younger than Dane, handsome and cock-sure of himself. Despite his somewhat narcissistic tendencies, everyone liked Kyle and his winning smile. "You look like you need to dance."

Jessica looked up at him through her lashes, taking just long enough to respond to put him slightly off-guard.

"How sweet of you to notice," she responded, slowly getting to her feet. It was obvious that Kyle had not expected her to consent; he blushed lightly and glanced around the room. It was common knowledge that Jessica Taylor was the boss' property.

The jukebox began pounding out some hard-driving eighties rock as Jessica joined Kyle on the dance floor. It felt good to let loose, to dance off some of the tension that had layered on them over the past several days. Kyle seemed quite taken by Jessica's attention, and daringly grabbed her with a challenge in his eyes.

"Ever do any dirty dancing?"

"Maybe you could show me," she replied playfully.

The music absorbed them, and the atmosphere dazzled Jessica, becoming more like a dream than reality; when she looked at Kyle, it was Dane's laughing eyes she saw. Within moments, her imaginary vision turned real as she caught sight of Dane leaning against the wall near the door, his arms folded on his chest, his smile dangerous.

She continued dancing with Kyle, who had not yet noticed Dane's appearance in the cantina. Jessica felt the heat of Dane's eyes on her, boring through her, threatening her. At last, the song wound down, and Kyle boldly kissed her on the cheek before returning to the jukebox to poke in some more quarters. He clearly enjoyed Jessica's attention; he hadn't, however, bargained on walking right into Dane Pierce as he turned to rejoin Jessica where she waited on the dance floor.

The wicked smile still on his lips, Dane put his arm around Kyle and walked him toward a table in the corner of the cantina. Although the music began again and conversations continued, all eyes were on them as they stopped to briefly discuss some unheard topic, Dane smiling, Kyle nodding, the latter's face uneasy and overly agreeable to Dane's suggestions.

Jessica watched the scene unfold with irritation. She hated Dane for interfering, hated his possessive way with her. She turned from the dance floor as Dane approached, but he caught her by the wrist and pulled her back. "If you want to dance like *that*..." he said, grinning as the next record to drop onto the player crooned a torchy tale of lustful blues. "Let me show you how it's done."

Dane took her into his arms, skillfully moving her around the floor in a blatantly shameless exhibition for the watching crowd; his hips moved against hers, his thigh sliding between hers as he dipped her backwards in an erotic maneuver that would have challenged Patrick Swayze's own moves. He held her there for a dizzying length of time.

She stared up at him, her hair wet and sticking to the perspiration on her face; she felt her damp shirt stretch down and taut across her breasts as her chest heaved with emotion. It was a picture of perfect control, Dane's control over Jessica.

He swept her back up, spinning her a half turn before stopping with his lips not an inch from hers. Mesmerized, she saw only Dane; they might have been alone in the room.

The song ended, and with it, the "spell." Jessica blinked, took a shaky breath and walked purposefully to the table and sat down. Dane followed, shouting his request for a drink to the bar and straddling a chair facing her. Immediately, two or three of the girls stood and moved to another table.

I'm Lauren Bacall, Jessica thought, I can be sultry. She narrowed her eyes and leaned her head back. *Too bad I don't have a cigarette – as if I smoked!*

She eyed Dane coolly. *I suppose I should go change into something less provocative,* she thought dryly. Still Bacall, she spoke. "How goes it, Pierce?"

"You tell me. We're ahead of schedule." The grin was unmistakably his most luscious. Jessica thought the room grew hazier, but she could see Dane's smile quite clearly. Truly a Cheshire smile, she decided. And he, a Cheshire cat, always moving around her, appearing and disappearing.

"What's next?" she inquired, thinking she even *sounded* like Bacall.

"Next, we make love on the beach." Jessica knew he was speaking of the next day's shoot; that weather permitting they would commence with the most difficult scene, at least for her. His comment had brought forth a vague, erotic image to her mind and an aching arousal to her body. The thought of Dane making love to her on the sand was more than she could handle without giving herself away. Masking her desire, she feigned belligerence and stood up to leave.

"Good night. I have to go before *I* say something *seductive*." Sarcasm coated her every word. Dane stood, ignored her barb and grasped her arm.

"Don't go." His voice cut the heavy air like a blade.

"Let go of me."

"Sit down." Again, the sharpness biting her, his hand brutally gripping her arm. Their eyes locked into a battle of wills. She slowly sat back down.

Dane thumped the wooden table with the heel of his hand. "Why do you fight me so? Why can't you accept the way I am, and treat me like you treat the others? Jesus, you act like I'm some kind of monster."

"You're not like the others," Jessica said flatly. Pain gripped her. She wanted to be honest, to tell him how she really felt, tell him that it was all she could do not to rush into his arms at his slightest look; that her outward disgust with him was only her feeble defense against the enormous power he held over her. That right at this moment she wanted him more than anything she had ever wanted in her entire life. She suddenly felt drained and empty, and her voice was small and weak.

"Please, Dane, let me go." Jessica watched his eyes; her double entendre was lost on him. She lowered her eyes, felt the rum burning in her stomach.

Dane looked around. No one now seemed to be paying any attention to their intimate conversation. "I'll walk you to your room. It's bad outside."

"No, I'll be quite fine, thank you."

"Jessie, honey, you're toasted. Don't make a scene."

Outside, she fought him. "Don't touch me! I wouldn't want to *encourage* you."

Dane let her words go with the wind as he took her down the path to her bungalow. Once inside, they were both sobered by what they found. One of the palms in front of the small structure had toppled, crashing through the window and wall over the bed, destroying half the room.

"They'll just have to get me another room," Jessica asserted nervously.

"No more rooms. We've over-filled the place already."

"I can share with Melinda or one of the other girls," she reasoned, hurriedly pulling together her things, which was difficult enough in her emotional state without the addition of the wind and the sputtering, threatening raindrops that began to fall through the gap in the wall.

"Nope. You, me and Doug Lewis are the only ones with private rooms. Everyone else is already doubled or tripled up."

When she'd finished packing, Dane took Jessica to his bungalow, which was two rooms, the outer one he obviously used as a make-shift production office.

No sooner had they closed the door than the lights flickered and went out.

"Damn!" Dane picked up the phone, which Jessica deduced was dead from the way he slammed it back down. He withdrew his iPhone from his pocket. "Cell service is out, too."

Jessica bit her lip and reached out in the darkness, taking Dane by the wrist. He turned to her and squeezed her shoulder.

"Stay put, Jess, I'll be back."

She dared to peek out the window after he left. A single, emergency powered light illuminated the roof of the main building. The blackened sea writhed, a seething monster assaulting the shoreline just forty yards away. Frightened, she felt the desk for the phone, which was still dead. She then groped the dresser drawers, her hand finally closing on a box of wooden matches. With clumsy fingers she lit one and squinted at her watch; it was nearing midnight, 8:00 p.m. at home. Hopefully, the phones would be restored soon, and she could call Mac. She curled up on the bed and was soon asleep.

It was Jessica who woke first, her head dizzy and aching. She looked around and saw Dane sleeping in the chair, an empty bottle in his hand and the remains of a small candle on the dresser. She crawled across the bed and sat up, rubbed her eyes and adjusted her shirt. Looking at her watch, she saw it was eight o'clock. Bright sunlight poured into the bungalow. She listened intently, but no sound of wind could be heard. Instead, there were voices outside.

She reached across and shook Dane's arm gently. "The storm's gone."

Dane started as if he'd been shocked and then shoved his hands into his hair. "What the fuck did I do to my head?" he moaned. He looked at the bottle on the nightstand. "Jesus H.—! What time is it?" He closed his eyes in pain.

"Eight a.m." Jessica waited for another outburst of obscenities. Instead, Dane stumbled to the door and opened it, leaned out and stared up the beach. Five or six people were gathered a few yards away, sunning themselves on the purged sand. Farther down, he could see crew members setting up the day's shoot and rigging the *Pacifica*, still in one piece. He rubbed his eyes, and when the crew noticed him, they applauded. He promptly flipped them off, his spirits lifted by the sight of the perfect weather, and his working crew.

He returned inside and faced Jessica with a worn smile. "Sorry. I'm not at my best after sleeping with a bottle of rum."

"I should apologize. I was a bitch last night. I don't know what got into me."

"Same thing that got into me." He motioned to the bottle. "Alcohol can be a dangerous bed-fellow. Especially *this* rot-gut." He went to the bathroom to splash his unshaven face.

Not as dangerous as you are, she thought, but held her tongue. This week would be difficult enough without her fanning the flames.

Power was restored that afternoon, but shooting did not resume. Nor were the phone or satellite services repaired. Cell service was spotty. The storm damaged several vital pieces of equipment, and replacements had to be flown in from Los Angeles. But first, communication to the States had to be established.

Jessica tried to send first a text, then an email, to Mac, but without internet service, the messages failed. She hastily penned a letter, explaining the situation, but was warned that the letter would likely not arrive in even a week's time. Disheartened, she strolled away from the lobby and wondered what to do next; most of the company was taking the day off. Hotel carpenters were hurriedly repairing the storm damaged bungalows, so Jessica wandered down the beach, enjoying the mild weather and curiously eyeing the dense vegetation that grew down from the volcanic bluffs to the beach, leaving only about a hundred feet of sand exposed. She didn't bother turning around at the sound of the approaching Jeep; Dane, she knew, would catch up with her momentarily anyway.

"Want a lift?" he called, pulling the vehicle alongside as she walked.

"Not really."

"Come on. Doug and I are going for a ride. It'll be fun! I want to go round to Admiralty Bay."

Jessica sighed and held out her hand. Dane was delighted at her decision and turned the Jeep around, heading back toward the Marquis, where Doug Lewis was waiting.

"You've met Doug?" Dane asked.

Before Jessica could respond, Doug climbed into the Jeep and shook her hand.

"Of course, we've met. I'm the villain who can't wait to abduct the lovely Miss Sinclair. Glad to see you, Jessie."

They spent the afternoon exploring the small island. Admiralty Bay and Port Isabella, then on to Consequence Bay where whaling boats were moored in the small inlet.

"I can't believe they're still killing whales," Jessica said with a shiver.

"They don't get many, anymore," Doug answered.

They stepped over giant bones and strips of *baleen* strewn about outside the remains of a closed whale factory. The smell of the factory was still very much present, and Jessica begged Dane to move on, her arms crossing her stomach. Her morning hangover lingered.

The three of them piled into the Jeep and Dane took them up a narrow, unimproved road through the dense, jungle-like foliage, coming to a rustic cottage built into the rocky hillside. Portions of the home were originally caves, carved from the ancient volcanic rock of Amande. Dane thumped on the horn a couple of times before swinging himself out of the Jeep and helping Jessica to the ground.

A man appeared, his grin as broad as his hair was white.

"Dane! I knew you'd show up one of these days—how the hell are you?" He shook Dane's hand aggressively, simultaneously clapping him on the shoulder with his other.

"I'm great, Art. And you look like island life agrees with you...Art, this is Jess Taylor, and Doug Lewis. My cohorts."

Art Martino ushered the trio into his rock house and proudly expounded on its unique construction.

"Sherie's out at the market right now, but we've been expecting you, so I hope you're staying for dinner?"

Dane looked to Jessica, who shrugged slightly and looked to Doug.

"I could use a decent meal," Doug offered with an amused smile. "I'm getting a bit worn on corndogs."

Jessica marveled at the odd combination of Americana and West Indies culture that decorated the home. Since they'd chucked the Wall Street scene fifteen years earlier, the Martinos had built an entirely new life in Amande and would never go back. Sherie was probably fifty, Jessica assessed, but her casual, relaxed mannerisms and comfortable hospitality made her seem years younger. Was it the absence of stress, Jessica wondered wryly, noting the sharp contrast between Dane's weary, sometimes haunted look and Art's bright, enthusiastic demeanor?

"This looks great," Doug commented as Sherie loaded the dinner table with island delicacies. Doug, Jessica noticed, would try anything and ate heartily of every dish Sherie offered; Dane picked around, trying this and that, keeping up an endless stream of vibrant conversation with Art. Jessica secretly eyed each selection with suspicion, forcing herself to appear casual about the food.

"*Ecrevisses*," Sherie announced, passing a shallow bowl around the table.

Expectant, Jessica turned her eyes to Dane.

"Freshwater crayfish," he explained with a gleam, and Jessica nodded. "Think of it as baby lobsters."

Okay; this isn't too bad. Jessica chewed the shellfish quickly and swallowed, her heart sinking as Sherie brought forth still another platter of steaming...was it meat?

"Mountain chicken." Sherie smiled proudly. "Got the recipe from Madame Toussaint, in Port Elizabeth."

Ah, chicken. Something Jessica could deal with. And almonds, lots of them, around the edge. Of course, she recalled with a smile, almond trees grew all along the beach. "That looks good." She took a generous portion, hoping that her filled plate would preclude any more offerings. Dane smiled in approval.

Soon, the platter of "chicken" was bare, and Doug lamented that he'd never taste anything so good again.

"You're probably right. You won't find this kind of chicken in L.A., my friends. Or in New York," Art chided.

"Is that right?" Dane mused. "What's it called?"

"*Crapaud.*"

"It's hard to believe there's anything you can't get in the States," Jessica challenged with a smile.

"True. But these little buggers must be caught fresh. They're slippery, hard to find. Most of them are found on Dominica. They're even a delicacy here."

"Slippery? Chickens?" Doug asked.

The smile that had remained on Dane's face throughout dinner broke into a chuckle and he reached across the table to touch Doug's forearm. "Crap-*poe*; they're frogs, my man. Best damned bullfrogs you ever tasted."

"I will never, *ever*, forgive you, Dane Pierce." Jessica kept her voice low as they climbed into the Jeep later that evening. "You knew we were eating...bullfrogs...oh, God! And you never said a word!" Angrily she shoved him, nearly sending him out the side of the open Jeep as he laughed uncontrollably. In the back seat, Doug was moaning.

"I owe you one, Pierce," he warned. "Eating amphibians is against my religion."

"It was good, wasn't it?" Dane reminded them between giggles. "Tasted like chicken, right?"

"That's not the point! Oh, God, I'm going to be sick." Jessica closed her eyes and leaned back against the seat.

"Well, wait 'til we get back to the hotel. Jesus, you should have seen your expression!"

"I'm sorry if I offended your friends," she said dryly.

"You didn't. They're cool. They pulled the same shit on me two years ago, when I first came here to scope out the location." Dane reached over and slid his fingers across her stomach as he drove.

Torn between casting his hand away from her and relishing the warmth of his touch, Jessica decided on the former and grasped his wrist; before she could demonstrate her chagrin, however, Dane clasped her hand warmly in his, then brought it to his lips. "I'm sorry, sweetie," he murmured against her palm before kissing it. "I knew you weren't feeling well. I messed up."

"It's all right, sugarplum," Doug answered from the back, his voice a mockingly high pitch.

Dane's apology warmed Jessica, despite the nausea grinding away at her insides.

At the hotel, Dane helped her from the Jeep and tried to take her into his arms. Jessica wrestled away from him and ran from the Marquis parking lot all the way to her cabin, arriving just in time to rid herself of the *crapaud*.

Later that evening Jessica heard a commotion outside her bungalow. Through her window she could see a small group of people gathered near the entrance to the cantina, Dane's tall figure unmistakable in the middle. Still not feeling well, she grabbed her shawl and left the room.

Dane waved when he saw her.

"You won't believe this one, sweetie." He handed her a folded sheet of paper.

"What is it?" Before Dane could respond, she realized it was a printed copy of an email. Her eyes widened when she saw the sender's name: The Academy of Motion Picture Arts and Sciences. Quickly she scanned the brief notice. Her mouth opened in surprise.

"They want to know if you can hook up a live feed to the States?" Jessica re-read the telegram again. "Does this mean what I think it means? Oh my God!" She rushed him with a hug, and he laughed out loud.

"Can you believe it? An Oscar!" Dane spun her around, still laughing.

Kyle was beside himself, standing nearby grinning ear to ear. With an "air" microphone, he turned to the group of well-wishers with a mock serious tone.

"And now, coming to you live from the God-forsaken island speck of Amande, we bring you, Dane Pierce."

Dane threw back his head and shrieked. "*Bellerive!* This is...insane!"

Jessica was genuinely happy for him. Nonetheless, she declined his offer to celebrate later in the cantina.

SEVEN

Boys Will Be Boys

Fortunately, the weather held, and the equipment arrived on Tuesday. Dane's optimism ebbed slightly as they fell behind schedule. Phone service was partially and sporadically restored, and Jessica tried in vain to get through to either Mac or Roxanne.

By Monday night, Mac had become increasingly anxious about Jessica's failure to call. The weather service said that several of the Grenadines' tiny islands were damaged by the storm and that phone communications, including cellular, were intermittent at best. On Tuesday, he began trying to call the hotel with no luck getting the call past a long-distance operator. So, it was with great surprise to Mac that on Tuesday afternoon someone at the front desk of the Marquis finally answered the ring.

His joy at connecting was soon dashed by the news that Miss Taylor had checked out of her room. After further delay, it was determined that Miss Taylor had moved into Mr. Pierce's suite, and she was currently not in. Mac hung up the phone in confusion. He stared at the instrument, frowning, trying to make sense of what he'd been told. There must be a mistake, he reasoned, and dialed the hotel again. But it wasn't in the cards for him to get through a second time. The service was no longer available.

His mind burning with obscure thoughts about Jessica and Dane, Mac strode to the garage and uncovered a Honda 750 parked in the corner. Quickly donning his helmet, he opened the garage door and started the Honda, which sputtered and complained at first from lack of use, then rode down the leaf-strewn driveway and out into the canyon.

He drove until he came to the beach, where he stopped and strapped his helmet to the side of the bike before continuing, illegally, down the strip of wet sand near the surf. Thoughts of Jessica filled his head in flashing visions; sitting across from him on a blanket in Santa Barbara; taking Megan's hand along the Oxnard pier; tearing down Laurel Canyon in the blue Miata, her hair dancing wildly behind her in the wind. He smiled at the visions of Jessica sharing ice cream with him late at night and the lunch in his dressing room; but the smile faded with the memory of her crying into his shirt after walking out on Dane Pierce.

Finally, he parked the bike and sat down in the sand, watching the sun begin its nightly dip into the water. "I can't do this," he thought out loud. "She must know what she's doing." *Don't get involved.* He squinted at the water, but the visions in his head wouldn't stop. He remembered the fear in her eyes when he'd asked about Pierce, the night before he'd left for Germany. Mac unconsciously grasped a handful of wet sand as he thought about Pierce's cocky arrogance and callous treatment of Jessica's heart.

"No. I can't do this."

As the stars began to appear, he got on the bike and drove slowly home.

Tonight, the big house seemed tight and confining after his ride. He went to the kitchen but found nothing there that would fill the emptiness he knew was not really hunger. In the bathroom, he stared at his own features in the mirror. "Get a grip, Mac. You're freaking out over nothing." He needed to do something, something to kick-start his engine and burn off this unreasonable anxiety eating away at his insides.

Mac picked up the phone and dialed. "Hi Roxie, it's Mac. Have you heard from Jess?"

"No, haven't you?"

"No. Look, I have to be gone for a few days. If she should call you...tell her I'll try to get through to her when I get home."

"Sure, Mac. Where are you going?"

"Colorado." He didn't elaborate and hung up without further conversation.

Aspen, Colorado, was a cold place about now. February had brought an abundance of snow, and Mac met old ski buddies for three days of downhill racing fever. It felt good to be frozen and exhausted, he decided, after the first two days of strenuous skiing. It felt good to be among people he understood and who enjoyed the simple pleasure of slicing brisk air with a warm body at sixty miles per hour. He gained back some sense of self, honing his skills on the slopes for still another day before retiring his skis and flying back to Los Angeles. And although he felt he'd renewed his perspective, his heart was heavy as he entered the dark house.

His cell phone buzzed. A voicemail was pending.

"Hi Mac, it's Jess...sorry I missed you, boy am I sorry! I guess you must have heard about the storm. It's taken days to get a line out of this awful place, my iPhone is useless. Um...Our luck's been both good and bad out here, of course the weather's been a constant problem. Part of the hotel was destroyed, and they've changed my room twice, can you believe it? Oh Mac, I've only been here ten days and I can't wait to get home. The bugs here are huge and ugly, and there're these weird little lizards everywhere. The food is gross, I can't eat it, and everyone drinks rum all the time, and... I hope everything's okay with you. It's noon here, so I guess it's...eight a.m. there, I thought I might catch you, but

I guess not." There was a pause while she said something incomprehensible to another person. "Well, I have to go now, I'm being paged. Ha! As if they had anything so "high tech" here! I sure hope you get this message. I miss talking to you. I guess this place is supposed to be beautiful, but I think it depends on who you're with, y'know? Take care, Mac, I'll call again. Bye."

Mac listened to the message again. He sighed. He chewed on his lip, tapping his desk nervously with his fingers. She sounded homesick and anxious. So maybe she wasn't sharing a room with Pierce after all.

Collapsing on the couch, he once again turned on the television. He'd all but ignored the fact that tonight was Oscar night in L.A. Although he had attended in past years, it meant little to him. Even his own Emmy statuette bore no great distinction in his house. The glitz, the egos and the phoniness of it all depressed and offended him. But as Whoopi Goldberg introduced Harrison Ford to announce the Best Actor nominees, Mac leaned forward as Dane's name was read.

The other four nominees were sitting within the Kodak Theater. Dane, of course, was shown in a still inset, dressed in his pirate threads. Intrigued, Mac could not force himself to turn off the tube.

Ford's looking surprisingly good, he thought, purposely distracting himself from the anticipation he hated to feel. And yet he *knew*, before the infamous envelope was opened to reveal Dane's name. He picked up the TV controller.

"We have Dane on a live remote." Harrison Ford was saying. Mac stayed his hand. "Dane? Are you there?"

Mesmerized, Mac's eyes grew wide. There was Dane, standing in a bar with revelers all around him, cheering and holding up beer steins. And beside him, Jessica.

Mac rubbed at his mouth. He couldn't hear what Dane was saying as he stared at Jessica. She looked thin and pale. *And TV is supposed to put weight on?*

Dane's acceptance was brief, and Whoopi returned to the screen. Mac switched off the television.

He picked up the phone and looked down at his watch. Slowly he cradled the instrument, then paced to the back windows, not seeing the pool outside but instead seeing Jessica; surrounded by ugly lizards, vulgar, rum-drinking grips and roadies...and Dane Pierce. Had she purposely left his name out of her message? Retracing his steps, Mac again picked up the phone and called the airport weather station. After making a few notes, he went to his room and repacked his bag.

His logical mind admonished him for his poor judgment, but he stubbornly replaced his sweaters and corduroys with T-shirts and shorts, stuffing his bag hurriedly. With a little luck and clear skies, he could land in "the Windwards" within twenty-four hours.

·❤·❤·❤·❤·❤·

The twin engine Piper Cheyenne touched down on the rudimentary runway at noon Tuesday afternoon. The last leg of the flight, Miami to Amande, had been a grueling six hours; 1600 miles over water with only one brief set down for fuel in Barbados. Mac jumped out and tethered the small plane to the guy lines, then shook out his legs and grabbed his bag. A departure from the cold of Aspen, the Caribbean air was warm and breezy.

The airstrip seemed deserted. He walked toward a ramshackle building where an old car had obviously been parked for a decade. He was pleased to find the porch occupied by an island couple, who eyed his blond hair, sunglasses and leather jacket suspiciously. "Hello?" he began, removing the glasses.

There was a flurry of native conversation before they continued staring at him. "American," the man finally offered.

"Yes, American. I'm here to find my American friends, they're making a movie?"

The woman stood up and walked around Mac, inspecting his black Levis from all sides. She squinted into his face then turned excitedly to her companion. "Doktor Jim!"

Mac looked away, shaking his head with a smile. Even here, where it would seem television might be a luxury, this woman knew him. He tried again. "I need a ride...car...automobile...to the Marquis."

"Ah, Marquis! *Oui, les Américains...*"

"Good! Can you take me there?" The woman nodded happily, thrilled at the sight of an American television star asking her help. The man didn't move from the porch, only grunted when she told him she was taking the movie star to the hotel.

At the front desk, Mac ignored the "No Vacancy" sign and asked for a room. The clerk eyed the quality of Mac's jacket and flight bag greedily. "You are with the Pierce people?" he asked.

Mac weighed his response carefully. "Well, sort of." He pulled a hundred-dollar bill from his wallet and subtly folded it lengthwise.

"You are in luck, Monsieur. We have been full, but I think we can accommodate you." The clerk grinned broadly.

Exhaustion was a mild word for Mac's condition; he'd had little rest since his impromptu skiing trip and now, a thirty-six-hour flight from Los Angeles to the Grenadines. He showered and stretched out on the bed and was asleep in thirty seconds. He'd find Jessie tomorrow.

Mac did, indeed, sleep until the following morning, waking at six and needing to run. He looked out the window and whistled softly to himself. This coastline was one of the prettiest sights he'd seen, the sands glistening white, the water purest blue. He donned a black athletic shirt and running shorts. His legs were sore from skiing, and he had a good start on a tan, he noticed as he stretched and warmed up for the run.

The air was still reasonably cool as he jogged along the beach. He chose the direction opposite from where the filming was obviously in progress; he wasn't ready to run into Dane Pierce yet. He felt good, and as he ran his mind turned to Jessica and anticipation began to needle him. How would he explain his visit? I don't have to explain, he decided. *I'm on vacation.*

The sand was beginning to warm up. Wardrobe people were dressing Jessica in rags, her costume for today's shoot. She bit her lip silently as the shredded dress was tied to her nearly naked body. No time for modesty, she reprimanded herself, but felt uncomfortable just the same. Today they would shoot the scene between Mariah and Roger, whom, wandering around the island after the shipwreck, find each other and run the gamut from excitement, to anger, to pain, and finally to passion driven by fear and isolation. At least that was how Jessica perceived the transition. Dane, however, would probably play it differently. She grimaced at the thought that they'd never rehearsed this difficult, and crucial, part of the film.

Fortunately, their ultimate union was only implied, occurring "off-camera." Dane allowed that he wasn't into epic-porn and had this part, as many others, of the screenplay rewritten. Jessica's hand absently pressed to her stomach, where a growing tightness made her feel weak.

It wasn't enough that she had to face today's trials; she was worried about Mac, finding it inconceivable that they had not connected for well over two weeks. Indeed, it had been a month today since their rainy morning good-bye.

Jessica assumed her position on the sand. All around her, in a tight circle, were cameras, lights, reflectors; cords, microphones on beams; a camera boom and truck; and people, all waiting for the director to call *Action!* and the fire between Mariah and Roger to begin.

Her "dress" was wet and sandy. Her skin was too brown for a Boston aristocrat, but Dane had jokingly claimed "poetic license" and dismissed it, adding that the audience would only find her California tan even more appealing. Dane, too, was bronzed from his time here on the beach, although Jessica noted ruefully that his attire was not nearly so abbreviated as hers.

She looked around for him now, wondering what was taking so long. As always, he was a director first and was setting up the shot from above on the truck. The sun blazed behind him and she shielded her eyes to see. *So many people.*

"Back off, folks," Dane shouted from the truck, as if reading her mind. The circle loosened as those not truly required backed away. "Okay, we're ready." He jumped to the sand in an Errol Flynn move and hastily donned a torn white cotton shirt.

They had already shot the best part in Jessica's opinion, that of the mind games and highly charged dialogue between the two. Now, stretched out on the sand, Mariah would fall prey to Roger's overwhelming sexual charisma.

"We'll get out of here soon, Mariah, I promise." Roger takes her into his arms.
And Roger had Dane's green eyes, ardently staring into hers. Jessica was amazed at how easy it was to act with Dane. Her anticipated panic disappeared; Dane waited for her to respond with her line.

"It won't be soon enough," Jessica announced, then giggled, and the entire crew broke out laughing as they caught on to her ad-libbed line. Dane, too, laughed and he dropped her into the sand, then pretended to strangle her.

He shot a look to the assistant director, then the main cameraman. "Screw the rehearsal. We're going to tape now. Jess and I know how to do this."

The cameras began rolling. He repeated his line, and this time Mariah turned soft brown eyes up to him.

"Maybe we were meant to be here, Roger."

Jessica was not at all surprised at the urgency with which Dane allowed "Roger" to kiss her. His hands caressed her body in slow, erotic moves, and lenses zoomed from various angles. Soon Jessica realized that even Dane had not planned on becoming this involved with the scene. She was ultimately reminded of their night together; she could feel his body reacting to hers and she prayed that either the Assistant would end the scene, or that all these people would disappear. Finally, someone above her yelled "Cut print that...perfect." The requisite applause from the watchers followed. Dane lifted his face skyward, as if disoriented, then his eyes smiled.

"Wait! We have to do it again. I wasn't ready."

"Forget it!" Jessica shouted, pushing him off her into the sand. She sat up, trying to brush the sand off what was left of her dress. The group disbanded, but Jessica remained sitting in the sand with Dane, who sat staring at her with a whimsical smile.

"It wasn't so bad, was it?" he asked.

Jessica studied Dane for several seconds before responding.

"Honestly?"

"Honestly, of course,"

"It was...tolerable." *If he only knew,* she thought.

"We can finish it, if you want." His eyes challenged her, his fingers plucking at the ties on her dress, stretched taut across her small breasts.

She sighed, standing up and shaking out her skirt, then voiced her thought of the week before. "You never give up, do you Dane?"

"Never," he said with a grin.

He stood and they walked slowly toward the *Pacifica*, where the next shoot was being readied. He tried to put his arm casually around her as they walked, but she pushed him away. He laughed. "You," he accused, "are a constant pain in the ass."

"Thanks, so are you," she retorted. He laughed again, good-naturedly, as they reached the crowd setting up.

"It'll be at least an hour before they're ready," he observed. "I'm taking a break. Join me in the cantina?"

"No, Dane. I need a shower and a rest. See you later." He was wearing her down, and even though the dreaded ordeal was over, the tightness in her stomach had only increased and she felt dizzy.

Jessica trudged back down the beach toward the small group of hotel bungalows, and reaching hers, entered the unlocked cabin and fell to the bed. She stared at the motionless ceiling fan above her, and at the hasty, unpainted repairs; she shuddered, remembering the terrifying night of the storm.

Jessica sighed deeply. She'd left two more messages on Mac's voicemail, and still he hadn't returned her call. She had finally called Roxanne and had conversed bleakly with her message center as well. She felt weary and alone. Her performance, at least, satisfied her, for she was growing confident that Dane and the others were impressed with her talent. This afternoon, they would join Doug Lewis and begin rolling the cameras aboard the *Pacifica*, as the evil Eric Van Dorn would attempt to spirit Mariah away from the illustrious Roger Boyer.

I must take a shower. Weakness overtook her and she wondered when she'd eaten last. Since the episode at the Martino's, nothing had seemed good.

She struggled to stand up and began painstakingly untying the knots that held the costume together. A knock at the door startled her. What now?

"Island Pizza. Somebody here order a—" At the sound of his voice, she had the door open before he could finish. Jessica stared at him in disbelief, not speaking. She reached out and removed his cap and sunglasses, then wrapped her arms tightly around his neck in a rush that almost knocked him off the step.

"Oh, Mac," she whispered, slumping against him as she fainted into his arms.

Mac carefully moved her to the bed, then went to the sink and moistened a towel. Gently wiping her face, he became concerned at how thin and worn she looked. "Damn it, Jessie, what have you done to yourself?" he admonished aloud while taking her pulse. Through the shreds in her dress, he could see her ribs.

Now alarmed, Mac wasted no time. He picked up the phone and demanded that the front desk summon an ambulance. Then he stepped outside and grabbed the first person passing, a property man, and asked if there was an American doctor traveling with the production. "Get him, *now*. Miss Taylor is ill." The tone of Mac's voice was enough to send the man off in a dead run for the *Pacifica*.

Mac returned to Jessica and caressingly pushed the hair from her face. She opened her eyes drowsily and tried to get up. "I'm fine, really," she whispered. "It's just the frogs..."

Mac gently pushed her back down on the bed. "Lie still."

"What...what are you doing here?" she asked softly.

"Taking care of you, as usual." He smiled, wiping her brow with the cloth.

Jessica sighed and again lost consciousness.

Soon, the cabin was buzzing with people. The doctor and several crew members had arrived, but Mac admitted only the doctor. At the door, voices were hushed whispers: "Somebody better go get Pierce." Everyone had an opinion, and Mac shut out their voices as he anxiously watched the doctor examine Jessica.

A commotion announced Dane's arrival as he pushed his way into the room. His glance at Mac was cool and non-committal as he turned his attention to the doctor. "What's wrong with her, Doc?"

"Best I can tell, dehydration, possibly heat prostration, exhaustion...hell, she could be pregnant. We should get her to a hospital for treatment and tests." The louvered door provided minimal privacy and the speculation quickly circulated. At this news, Mac looked openly and coldly at Dane, his anger barely controlled. Dane absorbed the look, then abruptly left the room. Mac could hear Dane ordering the crowd to move away as the ambulance approached the hotel.

They sat at opposite ends of the narrow waiting room. The "hospital" was more of a clinic, and its architecture was as dated as the hotel's, but the care and technical expertise seemed adequate. Doug joined them, along with a half dozen others, including Jessica's stand-in, Melinda. No one spoke for what seemed to most like hours while they waited for word about Jessica's condition. Dane became increasingly agitated and began pacing the room.

"Why don't you just go take a walk," Mac suggested, almost saying "a hike," but thinking better of it.

"Is that what *you'd* do, MacKendall? Can I learn something from Mr. Perfect? 'Cause if so, I'd better listen up, huh?" Dane's tongue was biting, and Mac could stand no more. He jumped up and approached Dane.

"Well maybe you do have something to learn, Pierce! Did you ever stop to think that perhaps a human life is a little more fragile and precious than your lousy movie? It wouldn't have taken a lot of perception or sensitivity to notice she wasn't eating unless you're so hung up on sex and booze and fame to care... What the hell were you thinking about, man?"

"Hey-hey-hey..." Doug stood up and got between them, as it appeared that at any moment, Dane would throw a punch at Mac. "Look, we're all upset about Jess. But it won't do her a lick of good for you boys to be killing each other out here."

Mac immediately turned and went back to his seat. Weary, he ran his fingers through his hair and stared hotly at Dane, who'd remained standing with his fists tightened in rage. Doug clapped Dane on the back.

"Let's get some air, friend."

With a cold glance at Mac, Dane allowed Doug to lead him away.

Melinda, who'd witnessed the display of tempers, moved to sit next to Mac. She took out a cigarette and smiled at him. "You're Cory MacKendall, right?"

"Yeah." Mac was in no mood for conversation. "You can't smoke in here."

The young woman stashed the cigarette back in its pack. "You're the first person I've ever seen go up against Dane. And I've known him a long time. Way to go, Cory."

Mac nodded. It was about time somebody did, he thought.

"Are you her old man?" the girl continued, motioning toward the room down the hall to where Jessica lay, still unconscious.

"Her *what*?" Mac frowned at her.

"You know, are you two, like, a thing? Dane's very jealous of you."

Mac sighed and shook his head in disgust. This was too much. Melinda finally took the hint and moved away, cigarette pack in hand.

Another hour passed. At around one in the morning, Dane returned to the clinic alone, looking distraught and unkempt. He sat down, then stood up and walked over to Mac. "You wanna get some coffee?" he asked, his face a mask of exhaustion and despair. Mac stared at him, then nodded and they moved to the small cafeteria down the hall. The room was empty except for the two of them.

Mac apologized first. "I'm just worried. She doesn't take care of herself."

"I can't believe I didn't know this was happening. I noticed the weight loss, but thought she was just worried about the cameras, you know." Dane looked far away, absently biting his thumbnail.

Mac studied Dane's haggard face over his coffee. A sense of compassion grew as he realized that Dane might be suffering as much as he was over Jessica's health. But the feeling slipped away as Dane returned from his thoughts.

"Why are you here, anyway?"

"I'm on vacation. I thought it would be a kick to watch the filming."

"You mean, you wanted to keep an eye on Jessie, right?"

Mac didn't answer. Why did Pierce insist on needling him? Still, Dane continued. "Whatever. She'll be okay. I'll see to it that she gets all the cheeseburgers and fries she can hold."

Mac gave him a look of disgust. "Jessie doesn't eat that crap. You obviously don't know her very well."

"Ah. And you do, I suppose? Oh, yeah, you shared a refrigerator with her for a few weeks, right?" Dane looked away, his air aloof and condescending. He lowered his voice, as if they were not alone in the empty cafeteria. "Not quite the same as sharing her bed, is it?"

"Don't even go there." Mac squinted at Dane, new anger coursing through him.

"But I have been there. I'm going to give you some advice, MacKendall. *Good* advice. When she comes out of this, and she will, you'd better get off your Boy Scout butt and give her your best shot. Because if you don't, I will." His voice was still low and casual, his keen eyes menacing.

"Well, Pierce...I thought you already did that, and the way I see it, you blew it," Mac said coolly.

"Maybe I did," Dane nodded, absently turning his attention to arranging the tableware. "But she has this...weakness for me, you know." He looked up at

Mac.

Mac met his eyes briefly before looking away. Dane was pushing, and Mac's temper moved toward meltdown. "Her only mistake was in crossing paths with you."

"At least *I* made love to her," Dane challenged, his intense eyes glinting. And then it happened; Mac's fist shot out like a tripped mousetrap spring, connecting with Dane's jaw and sending the latter out of his chair and sprawling onto the floor. Despite the obvious pain and blood in his mouth, Dane tested his jaw and smiled up at Mac, who stood over him in instant, abject remorse.

"Nice hook, MacKendall." Dane held out his hand for Mac to help him up. Mac immediately extended his and pulled Dane to his feet.

In the men's room, Dane washed his face as Mac leaned against the wall, feeling worse than ever.

"I don't know what to say, man," he managed.

Dane pulled his dripping head from the sink and shook the water off. He blinked, then looked at Mac. "Say, you love her, *man*." He checked his face in the mirror, still talking to Mac. "Tell her, like you just told me." He turned around to face Mac. "Only don't hit her."

Mac didn't answer.

They returned to the waiting room to find a nurse inquiring after them. "Who is Mr. MacKendall?"

At this, Dane slapped Mac on the shoulder and walked to the door. "I'll be around."

Mac's heart began to race and the aching in his legs disappeared as he followed the nurse down the hall to Jessica's room. She adjusted the curtain, pulled around Jessica for privacy, and promptly left the room.

Tentatively, Mac stepped around the curtain. Jessica lay still, pale and dressed in a hospital gown. The IV attached to her arm gave her an even more fragile look. She appeared to be sleeping. After a moment of assessing her appearance, he touched her face lightly with his fingers, gently moving away a stray strand of hair.

She opened her eyes and turned to gaze upon him. "You really are here. I thought it was a dream." Her voice was small and soft. She was obviously weak, but there was no mistaking her subtle gesture as she lifted her hands to reach out to him. Mac was already there, sliding his arms around her, holding her tight.

"Mac, what's wrong with me?" she whispered close to his ear.

Mac pulled gently away from her, locking his eyes onto hers. "Nothing too serious. You seem to have forgotten that you have to eat and sleep occasionally to stay alive." He couldn't help the bit of sarcasm that had crept into his voice, letting her in on his disappointment. "You'll be fine. You just need some time off."

Tears came to her eyes, and she swallowed hard. Her voice was strained. "I still can't believe you're here. I've missed you so much, Mac, I've been calling you..."

"Shhh...I know." He wiped her tears away, then awkwardly cleared his throat. "Pierce is here, I'm sure he wants to see you."

"Stay with me, Mac." He heard growing panic in her voice.

"I'll be back, but you should see Dane." He wet his lips nervously and started to leave. But she was grasping his hand, if weakly, and he returned to her side.

Mac gazed down at her small figure, her beloved eyes begging him to stay. Without a word, he leaned down and slipped his fingers beneath her head, impulsively moving his lips to meet with hers. Tenderly, deliberately, Mac kissed her, and what began as a simple kiss on the lips quickly swelled into a fully realized gesture of ultimate affection.

Startling even himself, Mac pulled away, an embarrassed flush to his face. Clearing his throat, he backed toward the door. "I'll be back; I won't leave you, Jess."

Outside, Mac found Dane staring at the surf. He grimaced at the sight of the pale purple stain on Dane's cheek, then turned his own eyes to the ocean before them that neither truly saw. Without a word, Dane left Mac to brood alone.

To a stunned Jessica, the encounter was over almost before it had started. Mac's whispered words touched her somewhere deep inside. She couldn't remember him ever having kissed her like that. She touched her fingers to her lips, seeking some evidence that his loving touch had not been only some elaborate hallucination.

She watched as Dane strode into her room, her mind still absorbed by the sensation of Mac's kiss. Dane seemed uncomfortable in his own skin; the pain reflected in his face growing as his eyes took in Jessica and her surroundings. Hastily she swiped a stray tear from her cheek.

He immediately bent to kiss her forehead, then sat on the edge of the bed.

"I've sent out to Miami for a couple of Big Macs and fries...you want a chocolate shake with that?"

Jessica sniffed and managed a small laugh. She made a fist and tried to punch him, but Dane intercepted her hand, opened it, and kissed her palm. "Can you ever forgive me, sweetie?"

"For what, Dane?"

"For letting this happen." He bowed his head, his eyes looking down at her small hand in his.

Jessica slowly reached up and drew her fingers into the long, ashen hair at the back of his neck, winding the strands around them. "You can be a real pain in the ass," she paraphrased his words of the day before, now gripping the locks and tugging them gently. Dane kept his eyes level. "But you didn't do this to me."

Dane's vulnerability was obvious. He sighed, and she let go of his hair, tenderly replacing her grip with a caress down his bruised cheek. He leaned toward her face, but held back, opting instead for a smile and a comfortable way to change the mood.

Before she could ask him what had happened to his face, he lifted the sheet and gazed underneath it. "A little scrawny, but everything seems to be there." He grinned at her, then looked around uneasily. "Look, I'd better go. You should rest. Are you okay, babe?"

Jessica nodded. "Not poisoned, not pregnant, not dying. Dane, thanks for worrying about me. But don't. It doesn't become you."

She could sense that her comment hurt him, and she struggled to sit up.

"No—no," he scolded, but she sat up anyway and put her arms around him, ignoring the needle in her arm.

Dane stepped out into the cool night air. Despondent, yet wired. There would be no sleep for him tonight. He headed for the cantina, hoping to meet with a bottle of comfort to bed down with. Instead, he encountered Mac walking about outside alone.

"Yo. MacKendall. Have a drink with me."

Mac stared at him, in clear belief that Dane had lost his mind, then looked into the midnight sky at the multitude of stars forming a tropical canopy over them. As if spying some signal there, he consented and fell into step with Dane as he walked to the cantina.

Inside, only a couple of die-hard locals lounged under the fans and most of the smoke had dissipated after the crowd had dwindled. The bartender regarded them without much interest, routinely setting drink napkins before them.

"What do you wish, Monsieur Pierce? Rum tonight?"

"Set us up a couple of shooters." Dane pulled a large bill from his wallet. "And keep them coming until this runs out." He glanced at Mac who nodded in silent agreement at his choice. "And Maurice, don't forget my limes this time."

"No problem, Monsieur. I have many limes tonight."

"Good. And pal, if I pass out before the dough's gone, keep the rest, okay?" The bartender grinned. He knew the wealthy American would not pass out before the hundred was spent; he drank them too fast.

Dane held up his first drink before Mac. "To women, God love'm. *Salut!*" Mac humored him, raising his glass in a mock toast. Dane tossed down the tequila without a blink, demonstrating the technique to Mac, who followed suit. He laughed at Mac's surprised expression, and the bartender filled the glasses again. "Great, huh?"

Mac nodded again, unable to find his voice after the tequila had seared his throat.

"God I could go for a cigarette," Dane confessed.

"I didn't know you smoked," Mac managed, eyeing his second shooter with dread.

Dane put away his second and turned to Mac. "Quit five years ago. But times like these I could just about light up a whole damned pack. It's her fault. *She* makes me crazy." He grinned at Mac. "Go ahead. The second one's easier, honest. And by the way, pal, the salt goes *before* the lime."

Mac hesitantly picked up a slice of lime and glanced at the salt, then shook his head and tossed the lime back into the bowl. He paused before bringing the tequila to his mouth and turned to Dane. "Shit, Pierce, why am I doing this?"

"Because you're fucking miserable, that's why. We're both a couple of sorry assholes."

"Oh. Right." Mac nodded and downed the tequila. "You're right," he croaked, his gullet on fire. "Much easier." He attempted to clear his throat. "Look, I don't want to talk about Jess, okay?"

"That makes two of us, pal," Dane nodded and slapped Mac hard on the back. "Maurice! Another, *s'il vous plait!*" He paused before throwing back his third. "Maybe I should just throw in the towel."

Mac held the shot glass delicately in his fingers, marveling at the damage such a small amount could do to his stomach. "What towel?"

"She's never gonna forgive me anyway." Dane looked up at the fan, pouring the liquor into his mouth and holding it there for a moment before swallowing it. "I'm a bad decision, all around."

"I thought we weren't gonna talk about her."

"Not that you're such a prize, either."

Mac shook his head and sipped at his drink.

And so it went. Mac lost count at around six, but he was later told that Dane had bested him by two or three shots and had somehow managed to get Mac to his cabin.

EIGHT

Hearts Asunder

Jessica was released Thursday morning in the care of Pierce Productions. Although Dane had made the decision to halt the filming, Jessica insisted they resume immediately without her and shoot what they could with Melinda. They were already behind schedule, she pointed out. Her strength returning, she stood barefoot in the sand, waving her arms and arguing with him to "get his act together."

"I want to go home, Dane," she pouted. "So we need to wrap this up!" She snapped at him jokingly, grabbed his chin and shook his face back and forth.

"Ouch! Settle down, spitfire." His hand went to his jaw.

"You never did tell me what happened to you," she inquired, referring to the bruise, now camouflaged with make-up.

"Mac hit me," he boasted proudly, like a small boy tattling on his brother.

Jessica turned to Mac, who had been silently listening to the argument transpiring outside Jessica's bungalow. He sat in the sand and leaned against the cabin, a wet towel draped over his head.

"What?" Jessica's mouth dropped. "Mac?"

Mac lifted the towel and squinted at her, shrugged, then replaced the towel. She turned back to Dane.

"Why?" she demanded, her eyes shifting between the two men.

"Because," Dane began, and Mac pulled the towel from his head, his bloodshot eyes watching guardedly. Dane looked to Mac before speaking. "Because I was being an asshole, as usual." Dane laughed. "You okay, Mac?"

The towel back in place, Mac shook his head "no."

"Well, you kids have fun. I gotta go see a man about a boat." Dane headed off down the beach, the *Pacifica* his obvious destination.

Jessica coaxed Mac inside the bungalow where she dumped two aspirin tablets into his palm and offered him a sip of bottled water.

"This is monstrous," he moaned. Jessica crawled onto the bed behind him, placing a pillow across her legs and then pulling him back to lie with his head on her lap. Without another word she began massaging his temples, his forehead, the back of his head. Mac stared at her briefly before closing his eyes.

"Why *did* you come?" She slid her fingers along his jaw, his neck, his shoulders, slowly chasing the pain from his body.

He sighed before answering, his eyes still closed. "Someone had to catch you when you fainted."

She pushed hard on the back of his neck, kneading the tense muscles, and Mac groaned. His hair, still damp from the shower, fell over her hands and covered them.

"Well, it doesn't really matter," she said. "But you sure came a long way, all alone. He didn't answer and she paused, leaning close to his face. "Mac?" She smiled at the peaceful expression on his face, then eased herself out from beneath the pillow and stretched out beside him on the bed. She stroked his face and pushed back the locks of hair she had disheveled, caressing his cheek in the process. "You are the best man I have ever known, Cory MacKendall. The best." She leaned over him now, kissing his forehead and his cheek before pausing to hover just above his lips in indecision. Giving way to the moment, she pressed her lips to his, delighting in the feel of them, even passively. It was a magical moment, like a fairytale kiss.

Filming resumed that afternoon. Jessica paced around off-camera, restless and wanting to get back to work. "I'm really fine," she insisted to anyone who would listen, but Dane was adamant about her not returning just yet. Mac, too, was restless, and that night suggested that he and Jessica go for a walk. He wasn't into the noisy, smoky cantina scene, and thought the exercise would do them both good.

"Pierce says you can get back to work tomorrow," Mac announced as they walked down the wet sand.

"What? When did he say that?"

"He wanted my permission."

"And you said..."

"I said I wasn't your keeper. I said if you felt okay, it was up to you."

The breeze was still on the warm side. Jessica had wrapped a long, sheer gauze skirt around her one-piece, floral bathing suit. Mac's island-print cotton shirt was unbuttoned over white draw-string beach trousers, his hands thrust deep into the pockets. The moonlight was made to order.

Jessica had never fully appreciated his well-toned muscles and firm, trim physique. The breeze caught his hair, alternately exposing and covering his tanned brow. Mac strode casually along, his demeanor thoughtful; yet despite the easy pace, he seemed tense, and Jessica wished she could reassure him somehow. But a new feeling had moved into her heart. An awareness that had not been there before; a risk was now present. She could no longer find the easy, familiar comfort that had existed between them. It disturbed her that she could feel self-conscious in his presence, after the weeks of living under the same roof, the playful bantering, the late-night talks and early morning meals—they had been emotionally intimate, and now, suddenly, she was confused, even embarrassed by the feelings stirring within her.

Mac's mood was somber. "Jess, I'm going back home in the morning." He said it without looking at her. He continued walking, hands still buried, but she stopped short. He turned back, and Jessica could feel the color rising in her cheeks.

"Oh," she responded, the old tightness returning to her stomach. She waited expectantly for an explanation. Mac appeared troubled and uncomfortable.

"I just need to be alone for a while, I can't explain. You finish the film, and when you come home," he paused a moment to form his words, "maybe we'll have a lot to talk about."

"Are you...upset about something? Have I done or said something wrong?" she began tentatively.

He smiled, a fleeting, remorseful look before taking her hand and gently urging her to continue walking. He didn't speak again, and she decided not to ask about the fight with Dane. It was clear he didn't want to talk, and she would give him this. And despite the warmth of Mac's hand, the long, sensitive fingers wrapped so firmly around her own, Jessica felt as if she was walking with a stranger.

At her door, he did not kiss her goodnight. Instead, Mac imparted the same, painful smile he'd flashed briefly when she'd questioned his motives for leaving Amande; and after quietly making her swear to take better care of herself, he closed her door and walked away. She lay awake for a long time, confused and saddened by his words.

·❤·❤·❤·❤·❤·

Jessica tumbled from her bed at 6:30 a.m. and hurried into a pair of jeans, stuffing her cotton nightshirt into them and shaking out her hair with her fingers. She did not even stop to glance into the mirror before rushing out the door and running barefoot across the sand to Mac's bungalow. She knocked but entered the unlocked room without waiting for a response, only to emerge seconds later. She ran all the way to the main building, breathless as she approached the front desk.

The night registrar was just preparing to leave, and he stared at her disheveled appearance with curiosity.

"*Monsieur* MacKendall?" she inquired, panting.

"*Oui, Monsieur* MacKendall has checked out, *Mademoiselle*."

Jessica's face fell and she closed her eyes, still trying to catch her breath. She turned slowly and headed toward her cabin, only to walk past it and down to the surf, where she squatted to touch the cool water with her fingers.

"He took off an hour ago."

Dane stood beside her, wearing only blue jeans and a serious expression. "I gave him a lift to his plane."

She could not disguise the sorrow in her eyes as she looked up at him, nor did she try.

"What did he say?" she asked softly.

"He wasn't exactly talkative." Dane replied. "I'm sorry."

"About what?"

"It's probably my fault he left. I sometimes don't know when to shut up."

"No, Dane, I don't think it was you. If Mac had a problem with you, he would have made it known. He's very straight forward, with most people."

"Well, you got that right," he replied, absently touching his cheek.

Jessica wasn't listening, however. Not to Dane, anyway.

I won't leave you, Jess.

Jessica returned to work that day, and after two more weeks of fifty-nine cast and crew members sweating out in the Caribbean sun, the film was completed to the satisfaction of Pierce Productions. Jessica had finished out her role admirably, taking great pains to improve her health and sustain a stable attitude in the face of her emotional disarray. There had been a change in her, and in Dane, too, noticeable by everyone involved with the project.

She kept more to herself; he was subdued. The constant stream of sexual innuendoes ceased, and he treated his leading lady with dignity and respect. All were agreed that the balance of the filming had gone much smoother without the undercurrent between them.

Finally, on this hot Wednesday afternoon, the announcement was made around three: it was a wrap. *Lost Season* was in the can. A celebration was immediately planned for that evening. Jessica sighed in relief that home was almost in sight; she would leave on the first plane out tomorrow. After exchanging happy pleasantries with other cast members, she began fighting the sand back up the beach once more to her bungalow.

Dane rushed to catch up with her. "Miss Taylor? Could we have a word?"

Jessica turned and smiled. "Yes, Mr. Pierce?"

"You'll be at the party tonight?"

"Ah. I don't think so, Dane."

"You have to be there. It's in your contract." He grinned. During the last several weeks, he'd grown a mustache as Roger Boyer, and while Jessica found it rather becoming on Roger, she decided it detracted from Dane's seductive mouth. Momentarily hypnotized, she reached up to touch his upper lip with her fingers and slowly shook her head.

"When is this coming off?"

"For you I would shave my ass."

She couldn't help a giggle at his unexpected response. He squinted at her in the sun, and, as if sensing a concession, touched her forearm. "Good! Seven o'clock, casual attire, no-host bar."

This made her laugh, and he boldly reached out and pinched her cheek gently. "That's my girl. See you later."

In her room, Jessica fell backwards onto the bed and again focused on the ceiling fan. This awful room was about to become history. This cramped, stuffy little cell had seen it all, especially the tearful nights after Mac had flown out of her life for some terrible reason she couldn't fathom. She'd cried until her eyes ached and wondered repeatedly why he'd gone so abruptly, so unhappily.

But she would not succumb to that misery now. She turned on her side, grasped a pillow to her chest and fell asleep. Her dreams were a mural of scenes from her worst thoughts; Mac, angry with her, and Dane's dancing eyes, taunting her. She awoke with a start and quickly looked at the clock: 7:45! She couldn't believe she had slept three hours. A glance out the window provided a view of a bonfire, just yards down the beach, and forty or so people gathered to roast a pig. A steel drum band was just warming up and several party animals were dancing in the sand.

She rubbed her eyes and sighed. The scene looked festive and gay, and she decided she'd go for it. But first, she must call Mac and tell him she was coming home. He would want to know that, in any case.

She dialed the familiar number, regretting that it was only 4 p.m. at home. He might be out.

"Hello?" Jessica's eyebrows went up as she heard a woman's sleepy voice answering her call.

"I'm sorry, I must have misdialed. Is this 555-6849?"

"Um...Yes." Silence. When Jessica didn't speak, the woman went on. "If you're calling for Cory, he's...not available."

Jessica was stunned. She had to think fast and found a voice she didn't know she had. "No—I was calling for Jessica."

"She doesn't live here anymore." The woman said flatly before hanging up the phone.

Jessica put down the receiver slowly, finding it difficult to cradle it properly. She stared at it, confused. "No," she whispered. "I don't believe it."

She looked into the mirror, seeing Mac's face there instead of her own, an unknown woman in his arms. Nausea overcame her and she ran for the bathroom.

Forty minutes later, Jessica emerged from her cabin, freshly showered and wearing a wrap around, spaghetti-strapped Hawaiian shift. She was barefoot and carried a rolled-up blanket under her arm, walking smoothly and unhurriedly toward the partiers down the beach.

"Hey—it's the Oscar nominee!" someone shouted.

Confident. I'm confident and Dane thinks I'm beautiful. And I'm not committed, not to Mac or anyone else. She greeted people and returned their congratulations as she moved through the group. Slowly but deliberately, she made her way to the gaping ice chests filled with beverages for the party and selected an almost full bottle of cold Chardonnay. Turning back toward the fire, she sought Dane's eyes and walked back. *I can do whatever I want.*

Dane, sitting near the flames, gave her an appreciating grin. He was the perfect picture of the successful young director, greedily enjoying the spoils of his latest achievement. He looked handsome and dangerous, Jessica thought, in his half-buttoned, white gauze shirt and tan shorts. Melinda, obviously "well into her cups," hung on him, and he kissed her periodically; yet his eyes followed Jessica as she moved, almost seductively, in his direction. And his upper lip bore no trace of the objectionable mustache.

Reaching the fire, Jessica paused for a moment, exchanging solemn, silent communication with him before she continued walking on down the beach into the darkness. A couple of revelers called out for her to join the dancing, but their words were lost to the warm off-shore breezes.

She walked until the fire was just a tiny, bright spot in the distance and she found a group of boulders protecting a small cove. She spread the blanket and turned around to face Dane, whom she knew would be right behind her. Wordlessly, she handed him the bottle and he twisted out the cork.

Dane took a long draught from the bottle, then handed it to her and she did the same. She pushed the bottle into the sand, then untied her sash and let the breeze blow the simple dress open, exposing her trim, naked body; her fingers began calmly and adeptly unbuttoning his shirt and pants, and soon they were both nude and facing each other on the blanket.

He did not smile or speak. He took her into his arms, gently at first, and kissed her as they sank to their knees and finally to the blanket, where their lovemaking quickly accelerated into a furious and exciting pace. She surprised him with the urgency of her demands, but this only enhanced the erotic aura that surrounded them, and he took her lead. Not looking for tenderness tonight, Jessica dug her nails into his hips as she pulled him against her, uninterested in the playful sensuality that Dane would have normally initiated.

"Whoa, baby...slow down," he cooed, chuckling to himself as he maneuvered her position below him. "We have all night. No need to rush."

Dane was very much in control, savoring her, unleashing upon her the passion that had been growing out of the tremendous tension between them since their arrival on the island weeks before. He possessed every part of her, kissing her, massaging her, biting her, and making her wait for the ultimate climax to their union. Roughly he pinned her arms above her head, and her struggle to free them drove him mad with desire; Jessica was wild with anticipation.

And afterward, after she had cried out in ecstasy and pain, Dane lay beside her, stroking her hair back in smooth, caressing movements, soothing her exhausted body and pounding heart. It was she who spoke first.

"What do we do next," she asked quietly, "now that we've made love on the beach?"

"You've wanted to go home since we arrived. Now you get your wish."

"What if I don't want to?"

"Don't want to go back to L.A., or home to Mac?"

She didn't answer at first. She traced his lips with her fingertip, and he grabbed it with his teeth. "Mac has...his own life, Dane. I know you have these ideas, but really, we're just friends. Mac is a kind, wonderful person, and I'm incredibly grateful for all he's done, but that's as far as it goes."

"Bullshit, Jessica."

"Do you never tire of using foul language, Dane?"

"What are you going to do when you get there, go back to being Jack and Jill?"

"I have to get a place. Move my stuff. I want to get a new project going, Teddy has several scripts for me; I have to keep working."

"Does Mac know you're moving out?"

"Of course he does. It was only temporary until I came home anyway. And you were right about his being involved with someone else, and about him denying it. She's answering his phone, so she damned-well exists."

Dane chuckled to himself. "Not jealous, are you? And anyway, I never said that," he corrected her.

"Sure you did, in the car that night."

"What I said, dear heart, was that he was involved with *someone*. Not someone *else*. *You*, darling, you're the one screwing with Mac's head." He leaned close and bit her earlobe.

"You're out of your mind," she retorted. His mouth was sending shivers down her back, and she turned and pressed her body against his.

"He never told you, did he? About why he hit me."

"No, and it isn't important. You can be really crude sometimes and although I've never seen Mac's temper driven so far, I'll bet you could do it."

He smiled at her. "I told him that you and I were...intimately acquainted...and that he'd better get into the running quick, or I would take you away." He watched her face for a reaction. "He was insane with jealousy. He hit me before I knew what was happening."

Jessica's eyes widened and she frowned. "How *could* you...You son-of-a-bitch! I don't believe you did that!"

"Look, it had to be done. I wanted to know if my instincts were correct. I have a rather personal interest in this affair."

"You baited him on purpose. Dane, you're worse than I thought." Her words were biting, but she was truly more interested than angry.

"Unfortunately for both of you sorry kids, he wouldn't listen. He has a certain...aversion to me. So, it'll be up to you to bring him around, Jess."

She scoffed at his suggestion. "Mac's got someone else, I told you. She's in his bed right now. I heard her voice."

"Look, if he's screwing some bimbo while you're gone, it's only because you've got him so wound up, he can't see straight. Jessica, sex without love is like...like a wrestling match with a big finish. That's all. For a guy, it can be...routine."

"A wrestling match? Is that what this is all about?"

"I wasn't talking about us." Dane rolled onto his back and stared into the night sky.

"Oh Dane," she muttered. "I wish things were different." Her voice took on a weary tone.

"Like how?"

"Like, I wish you and I... God! We're so incompatible, but..."

"But? What is it your little heart desires, sweetie?"

"I wish you weren't such a bastard, Dane. And I wish I didn't love you."

"*You* love *me*? Since when?" He smiled in apparent amusement.

"Since forever. And you know it. And you're being a rogue and a jerk and even an asshole doesn't change it."

His smiled waned and he sighed. "A rogue? Where did that come from? Look, Jessica, I need to be honest with you. I...hmmm. This is difficult." He seemed off guard for the first time. "I care...a great deal about you." He chose his words carefully, she could tell. "But even if I were free of my obligations, even if I felt worthy of you, I couldn't begin to make you happy. You said that yourself, to me, and you were right. And anyway," he hesitated, clearly weighing his next offering, "it was *Mac's* name you called out in the hospital, and... *his* name you whispered in my ear tonight. I know when I'm licked."

His words were like small hands gripping her heart and squeezing. Her face felt warm, her tears hot; and despite the painful words, he pulled her close again and began slowly, tenderly arousing her once more. This was it, the last time they would be together. They both knew it, and his own voice was tight with emotion as he whispered to her.

"No anger this time, darling, this is for *us.*" Hearts breaking, they made love again; and soon he wrapped the blanket around them. The ocean breeze had turned cool.

NINE

Homecoming

"I wish I could go with you to the airport, but I just can't," Dane said as they loaded Jessica's luggage into the waiting taxi. "There're a million things waiting to be tied up."

"Don't worry yourself, Dane. I'm fine, really."

"Be careful, sweetie." He hugged her in full view of the dozen or so people waiting to board the bus. This time there was no comic applause, and Dane lowered his voice. "Jessie, I'll be back Saturday. If things get tangled up for you, you're welcome to stay with me for a while, if you want. You'd hate it though; I'm not particularly attentive, as you know." He grinned. "I've already spoken with Peter. He'll take care of anything you need."

Jessica fought back the tears. Would she be crying forever? "Thanks, Dane. I think I'll be fine." She hugged him tightly, then turned to get on the airport taxi.

"I'll call you," he said.

"Don't make promises, darling."

Miami International Airport was a busy, scary place. It was 7:30 p.m., and Jessica found her cell phone finally had a signal. Weary, she found a seat, her body subtly reminding her of the marathon intimacy she'd shared with Dane. It's a wonder I can even walk, she thought ruefully. She dialed Roxanne's number. It was 4:30 p.m. at home, and she sighed with relief when her bestie answered.

"Jessie! Where are you? Are you home?"

"Not yet. Miami. Is everything okay?"

"Everything's ducky. Are you coming home?"

"That's why I'm calling. My flight gets in around nine p.m. I know it's a lot to ask, but—"

"I'll be there. LAX?"

"Yeah. Thanks a lot, Rox."

"No problem-o. But...did you call Mac? I would think—"

"No." Jessica paused, not able to explain why she hadn't called Mac. Of course Roxanne would expect him to pick her up. "Can you come?"

"I'll be there."

Jessica's mind was numb with overworked emotions. On the flight to L.A., she couldn't sleep despite her exhaustion. She lay back and stared out at the soft carpet of clouds below the jet, lamely trying to organize her jumbled thoughts and the unbidden images of the weeks passed.

Dane had roused her just before dawn from the sandy alcove where they had spent the night. They watched the sunrise together on the sand. He'd been more than responsive, but Jessica was consumed with melancholy. What was happening to her? Despite the tenderness Dane had shown her, the overtones of love he'd finally relinquished to her, she felt empty and dispirited.

The memory of her desperate, almost wanton behavior of the night before made her face hot with shame and spawned the even more painful memory of what had driven her into the lustful encounter with Dane: the phone call to Mac.

Jessica's insides tightened with grief. She unconsciously knotted the hem of her blouse into her fist. How could she face Mac?

It would be different if he hadn't come to the island. If he hadn't been so...loving. If he hadn't kissed her!

"Miss? Is everything okay?" A male flight attendant was leaning over her. She struggled to sit straighter and forced a smile.

"Sure. Fine, thanks." *Just peachy.* Involuntarily, her thoughts returned to Cory MacKendall. Was it possible that she'd called his name while making love with Dane? Her face burned again. The thoughts would not stop; her filmstrip mind was projecting a scene between herself and Mac. She ran her fingers through his burnished golden hair, around the strong shoulders and down his chest. She could almost feel his smooth, tanned skin and the firm strength of his muscles...

"No," she whispered, shaking her head. Her pulse raced at the thought of touching Mac, not in the casual way they'd always touched, but in a loving, intimate way.

"No," she repeated. These visions had to stop, *now.* Mac had another woman in his life, and she feared that even their friendship was at stake.

Weary with anxiety and physical fatigue, Jessica was only mildly relieved when the jumbo jet touched down in Los Angeles.

Roxanne wanted to know everything, every detail of her trip and about the film. Jessica told her about the bugs, the frogs, the storm; about the *Pacifica*, the damaged cabin and the cantina. As they turned into the subterranean parking underneath Roxanne's townhouse, she turned to Jessica. "And what about you and Dane?"

Inside, over hot chocolate, Jessica sketched out the details of her relationship with Dane, and Mac's surprise visit and hasty flight home. She guardedly asked if Roxanne had been in touch with Mac.

"We've spoken a few times. He's been really kind, listening to me rave on about my new business. He gave me the name of his attorney to help get my contract squared away. Why do you ask? Haven't you two kept in touch?"

"Not really." She broke down then and told Roxanne the awful story about the phone call and the woman.

Roxanne was thoughtful and offered no opinion.

"And worse, Dane's got this stupid idea that Mac's in love...with me!" She tried to look carefree about this information, but knew she'd failed in Roxanne's eyes.

"How does Dane feel about it?"

"Dane...well, Dane's Dane. He was actually really...good...to me just before I left." Her voice wandered off as she remembered the night before on the beach, and this morning's affection. "What are you thinking, Rox?"

"That you must call Mac, and soon. If he finds out you're home and you haven't called him...he'll be hurt." Roxanne pressed her lips tightly together and raised her eyebrows at Jessica.

"Right now I'd rather call my mother." Jessica replied, despondent. It was going to be a tough week.

They stayed up late, too late, as Roxanne had an early day ahead. But they talked about everything they'd missed of each other's lives and got just about caught up around 2 a.m.

"So, you been dating at all?" Jessica asked, tiredly pulling a nightgown out of her bag.

"Well, I didn't want to mention it, what with all that's going on with you," Roxanne began, pulling a blanket off the closet shelf. "I did meet someone."

"Oh, do tell, you brat! How could you even consider keeping it from me?" Jessica gave her a mock pout.

"His name's Tom Jarrick. I met him at Jennifer's."

"Oh, it's 'Jennifer,' now?" Jessica teased.

"Yes, dahling, Jennifer introduced us. He's a screenwriter. He wrote the screenplay for her next movie. He was there for lunch." She paused, hugging the blanket to her chest. "He's everything that every other man hasn't been. He's warm, sensitive and... mature. He knows where he's been and where he is and where he's going. He's divorced, he has a teenaged son, and yet he's still so young. He took me to Disneyland!" Roxanne giggled. "And, we didn't even have sex until the fourth time we went out."

"A new world's record." Jessica was warmed by this news, so happy for her friend, and a small flame of hope burned within her. She took the blanket and gave Roxanne a warm smile. "I can't wait to meet him."

Exhausted, Jessica soon fell into bed after planning for Roxanne to give her a lift to Mac's on her way to work in the morning. At the very least, she thought, I have to get my car.

"Thanks for driving me over here. God! Rox, I am such a wreck! What if *she's* there?"

Roxanne turned the lipstick-red Trans Am into the long private drive leading to Mac's house. "She won't be there now. And you have every right to be. Everything you own is in that house. You should have called, though." She stopped near the front door. Jessica sat, distraught, looking at the house she loved so much. "Uh, Jess, I know you're apprehensive about this, but I'm kinda late for work."

"I'm sorry. I'm going. Just wait until I get in, to make sure he hasn't changed the locks."

"Don't be ridiculous."

Jessica turned her key, and the door opened easily. She waved Roxanne off.

I'm just going to get my car keys and go. Then I'll call him later and we can arrange to meet to resolve...to resolve what?

She crept into the kitchen. Nothing seemed out of the ordinary. "Mac?" she called out, softly. No answer. The house seemed to be empty. On a whim, she went back outside and jogged over to the garage, unlocking the side door and peeking in. Both Mac's BMW and his truck were there, along with her precious little car under a canvas cover. She lifted the corner to be sure. The blue paint nearly glistened with polish, and she remembered leaving the car dusty and dull. So where was he? Running, probably. *Good, I can be in and out before he returns.*

She went back to the house and quickly trotted down the hall to "her" room. Nothing here had changed, except that a small stack of mail was on the dresser. She grabbed a couple of garments from the closet, then picked up the mail and returned to the kitchen. Smelling coffee, she noticed an almost full pot of fresh brew in the coffee maker. She frowned. Mac rarely brewed coffee for himself. While wondering about this new mystery, she gazed past the family room through the back windows to the pool, full and sparkling clean. Intrigued, she went out the back sliding doors to inspect this miracle. She bent down and tested the water with her fingers. Warm. Mac's been busy, she thought, then jumped at the sound of tires on the gravel near the garage.

She stood up just as Mac dismounted from his twelve-speed mountain bike at the side garage door. Panting, his Minnesota State tank shirt soaked, he stared wordlessly at her across the yard.

Jessica cleared her throat. "Hi," she called tentatively.

"Welcome back."

Not welcome *home*, Jessica noticed. He took the bicycle into the garage and returned just as she reached the back porch. He followed her to the kitchen.

Oh, my God, what am I going to say now? Jessica's mind froze with panic. This was it, the moment she had gone over and over during the last two weeks. "You made coffee," she started. "Expecting someone?"

"Yeah. You." His tone was non-committal. "You stayed with Roxie?"

"Well, she picked me up. I got in late last night."

"How was the flight?"

Jessica shrugged. "Fine, I guess. I slept most of the way," she lied. She poured herself a cup of coffee. "I don't suppose you want any right now?" she offered, glancing at his damp shirt and the perspiration on his face. His hair was awry from the ride, but his face was clean shaven. He crossed his arms and leaned back against the opposite counter, silently watching her.

"How are you?" Jessica asked softly. Boy, I'm original, she thought sourly.

"I'm—" Mac shrugged slightly. "I'm fair. You?"

I'm a complete and utter wreck.

"Fine." She wet her lips. "The pool looks great, Mac," *...and so do you.*

"Big job. They just finished a couple of days ago."

Their trite conversation unnerved Jessica, and her fingers trembled while holding her cup. She prayed he wouldn't notice. "So, how did you know I was back?" she asked quietly.

"Our pal Pierce woke me up this morning on the phone looking for you," he answered flatly. "I had no idea you were back." Mildly accusing.

On edge, Jessica became defensive. "I would have called you, but I thought you might be busy with, you know...other things." She looked down at the cup.

At her comment Mac sighed in disgust, raking his fingers through the locks above his ears in frustration. "You called here Wednesday afternoon, didn't you?" It was more of a fact than a question.

Jessica put the cup in the sink. "I have to go." She hurriedly gathered the mail and her keys and started for the door. Quickly Mac stepped ahead of her, blocking her way.

"Jessica, it's not what you think."

"Please, Mac, I *have* to go." She tried to go around him, afraid to hear his explanation. She nearly ran through the door, her panic heightened by his closeness.

"Jessie, we have to talk," he demanded, following her to the garage. "Don't go."

She pulled the cover off the Miata and carefully, if hastily, folded it up and put it on a shelf above the car. "The car looks super, Mac, thanks," she murmured, then got into the driver's seat.

He stood next to the car, angry and exasperated. "Pierce's waiting for your call. He plans to be back tomorrow, so you won't have long to wait." His bitter tone was not lost on Jessica. She flashed him an angry look and tore down the driveway, leaves flying furiously around her tires. Mac cursed loudly and kicked at the gravel in rage.

Jessica crossed the Valley and headed for the beach. She drove north and didn't stop until she reached Santa Barbara, where she rode around aimlessly. In Montecito, she found herself parked at the place where she'd picnicked with Mac. It seemed an eternity ago.

Her thoughts were jumbled and painful. Did Mac know about her night with Dane? Could Dane have possibly been so awful as to mention it to Mac? Had this new woman in Mac's life changed everything? She remembered, now vividly, the feel of his lips that day in the hospital, the slow and tender way he had kissed her. *Oh God, this can't be happening. I can't lose Mac.*

She drove inland and joined Interstate 5, then turned back south. It was late afternoon, and she took the Frazier Park turnoff that led to the mountain resort area just north of the Valley. Two hours later, she had paid for a week's rental of a small hillside motel cabin with kitchenette.

Jessica closed the door after the rental agent left and went to sit in the early evening hues of the sunset that warmed the small deck that faced a lake. A minor sense of accomplishment encouraged her. At least she had a place to stay, alone, for a while. But she would eventually need her laptop, her television, her desk. Not to mention her entire wardrobe!

She glanced vacantly through the envelopes she had picked up at Mac's; closing bills, mostly, on her utilities, junk mail and two personal letters. In surprise, she recognized the handwriting on the envelopes as Wesley's. She quickly opened and read them both.

In the earlier one, Wesley was brief and almost formal. He was coming to L.A. to look for work, would she like to get together? If so, there was a number to call. In the second, the tone was depressing and sad. He was not only out of work but sounded despondent over the breakup with a girlfriend; and he was losing his home to foreclosure. Jessica frowned at the sadness of this news. *Poor Wes.* She wished she could help him, but in truth, she just couldn't involve herself in anything right now. She put the letters into an empty kitchen drawer.

There was no landline phone and no cell tower close enough, so she decided she had better drive to Roxanne's and at least pick up her luggage.

"Where in the world have you been?" Roxanne's voice was a mixture of relief and irritation. "I've been worried sick."

Jessica colored. Roxanne had a guest, and her evening was obviously ruined by Jessica's disappearance.

"Sorry, Rox, I just went for a drive."

"Dane's called twice and Mac once. They are both worried about you. God knows why. I know you can take care of yourself, but Mac said you were upset when you left."

"I rented a temporary place. It's near Frazier Park, just for a short time, until I decide what to do." She glanced up as Roxanne's friend emerged from the kitchen. "I'm so sorry; really, I should've called you once I got service. I didn't think anyone would notice."

"Didn't think, huh?" Roxanne sniffed. She turned to Tom, who was watching the scene unfold with amusement. "My best friend, Jessica Taylor," she offered, "Jess, this is Tom."

Roxanne's gentleman friend stood and extended his hand. *Another tall one,* Jessica thought. And the moment she grasped his hand, she knew he was the right man for Roxanne. He had dark, curly brown hair and a full mustache, and warm, genuine brown eyes.

"Happy to meet you. And, happy you're alive," he said with a wink and a smile. Jessica's response was pre-empted by Roxanne.

"Jess, get on the phone and call them back. Both of them." Her words were an order, not a suggestion.

"Rox—"

"At least call Mac. Jessie," she pulled Jessica aside to the kitchen and her voice became a whisper. "Mac's in a bad way. I've never heard him sound like this. I could care less if you call Pierce or not. But Mac..." Roxanne shook her head and left the room.

Tightness constricted Jessica's chest until she could hardly breathe. Roxanne was right, of course, but how could she call him? She dug her phone from her bag, dialed Dane's home number and asked Peter to let Dane know she was doing fine and that she'd call him after he returned. Peter was happy to comply.

Calling Mac would be a different story. She went to Roxanne's bedroom and closed the door. Numbly, she dialed Mac's number, remembering the last time she'd done so. On the third ring, he answered. She wanted to hang up, to prepare something to say, but his voice had already grabbed her heart.

"Hi, Mac, it's me," she said quietly, calmly.

A long sigh. "You okay?"

"Sure. I drove up to Santa Barbara. I'm okay."

"Jessie, come home. We need to talk." He sounded tense.

"Mac, I need to get my stuff." She cleared her throat. "I rented a place today." Silence on the line.

"I can come by when it's convenient for you." Jessica rushed the words out before she lost her nerve.

Finally, he spoke. "If that's what you want." He paused, and Jessica squeezed her eyes tightly shut, anticipating his next words. "*Now* would be convenient."

She had never heard this hardness in his voice before. It scared her. "I can't come now. It's late. Tomorrow?"

"Tomorrow evening then. I won't be home until seven. Feel free to let yourself in."

"Okay. I'll see you then." Jessica bit her lip and ended the call.

Saturday morning dawned foggy and cool. Jessica drove Roxanne to the cabin in the woods. "It's just for now. There are only six units, mine is at the end of the trail." Roxanne reluctantly approved and the two of them rearranged the furniture and stocked the kitchen with food. Later, they took a hike up the mountain together, letting Jessica's problems take a back seat to the beautiful scenery and peaceful atmosphere.

"I love it here." Jessica sighed as they sat on a fallen log near the top. "I hate to go back."

"You shouldn't hate to—the cabin's adorable. And you could find something more permanent if you want."

"Yeah, I know. I'm just dreading facing Mac. I don't know what's going to happen. He is really, really angry with me."

"What in the world could he be mad about?"

"I've had nothing else on my mind for weeks. I think...I think we got too close. I must have scared him by being so clingy down in Amande. And worse, my hysteria over his...friend. Mac's not ready for someone like me to drop into his life. I love him dearly, as a friend, and I regret blowing it with him." She couldn't keep the sadness from her voice.

"As a friend?" Roxanne repeated quietly. "Jessica, this is Roxanne. Can you honestly tell me you're not attracted to Mac as more than a friend?"

Jessica closed her eyes. Her movie-screen imagination flashed Mac, yesterday morning, leaning against the counter; his runner's legs, the taut, muscular chest breathing hard from his morning ride; the sensitive, concerned eyes. She remembered how she used to tease him about showering too much and his obsession with keeping his hands and nails clean. Men's hands had always fascinated her, and Mac's were *perfect*.

Then the picture changed and went back to the hospital room in Amande, the recalled scene that had played endlessly in the weeks that had followed. *"I won't leave you, Jess."* And the kiss. The mind boggling, unexpected rush of emotion that had changed everything.

"Why?" she murmured to herself. She stared across the pines, lost in thought and mindless of Roxanne. "We joked about having slept together," she whispered. A desire suddenly engulfed her, a desire to see him, talk to him, and get everything straightened out. She wanted to be able to touch him without fear and smile and laugh with him again. She sighed, wondering if things could ever be the same.

They hiked back down, a more difficult feat than the climb. After one last look around, they locked up and headed back to the Valley.

She had trouble deciding what to wear, since she only had a few suitable items with her. Roxanne brought out a pair of black jeans and a fuzzy peach sweater, and although the pants were slightly loose in the hips, Jessica was satisfied with the look. It was six o'clock, and they threw together a salad and waited.

"Tom and I are flying to Tahoe next weekend," Roxanne told her.

"Oooh...sounds like fun." Jessica toyed with the salad, her mind obviously wandering away.

"It will be," Roxanne sang. Looking across the table at Jessica, she waved her hand in front of her friend's face. "Yoo-hoo, Miss Taylor, forget your lines?"

"I wonder what he did today. He doesn't work on Saturdays."

"And you're thinking he's with her." Now Jessica looked up at Roxanne's face expectantly, but Roxanne huffed out a breath. "There are a million things he could have done today. You're being hysterical. And you can quit looking at your watch," Roxanne suggested. "It's six forty-five. It's at least a half hour's drive."

Jessica went to the bathroom to freshen her makeup and hair. She started to nibble on her nails, then laughed and called out to Roxanne: "I can't even bite my nails, they're plastic!" referring to the acrylic fingernails applied in the Caribbean.

"You look great, except for the hickey on your neck," Roxanne advised. In horror, Jessica looked back into the mirror. She blushed, remembering the wild night on the sand. She borrowed some makeup and covered the mark sufficiently, she hoped.

It was dark when she arrived at Mac's. He was indeed home and answered her knock at the door. She could sense immediately that his mood had changed from the day before, and she followed him through the family room and outside to the pool. Candles were burning at a patio table where he had obviously just been sitting.

"It's beautiful, Mac," she spoke of the pool, now lit for nighttime, and the surrounding landscape lights in the garden. With an inside smile she remembered suggesting he get it finished, so *she* could swim. She sat down and allowed him to pour her a glass of Irish cream. "The good stuff, huh?" she joked, unintentionally letting down her guard.

He picked up his glass and held it up to toast. "To...tomorrow," he said simply, "and your new place."

Jessica stiffened slightly but sipped the drink, trying hard to control her anxiety.

"So, where is it?" he inquired. "Your place?"

"In the mountains. It's just a little cabin, actually." Jessica decided to let him go on believing it was more than just a motel.

"Santa Barbara?"

"Pine Mountain."

"Ah. Nice area. I hiked there once."

A bit of quiet. Then, "When would you like to move your things?"

"Any time," she answered softly.

"Next Saturday okay? I'm going to be pretty busy during the week."

Jessica took another swallow, then cleared her voice. "Look, Mac. About yesterday—"

His hand went to her wrist, the long fingers wrapping gently around it. Her pulse quickened and then seemed to stop, as if her heart had paused to listen also. He leaned slightly forward. "Let's forget it, okay?"

"But you were right, Mac, we do have to talk about...things." Her voice was small and hesitant.

"There will be time for that." He seemed certain and confident, and Jessica was awash with relief. Except...except his hand was moving from her wrist to her hand, which he took and held in both of his. "Just—don't—run away again." He had her attention and knew it. Her face burned. "If you do, I won't be your best friend." The serious brown eyes had a serious message for her, despite his childlike warning.

"You ran *first*." She'd said it before she could stop herself. Mac slowly released her hand and stood up, walking toward the pool with his back to her. Turmoil rocked Jessica, and she shuddered from the adrenaline surging throughout her body. Things had been going so well.

"You're absolutely right." He spoke to the pool. "The situation down there was making me face things I wasn't ready to. Unfortunately, my ego and my reason sometimes clash, especially when it comes to people I care about."

Jessica sat frozen in her seat. It was all she could do not to jump up and throw herself on him.

He returned to the table, offering a brief smile. "I'm sorry, I'm being melodramatic. I guess I'm on camera too much."

Still trembling, Jessica feigned a calm she couldn't begin to feel. Mac again took her hand, pressing it firmly between his.

"I'm sorry about yesterday, too. It wasn't you I was mad at." He brushed her fingertips with his lips. "It was me."

"Oh." Jessica swallowed, transfixed by the sight of his mouth kissing her fingers, speaking the words of redemption.

"You feeling better?"

She nodded. So complete was her preoccupation, she would have nodded at any question.

"Forgive me?"

Forgive me. Jessica stared at him for a long moment. The endless nights of misery, of wondering what she'd done to offend him, the practiced apologies never uttered, all came flashing by her as she looked into his eyes. Forgive *him*. She shook her head briskly, briefly, to break free of the memories. "Forgive you for what?" she whispered.

And then he smiled again, making everything as it had been before. Except for the gentle hand-playing, of course.

Still holding her left hand in his right, Mac drank down the rest of his drink.

"Before I forget, Megan sends her love," he said. "She can't wait to show you her *pierced* ears."

"You," Jessica began, pausing to clear her throat, "you were with Meggie today?"

"Of course," he said simply. "Where else would I be?"

"Oh, there are probably a million things you could have done today," Jessica replied, looking up toward the stars as she paraphrased Roxanne's words.

Mac only smiled softly, slowly shaking his head.

They talked for nearly an hour about the day he had spent with Megan, and Jessica's career plans after the completion of *Lost Season*. At around nine, he picked up their empty glasses and extinguished the candles. At his cue, she followed him back to the kitchen and then to the front door. It was clear he was dismissing her.

Jessica was bursting inside. She stood on the porch, filled with anticipation. *Touch me, Mac. Please. Anywhere. Any way. Make things right.*

Instead, he went back inside and immediately returned with an envelope. "Something for your new kitchen; open it when you get home." She bashfully took the envelope and put it in her purse.

"I'll call you before Saturday, Mac." She fumbled with the car keys.

He nodded and walked past her to the car, parked at the end of the walk. Turning, he casually sat back against the passenger door and shoved his hands into his pockets. Overhead, a three-quarter moon dusted the scene with silvery light. Jessica stood awkwardly on the brick walk, wondering what to do or say next as he silently considered her. She took a tentative step, glancing nervously at her feet, the words she wanted to say sticking somehow in her throat.

"Yesterday was one of the worst days of my life," she finally admitted. "I was so afraid that we might not be friends anymore. I don't ever want that to happen again."

"It was bad for me, too." He paused, searching for words himself. "Everything has changed, hasn't it?" he asked softly. Her lips smiled briefly, and she offered a subtle nod. "I don't know exactly how to be..." he confessed, now pulling his hands from his pockets and rubbing them on his thighs to dry his damp palms.

Hesitantly, she moved slowly toward him, stopping just inches from touching him. He brought his hands to rest, ever so lightly, on her hips; she could barely feel them.

"It's so strange, I keep feeling I don't know you the same way, anymore," he continued, his voice unsure.

"Do you want to know me?" she asked simply, bravely, her body rigid with expectation.

"Oh *yes*. Very much."

At his response, Jessica lifted her hands to his shoulders and ran her fingers over them, while at the same time pressing her lower body against his, hip to hip, thigh to thigh, knee to knee. The touch caused her to catch her breath. She continued dragging her trembling fingers down his shirt, absorbing his warmth, before returning them to encircle his neck.

"I'm a wreck," she confided giddily.

"So am I," he responded with a nervous chuckle.

His hands were now alive and finding the warm flesh of her back inside her sweater, pulling her tightly against him until her face was just before his. He stared into her eyes, and she wondered if he was trying to tie the past with the present, as she was.

Kiss me, Mac, kiss me now!

Mac could not keep a small smile from forming on his lips. Closing his own eyes, he dragged his lips slowly across hers, savoring their softness, delighting in their sweetness.

Jessica, too, closed her eyes, absorbing the loving affection conveyed by the warmth of his lips on hers. Bringing her hands to his cheeks, she stopped his wandering appraisal of her mouth and pressed her lips firmly against his. He needed no further encouragement; his lips consumed her mouth; slow, wet and delicious. Inside, her heart danced wildly, and her mind lolled in pleasure. Surely, she had never been kissed like this in her life. It was as if she'd never been kissed before, his touch filling her with the kind of excitement that comes with a *first* kiss, a first intimate encounter with a new love.

At last, he pulled his reluctant lips away from hers, leaving her breathless and flushed; then he hugged her fiercely, his breath hot against her ear, sending shivers around her trembling body. "Jessie, I've missed you so damned much." His voice was tight. "I wanted this...you...so badly. God, I hated leaving you there! But I just couldn't let myself compete. I was afraid." His words rushed out in an urgent whisper. "I didn't want things to change."

"I understand," she breathed, seeking his mouth again, making him kiss her again. Jessica was intoxicated with his fervor as he finally let go weeks of repressed longing.

Soon, too soon for Jessica, he retreated for a deep breath and smiled softly.

"Is this fun or what?" His tone was intimate, and teasing.

Finding it difficult to speak, she smiled shyly. "Why didn't you ever tell me you could kiss like this?" she managed, her knees weak as he still held her tight.

"And spoil the surprise?" He rocked her slightly in his arms. "Don't pass out on me again," he whispered, referring to his arrival on Amande.

"And miss you kissing me again? Not a chance," she murmured. Being in Mac's arms was undeniably the most wonderful, secure feeling she had ever experienced. She couldn't get enough of touching him, her fingers delving into his hair, caressing his face, finding the muscles in his shoulders. It was her vision from the flight home, but *real.*

"*Am* I going to kiss you again?"

"I think you'd better...if you really want to *know* me."

He smiled at her offer. And instead of replaying the passionate display of desire, he kissed her gently on the forehead, and cheek, and nose, casually adoring her face and ears with his lips.

He released her slowly.

"You'd better go now, it's getting late...and I need some cold water, a lot of it." Mac was clearly overwhelmed by the intensity of his own feelings, both emotional and physical. Things were happening far too fast for them both.

Jessica nodded, swallowing hard and again retrieving her keys from her purse. She slipped into the Miata, still breathless, and he leaned through the window to brush her lips once more. Despite the euphoria surrounding his affection, Jessica felt a remote disappointment that he hadn't asked her to stay.

As if reading her thoughts, he squatted next to the car and took her hand in his. "I won't be able to sleep thinking about you," he confided.

"Then, maybe we should...*not sleep*...together," she ventured, licking her lips uncertainly.

"On our first date? I'm surprised at you, Jessica Lynne." He feigned disdain, then winked at her while reaching up to tousle her hair. "Good night, love. Be careful."

She drove back in a fog. It was just over an hour to the cabin, but she hardly noticed the time as she thought about the evening's events and the days to come. Maybe Dane had been right, after all. It was all true; it was Mac she loved, Mac who truly loved her. All these months of being friends, confidants, companions—had set the stage for the truest kind of intimacy.

Once home, she went to the sink for some water. She felt giddy with emotion, and her throat was dry. Suddenly she remembered the envelope and rushed to retrieve her purse.

Jessica opened the envelope with trembling fingers. Inside, she found a single, small, yellow square of paper. A "sticky" note, on which she saw Mac's careful, neat printing, a combination of large and small capitals, that read, "Friday night—Dinner with Mac—7:30."

Jessica grinned and pressed the note to her chest for several seconds before sticking it to the refrigerator door.

TEN

Night Flight, Night Music

Jessica spent the next few days relaxing in and around the cabin. It was furnished; she had almost no furniture of her own. And now that her life was changing again, she reminded herself that this place was only a rest stop; she suspected that she would spend little time here. Looking around inside, she decided the place needed something lively, if temporarily, so she made one more list for another shopping trip to the general store at the bottom of the mountain. "Houseplants, Throw Rug, Firewood (ask if fireplace works!), Ice Cream, *Variety*—Call Teddy—Call Roxie!"

After shopping, she walked around the parking lot holding her phone in the air. "I wish they had reliable cell service up here," she murmured as she dialed Teddy's number.

Teddy wanted to meet with her as soon as possible. He had several promising "vehicles" for her to read. "Good stuff, Jess."

"And how are you doing, my friend?" she asked.

"Never better. You've given me credibility, Jessie. I'm getting work for some of my other clients as well."

"Great, Teddy. I'll see you Thursday, okay?"

Roxanne had a list of calls for her. "Let's see: Your Mom's practically livid, your sister's about to go into labor. Dane has called twice today, railing about something. Teddy's trying to reach you."

Jessica giggled. "I owe you, and I love you."

She would put off talking to her mother one more day, and Teddy was handled. She sighed and next dialed the unfamiliar number Roxanne had read off for Dane.

"Pierce Productions," a switchboard operator's voice. After heavy interrogation, Jessica finally got through to him. "Quick, my signal is spotty, and my battery is low."

"Jess, we have some bad film. I need you on the set at nine a.m. tomorrow." Dane's voice was tight and distant.

Jessica silently mouthed a few choice words. "What film?" she asked dully.

"That we shot before we left for the Caribbean. The Boston stuff." He was more than irate, and she patiently listened to *his* choice words for several seconds before interrupting.

"Dane, I...Dane? *Dane!* I'll *be* there!"

"I'm sorry, Jess." His tone changed. "Everything okay?"

"I'm great. I'll see you in the morning."

"Thanks, sweetie. And get yourself a damned phone that works!"

The costume and make-up people were all over her, lightening her skin tone and stuffing her dress. "We have to have you match the earlier shots." This work was simple compared to the long, grueling days on the island, and Jessica breezed through the retakes easily. Dane was pleased, and they walked together to the commissary for a quick mid-afternoon meal.

They ate lunch companionably, their conversation lively with talk about the trip and the film. Dane was highly animated, in the throes of excitement over wrapping up the film.

"So how come you're so chipper?" he asked, "All I've had is shit since I got back."

"No particular reason," she smiled back at him.

He leaned forward conspiratorially. "You and Mac finally getting it on?"

Shocked by his frankness, Jessica raised her hand as if to slap him. He caught it and held it back. "I'm learning," he smiled. "My jaw is still sore."

"Dane Pierce, you are the most disgusting, vulgar, slimy pig to walk this earth," she began, leaning forward for privacy.

"You mean to say you *haven't* gotten into his pants yet? My God, it took you no time to get into mine," he replied, laughing playfully.

Jessica stood up. By now, everyone in the lunchroom was watching them. "That's because yours were already down—around your knees," she asserted, emphasizing the last words and walking smartly from the room.

Dane watched her leave with admiration, subtly pleased with the change in her. He looked around at the others and smiled.

"That's Jessica—always rehearsing. She's really something."

"I'll bet she is," murmured one man sitting nearby. Dane chuckled to himself and finished his meal alone.

Friday could not arrive soon enough for Jessica. Thursday found her dragging home a stack of screenplays to read and a new dress for her date with Mac. Upon dropping her packages on the Futon, she remembered with despair that she'd again failed to return her mother's phone call. Well, it could wait until tomorrow; they were getting used to seeing her in the little market down the hill, but she just couldn't make the trip back to town again today. And anyway, her mother was just being her usual, hysterical self, Jessica was certain.

She was bringing in a few pieces of firewood when the manager walked up. "Do you need fresh linen?" she asked, a little out of breath.

"What I need is cell service," Jessica responded with a chuckle.

"If you've got a smart phone, we have internet, you know. You can use that to call if you have the right... what are they called? Apps?"

"You're kidding me. All this time."

It was noon on Friday before she had the wi-fi-based phone app working. Her first call was not to Mom but to Mac. "Give me directions and I'll pick you up at seven," he suggested. She had planned on meeting him somewhere in the Valley; it was another hour to the cabin, but he insisted, and she rattled off a verbal map to her woodland cottage. "Got it. See you later."

Jessica put the phone down reverently. She took a deep breath, then grabbed a couple of the scripts and headed for the tub.

Her dress was simple but quietly elegant. He had mentioned reservations at *Le Chene*, a dark, romantic restaurant in the foothills, and she knew the white knit dress with tiny silver threads was perfect; form fitting, with small, off-the-shoulder pouf sleeves. She'd had her long hair trimmed and curled, and tonight she pulled it to the top of her head and let the curls cascade down with thin silver ribbons.

He took a deep breath when she answered the door. A soft "whoa" escaped his lips as he looked her up and down.

She smiled and spun around for him with mock flourish. As she turned back toward him, he slid his arm around her waist and pulled her close for a brief hug and a kiss on the cheek.

Mac, too, was resplendent in a charcoal suit, sky blue shirt and, Jessica noted with gaiety, burgundy suspenders. "I really hate ties," he explained.

"I know *that*," she giggled. "Come and see my place." She gave him the grand tour, and soon they were riding back south in the BMW.

"I'll pass on the *Frog Legs Provençale*," Jessica said with a mock frown.

"Beef tongue, perhaps?" Mac teased. "How about *Sandabs Veronique?*"

"Chicken? Do they have just plain chicken?"

"Lobster. We're having *Lobster Le Chene*. Unless you'd rather have the Baby Salmon."

"Lobster is wonderful," she said, giggling.

"Start with the Baked Brie and Artichoke Vinaigrette," he told the waiter. "And I'll take a look at that wine list."

Dinner was easy and comfortable. Mac entertained her with comic stories about the haphazard workmen that had finished the pool, and she delighted him with her off-beat description of one of the screenplays she had been offered.

"Can't you just see me as a female *Mad Max?*" she laughed. "A machine gun in each hand?"

Everything seemed much as it had been between them before Amande, except for an underlying nervousness Jessica felt when she caught him looking at her just a little too long.

They ordered decaf coffee after dinner, and Mac became serious. "There's something I need to say, and it's not too pleasant, and I need you to...listen *and* hear me," he began. "It's about the girl who answered my phone."

"It's not necessary, Mac. Really," she began, but knew she wasn't very convincing with her cheeks burning pink.

"It was Lauren. She called me, claiming to be at an impasse in her life, you know, like maybe suicidal. God, I hate that word." He paused to gather his thoughts. "She asked me if she could come over, to stay and if I would help her get through it. She's been sleeping with some director, and they'd had a fight— small wonder—she said he meant her harm and that she couldn't be alone. I hung up, I struggled with it, and all I could think about was...what if she did it? How could I live with that? And she could do it, too, I'm afraid." He avoided Jessica's eyes, instead focusing on the credit card turning in his fingers.

"I called her back. I told her to come over, that she could stay until the morning, and I'd help her figure out what to do. She came, and things...just got out of hand." He wet his lips, then put down the card and looked directly into her eyes. And Jessica knew; she knew what had happened next. Her eyebrows lifted slightly, but somehow, she had already known the truth and it didn't hurt nearly as much as she'd thought it would. She couldn't let him continue the self-torture of his confession alone.

"And you and she...had a sort of wrestling match?" She offered her implied forgiveness, lowering her chin in question.

"I was still reeling from Amande." He squinted at the memory. "And she's a really mixed-up kid, Jess. She thinks that sex is the same as love and acceptance, from anyone. Which of course makes it even more awful that I did it because I don't love her. In a way, she's a victim, just like you felt Roxie was a victim." He sighed. "Lauren answered the phone while I was in the shower. I heard her hang it up as I was getting out."

"Was she...in your bed?" Jessica was astounded at her own question, but she had to know.

"No. It was...*she* was in the family room." His discomfort was tempered by amusement. "On the floor."

This news pleased Jessica immensely. On the floor. Like wrestlers.

"And when she left, did you say...will you be seeing her again?"

He looked almost offended. "Of course not." He took her hand, lacing his fingers with hers.

"She said I didn't live there anymore," Jessica told him, and she could not stifle a chuckle. "See what happens when you shower all the time?"

Mac's smile was like sunshine to her adoring eyes.

An hour later they were back at the cabin. It was cold in the little house, and Mac gave her his jacket and built them a fire. Jessica brought wine and glasses from the kitchen, and Mac flipped open the Futon in front of the fireplace.

"I know you don't really drink much, but I thought..."

"I'd love some," he replied, lying down on the Futon on his stomach, facing the fire. She placed the glasses on the hearth and poured them each some of the wine before joining him.

"Well, what do you think?" she asked.

"Of what?"

"Of my place."

After downing the wine and pouring himself another, he turned on his side and propped his head on his fist.

"I like it," he said, reaching to her hair and playing with the ringlets, "but I miss you, in mine." His simple statement meant a lot.

Jessica's stomach felt like cement. *Gosh, Jessie, this is just Mac, for goodness sake. Just Mac?* What *was* he doing to her hair?

"I need to get rid...of this." He answered her thought by deftly pulling the pins from her hair, allowing the curls to fall around her shoulders. "Much better," he murmured. His hand moved through the hair and down her back, pulling her close to him on the makeshift bed. "Don't be afraid of me, Jessie," he said softly.

She could not answer. This was scary, this was new. This was *different*. As excited as she had ever felt at Dane's touch, this was ten-fold, ascending all she'd felt before, and she could barely handle it. She wished she had drunk her untouched glass of wine.

"Did I ever tell you how truly beautiful you are?" He whispered in her ear.

"No," she replied, breathless. "But then, it's not like you to say such things."

"And how would you know that?" He smiled lazily.

It was true. She had never seen his romantic side. Never experienced the sensual side of this man who had shared her pain, her secrets, her fears.

His lips traced a path from her ear to her mouth, and she felt she would die with anticipation. His arms held her closer now, and his kiss was soft, and deep, and enduring. Never in her wildest imagination could she have suspected her former roommate of such talent. His lips caressed gently, kissing her again, and again, much to her ultimate joy. He didn't paw her or push her; instead, he behaved as if she was sixteen and breakable. And she loved it.

He stopped briefly to look into her face with a sudden smile. "Should we be in the back seat of my car?"

"Anywhere but your family room floor, *Cory Lee*," she whispered, her fingers toying with the burgundy suspenders. She could sense his excitement building with hers as she lay back and he lowered his lips to her throat, kissing down to the neckline of her dress.

"This is great. Why didn't we ever do this before?" he murmured. "All those weeks we could have—"

Suddenly, Jessica's normally silent cell phone shattered the ambiance and they both started, then looked at each other. Jessica scrambled up to answer it. Who could be calling this late?

Mac collapsed back on the bed. "If that's Pierce, he's a dead man," he called, throwing his arm across his eyes.

Breathless and flushed, Jessica answered the phone. "Oh no, no... not *now.*" Jessica glanced back at Mac, who jumped up to join her. "God, I'm so sorry I forgot to call...of course, I'll be on the next flight. I'll be there, Mom, tell Chrissie not to worry. Jesus—! Um, I'll call from the airport...I'll take a taxi to the hospital."

Jessica's head swam. This was not the news she wanted; the timing couldn't be worse. Mac stood behind her and held her lightly around the waist.

"Okay Mom, tell them to hold off as long as they can. I'll call if there's a problem. And tell Chrissie I love her."

She hung up and turned to Mac, tears blurring her vision. "Chrissie's in labor. They need to do a section—a cesarean, she'll need blood, mine—I promised her mine, she's so afraid of getting bad blood." Her words were jumbled, and she was shaking badly.

"Calm down, baby, where is she?"

"Brighton. Utah. They don't want to start until I'm there. They're going to try to wait, try to slow down the contractions. She's already in pain." She pressed her hand against her forehead, and he held her. "I promised her I'd be there...oh, God. I should have called."

Mac was in control. "Brighton. That's near Salt Lake. Go pack a bag, quickly." He turned her toward the bedroom and gave her a gentle push, then picked up the phone.

She was only remotely aware of his conversation. "...need to call in a big favor...I need the Gulf...now, tonight. And a pilot, I can't fly. Salt Lake. Thanks a million...meet you at Burbank. Forty-five minutes."

Jessica dried her face and emerged from the bedroom. "Are you trying to get reservations? I'll never make it," she cried.

"We *will* make it," he stated, putting on his jacket and putting out the dying fire. And they were on their way down the dark mountain.

"That's Las Vegas," he told her, pointing out the small window in the Gulfstream III jet he had borrowed from "a friend." The craft was a luxury edition; they sat in leather captain's chairs drinking champagne. Mac had called in a very nice favor indeed. He'd also had a change of clothes in his trunk, which he brought along with Jessica's hastily packed bag.

"Oh my God, can I give blood if I've been drinking?"

"Would you relax?" He smiled at her. "I'll bet your sister would laugh out loud if she could see you." He tried to put her at ease. It was a two-and-a-half-hour flight in this, one of the fastest corporate jets available. He took her hand and kissed it. "Things will be fine."

Mac called ahead on the "Jetfone" and a friend of her sister's met them with a car. They rushed to the hospital where Christine had been taken for the surgery.

Inside, Jessica ran to her mother in the waiting room. After embracing and wiping tears, Jessica asked, "Where's Sissy?"

Her mother motioned to a nearby door and turned to peer at Mac, who had quietly followed Jessica into the room. "My God, Jessie, you've brought your own doctor?" she said with a laugh. Mac scratched his eyebrow self-consciously, then extended his hand. "Mac MacKendall, Jessie's...escort."

"Can I see her?" Jessica was impatient.

"Nick's in with her. They're prepping her," her mother responded.

Janet Taylor was a petite woman but had a significant presence. With graying brown hair and sharp, deep brown eyes, she posed a stereotypical picture of anyone's third grade teacher.

A doctor approached and eyed Jessica with interest. "You must be Christine's sister?"

At Jessica's nod he beckoned her to follow. She grabbed Mac's hand and to his surprise, dragged him along to an examining room where a nurse drew blood from Jessica's arm.

"It's just precautionary. We'll take a sample now, but we probably won't need any significant amount of blood." Jessica giggled nervously as Mac feigned dizziness while watching the blood flow into the receptacle.

"The doctor recognized you. You must resemble your sister," Mac pointed out as they later walked back toward Christine's room.

"I do, somewhat." Jessica laughed, pushing the door open. Mac's eyes rested immediately on the attractive girl in bed; her face, though pale and damp with perspiration, was Jessica's face in exact detail; her hair was a shade lighter and in shorter, wet curls; her eyes were weary yet bright, and they, too, were Jessica's eyes. "We're identical twins," Jessica said over her shoulder, rushing to her sister's bedside, crying and hugging her at the same time. She missed Mac's shocked expression, but Nick greeted him warmly.

"Nick Reeves, Jessie's brother-in-law," he explained and extended his hand.

"Mac MacKendall."

Just then, another nurse entered the room. "We're ready to go to the O.R.," she said cheerfully. Christine moaned. "While we're getting them set up, you scrub and get changed," the nurse told Nick. Nick looked panicky and Mac helped usher him out of the room; Jessica could hear Mac's voice trailing away as he recounted for Nick the details of Megan's birth, one of his favorite subjects, offering words of comfort and support.

Nick Reeves was what Jessica termed "fiercely attractive," with black hair and striking dark eyes on a rugged, outdoorsman's face. A strong, assertive mountaineer, there was nothing Nick was afraid of. Nothing, except babies, of course, and childbirth and anything else he could not prevent from hurting Christine. He needed a shave and sleep badly but would not leave her side for a moment during the surgery and delivery of their child.

Mac parked himself in the waiting room, patiently answering Jan Taylor's questions about "Doctor Jim," and adroitly avoiding those about his relationship with Jessica.

"She can be strong-willed, Mr. MacKendall. She let go of a fine thing once before." There was no mistaking Mrs. Taylor's affection for the long-absent Wesley Elliot.

"You keep in touch with Jessie's ex?" Mac questioned her, figuring it was her turn to squirm.

"Wesley calls periodically to inquire after Jessica," she stated matter-of-factly.

Curious, Mac thought. Jessica had said she hadn't heard anything from Wesley herself in years.

Soon, Jessica walked into the room and Mac leapt to his feet. Her mother's eyes were fixed on them as he tenderly assessed her condition after the transfusion that was needed after all.

"I'm fine, just a little weak...but they gave me a cookie." She smiled brightly up at Mac while he examined her arm.

"Nice bandage, goes well with your dress." Then, more quietly, "Did I tell you how luscious you look in that dress?" He put his arm around her and walked her to sit beside her mother.

"You okay, honey?"

"Sure Mom, never better."

"I can see that," Jan responded, taking obvious note of the protective way Mac held his arm around Jessica's shoulders. "Too bad you couldn't come for Christmas," her mother began. "In my wallet I have some color snaps of Chrissie and Nick, and some clippings of you from *People Magazine*. Oh—Paul sends his love."

Jessica and Mac were both sleeping when Nick came bounding into the room an hour later, passing out bubble gum cigars to the few people lounging around. Reaching his mother-in-law, he dropped to one knee and silently handed her a pink cigar.

"Hallelujah!" she hollered, grabbing him and beginning a hugging and laughing spree that lasted several minutes.

Finally, Nick came to Jessica and Mac. "Chris is sleeping now. The baby is in the neo-natal ICU, I guess they sometimes do that when it's, you know, a C-section." He pressed a set of keys into Mac's hand. "It's the blue Jeep near the emergency entrance. Jess, you still know how to get to the lodge?"

"I think so."

"Tell Jeff at the desk that I said to give you the Zurich, and we'll see you tomorrow. I mean, later."

"Thanks, man," Mac said, clapping Nick on the shoulder. "Dad."

They stopped briefly at the nursery's neo-natal unit, and the nurse rolled the bassinet to the window. "Baby Girl Reeves" was tiny, and pink, and precious.

"I guess you and Linda didn't want any more children after Megan," Jessica said, adoring eyes fixed on the infant.

"Linda certainly didn't. Not long after Megan was two, we went to see a surgeon." He squeezed her hand. "I would have liked to have had a son. She didn't want to go through it again."

It was another hour before they unlocked the door to the "Zurich," revealing the lodge's finest luxury suite, complete with wet bar, private Jacuzzi tub, streaming movies, stereo system and a round bed. Mac went to the bed and sat down, bouncing on it and flashing Jessica a most innocent look. She punched buttons on the stereo, and on a whim, turned and raced over to him, tackling him backwards on the bed. Not to be outdone, he rolled them over and stretched out on top of her, clasping her hands and kissing her.

"Mmm..." she moaned, pulling her hands free and wrapping them around him. She was instantly aroused, and only by his kiss. "I want to know who taught you to kiss like that."

"My high school psych teacher." Despite his mischievous smile, Jessica believed him, her eyes wide. "She taught me a lot of things."

"Like what else?"

"Like, always worry when your girlfriend's mother is sleeping down the hall."

Jessica giggled, her fingers nimbly unbuttoning his blue shirt. "She's not sleeping down the hall, and since when am I your girlfriend? Aren't you supposed to give me your high school ring or something? Or did you give it to your teacher?"

"I have something else in mind to give you." Mac bowed his head to kiss the soft, modest cleavage exposed above her dress, pushing the neckline down with his chin as far as the material would stretch. The hot moisture of his mouth against her breast prompted an involuntary shudder.

Jessica could feel her body responding, every cell reacting, a deep stirring growing within her. Mac, too, was aroused and she instinctively moved beneath him, pressing against him for more stimulation despite their restrictive clothing. Mac lifted his head and adjusted the neckline to cover the damp, rosy subject of his attention.

"So, who taught you?" Mac asked softly, dropping more small kisses on her mouth and cheek.

Jessica smiled, ignoring the question and slipping the suspenders from his shoulders before pulling the shirttails from his slacks. "I want you," she whispered, sliding her hands inside his shirt and around his back.

"And I want you." Mac pulled away now and stood up. "But I need a shower."

Jessica sighed in exasperation, watching as he quickly removed his shoes and socks and unzipped his pants, then stepped out of them and carefully draped them over a chair. His eyes never left hers as he silently unbuttoned his cuffs and removed his watch.

Lying on her side, Jessica slid her knee up seductively, watching Mac's unwitting striptease with mild vexation. He smiled at her small attempt to deter him. Still somewhat overwhelmed by the events of the past hours, annoyed and enthralled at the same time, Jessica was fixated on his short, blue, knit Jockey boxers.

He caught her looking. "Medium," he said, pulling the waistband out just slightly. "Although my jeans are thirty-four's." He leaned over her for a kiss, and she lay back, allowing her hem to slide all the way up her thighs.

"I know," she murmured against his lips. "I did your laundry more than once."

He pulled away again. Winking at her obvious confusion, he went to the bathroom and started the shower, leaving the door ajar. The digital clock on the stereo displayed 4 a.m.

A girl can take only so much, Jessica thought defiantly, quickly slipping out of her dress and undergarments. She silenced the phone and turned off all the lights. There were numerous skylights in the ceiling of the suite, and an almost full moon cast a dreamlike frosting on the rooms.

She tiptoed into the bathroom and flipped off the light switch.

"Hey—!" Mac exclaimed, then opened his mouth in admiring awe as Jessica daintily stepped into the shower with him. The moonlight revealed her to him in a surreal fashion, illuminating the water droplets that licked at her body. Her fingertips reached tentatively to touch him, her long nails combing through the sparse hair on his chest. The bar of soap in his hand found her throat, slowly sliding down and around her breasts as his mouth moved steadily toward her lips; all the while hot water pelted their bodies in a sensual waterfall of bliss. Still kissing him, she took the soap from him and seductively lathered his body, his skin and muscles a delight to her anxious fingers. Soon, they were one soapy, sensuous mass. He lifted her without effort and her legs wrapped around him reflexively. Bracing her against a small, tiled bench that seemed incredibly perfect for their intention, Mac closed his eyes as she guided and accepted him; they moved in unison, steam filling the air around them.

Nothing this wonderful could really be happening, Jessica thought fleetingly, feeling as if she and Mac would be joined this way forever. Their passion was heightened by the interruption of their earlier encounter at the cabin and enhanced by their mutual feeling that this was meant to be. He murmured endearments, she whispered his name, repeatedly. The music, the water, the rhythm...his monologue of loving words. This, most surely, was the real thing.

No confusion, no regret. No anger, no pain. Jessica was brought to the limits of sensuality, the edge of sanity as she and Mac shared the ultimate act of love.

Later, Mac shut off the water, Jessica clinging to him possessively. "Now that...was a nice shower," he murmured. Jessica moaned softly, unwilling to come down from her euphoria.

"I don't believe this," she said simply.

"Neither do I."

They began to laugh, and, after carefully wrapping her in a thick bath towel, he carried her to the bed and laid her down, his hair and torso dripping wet.

They lay together for some time, their wild energy dissipating as he slowly and painstakingly blotted the moisture from her skin.

"Are you tired?" he asked suddenly.

"No, not really," she answered, fully enjoying his fond attention.

He reached for the phone and pressed some numbers.

"Yes, what are the chances that we can get some ice cream up here? Yes, I realize it's almost five o'clock. We're...early risers and we eat ice cream for breakfast."

Jessica broke into a fit of giggles.

"MacKendall...yes, guests of Mr. and Mrs. Reeves...ah, that would be nice. You do have Cookies 'N Cream, don't you? Well, maybe you could *find* some. We'll wait. Excellent. Thank you."

"You are something else." Jessica laughed. "They must think we're crazy."

"We are." He went to the closet and retrieved two chocolate brown velour robes and tossed one to her. She put it on and followed him through the sliding glass doors leading to a large patio.

The first gray rays of light were visible in the east over the Wasatch Mountains. The air was cold, and crisp, and sweet. "This is real air, Jessie. Not that mixed bag stuff we have in L.A." He sat in a patio chair and pulled her onto his lap. "I wish we could stay here a week."

She put her arms around his neck and pressed her forehead to his. "Yeah?"

"Yeah. And make love all...the...time." His voice was low and seductive. He kissed her softly. They sat together in silence watching the gray light become pink light. The quiet augmented their mutual feeling of contented comfort, their thoughts singly on each other, and on the miraculous change in their relationship.

"I wanted you the first time I saw you." Mac said quietly. "You were so wound up."

"In my kitchen. At Christmas."

"No. Before that. That morning you came for the audition that wasn't."

She turned and straddled her knees around him, leaning down to kiss him again. "I could kiss you forever."

"I could live with that."

A knock at the door inside brought them around. "Ice cream time." Mac found his wallet and pulled out several bills. Jessica answered the door.

The young man with the tray was obviously stunned by Jessica's appearance. "Mrs. Reeves?" He glanced at her slender figure. "Whoa...impossible." Terribly confused, he looked at the slip of paper on the tray, trying to read the words in the dim light. "Mrs. MacKendall?"

"Thank you," Mac said, taking the tray before handing the boy some cash. The courier shook his head, then looked at the ten dollars in his hand. "Hey, this is really cool...uh, Mr. MacKendall, I mean, if you need anything else, just ask."

On the bed, they took turns feeding each other playfully, and when it was gone, they lay back down and made love again.

"I can't believe you attacked me in the shower." Mac's fine, sensitive fingers were playing across her chest as he parted the brown robe, exposing the milky white part of her that had not seen the Caribbean sun. He leaned down and pressed his lips to her breast, slowly, tenderly expressing his renewed desire for her. His still damp hair touched her chest, and she shivered slightly.

"You kept me waiting. On purpose," she accused. She felt, rather than saw, his confirming smile against her skin as he continued to explore her body.

"I needed a shower, *ma petite*." The warmth of his words, now spoken into her ear, made her jerk with another shimmering spasm down her spine. "You're cold?" he teased, moving to lie on top of her. He laced his fingers tightly with each of hers, pressing her hands into the pillow, peering deeply into her eyes once again. She sensed his restraint of some comment, some endearment which he was not yet ready to impart.

Jessica was filled, overfilled, with desire and love for him. She strained against the pressure of his hold on her, lifting her chin to capture his lips with hers. He took her on, exploring her mouth with his tongue, giving her what she craved. She had never known kissing like this.

Pulling away quickly, Mac grinned at her. "You've been seriously deprived of proper kissing all your life, haven't you?"

"Yes," she panted. "Let go of me so I can attack you again."

"No. We do it *my way* this time."

It was beyond Jessica that she could be made to feel so wonderful. She could not help but compare this experience with the ones with Dane. Dane was... sexual, even erotic. He knew her buttons and soft spots and knew her desires, instinctively. He performed on her, rather than with her, his own desire heightened by his success in arousing her. He seemed almost like a well-defined, sexual machine, exacting perfect control over her.

Mac cared little for such control. His actions were driven solely by his devotion and adoration for Jessica. He gave of himself equally to his taking from her, with no premeditation, planning, or expectations. Just spontaneous, generous love, and they enjoyed each other completely.

As the sun's light finally poured into the suite, Mac drew the dark draperies across the windows and they slept, entangled in affectionate comfort. It was noon before they awoke, delighted with the sight of one another. Now they welcomed the sunshine into their room, and Mac stood over her as she lazily stretched on the bed.

"What are you looking at?" she teased.

He sat down and lifted her hair to inspect her neck, turning her chin from side to side.

"I wouldn't want to have marked your lovely skin."

She looked up at him, suddenly alert to the fact that he was referring to Dane's parting souvenir of the island. Obviously, he had seen it that morning in the kitchen. A million years ago. She started to speak, and he pressed a finger to her lips.

"That was then." No other words were necessary, it was clear.

ELEVEN

Trials and Truces

Jessica spent as long with her sister as the hospital would allow. They talked about their different lives until they were each hoarse, the subject ultimately turning to the new little life to be christened Angelica.

"Well, we're really different now, Sissy," Jessica sighed. "You're a mom."

"You will be someday, Jess." Chrissie grasped her sister's hand.

"I almost was, once...but lately I've been glad, sort of, that it didn't work out. It just wasn't meant to be. If I hadn't miscarried, I'd probably be a fisherman's wife cleaning crab with five kids clinging to my apron." The girls laughed.

"And instead, you're being courted by all these Hollywood studs." Chrissie poked at Jessica's stomach.

"No, only one, Chris. There will be no others."

"Sounds serious. Is he as wonderful as he is handsome?"

"He is," Jessica said softly, her eyes becoming blurry, "everything."

"God, you sound like me when I met Nick. I hate to say it, Sissy, but you didn't act this way about Wes. Are you going to marry him?"

Jessica looked down at her lap. "If he asks me, yes. But knowing Mac, it could be a while before he decides something like that." She smiled. "I can wait. The way I feel right now, I would wait forever."

"Oh, Jess, please! You're making me sick." Chrissie laughed.

"Nick's giving him the grand tour of Salt Lake."

"Yeah, he was thrilled at the opportunity to get out of here. He hates hospitals. And, he likes Mac."

"You lightened your hair; it looks great."

"I had to do something. I'm afraid when *Lost Season* opens, I'll have no peace."

"Could be good for business," Jessica teased, then added, "I'll send you one of those big noses with the glasses."

"You seem a little underwhelmed today, Sis, is something wrong?"

"Just...Mac has to fly back to L.A. this afternoon, and I'm bummed."

"Go with him."

"No! I want to be here with you for a few days, honest. Mac and I have a whole future ahead of us."

"Oh, for Pete's sake, Jess, go home with Mac. I'm fine, really."

"Forget it, Chris, I've already purchased a ticket home on Tuesday. Mac's doing this environmental TV special and he's busy, otherwise he'd stay, too. This trip wasn't exactly planned, but we want to come back up later this year."

She argued with Mac about taking him to the airport. "You should know by now that I can take care of myself. You can't be worrying about me. I'm taking you to the airport, and that's final." He shrugged and gave her an exasperated, if loving, look, and they left for Salt Lake International.

It was more than hard to say good-bye. "Seems like we've done this a lot," she said, trying not to cry.

"You'll be home Tuesday, right? I wish I could stay, but yesterday was Megan's birthday, and I promised to take her to the Music Center this evening." At Jessica's puzzled look, he continued. "She's precocious, I told you. It's a children's opera."

"That means Angelica was born on the same day as Megan." Jessica was losing the battle with her tears, and he hugged her.

"Call me, okay? Every night until you come home."

"Sure," she sniffed. "You're working, right?"

"Yeah, but not late hours. You be careful, okay?"

She nodded over his shoulder. Blinking away her tears, she caught sight of someone across the crowded terminal staring at her. The face seemed hauntingly familiar, but different...

Mac felt her stiffen and looked in the direction of her gaze. "What is it?" They both glimpsed a man in the crowd, some twelve yards away, watching them. Very tall and thin, he had shoulder length reddish-blond hair, a mustache and several days' start on a beard. As his eyes met Mac's, he turned and disappeared into the throngs of passengers.

"Just thought I saw someone I knew, but I was mistaken," Jessica said. "You be careful, too."

Standing in the middle of the airport, they kissed until the ominous voice of the airline called his flight for the final boarding.

Jessica spent the next three days dividing her time between visiting Christine and helping at the lodge. In another era of her life, she would have stayed at least two weeks. She loved children and would have enjoyed helping with the baby. But her mind was filled with images of Mac, and it was difficult to stay.

As it turned out, she extended her stay until Wednesday morning, for the hospital released Chrissie on Tuesday evening and a small celebration was held at the lodge. She continued to occupy the suite, despite her protestations to Nick that it was an unnecessary luxury. She called Mac each night as promised, and he told her all about Megan's birthday and the opera and the "special" with which he was involved at the studio. Just the sound of his voice mesmerized her; closing her eyes she could see him in the house, talking to her on the phone.

Tuesday night after the party, she tiredly returned to the suite and on a whim, turned on the Jacuzzi jets in the spa. The hot bubbles felt good, and she called Mac from the phone she'd brought with her to the tub.

"Don't you dare tell me you're not coming home tomorrow," he warned her.

"Not on your life. My flight gets in at ten in the morning."

"You know I can't be there...but I'm sending Henry, you remember him, don't you?"

"Of course. That's wonderful, I appreciate it." She sighed. "I'm in the Jacuzzi, Mac."

"Don't say that," he moaned. "God, I miss you, babe."

She giggled softly. "Good. Because I'm going to jump on you tomorrow."

It was difficult, at the last minute, to leave Chrissie and the others. Her mother admonished her for staying so briefly, but Jessica swore that she'd return in the late summer or fall and stay a couple of weeks. She also promised to visit Seattle soon, suggesting the family get together there for Thanksgiving. Or better yet, everyone could come to L.A. for Christmas. Her mother scoffed but hugged her with tears in her eyes.

"I'm sorry if I might have offended your young man, Jessie. It's just that Wesley has missed you so." She appeared to stop short of saying more than she wanted to.

"What, Mother, what about Wes?"

"Nothing. I just meant that I'm not used to seeing you with someone else."

"Mother! It's been five years since Wesley and I divorced!" Jessica cried in frustration. "And Mac is ten times the man Wesley was."

"*Is*, Jessica, he's not dead, although you might think so." Her mother seemed overly concerned about her ex-husband. "Anyway, Mr. MacKendall seems to be a nice young man, Jess, for an *actor*."

"What is that supposed to mean?" Jessica threw her hands up, exasperated. *And she wonders why I don't always call her back.*

"Mom means well, Sis," Chrissie consoled moments later as they said their last good-bye. "She's just living in the past, when we were all together, and you and Wes used to come over for dinner every week...she remembers those as the good old days, and she equates your career with the demise of those times."

Jessica nodded. "I know. She just gets to me sometimes...And it bugs me that Wesley calls her all the time." Glancing at the clock, she cleared her frown. "Look, I have to go, or I'll miss my plane."

The sisters hugged, cried, and promised to stay in touch. Jessica said she'd remember to forward the "disguise" as soon as the picture hit the theaters.

Nick drove her to the airport, and while boarding the plane, her excitement began to build. She was going home, to Mac this time.

Mac's right about this poor air, she thought, as the United wide body approached L.A.'s International Airport. But nothing could dampen her spirits now.

Christine had unloaded a few dresses on her, one of which was perfect for today: a springy, flowery sun dress with a full skirt and fitted bodice, accented by a solid red belt hugging her trim waist. Red pumps completed the outfit. "Take them Jess, they're not much use around the mountains here," Christine had told her. And from the airport gift shop, Jessica added a perfect straw hat with a red hatband.

The jet landed without incident, and Jessica sighed with relief. Her hasty trip meant no luggage, everything being in the carry-on over her shoulder. Although she wasn't quite sure where to look, Henry appeared out of nowhere and ushered her gallantly to the waiting limousine.

"Where to, Miss Taylor?"

"Well..." She grinned at Henry. She had a plan, and he grinned back. "Do you think you could get me past the gate at Castle?"

"Mac working today? I think we could sneak you in." And they were off.

Jessica's stomach was aflutter. She twisted the strap of her bag nervously. *Oh boy-oh boy...come on come on come on...*each red traffic light lasted an eternity.

At Castle Studios the guard waved them in. "Should I wait, Miss Taylor?" Henry asked.

"Uh...no. I think I can get another lift, thank you." She smiled brightly, and Henry chuckled. He helped her out at the door to the sound stage where Mac's BMW was parked outside. The red light was flashing, and Henry started to say something.

"I *know*." She smiled, and Henry drove away. She paced, and the minute the light went off, she hurried inside.

The stage was set up for an interview, talk-show style. An observation booth loomed twenty feet above the set, to one side, wherein sat the producer and director. They talked to the cast and crew via a loudspeaker system overhead.

"Okay, let's try it again," the voice boomed. A bell rang. Jessica slowed her pace, her heels echoing loudly as she approached the stage. Mac was sitting on a couch, apparently interviewing a woman about toxic waste as slides changed behind them on a large screen. He caught sight of Jessica and jumped to his feet.

"Wait, Bert, wait!" he called. Leaping off the stage, he ran toward Jessica and swept her up into his arms, lifting her off her feet and spinning her around, all the while kissing her hungrily. Everyone else in the room watched, and above a spotlight was trained on them by a humorous light technician.

After several moments, the man in the booth clicked on his microphone.

"Excuse me, uh, Mac, could we continue sometime today?"

Mac waved his arm and eventually put Jessica down.

"Can you take a break?" Jessica whispered.

"I..." Mac looked up at the booth, frowning, "...don't know."

Although he could not hear their words, the director's voice came again. "Take five, Mac."

"Fifteen, Bert?" Mac called back.

"Ten maximum. Maybe you won't be so *worthless* when you get back, huh?"

"Ten minutes." Mac looked at his watch and glanced down at Jessica. A smile curled on his lips, creating the boyish dimples she adored. "This could be a new record...come on."

He took her hand and they ran from the room, much to the merriment of the crew. This stage was farther from his dressing room than the *Doctor Jim* set, and they were panting when they reached it, Jessica carrying her heels as she ran in her bare feet.

Mac closed the door and threw the bolt. Jessica reached behind her and began unzipping the flowered dress, and Mac approached her.

"Ah ah ah ah, *my* turn this time."

Their chests heaving from their abrupt getaway, they undressed each other quickly, laughing at their own adolescent behavior. Then they were on the small bed, instantly falling into a playful, loving game of passion and desire, delighting one another with sensual pleasure.

"Not much opportunity for foreplay," he laughed, turning on the shower minutes later.

"Foreplay was over when you touched me the first time," she confessed.

"That good, huh? Damn." Then, more seriously, "I missed you so much; it seemed like forever."

They washed any physical evidence of their encounter from their bodies, but there was no mistaking the obvious glow in their faces as they returned to the set, hand in hand, calm now. They had been gone twenty minutes.

"Nice of you to rejoin us, Valentino." The voice invaded their private good-bye, but Mac ignored it; his attention was directed at fussing with Jessica's hair.

"Henry dropped you off...you need my car?"

She nodded and slipped her hand into his pocket, seeking the keys. She pulled them out and he took them, attempting in vain to separate two halves of the key chain. Jessica took them back and unhooked them easily. "Guess I'm still worthless," he joked. "Where are you off to?"

"Paramount, first, I have to check in. I was supposed to be on the set yesterday, and Dane will have my head on a platter. I have to do some shopping, then I'm going to the cabin."

"You're coming home...*back*...to my house tonight, aren't you?"

"If you want me to." She smiled coyly. "I should be there around seven-thirty or so. Let's make...dinner...together."

He kissed her again. The voice of God thundered.

"MACKENDALL! Jesus, his hair's *wet*. Miranda, get a blow dryer out there."

Paramount Pictures was only three blocks away. Castle had, in fact, once been part of Paramount. The BMW seemed to drive itself and she cruised onto the grounds filled with a sense of glamour. "This could be a wonderful habit," she thought, parking in her usual spot near the door.

The red light here was also flashing. "Damn!" she cursed, her patience waning. Finally, she pulled the door open anyway and walked in. She could see Dane instantly, his presence commanding as he directed a scene set in an early Bostonian bank.

"Cut it there," he shouted, spying Jessica as she approached, again carrying her shoes. "You trying to ruin my picture? Is that what you're trying to do?" He feigned irritation, and she smiled brightly at him.

They had not seen each other since she'd walked out on lunch the week before. She liked the easy, comfortable relationship that had developed.

"Five minutes, everybody." The crew broke and people started moving about. I'm really causing problems today, Jessica thought with amusement.

Still glowing with "afternoon delight," she wondered if Dane could tell.

"So, where the hell have *you* been?" he asked, toying with the straps on her dress.

"In Utah. My sister had her baby."

"Yeah. Well, those things happen. Luckily, I didn't really need you yet...*here*, that is..." now his fingers were tracing the neckline and she absently, routinely, slapped them away. "But I will need you on Friday, for certain...Got that? Don't let me down, sweetcakes."

"I won't," she smiled warmly. Too warmly. He leaned closer and looked into her eyes.

"You did it, didn't you?" the smiled broadened, the green eyes twinkled.

She nodded. He straightened the dress and cleared his throat. "Well."

Jessica reached up and whispered in his ear. His eyes opened wide.

"In the shower? In the freaking shower? Je-sus!" He looked around in comic disarray. "You never did *me* in the shower." Despite his apparent merriment, he kept his voice discreet.

Jessica could not help but giggle at his lame portrayal of disgust.

"And I thought I had you set for...at least a month. You must be insatiable." His smile was bittersweet. "I guess ol' Mac's got something going after all. Lucky bastard."

"Dane, you are the second most wonderful man in the entire world." She put her arms around his neck and hugged him affectionately.

"Somehow, second best with you just doesn't cut it, sweetie."

"He loves me, Dane. He really loves me."

"Did he tell you so?"

"No, not out loud..."

"Make him do it, Jessie. Make him tell you." This, apparently, was her new assignment. "In fact, tell him 'no more screwing' until he does."

Jessica laughed at his demands. "I have to go." She brushed his cheek with her lips and pulled away. He grabbed her hand and stopped her.

"Hey, Jess, there was a guy here this morning looking for you."

Jessica stopped in her tracks. "Who?"

"I don't know him. Whenever anyone asks for you, they get me. Kinda scraggly guy, blond, tall...with a deranged look. Probably just a demented fan of yours," he said with a grin.

"You're joking, right?"

"Well, he did look like he hadn't slept in a long, long time. But shit, I probably look like that right now. Anyway, I told him I didn't know where the hell you were."

She nodded, her expression subdued. "Thanks, Dane. See you Friday."

Jessica's blush faded as she drove thoughtfully across the Valley. Dane was right, the man asking for her was probably just some weirdo who had seen her recent pictures in a magazine. But there was something at the cabin she had to check. Later.

First, she stopped at Mac's house and let herself in. She roamed about the big house, seeing it in a new light. She wondered if he wanted her to stay, to forget anyplace else and just live here.

In Megan's room, she found a tape measure and began measuring the windows and the antique canopied bed. She made notes about everything in the room, then went to the kitchen. With a bowl of cold, fresh strawberries in front of her, she outlined plans for decorating the little girl's room with frilly eyelet and fantasy fairy princesses.

Jessica jumped at the sound of a car parking on the gravel. She hurried to the window, peeking around it, her heart thumping. A rusty old station wagon had stopped near the front door, and someone was taking something out of the back.

Suddenly, unreasonably terrified, she ran to the small study and closed the door.

She waited. Whoever it was, they weren't particularly quiet about entering the house. Then she heard a new noise: the sound of Gretchen's vacuum cleaner in the hall.

She sighed deeply. *What's come over you, girl?* She walked out of the study feeling stupid. Gretchen started at the sight of her, and they both laughed.

On the kitchen counter she retrieved her keys and found two envelopes addressed to her next to the coffee maker. One was from Pierce Productions. It was a check for three thousand dollars, a reimbursement for travel expenses. Her eyes widened. *I can really use this.*

The second envelope was more disturbing. Another letter from Wesley.

"...too bad I will miss you. I understand you are in Salt Lake with Mom and Chris, and I am here in L.A. for a few days. However, by the time you read this, I will be well on my way back to Seattle. The University is holding a job for me, and I've got to get back."

Jessica sighed with relief. She really didn't want to see Wesley right now, and it was good that he was being offered a job. She put the envelopes into her purse and after paying Gretchen, left the house again.

She spent the late afternoon shopping for materials for Megan's room. Her spirits again high, she also bought an expensive sewing machine and asked that it be delivered to Mac's house on Saturday.

It was nearly seven when she turned the BMW up the last steep drive toward the motel cabin. She didn't really need anything here, but she wanted to check things out anyway and water the plant. The BMW's headlights shone on the little blue car parked in the attached carport. She left the Beemer in the driveway.

If this were really my place, I'd build a door into the room from the carport, she thought tiredly. She turned the key and went inside. She was not even remotely prepared for what she found.

Jessica's eyes fell first on the Futon she and Mac had left open on the floor. It had been slashed to shreds and great tufts of stuffing were strewn around the floor. The sliding glass doors to the patio were open, and the breeze blew around thousands of pages of script, unbound and lying in heaps. The new plant had been dumped.

"Oh my God..." Her heart began beating triple time. She cautiously made her way to the kitchenette while digging into her purse for her phone. She had to dial several times before her shaking hands could get Mac's number correct. He answered cheerfully.

"Mac...it's me...something's happened." She was sobbing and losing control fast.

"Honey, calm down, what is it? Are you okay?" Mac's voice sounded his alarm.

"Someone's...been...here...Everything's trashed." Her eyes were wide with terror as she surveyed the room. "It...it's awful."

"Did you call the police?"

"No."

"Jessie, listen to me. I want you to get back into the car. Are you there? Get in the car and drive down to the market. They should still be open—"

"Y-yes, I think so...'til nine or so."

"Good. Just go, *now*. I'll be there as fast as I can. Stay calm, baby."

Numbly, she put the phone down. Instead of rushing outside, she opened the kitchen drawer and removed the two letters she'd put there last week. Through blurry eyes, she examined the postmarks. The first was from Tacoma, Washington; the second was postmarked San Francisco. Jessica sniffed and pulled the third letter from her purse, the one she'd picked up today at Mac's. In horror she read, "Salt Lake City, Utah" stamped across the top. "Oh God," she whispered.

Now she moved into action. Grasping the letters and her keys, she ran from the house, quickly crossing the driveway to Mac's car, and gripped the door handle. She turned to look at the carport and stopped. *The interior light in the Miata was on.*

She hesitated, staring at her car as if hypnotized. *Don't be stupid, Jessica,* a voice screamed in her head. But it was too late. A large hand clamped over her mouth from behind, stifling her scream and cutting off her breath. Struggling, her captor roughly dragged her around to the passenger side of the black car and a familiar voice whispered harshly in her ear.

"I like the Mazda, kitten, but let's take the pretty boy's Beemer. We could use a little style going out."

She wasn't going without a fight, and she twisted violently as he tried to force her into the car. Grabbing her purse firmly, she whacked her attacker on the head in vain, spilling the contents onto the driveway. Finally, he struck her hard across the face, knocking her senseless. Slamming the door, he ran around the car and got into the driver's seat, adjusting it for his long legs. He took the keys from her clenched fist and drove into the blackness down the hill.

Mac felt terror of his own. He raced to the garage, deciding as he ran that the bike would be fastest. He jumped onto the Honda and tore out of the estate, leaving his helmet behind. The Hollywood Freeway seemed too busy for a Wednesday night. Speeding to seventy-five mph, he kept a mindful eye out for the California Highway Patrol; he couldn't afford to get stopped. He edged the needle up to eighty. He breezed through the pass into the Santa Clarita Valley, weaving carefully around the big-rig trucks exiting and entering from the merging freeways at the crest.

His heart cramped painfully. The wind blew madly through his hair, and his mind was filled with the sound of Jessica's terrified voice. It would take forever —too long—to reach Pine Mountain.

The little market was empty, save for the proprietor and his wife. "Sure, we know Jessie, comes in here all the time to use the phone. Ain't seen her around for a few days, though."

Mac was back on the bike in seconds, winding up the dark, narrow road to Jessica's motel cabin.

He hadn't paid attention to the carport before. The driver's door to the Miata was ajar, and the interior courtesy lights were on. He looked over at the cabin; the front door was closed, and kitchen lights glowed through the window.

"Jessie!" he shouted. He rushed to the door and found it unlocked. "Jessie!" he called again, knowing already it was for naught. The BMW was nowhere around.

Inside, he surveyed the room and the mess. The wine glasses they'd left in haste were shattered on the hearth. The sight of the slashed bedding made him ill.

He quickly toured the house, finding all the damage to be in the front room. He stared in vain at his cellphone, and the "no signal" icon.

After failing to raise anyone at the manager's cabin, Mac wasted no time in getting back to the general store. The Kern County Sheriff's Department took the details and advised him that deputies in the area would meet him at the motel.

Roxanne was his second call. He sketched out what had transpired, and Roxanne was in tears. He promised to come to her place as soon as he'd finished giving his report to the sheriff's deputies who were on their way.

Mac's jaw worked as he considered his next thought. Rubbing his closed eyes, he forced the words out.

"And Roxie, get a hold of Dane Pierce."

Dane arrived at Roxanne's just as Mac was parking the Honda at the gate leading to the townhouse steps. They exchanged nods and entered as Roxanne held the door open, her face ashen and streaked with tears. Inside, Tom Jarrick was pacing. The three men shook hands.

"Does anyone want anything to drink?" Roxanne asked tensely. She and Tom had already put away a bottle of Chardonnay prior to Mac's call.

"Got any whiskey, Roxanne?" Dane asked. She nodded and poured him a glass with ice.

"You won't be much good to us if you're drunk on your ass," Mac warned.

Dane stared at him levelly and downed the whiskey without replying.

"What did the sheriff have to say?" Tom wanted to know.

"Haven't a clue. These guys weren't exactly detective types, if you know what I mean. We found several things from her purse on the driveway, including her phone. They dusted everything for prints; they put out an APB on the Beem. And that's it, besides taking a photo with them of Jessie."

"Is there anyone that may be interested in Jessica? Old boyfriends, scorned lovers?" Tom's years as a mystery buff were helpful. "Maybe crazed admirers?"

Dane snapped his fingers. "That guy—this morning."

"What guy?"

Dane told them about the visitor to the set. "A real loser—long hair, kind of orangish-blond, unshaven. His eyes were—"

"Hazel and kind of vacant, right?" Mac asked suddenly.

"Yeah."

"And real tall and skinny?"

At Dane's nod, Mac continued. "He was at the airport, in Salt Lake. Holy shit, he's been stalking her." Mac turned to the window and rubbed his forehead wearily. Things had taken a decidedly horrifying turn.

"Now we're getting somewhere," Tom said.

"She knew this guy, I could tell. She said she thought she'd seen someone she knew, but was mistaken," Mac recalled.

"Roxanna, you've known her a long time. Does this sound like anyone you might know?" Dane ventured.

Roxanne frowned, slowly shaking her head. "She hasn't dated much since her divorce. This guy doesn't sound like someone she'd date, anyway."

"There's got to be something we're missing. I'm going back up to the cabin. I can't just sit here," Mac said in agitation.

"I'll go with you." It was Dane who rose, and Mac looked at him thoughtfully.

"Okay. Rox, you and Tom sit tight. If she should get an opportunity, she might call here."

His comment again brought tears to Roxanne's eyes, and Tom held her tenderly. "Call us if you find anything," Tom told them.

The two men jumped into Dane's Porsche and sped away.

"I really appreciate your help, Pierce," Mac said.

"Hey, believe it or not, Jessie is important to me, too."

They spoke little on the way. In Pine Mountain, downshifting into first gear, the Porsche began to climb the hill. Dane parked the car on the driveway and stared at the group of small cabins, then back to the view of the town below.

"Awesome."

Armed with a large, bright lantern, they began searching the carport area first.

"Look at this." Mac rushed over to where Dane gestured. "Looks like someone was standing or squatting behind these boxes. The bastard was hiding here." The flashlight revealed clear, large footprints in previously undisturbed dust on the floor.

Inside, they painstakingly sifted through the shredded Futon and the scripts, sweeping up the glass and righting the plant.

"Cute place. Looks like her," Dane commented.

Since the lodging was obviously temporary, very few personal items were in evidence. And apart from one open kitchen drawer, everything else was neat. Discouraged, they went back outside, carefully checking the ground, the patio and the shrubs for anything the sheriff's team may have missed. Brushing the bushes around on the far side of the Porsche, Mac spotted something caught in the branches, lower on the hillside.

"Bingo." Envelopes, four of them. They took them inside to examine in the kitchen light.

The first contained a check, ironically bearing Dane's signature. The second, a bill. The other two were not so innocuous.

Mac sat at the table leaning his face into his hands as Dane read Wesley's letters aloud in a dull monotone.

"...*but you, kitten, finally have all the glamour and success you've always wanted, and I know now that it was I who was holding you back, that it was always you with all the talent...so life goes on for some, doesn't it?...*Geez, this guy's a nut case." Dane's voice sounded truly fearful for the first time. He swallowed and continued reading.

"...*it wasn't enough that you cast aside the blessed life I put inside you, I wasn't good enough for you either, was I? But I have changed, and I think you'd be pleased...*"

"I can't believe this is happening," Mac murmured.

"Okay, okay. We've got to get a handle on this guy." Dane ran fingers through his hair. Mac looked at him, watching for an idea to surface. "He's her ex, right?"

Mac nodded. His mind was burning with the words from the letter. Dane took a deep breath, flexing his fingers.

"First, we notify the sheriff of what we've found. Then," he said, looking steadily at Mac, "we go after this fucking lunatic. He can't be far, right? And he's in your car."

The sheriff's deputy on the phone seemed unimpressed with their discovery. "Yep. The estranged husband story."

"Divorced! Divorced for five years! Look, I'm giving you vital information here!" Mac was losing control and hung up. The shopkeepers, their expressions worried, silently stood by. Taking a deep breath, Mac called Roxanne. He forced his voice to sound calm, his eyes watching Dane pace around the store. "Roxie? Mac. Describe Wesley Elliot as you remember him."

Dane stopped pacing and observed Mac's reaction. Mac nodded. "Uh huh, okay. Where can we get a picture of him?"

"I have several," Roxanne was saying. "I can't believe this. It's hard to imagine Wesley looking like that. I, uh, can scan some of these..."

"No, we're coming back there anyway." Mac hung up the phone and they were off.

They drove back to Roxanne's in silence. It was midnight, and the LAPD had sent two officers to Roxanne's at Tom Jarrick's request. They were asking for photos of Jessica and Wesley, and a description of Mac's missing car.

"He won't get far if he stays with the vehicle. An 850i is a flashy, visible, car. And with a vanity plate that reads "DR J," he's liable to ditch it soon."

Mac gratefully accepted a cup of coffee from Roxanne, and he and Dane sat down to a table spread with photos of Jessica and Wesley, dating back to their junior year of high school. Mac turned to Dane, his eyes filled with exhaustion and grief.

"This is really shitty, isn't it?" He referred to the photos of the smiling, fresh-faced teenagers. He picked up a particularly handsome picture: Jessica and

Wesley's wedding photo. "I can't do this," he muttered, standing and turning to the window.

Dane sighed and hastily picked two or three pictures. The officers took them and promised to call with any news. "These will be on the wire in minutes. Your friends at Kern County Sheriff's Department will pick them up too, along with LASD, and the media will probably have it by morning, Miss Taylor being a celebrity and all."

Everyone nodded numbly and Roxanne thanked the officers. There remained a bleak silence in the townhouse. Roxanne went to the couch and curled up next to Tom, who sat thoughtfully pulling on his mustache. Dane sat staring at the remaining photos on the table, lost in his own thoughts about what to do next.

"Until we know more, about all we can do is wait." Tom sighed heavily.

"I'm going home," Mac announced. "If anyone hears anything...?" There was silent agreement that each would call the other with any news at all. Dane followed Mac outside.

"Look, MacKendall...I know we haven't always seen eye to eye, but you've gotta let me know if anything happens," Dane began.

"Of course, man," Mac replied, looking away.

"Let me give you my number."

"I have it. Jessie *programmed* my phone...you're number five." His voice reflected a touch of irony.

Dane sat on the Porsche's fender. "That's funny, this morning she told me I was number two," he said in amusement, referring to Jessica's affectionate declaration.

"You *did* see her today?"

"Oh, yes. Yes, I saw her." Dane smiled into the distance. "She came bounding onto the set, ruining my take, all bursting with romance...over you, asshole."

Mac said nothing. He was getting used to Dane's mouth and was finally realizing that vulgarity had nothing to do with what Dane meant to say.

"She—was—radiant." Dane continued.

"She's always radiant," Mac said softly.

"She was getting *wet*, just talking about you, man. I gotta hand it to you, Mac." Dane's eyes finally focused on him. "But I guess I had my chance, didn't I, as you so astutely pointed out to me on the island?"

Mac thought on this, unsure if he should venture into what he really felt. Perhaps Dane was baiting him again. In retrospect, and under the circumstances, everything was irrelevant anyway.

"Do you think you really gave it a chance, Pierce? Honestly?" he asked.

Now it was Dane's turn to digest Mac's words.

"No. I couldn't allow myself to let a woman like Jessica, or any woman for that matter, get under my skin; not at this time and place in my life. Believe me,

I wanted to, but..." He smiled briefly at Mac. "You're right, as usual, my friend."

The early morning air was cold and damp, and clouds had moved in overhead. California's fickle April weather was upon them. "I never thought I'd be sorry to see rain." Mac cleared his throat.

"Get in. I'll drive you home," Dane offered. "You have no helmet or coat."

"I'll be okay," Mac declined.

"I insist. You live only a couple of miles from me. We'll get the bike tomorrow."

"Your kids been sitting here?" Mac complained, adjusting the seat backward to accommodate his legs.

Dane smiled. "Yeah, but it was Jess who moved that seat last, the last time I took her out. Before we went to the island. Surely you remember?"

Mac remembered well. It seemed like ages ago. She had come home in tears.

"She was already in love with you then, Mac." Dane chuckled, recalling the evening. "I really wanted her to come home with me. At the time, I fancied her the salvation to my private hell...but she wouldn't have it. Not with Mr. Right waiting at home." Dane let out a long breath. "Look, man, I'm an a—"

"An asshole, yeah, I know," Mac said tiredly, then laughed under his breath with giddy amusement. Dane joined him and they released some of their tension laughing. Soon, Dane was on another wavelength.

"You're divorced, right?"

"Yeah. Two-and-a-half, maybe three years."

"What happened?"

Mac paused before answering, wondering if he should share a truth with Dane that he hadn't even told Jessica.

"Unfortunately, while I was playing doctor, so was she."

Dane looked at him in surprise.

"Of course, I was the last to know. Megan had just started walking, one day she took a tumble, and I got a frantic call from this jerk, Linda was freaking out...he was there, in my house." Mac shook the memory from his head.

"You loved your wife," Dane stated quietly.

"I did."

"Was it tough? Your divorce?"

"It was hell. I almost forfeited my custody rights by failing to appear in court. She told the judge I was always working. She was right, I guess...Luckily, I had a good attorney. Linda had me by the balls."

"Do you ever see her?"

"Every other weekend when I pick up my daughter. We're okay now. She's calmed down. And she knows in her heart she could never keep Megan away from me." He paused reflectively. "It's funny, I see her now almost as much as when we were married." He looked at Dane. "You?"

"My wife's suing me for a bezillion dollars. She's turned my older daughter against me, erased my younger one's memory of me, and enrolled my six-year-old son in a lousy military academy."

Mac whistled.

"That's not all. She's changed the locks on our home. She's screwing some twenty-five-year-old law student, a tennis pro who I used to pay to coach my kids, and she's pregnant. And of course, the whole thing is my fault. Next thing I know, she'll be spilling her guts to Oprah Winfrey, for Chrissakes."

"Your fault, huh?"

"I wasn't the best husband...or even a good one. When I was making *Sioux Nation*...aw, shit. Let's just say I'd better forget about ever getting into politics."

Mac was quiet while he deduced the meaning of Dane's admission. Finally, he shook his head. "What is your attorney doing about all this?"

"Right now? Sitting on his ass in Caracas."

"I'll give you my attorney's card, he's in Encino. Tell him I gave you his name. He's the best," Mac offered. "Linda's lawyer had my assets frozen, and nearly had the studio convinced they should pull the show. George will put a stop to that shit."

"I will. Thanks, man."

Mac believed Dane's appreciation was sincere. It felt good to them both to be talking about something else, despite the ugly details of Dane's divorce. It was at least a *known*, with a predictable outcome. Jessica's abduction was a horror they could not so easily face.

Dane stopped the Porsche at Mac's front door. "I'm shutting down the film for today."

"Can't they shoot without you?"

"Only the small stuff. I have too much invested in this film to let incompetence screw it up."

"I hear you." Mac got out and Dane jumped out also, leaving the engine running. He came around to Mac and stood before him, his hands stuffed into his pockets. A light drizzle was evident in the Porsche's headlamp beam.

"Hey...we'll get her back, man." The two men glanced nervously around, lost in mutual misery over Jessica.

Mac nodded in agreement, but doubt clouded his face.

Dane slowly extended his hand, and Mac grasped it. "Call me. Number Five."

TWELVE

Always My Own

The fog turned into rain as the tan Mercury Cougar limped into Oxnard, muffler smoking and Washington license plate swinging on one screw. Dents blemished one side of the car, and a lone wiper scrapped noisily across the driver's side of the pitted windshield. Gray morning light accompanied the rain; the coastal town was still sleeping.

Jessica stared out the window in cold, exhausted silence. The salty, metallic taste of her own blood still in her mouth, she wet her lips repeatedly while twisting her wrists inside the clothesline rope that bound them.

Wesley hummed an unrecognizable tune to himself as he drove closer to the shore, down a street of mostly rental beach houses all in a row, seeking a specific one.

"Here it is, kitten, honeymoon heaven." He smiled, turning the thrashed car into an open garage. Quickly closing the garage door, he helped Jessica from the car and hastily ushered her inside.

"Still looks the same, doesn't it, Jess?" he asked, dragging her across a living room to a wall of glass looking out at the gray sea. She didn't respond, and he twisted the clothesline abruptly.

"Yes! Yes, it's still the same." Tears sprang to her eyes at the pain in her wrists. He released her onto a couch.

"We were lucky to get it on such short notice. Of course, mentioning your pretty boyfriend's name and VISA number didn't hurt."

"How...how did you get Mac's credit card?" she asked wearily.

"At the airport. He wasn't smart. Left his card in the tray a little too long," Wesley responded, his last statement pronounced in a sing-songy voice.

"Wesley, please untie me."

"Not yet, kitten. I want you to get used to being here first. That's how you train a stray cat, right? Ah, this was it, all right. This was where you and I...first got it on. I'll never forget how scared you were, Jess. But you're not the timid little virgin anymore, are you? Not with all those rich Hollywood pigs jumping in and out of your bed. How does it feel, getting poked by a...*real...star?*" he asked, his eyes wide and his voice taking on a mocking, dreamlike quality.

"Guess it'd be hard to go back to a punk like me, huh, Jess? Oh, but I've learned a few new tricks. Living on the streets, like I have, you learn a lot. From pros. I bet I could turn on your lights again, kitten."

Jessica's stomach churned. She was beyond crying, only filled with revulsion and worry. How could she escape? Wesley was obviously quite mad, and she knew she must remain calm and try to outsmart him somehow. But if he meant to have sex with her, all sense of reason and rationale would leave her. She simply had to stay in control and divert his attentions elsewhere.

"What are you going to do, Wesley?" she ventured.

"Our daughter would have been eight years old, Jess. Eight years. What a waste...all because of that damned play you insisted on being part of. You wouldn't let up, hours and hours on stage, rehearsing until you dropped. Until you killed our child."

Oh God, this is getting bad, thought Jessica.

"But we can try again, Jess. And keep trying, until we get her back."

Nausea welled at the thought of Wesley touching her like that. It was hard to remember a time when she responded to Wesley's touch. Desperately she sought a line of thinking, something to get him going another direction. But he suddenly turned.

"I'm hungry. There's food in the kitchen. You want a sandwich?"

She shook her head. She knew if she ate, it would come right back up. Maybe that wouldn't be so bad, she thought wryly. *Maybe he won't rape me if I'm vomiting.*

He left the room, and it seemed only seconds before he returned.

"Hated giving up the BMW," he said, while chewing. "But it's really not my style. Now, your *other* boyfriend has a Porsche. *That* would be worth keeping." He leaned toward her as if in confidence. "So, which one's better?"

"What do you mean?" she asked dully.

"Which guy? You're doing them both, right?" He took another bite of sandwich. "I gotta admit, you don't waste time sleeping your way to the top. My money's on the guy who did the pirate flick. The Porsche-dude. Does he bring his saber to bed? Ooh..."

Jessica remained silent.

"Hey, Chrissie's daughter is beautiful, huh?"

Jessica was relieved that he'd changed the subject but did not answer.

"*Isn't* she?" he thundered, his threadlike patience ebbing.

"Yes!" Jessica's mind raced, again wondering how to redirect. Her eyes fell on his silver belt buckle, bearing the insignia of a Vancouver diving association.

"Wesley, tell me about Vancouver," she began.

"Vancouver. Hmmm. Cold, wet. Beautiful trees. You should see my house, Jessie, you'd love it."

"I bet I would," she replied, trying to sound interested. He'd obviously forgotten that he'd told her about the foreclosure. She humored him. "Does it face the Sound?"

"Oh, yeah...and you can fish right off the deck. In the morning, the Sound is like glass."

"Take me there, Wes, I want to see it."

He looked at her for several moments. "Really?"

"Yes, really. It would be great to get out of California, away from the heat, right? The crazies?" She paused only a moment. "Do you have any cash? Can we make it?"

"Well...I was hoping you had some money we could live off of, for a while."

"I do, but not with me. All my credit cards are at M—" she cleared her throat. "My place. I didn't carry them to Utah." He looked discouraged. "But I know where we can get some—plenty, of money." *Here goes*, she thought.

Wesley looked intrigued. "From your pretty boyfriend, of course," he answered. "You think I didn't already think of that? Oh, he'd pay dearly to have his little bed warmer back, wouldn't he? But he won't really get you back, will he?" He laughed excitedly, walking aimlessly around the room. "Yeah, yeah! We'll fool him into thinking I'll exchange you for the dough. But you and I will be on our way to Canada!"

"Brilliant. He..." Jessica swallowed hard, executing her most difficult role yet. "He's not that great, anyway, Wes." She mustered her strength and smiled haughtily, her smile driven by his stupidity and the prospect of outsmarting him, rather than her callous words. "Let's call him."

"No! Not yet." Wesley tangled his fingers into his unkempt hair. "I want him to sweat a little." Jessica nodded in false agreement. "No, let's let him get good and worried first."

·❤·❤·❤·❤·❤·

At Mac's house, his phone was ringing. He leapt from the couch where he'd collapsed and slept sporadically and fitfully in his clothes. His face felt heavy with fatigue and he shook his head to clear it before answering the phone.

"Mr. MacKendall, Sergeant Denehy, LAPD. Your car's been found."

Hope rose into Mac's throat. "Where?" he asked quickly, his voice still gravelly from sleep.

"On a side street in Santa Paula. Just east of Oxnard on Highway 126."

"Anything else?"

"Yes...we're running some tests on something that appears to be dried blood. Just a small bit."

"Don't move the car. I want to see it where it is."

"Fine. You'll have to get it released in Ventura anyway, it's out of our jurisdiction. We already have a make on the prints taken from the steering wheel. They match the ones Kern County took from the cabin last night. We're waiting for information from Seattle police regarding this Elliot fellow. He has no priors in L.A., there's no positive ID yet."

"Okay, thanks Sergeant." Mac hung up, his movements slowed by his thoughts. Picking the phone back up, he pressed "Autodial," then "five" and waited through several rings. A British man answered, and obligingly went for Dane.

Dane sounded groggy. Apparently disoriented, he couldn't understand what Mac was saying.

"Dane, listen. They *found my car*. In Santa Paula. I'm outa here. You want to go?"

After a brief pause, Dane responded. "Yeah. I'm in. Where can I meet you?"

"I'll pick you up in thirty minutes. You're at the top of Benedict Canyon, right?"

"Last time I looked," Dane groaned. "Hang on."

Mac carried the phone to his bedroom in search of his shoes, listening as Dane rattled off directives to someone.

"Could you...please...get me some coffee? Brew it twice and throw in some sugar and a shot of Wild Turkey...thanks, Pete." More shuffling, then, "Sorry, dude. I'm clawing my way back up here. Come on by, I'll be ready."

Thirty minutes later, Mac was outside, honking the horn on the truck. Dane stumbled out, combing his wet hair. He stopped and stared.

"What the hell is *that?*"

"It's a 1953 Ford, and she's cranky, so get in before she quits."

"Let's take my car," Dane suggested.

"No. We can't be conspicuous. Get in."

Dane climbed reluctantly into the cab, closing the creaking passenger door with a rattly slam. "Nice," he said through a grimace, and Mac laughed out loud, putting down the throttle. The truck leapt forward, throwing Dane back into the seat.

"442 engine," Mac told him over the din of the truck's throaty muffler.

"Sounds good to me." Dane leaned back, closing his reddened eyes.

Mac stole a sideways glance at Dane. "Hurts, huh?" Dane only groaned, obviously nursing a hangover.

They didn't talk much on the way to Santa Paula until Mac finally spoke, his voice grave.

"They said there was blood in the car."

Dane's eyes opened. "No shit."

"Just a small amount." Mac paused. "Dane, if we find this guy first, I'm going to kill him."

Dane turned to stare at Mac for a long moment. "I'm with you, man," he murmured.

The BMW was easy to find. A blue and white patrol car with flashers on was parked at the corner, fully visible from the highway, and Mac's car was behind it. The truck backfired as he turned off the ignition.

"Inconspicuous as hell," Dane muttered, jumping from the cab.

The two met with Ventura officers and examined the car. In answer to Mac's inquiry, they showed him two or three drops of dried blood on the edge of the passenger's bucket seat. Mac's eyes smoldered as he signed a release for the car and provided the obligatory identification for the police.

"Can we leave it here for a couple of hours?"

"I'm afraid law enforcement needs to impound this vehicle," the attending officer said. "As it was used in a capital offense. But I can't be bothered with watching it until they get here, and as it's not illegally parked...well. I know *I* wouldn't leave a car like that around here but suit yourself."

Leaving both the BMW and truck, the two men crossed the highway and entered a coffee shop. It was several moments before either spoke, long after their coffee had arrived. Dane reached into his hip pocket and pulled out a small packet.

"I borrowed these last night." He spread several photographs on the table, Solitaire style, before Mac. "I know you're not real fond of these," he said, a smirk on his face. "But there just might be something here."

Mac frowned, examining each in turn. "Most of these seem to be taken at the same time...somewhere at the beach. Look, here's Roxie, too."

Dane nodded. "I spent a good part of the night looking at them myself."

"What's this?" Mac pointed to a long structure in the background of two of the photos.

"You're not from around here, are you?" Dane grinned at him.

"Minneapolis."

"It's Channel Islands Harbor."

"Where is it?"

"About ten minutes from here."

Mac's eyes widened. The two stared at each other momentarily. "Let's call Roxie first. I called her right before I left to pick you up, and she promised to stay by the phone. She may remember some details about this trip," Mac decided. He stood, feeling his pockets for his phone. He went outside the make the call.

Soon, he returned. "No answer. It's a long shot anyway, and I need another cup of coffee."

Roxanne stood in the kitchen making coffee, as Tom sat reading the front-page story of the Times concerning Jessica's disappearance. The phone's ring caused them both to jump, and Roxanne grabbed the instrument with trembling hands.

"Hello?"

"Rox? It's me." Jessica's voice was artificially calm.

"*Jessie?* Are you all right? Where are you?"

Tom was immediately on his feet and reached to press the "record" button on the machine connected to the telephone.

"I—I'm fine, Rox. Is Mac there, by any chance?" Her voice was small and steady, as if she were talking to a child.

"No honey, not right now, but I can reach him...did you try his cell?"

"I need to talk to Mac," she repeated.

"Jessica, listen to me. Are you with Wesley?"

"Yes, it's been raining here. When do you expect him back?"

"Has he hurt you?"

"No, no problems, I just need to talk to him. I need some money for a vacation; like 'last summer—'"

At this comment Wesley grabbed the phone and back-handed Jessica hard across the face, sending her tumbling to the floor.

"Roxanne, this is Wes. How ya doin', sweetheart? Long time, huh? Hey, I got a message for good old Doctor Jim. You tell the pretty boy I want...five-hundred thousand dollars, in unmarked, old bills, if he wants his little tramp back. And tell him she'll know some new tricks when she gets back, so it'll be worth the money. I'm going to teach her a new trick for each moment he delays. And she's going to teach me a few of his." Wesley chuckled. "Hey, and no police. Jessie doesn't like getting smacked around, know what I mean? I'll call again later. Make sure he's there."

Roxanne grasped her stomach. "Wesley, don't do this. Jessica hasn't done anything wrong...let us help you, Wes, oh, please, don't hurt her..." But the line was dead. Roxanne crumbled to the floor in a tearful, anguished ball.

"This is good, Roxie, at least we know she's okay. I don't think he'll really hurt her. Maybe we should call the police." Tom lifted her up to the couch. "Do you have Mac's cell number?"

"He said no police!"

Tom went to the phone, but before he could dial out, it rang again.

"Hi Tom, it's Mac. We're in Santa Paula, and—"

"Thank God, Mac. I was just going to call you. Jessica called here looking for you." Tom carefully detailed the conversation, even playing back the tape so that Mac could hear it over the phone. Mac squeezed his eyes tightly shut and leaned his forehead weakly against the wall outside the diner. Across the restaurant Dane watched Mac's actions with alert eyes.

"Tom," Mac's voice was almost a whisper. "Let me talk to Roxie."

"Putting this on speaker," Tom said.

"I'm here, Mac." Roxanne's voice was choked with pain.

"The photos you brought out last night; several are taken on the beach near Channel Islands Harbor. Do you remember anything about that day?"

"Well, Wesley's uncle had a beach house there, back then. In high school, we used to cut class in our senior year occasionally, and we'd go out there and fool around. You know, we'd get beer and stuff, and just...fool around. Jessie and Wes got a little...too involved there once...In fact, she used to say we were all like that old movie *Last Summer*, with Barbara Hershey and Richard Thomas." Roxanne paused, then exclaimed, "That's where she is! That's what she meant by mentioning 'last summer'!"

"Where is it? Can you remember how to get there?" Mac's voice was tight. He couldn't breathe.

"Gosh, it was right on the beach. It was a blue house, *then*...with a double car garage facing the street. It had a sun deck on the roof, but a lot of them did." She wracked her brain. "Oh! It had this funny little weathervane shaped like a pig. That's all I remember, Mac, sorry."

"That's plenty, Roxie. Stay by the phone, okay? I don't know about calling the police. They probably won't do anything anyway."

Back at the table, Mac threw down eight dollars. "Let's go."

"Where to?"

"The beach."

In the truck, Mac filled Dane in on the phone call from Wesley. Dane flushed with anger. "Does he have a weapon?"

"I don't know. We'd better assume that he does."

"We should call the police, you know."

"He said no police." Mac's jaw worked and he stared straight ahead. "I can't risk making this worse for her."

In minutes they were rolling through the small community of Channel Islands. There were few streets with houses on the beach, and these they drove down slowly and carefully, watching for any sign of something amiss. Roxanne had been right; most of these houses looked just alike, and none had a pig on the roof, although several did have weathervanes.

The gray clouds parted, and sunshine began peeking out. People walked on the sand. Children ran about with their dogs. Mac parked the truck mid-block and struck the steering wheel with the palm of his hand. "Damn!"

"Did you expect to see ol' Wesley sitting on the porch holding an AR-15 or something? Come on, Mac. Drive down the street once more."

Mac sighed and eased out the clutch. The truck balked and shot a loud bang out the back. Dane grimaced and shook his head.

Jessica heard a familiar sound in the street. Her cheek swollen and her lip bleeding, she tried to see out the front window unnoticed. She kept her face expressionless as her eyes lit on the truck driving slowly past the house. Her heart leaped and her pulse quickened, but she kept her eyes dull and uninterested.

Wesley dragged in a knapsack from the garage, which he dumped on the floor before her. Maps, trash, granola bars. And a semi-automatic handgun.

This he picked up, the obvious target of his search.

Jessica's eyes grew round. In college, she and Wesley had protested guns. She felt faint. She had had no doubt that Mac could overcome Wesley if he managed to discover where she was, but a gun? How could she warn him?

"You...never...liked guns, Wes."

"That's another thing I learned on the street. The only thing that has more power than money, is a gun."

Outside, the faded vanilla Ford parked across the street.

"Wait a minute." Mac was thinking again. He looked up and down the street, squinting to focus on each rooftop. "No pigs, but there are two houses without weathervanes at all. The one on the end, and this one. And the one on the end has no sundeck."

Dane looked to verify his finding. "Wow. *That's* telling."

Mac gave Dane a hostile look. "It's possible, isn't it? Let's knock on the door."

"Let's *not* knock on the door...are you nuts? If he *is* in there, and he's probably dangerous, he isn't going to want to see your face *or* my face at his front door. Right?"

Mac looked back toward the house in question.

"Am I right, Mackey, old boy?" Dane turned to face him and leaned back against the door. "So, we wait. And watch. Or we call it in."

"I thought we agreed we couldn't do that."

"We did not. You said we shouldn't. I'm not so sure, now."

"Not me, man. I'm gone." Mac reached behind his seat and pulled out a baseball cap. Dane watched with interest as he first tied his hair into a rubber banded ponytail, removed his outer shirt and pulled on the cap. Putting his sunglasses in place, he opened the door.

"Now how *do* you do that? Mine just won't behave..." Dane tried comically to pull enough of his hair together to make a queue. "So, Mac, where're you going, all dressed up?"

"To the beach, man, gotta work on my tan. Watch the truck for me, *dude*." He tossed the keys to Dane. "And the house. The horn does work, by the way; don't be afraid to use it, if you know what I mean."

Inside the house, Wesley was drinking from the mouth of a cheap, gallon bottle of wine. He took a long gulp and turned on an old radio, his impatient fingers spinning the dial in search of something to suit his mood. Finally opting for a romantic instrumental, a familiar tune once attached to a long-forgotten movie, he began to hum along. He untied the bonds on Jessica's wrists, then pulled her up and forced her to dance with him. He wrapped his arms around her neck, the revolver close to one ear, his lips against the other.

"*Always... always my own...*"

Jessica shuddered as the moist heat of his off-key song engulfed her ear. "Remember how we used to dance, kitten? *Allll...ways...*"

Outside, Mac was cruising the beach.

Mac caught a Frisbee and tossed it back to some children playing on the beach. Sauntering casually down the sand, he slowed his pace as he neared the house he suspected imprisoned Jessica. He picked up a few stones and began skipping them into the surf, glancing over his shoulder periodically. When he was reasonably certain no one was watching, he crept closer to the house and stealthily climbed onto the patio deck facing the sea.

Breathing hard, he kept a watchful eye on the beach for anyone who might find his behavior suspicious. He was in luck. He pressed his back to the house between two windows, then turned slightly to peer inside.

Sheer curtains hung in the window, but there was no mistaking the figures inside; Jessica, dancing with Wesley, looking either drugged or dazed or both. And Wesley, a deranged smile on his lips and a gun to Jessica's head. Mac's heart convulsed painfully at the sight; he quickly turned back around and flattened himself against the house.

"I'll kill him," Mac whispered to himself.

He craftily made his way back to the sand, unseen by anyone and turned to stare at the house again. His eyes were trained on the roof, his mind working fast.

Quickly he jogged back down the beach, cutting across the street farther down and returning to the truck. Panting, he got in and turned to Dane.

"She's in there." His chest was heaving hard, more from emotion than exertion.

Dane's eyebrows lifted. "Son of a bitch; you were right! What do we do next, Doc?"

"We have to move carefully. He has an automatic pistol against her head."

Dane colored noticeably. "We need a SWAT team. Hell, we need a damned militia! Where are the police?"

"We're going to smoke him out." Mac said in a low voice. Cold. Deadly. Dane looked at him in surprise.

"You're serious."

"Damned right. Every moment Jessie is in there, he could be hurting her. Killing her. You want to wait around for Dudley Do-Right?"

"I was thinking maybe the National Guard," Dane murmured, getting out of the cab with Mac, who went to the truck bed and opened a built-in tool chest. He pulled out a pair of wire cutters. Dane watched with curiosity as Mac also drew out a pair of work gloves. "What, pray tell, are you going to do now?"

"He's going to call Roxie back, right? But if the phone's dead, he has to leave the house to make the call."

"What if he has a cell?"

"He's a homeless vagrant. The house has a landline."

Dane considered. "Okay, but he won't leave Jess there."

"We don't know that. In any case, we have to get him to move, or catch him off guard. Dane," he stopped and peered directly into Dane's eyes. "I'm prepared to walk into that house and beat the shit out of him, gun and all, if I have to. I'd just rather not get shot at. So I need you to spot me while I go up on the roof and cut the cables."

"Mac. I get it. You're a hero. But look, man, we're actors. This isn't a movie set, and that piece he's holding isn't a prop gun."

"You wanna leave? Go." Mac started to move on, but Dane grasped his shoulder.

"All I'm saying is, you won't be any good to her if he shoots you. Let me call in local law enforcement to handle this."

"Do what you want." Mac again pushed past Dane and retraced his path to the water side of the house.

With a huff, Dane followed. "Maybe Jarrick called them," he muttered.

The patio Mac had watched from was a deck, raised off the sand, and they temporarily hid beneath it. Once assured that no one was watching, they slipped around to the side of the house, stopping before the electrical breaker box. The tiny padlock on the box door was thick with rusty corrosion from the salt air. Quickly Mac cut through the worn lock and opened the door, deftly finding and switching the main breaker to "off." The faint sound of the music inside died away.

Back on the deck, they made themselves hidden from the occupants of the house. Mac pushed the clippers into his hip pocket and on signal from Dane, began pulling himself up a steel pipe bolted to the corner of the house. Dane scowled up at him in the bright sunlight, peeking in the window periodically and nodding at Mac.

Wesley had stopped dancing and was picking up the radio, shaking it before thrusting it against the wall in anger. On the roof, Mac systematically cut the wires to the phone, then edged his way back down the pipe. "What are they doing now?" he whispered.

"He's making her sit on the couch." Dane frowned. Mac joined him to watch as Wesley seemed to be making overtures to Jessica on the couch. The couch faced perpendicular to the back windows, and Wesley's back was to them.

Jessica was weak from fear, lack of food and sleep. She felt she would drift away at any time. The sleepless night spent in Wesley's car and the sheer terror of the ordeal had taken its toll. She decided she had hallucinated the sight of Mac's truck passing by. Her mind spun dizzily. "I'm hungry."

"You should've said that when I was making sandwiches," Wesley responded, his fingers gliding delicately down her arm. He leaned closer and licked her ear, the gun still held close to the other side of her head.

"I need to eat," Jessica repeated, stiffly trying to remain coherent. The smell of his alcohol laden breath only served to make her more ill.

With a sigh of disgust, Wesley went to the kitchen.

"I'm going in," Mac started, and Dane moved to block him.

"Not yet, man. Stay cool. You know he's coming right back...If we can wait this out, he'll either go for a phone, or he'll pass out. He's guzzling wine. He'll get sloppy."

"Okay. But if he touches her, I'm going in."

Dane nodded. "Everybody loves dead heroes."

They sat down on the deck and leaned against the house, just under the curtained window. They waited several minutes.

"How long do you want to sit here? This is making me nuts." Dane adjusted his position. "Not exactly comfortable."

Mac stared out at the sea, frowning behind the dark glasses. "It's possible Tom called the sheriff, but I'm afraid if Elliot sees a patrol car, he'll go berserk. I wish we could get this over with before that happens. Let's just wait awhile longer."

"Here." Wesley handed Jessica a sandwich. She took it, moving in slow motion. She took a bite but could taste nothing. Slowly she chewed, and swallowed, and took another bite as Wesley paced nervously about the room. "It's time to call again," he decided. He picked up the phone next to the couch, listened, then impatiently pounded buttons trying to get a dial tone. Finally, he slammed the receiver down, in fury.

"What is happening to me?" he screamed, his anguished fingers again clawing through his tangled hair. The gun had been tucked into the waist of his pants and was partially hidden by the rumpled Hawaiian shirt he wore loosely buttoned. "I need to get to a phone."

Jessica rose weakly to her feet and hesitantly moved slowly across the room.

"Where are you going?" he shouted at her.

"I'm sick," she murmured, making her way toward the bathroom.

Wesley's face showed confusion and he began pacing again.

"We've got to get out of here. I can't...I can't think here. But...we need the money, the money, that's right. We gotta get the money from the punk with the car. Yeah..."

Jessica reached the bathroom just in time to empty the contents of her stomach into the bowl. She stared blankly into the mirror. She didn't see the purple bruises on her face or the dried blood on her cheek. Her mind took her back to the Caribbean, the day she'd left the small clinic after her collapse. *Your blood sugar is unstable, Miss Taylor. I'd have your regular physician do a thorough test when you get back to the States,*" the doctor had warned her. She had neglected to see her own doctor, of course. *Well, I guess I've been a bit busy. A bit busy...*she laughed, a shrill, hollow laugh borne of her disengagement with real life.

She emerged from the bathroom to find Wesley hurriedly re-packing the bag he'd dumped out. "C'mon—we're leaving."

"No," she moaned softly. "I need to lie down."

"Gimme a break. You can lay down in the car."

While he fussed with the bag, she walked to the back windows and stared out at the ocean. Still nauseous, she held her arms across her stomach and leaned tiredly into the window frame. Suddenly, movement outside caught her eye. Someone was on the deck. Her eyes widened and she peered down, leaning close to the sheer curtain. She saw nothing. Just her imagination again.

"Come on!" Wesley called to her, and they left by the kitchen door to the Cougar in the garage.

"She was right here." Mac groaned. "I could have touched her."

"They're leaving. We have to hurry."

The two raced to the truck, unseen by Wesley who was already steering the Cougar down the block. They followed a short distance behind, and in a few blocks, parked behind the small corner convenience store where Wesley had stopped.

Jessica stayed in the car while Wesley made the call from an old pay phone on the front of the market. She could feel her stomach churning again, and she struggled to get out of the car and enter the market.

Wesley slammed the phone down. "It wouldn't connect, damn it," he said, too loudly, following her into the store. "And where the hell do you think you're going, kitten?" He grabbed her roughly by the forearm.

The shop owner said nothing, watching them through his lowered eyelashes, noting the marks on Jessica's face and wrists.

"Do you have...a restroom?" she asked softly.

The proprietor shook his head indifferently.

"I'm sick, and I would rather use your toilet than your candy rack," she continued, holding her stomach, still speaking in a low and soft tone.

At this, he motioned silently toward the back.

"Thank you." She started for the door marked "Employees Only" and Wesley let go of her arm.

"Don't screw around, understand?"

Jessica ignored him and kept walking. Wesley toured the small store, the shopkeeper's eyes riveted to him the entire time.

"Gimme one of those frozen slushy things," Wesley demanded, approaching the cash register.

The proprietor pointed to the "self-serve" sign over the machine. As Wesley turned, he spied the gun in Wesley's belt. Silently he pressed a button under the counter.

Mac opened the rear door to the store slowly and carefully, quietly stealing inside with Dane close behind. They hid in the shadows as someone emerged from the tiny lavatory near the back door. At the sight of Jessica's pale, bruised face, Mac reached from the storage room and grabbed her, quickly covering her mouth with his hand and turning her face towards his for her quick recognition. Tears of relief flooded her eyes; tears of outrage came to his as he wordlessly examined her.

"He's going to pay for this," Mac whispered icily.

"What next, Doc?" Dane licked his lips nervously, eyeing Jessica himself, a touch of melancholy in his gaze.

Before Mac could answer, Wesley's voice boomed toward them from the store. "JESSICA! Shake a leg, baby. We gotta go!"

"We can take him, Dane. Put Jessie in the truck. I'll stall him, I'll put him in position. You come around in the front and back me up." He passed Jessica from his arms to Dane, who looked uncertain.

Jessica grabbed Mac's arm. "No—Mac, he has a gun. He'll kill you both. Let's just get out of here," she begged.

"And live in fear that this will happen again? No way. *Go.*" Dane walked Jessica quietly out the back door.

Mac crept toward the door into the market. It was a hinged, cafe style door, and he peeked over the top looking for Wesley, who was thumbing through a magazine at the newsstand. Mac took a deep breath and pushed open the doors.

The shopkeeper looked up. He started to protest about Mac's use of the back door but closed his mouth after interpreting the look on Mac's face.

Mac strode to the newsstand and stood next to Wesley, who turned to glance at him before looking back at his magazine. There was no recognition.

"I'm going to give you a choice." Mac's voice was as cold as steel and just as hard. "You can hand me your gun and sit down on the floor, or you can try to kill me before I kill you."

Wesley dropped the magazine and looked again at Mac, who was removing his sunglasses. The surprise in Wesley's eyes turned to a wild, excited smile. "Well, Mr. B—M—W! How nice of you to show up! You got some cash for me?"

"The only thing I have for you is this." Mac's right fist slammed into Wesley's gut and Mac felt ribs crack under his knuckles. The punch landed Wesley against the closed side of the front door, and as Mac shook out his stinging hand, Wesley reached for the gun in his belt.

The shopkeeper went down behind the counter. Wesley extended both arms, leveling the pistol directly at Mac, standing not ten feet in front of him. The wine and Mac's assault had left him unsteady, but he fired off two rounds in Mac's direction just as Dane leapt onto his back from behind, wrestling him to the floor. Mac rushed him from the front. His eyes wide and his hands shaking, Dane grasped the gun and tossed it across the room, then deftly pinned Wesley's arms behind his back as he struggled.

Mac was blind to everything except Wesley's hateful figure, his fury driven by the memory of the marks on Jessica's arms and face. He struck Wesley repeatedly until his fists were bloodied and his target began vomiting up the cheap wine. Dane loosened his grip and Wesley fell into the mess. Panting, Mac was remotely aware of police officers filling the small store, and of being helped to his feet by Dane. Dazed and momentarily disoriented, he looked around at the shattered frozen food doors and exploded potato chip bags. And then he noticed the officers' drawn revolvers aimed at his chest.

In disbelief Mac watched as Dane Pierce slowly raised his hands and placed them behind the back of his head. He suddenly realized that the cops were demanding the same of him. The shopkeeper was, of course, telling his version of the shooting, and still another uniformed officer appeared, leading Jessica into the front parking lot.

Outside, they were searched and questioned. Another police vehicle arrived, this one unmarked. The man behind the wheel flashed his badge to the Ventura County deputies, then walked to where Wesley Elliot was just coming around.

"Denehy. LAPD. This man is wanted for kidnapping, assault, and, it would appear, attempted murder." He turned to Mac and Dane, now handcuffed and leaning against the patrol car. "These gentlemen are not a threat. Please release them."

"Thank you," Mac murmured, rubbing his wrists. He looked around for Jessica and found her, still being interrogated. An ambulance was speeding through the intersection and into the small parking lot.

"Hey, we did it, man." Dane extended his hand in an offer of brotherhood. Swallowing hard, Mac nodded and clapped his hand onto Dane's.

"Is she okay?"

"She's okay. The ambulance is just routine. Looks like you need a Band-Aid or two, though." Dane pointed to a three-inch gaping wound on Mac's bare shoulder, where a bullet had burned past him. :

"Whoa..." Mac grimaced. "I didn't even know."

"What a hero! Too bad the cameras weren't rolling!" Dane joked.

"No, you were the hero, man."

They watched together as Wesley was handcuffed and read his rights.

Unable to wait another moment, Mac rushed to Jessica. They embraced for an eternity, not speaking, until Dane finally tapped on Mac's good shoulder. "The medics are here. You have to give her up for a few minutes."

While Mac and Jessica were being tended by the paramedics, Dane called Roxanne and relayed the news.

Jessica watched sadly as they ushered Wesley into a patrol car. He gave her a level stare before ducking into the backseat, and for just a millisecond in time, Jessica thought she saw a glimmer of sanity and remorse. She leaned tiredly against Mac and waited until the police had enough information to release them.

The three pressed into the cab of the truck and Mac drove back to Santa Paula. Jessica was asleep almost immediately, leaving both men to their own thoughts. A fog was just settling on the sleepy little town as Mac eased the truck against the curb behind the BMW. Mac handed Dane a set of keys.

"Ah, gee, I was hoping to get the truck," Dane lamented comically.

"Just take it home. I'll get it later."

Dane pulled gently away from Jessica, who slept limply against Mac's bandaged shoulder.

"Hurt much?"

"Naw. They shot some 'controlled substances' into me, I think."

"Wish I had some." Dane looked down where Jessica's hand was folded into his. He lifted it to his lips, his eyes locked onto Mac's. "Take care of her, all right?"

Mac nodded silently and Dane got out, walking around to the street. Mac held out his fist through the truck's window, and Dane bumped it. "You saved my life today," Mac said simply. "I'm in your debt."

"No sweat, man," Dane answered. "Anyway, I did it for Jessie, not you, *asshole*." Green eyes smiled at brown.

Mac returned the smile. He would not soon forget Dane Pierce's actions of this day.

As the tired rumble of the Ford's engine died away in the MacKendall driveway, Jessica opened her eyes. Unseeing at first, she sat bolt upright until she felt the comforting reassurance of Mac's arm around her.

"We're home, babe."

Inside, Jessica peered around the house with sullen eyes as Mac stood by.

"Don't suppose you're hungry," he murmured, watching her eyes for some light to return.

"No. I just need a shower."

"Sure. You need any help?" Mac touched her lightly on the shoulder and she jerked, then turned a weak smile his way.

"Sorry. No. I'll be fine. I just need...a few minutes."

He watched her walk into the hall leading to the bedrooms. The sight of her cotton dress, so sassy and attractive yesterday—indeed, he had helped her put it back on in his dressing room! —now stained with blood and wine, made him newly incensed. He leaned against the kitchen counter and pressed his hands over his eyes as the vision of Wesley Elliot returned. The anger threatened to boil up again, the same consuming rage that had driven his fists into Wesley's body, alarming even Mac himself by its intensity. Quickly he opened his eyes and stared at the backs of his hands. His fingers still bore traces of Wesley's blood.

Jessica scrunched the dress into a ball that fit perfectly into the bathroom wastebasket. She made the water hot, almost scalding, to purge away the nastiness, the poison that covered her body.

When at last she felt clean, she went back into the bedroom that had been hers for two weeks, before her trip to the Caribbean. She stood beside the great mahogany dresser that graced the wall opposite the four-poster bed and pulled open the heavy middle drawer. Of course, her clothes were still here, undisturbed, absorbing the fresh scent of the elegant camphor drawer lining. She pulled out a long, soft, white T-shirt and slipped it over her head.

She didn't bother to dry her hair. Approaching the bed, she reached for the corner of the plush patchwork comforter but hesitated. She heard the shower running in the master bathroom. Instead of pulling the covers down, she let her hand drag along the comforter, pretending to straighten its already smooth appearance. Then quietly she crept through the adjoining doorway.

His bed was already turned down. Suddenly, it made no sense to her at all to sleep anywhere else. There was a tiny lamp on the nightstand that resembled a candle, and this she left burning. Curling her knees to her chest, she closed her eyes.

It was not long before he was beside her, taking obvious care not to disturb her sleep. But Jessica reached for him in the darkness.

"I wish there was something I could say," he began, tenderly pushing her damp locks away from her forehead.

"I can say something. Something like—thank you for saving me."

"You must have been so scared." Mac made no attempt to disguise the anguish in his voice.

"All I kept thinking about was us, about how wonderful everything has been, how we're finally together, and he, he, was going to destroy it all." A sob broke into her words. "And then, when you came, I was so afraid he would hurt you."

"Shhh. It's over now. He'll never hurt us again."

"But he tried to kill you! How could I have lived with that?"

"He didn't." Mac stopped stroking her face and took a deep breath, which he let out slowly, laboriously. "Do you understand that there were no choices for me?" His voice was soft but strong with conviction.

Jessica frowned at him in the darkness, trying to read his eyes and make sense of his words.

"Do you understand that my love for you is far greater than any fear, any risk I might have to face?"

Jessica was again rendered speechless by the tightness in her throat. She tried to whisper his name, and he pulled her slowly and gently against his chest where she sobbed.

He made no attempt to quiet her grief, running his hands up and down her back with long, loving caresses. And when the sounds of her suffering finally faded away, when her veins again began to pump warmth and balance back into her body and mind, she allowed herself to bask in the security of his arms.

"You must be exhausted," she whispered at last.

"I am close to comatose."

"Before you go to sleep, may I ask you one thing?"

"Anything, my darling. Anything at all."

"Did you, a few minutes ago," she paused, her voice small and childlike. "Did you really say you loved me?"

She felt rather than heard him catch his breath ever so slightly, and she held her own in anticipation of his response.

"Was that me?" He kissed the top of her head. Then he lifted her chin to peer into her eyes and his tone became serious. "I love you more than anyone ever has, or anyone ever will. And I should have told you that a long, long time ago." A bemused smile graced his lips and he kissed her on the nose. "But you want to talk about scared?"

Jessica heard the phone ringing but refused to open her eyes. Still captive by some rapturous dream, she slipped back into the arms of sleep, comfortable, protected. And after an unknown time had passed, minutes, possibly hours, she reluctantly stirred.

He was still beside her. Without opening her eyes to the sunlight that peeked through the slender gap in the draperies, Jessica reached out with her fingertips, touching his bare chest with delight. Slowly she traced a path up to his throat, his jaw, and his cheeks. She felt him smile. She smiled back.

"This is nice, huh?" he whispered.

"Mmm."

"I like going to sleep knowing where you are, safe and warm," he continued. Jessica nodded. "I like waking up beside you." Mac leaned close to nuzzle her ear. "And I like the feel of those sexy legs wrapped around mine."

"I thought those sexy legs were yours," she whispered back, starting to giggle.

"Could be," he responded, sliding his leg along hers. "So, what do you think?"

She opened her eyes now, craving a view of his face.

"About what?"

"About waking up with me every day?"

Jessica gazed at her roommate-turned-lover with new affection. Suddenly consumed with emotion, she recalled his loving admission of the night before. The worst day of her life had given way to one of the best. He really wanted her to move in with him.

"You're sure?" she asked, selfishly wanting him to repeat his request. She was already certain of his sincerity.

"I never wanted it any other way."

Carefully she threaded her arms around his neck, mindful of the bandages covering his shoulder. She kissed his cheek warmly, then whispered into his ear.

"I thought you'd never ask."

Thirteen

Misconceptions

I t had been four weeks since the brutal interruption to Jessica's life and things were finally beginning to settle into place for her. Mac had her car and her few belongings picked up from the cabin; neither of them wanted to set foot there again.

Although Jessica intended to rush into another project, to get "back to normal" after her ordeal, Mac warned against it and tried to keep her from accepting too much responsibility, too soon. So, she sat and read scripts, spent hours completing Megan's room, and occasionally sat with Roxanne while she sewed.

Ultimately, Jessica took over as mistress of Mac's home, organizing and directing the completion of the renovation and decorating. She kept meticulous records of the progress and detailed activities on the kitchen calendar.

The calendar fascinated Mac. He had always considered himself organized, but only to the degree of a wallet bulging with small slips of paper bearing important notes that were virtually impossible to read. Here, on the thirty-one days that comprised May, Jessica had mapped out their every move. And one such entry gave him pause. On May 27th, Jessica had written "Chrissie."

Thoughtful, he picked up the phone, glancing out the kitchen window for Jessica's car. She was off on a shopping run, and due home any moment.

"Roxie? Mac. Fine, babe, listen. Got a question for you. Isn't Jessie's birthday this month?"

"Uh...so it is, I'd forgotten. In about two weeks; May 27th. Why?"

"Because you and I are going to throw her a party."

"Wow, Mac, that's a great idea!"

"Can I count on you to help?"

"You name it." They chatted for a half hour, planning a big event to celebrate Jessica's 29th birthday, complete with live entertainment and dancing. "She will be knocked out, Mac. She'll love it."

"I gotta go. She just drove up. We'll talk later."

Jessica stumbled in the front door, unable to see over the heavy, over-full bag in her arms.

"Here, let me get that," Mac offered, taking the bag to the table. "Wow, what's in here?"

"Window hardware, for Meggie's room, and bookends, and a picture frame, and a mirror." She dropped into a chair. "I'm wiped. Would you mind if we didn't go out?"

He smiled and massaged her shoulders. "Mind? No, that's okay. I'll just open a can of Spam." Jessica made a face and he chuckled. "I'll make something. You...go do girl things."

At dinner, she didn't eat much.

"Guess I should have made the Spam," he ventured.

"I'm just not feeling too well. I think I'm getting a cold or something."

A week later Roxanne called and declared they needed a "beach day."

"Can't do it. I'm sick," Jessica complained.

"Too sick for the beach? What's wrong?"

"Flu. I've had it a week, can't shake it."

"What kind of flu?"

"Nothing will stay in my stomach, Doctor Boudreau."

"Jess, a week's a long time. Go to the doctor. Maybe they can give you something." Roxanne's voice held concern, but Jessica dismissed it.

"I'll be okay in a day or so, I'm sure."

"How's Mac?"

"He's fine. He's...wonderful. I keep hoping he won't get this, but the way he hovers over me, it will be a miracle if he doesn't."

"Could it be something you picked up on the island?"

"Gosh, I hope not." Jessica considered this possibility.

"Make an appointment. Now," Roxanne ordered. "I'll drive you, let me know when you go."

Roxanne excitedly completed arrangements for Jessica's party later that week. "The Elysian Country Club and Resort has a room, it's modest in size but perfect in atmosphere," she told Mac over the phone. "Glad you got in touch with Chris and Nick."

"They were happy to come down. It's Christine's birthday, too, of course." Mac said. "So, I'll just bring her to the party room after dinner. Will that work? And no shouting 'surprise,' okay? She'd hate that."

"Fine. Oh, sorry, I have another call. It's probably your girlfriend calling, so I'd better go."

Jessica was relieved when Roxanne made good on her promise to accompany her to the doctor. The waiting room was nearly empty.

"I hope he can straighten me out. Mac's taking me out tomorrow night, and I must be well. It's supposed to be special," she confided.

Roxanne gave her a broad smile. "He's one in a million."

"Miss Taylor?" The nurse directed Jessica into an exam room.

Dr. Anderson was a kindly, old-fashioned doctor, and Jessica had been seeing him for several years. He asked her many questions, peering into her various orifices and feeling her glands. He pressed here and there on her stomach and abdomen and sat back.

"When was your last monthly?"

Jessica colored. She hated the unavoidable question, even more so now because she couldn't really remember.

"I was in Amande, I think. Gosh, it's been...it was around March 5th...I think."

"Hmmm. No spotting, nothing?" He looked at a chart. "That's over ten weeks, Jessica."

"You know me, Doctor Anderson. I've never been what you'd call *regular*. And I've been through a lot of...stress lately."

"I heard. I'm truly sorry about that. Well, your blood sugar's been stable, at least." He sighed, then turned to his nurse. "Get me a pap kit. I'm going to do a pelvic. And get a specimen from her when I'm done."

Jessica grimaced. This was not going well. The doctor examined her internally, then again pressed around on her abdomen. "Hmmm," he murmured again. He stood up abruptly. "Get dressed, then I'll see you in a few minutes."

Jessica turned ashen as the nurse directed her to the doctor's office. "What is it, Doctor? Just tell me. I can take whatever it is. My grandmother had—"

"Hey! Sit down, Jessie."

"It's bad news, right?" Her hands trembled.

"Most people don't think babies are bad news, but these days I never know. Especially among young, *unmarried* actresses."

"Babies...what do you mean?"

"How can I be clearer? Let's see. How about, You-Are-Pregnant?"

Jessica froze in her seat, her mouth partially open, her face a perfect picture of shock.

"No," she said simply. "No, Doctor, that's not possible." Her voice didn't sound like her own.

"Do you know how many women have said that to me? They haven't proven immaculate conception yet, at least not in this century." The doctor chuckled, then squinted at her. "Not planned, I take it? Are you okay, do you want some water?"

"I have to throw up," she whispered.

"Jessica, I'm having Tami make up a prescription for pre-natal vitamins. And I'd like to meet your...young man, at some time during your term. Do you have any questions?"

Yeah. What young man? Or better, which?

In the waiting room, Roxanne leaped up at the sight of Jessica's white face. She said nothing at first but drove her to a nearby Starbuck's. They sat in silence until Roxanne grasped her hand across the table.

"Okay, kiddo, spill it. What gives?"

Jessica stared at Roxanne, knowing her face reflected her internal turmoil. Her search for the right way to break the news proved futile.

"I'm pregnant," she murmured.

Roxanne's mouth fell open. "What? How?"

"I...don't...know." Jessica pressed her fingertips to her temples. "Oh Roxie, why is God doing this? Hasn't enough bad stuff happened to me to warrant my having Mac's love? Can He really take that away from me now?" She sniffed and dabbed her eyes with a paper napkin.

"What do you mean? I thought you said you were...safe." Roxanne began awkwardly.

"Dane and Mac both told me they couldn't have children. Either one of them lied, or one's mistaken, and I've no way of knowing which one...oh God, I'm going to die...I can't lose Mac, Rox. I'll kill myself; I swear it."

"Calm down. Think this out."

"There's nothing to think out. Something has gone terribly wrong. Mac will never forgive me."

"Mac loves you more than life itself. He proved that to you last month. I can't believe he wouldn't understand, or at least try to."

"How could I possibly ask him to accept the fact that I might be carrying Dane's child? It would ruin him."

"You'll just have to tell him. You know you must. You're *not* considering an abortion?"

"No! I could never do that. I'll raise this baby alone if I have to." She dried her eyes again. "But I can't tell him tonight. I just can't. I have to get used to the idea, to formulate what to say."

Roxanne bit her lip.

"Rox, please don't say a word to anyone, not even Tom, okay?"

"Of course not. Everything will work out, hon, you'll see." Roxanne embraced her warmly.

At home that evening, Jessica stood in the bathroom, staring at her nude body in the mirror. She turned from side to side. The doctor had estimated her to be seven or eight weeks along. She decided she looked okay, just a little softer. She sighed and stuck a saltine in her mouth. Mac worked late, and she purposely feigned sleep when he joined her later in bed.

Saturday afternoon Jessica felt better physically but worse emotionally. After feigning joy over mutual birthday wishes with Christine on the phone, she somberly dressed for their night out. Mac had asked her to wear the simple white and silver dress she had worn on their wild flight to Utah, and she agreed easily. Normally she would have balked at wearing the same dress again, but this was just one less decision for her to make tonight.

Roxanne had come by to fix her hair earlier and was off in a rush for a date with Tom.

"Are you ready, gorgeous?"

"I don't feel gorgeous."

"You feel well enough to go?" Mac approached her, lifting her chin to peer into her eyes.

"Yeah, I'm much better. Thanks."

"What did the doctor say?"

"You're wearing a tux!" she exclaimed, evading his question. "I love it."

"Dashing, right?" Mac grinned at her and pulled her close for a hug.

"You are dashing in a ragged T-shirt, my darling." Her eyes misted over looking at him. After tonight, she might not have the luxury of flirting with him again.

"You sure you're okay?" His eyes were soft with concern.

"I'm...*perfect*. And..." she reached up to straighten his bow tie. "...I love you. Did you know that, Mr. MacKendall?"

His cheeks colored in response to her simple declaration. Jessica swallowed and looked away for a moment, then continued with a forced, bright smile. "And I will love you, always." She again fussed with his tie and he leaned forward and kissed her gently.

In the driveway he helped her into a new, white Lotus Elan. The BMW had been sold, now just a bad memory of their night of terror. Their reservations were for 7:30 p.m., and they were promptly seated near a picture window exposing a view of the entire, twinkling city below. A single candle cast its warm light on their faces. Mac was unusually ardent, alternately complimenting and teasing her and repeatedly taking her hand. He seemed anticipatory, Jessica thought glumly. She had vowed she'd tell him tonight but would wait until after the evening ended. Why spoil a wonderful time?

"So, what are your plans?" he asked her.

"What do you mean? For next week or next year?" *Well, I thought I'd have a baby first, then...*She smiled with difficulty, the irony of his question overwhelming.

He smiled back, but his eyes were more serious than hers. "Let's start with the rest of your life," he suggested.

Jessica stared at him, her smile static on her lips. She cleared her throat. "Well..." Her mind raced. "You know I want to keep making movies." She felt him take her hand, again.

"Okay, that's a start," he said softly. "What about *us*?"

"Well, what *about* us?" Her stomach was becoming increasingly nervous.

He pulled her hand to his lips. "Are you happy with the way things are?"

She looked into his eyes. "Happy...is a pretty weak word for the way I feel, Mac. Ecstatic, euphoric, maybe..."

"Secure? Content?"

"I suppose." Now off guard, Jessica wondered where he was leading.

"How would you feel," he said, pausing to fish a small velvet bag from inside his breast pocket, "...about spending the next fifty or sixty years...with me?" He produced a tiny gold ring, set with diamonds around the entire circumference, and slipped it easily onto her finger.

Jessica's lips parted slightly in awe. Literally stunned by his question, she lost her voice. She gently pulled her hand away from his, slowly turning it to examine the ring on her finger, touching it with her other hand reverently.

Her face colored. "Oh, Mac," she finally whispered.

"Help me out, here, Jess, I need a little more than, 'Oh Mac.' Those don't look like tears of joy."

He leaned down, trying to interrupt her gaze at the ring.

She turned her sorrowful eyes to his questioning ones. Her stomach lurched. "I...I don't...I don't know what to say," she said, sobs beginning to erupt in her chest.

"You don't? Well, of course if you need to *think* about it..." His voice trailed away as he studied her stricken face. Puzzled, he touched her cheek. "Jess, what's wrong?"

"I...need to go...to the ladies' room..." She stood up and hurried away. After a moment's reflection, Mac got to his feet and pursued her through the restaurant.

Jessica flew through the restroom door and turned quickly to lock it behind her. She fell against it, her body wracked with sobs. From the other side, Mac could hear her crying and he turned the knob.

"Jessie, let me in."

She held her breath, trying to hold back the sound of her grief, and he pounded on the door.

"Jessica, damn it, open this door!" She could not believe Mac would cause a scene in a place like this, but there he was, hollering at her through the door.

With shaking hands she hastily unlocked the door and Mac exploded into the room. His face was hot with concern and irritation; he grasped her by the shoulders as she leaned against the wall. Her eyes wide and still producing tears, she regarded him painfully.

His voice was low and tight with restrained concern. "It's okay to say 'no,' Jess, but God damn it, *don't run away from me*. It *destroys* me." He loosened his grip, his rage diminishing with the realization of her fear. "Jessie, baby, I *love* you! Jesus, if something is wrong you need to tell me. Nothing could be *that* bad..." He searched her eyes in desperation, finding only grief laced with tears. She didn't answer him, only sobbed in uncontrolled misery. She turned her head away and down toward her shoulder.

In frustration, Mac gently grasped her jaw and turned her face toward his. "*Talk to me*, Jessie, this isn't fair."

"All right! All right! I'm pregnant, okay?" She shouted the words into his face, as if shouting would banish the awful feeling from her body.

Mac reacted as if the world had stopped turning. His eyebrows lifted, and he stared at her in unabashed astonishment. Jessica again turned away.

"So it's okay if you don't want to marry me." She wept quietly.

Mac released her and turned to fall weakly back against the wall next to her.

"So. This is apparently distressing news."

She tried to speak calmly, but her heaving chest wouldn't cooperate and her words were lamely broken. "Oh Mac, I'm...so...sorry...I don't know how...or when..."

Silent, Mac stared at nothing before him for several moments. The only sound was of Jessica's traumatic sobbing.

"What I am hearing here, is that this child must belong to Pierce."

"No...it...it can't...be..."

"What makes you say that?" Mac rubbed his eyes wearily. "We both know what went on in Amande."

Jessica flushed a deep rose. "Amande." *God, please stop this nightmare,* Jessica prayed. "Mac, what happened in Amande...could not produce a child. Dane had the same surgery you had." Her voice was barely an embarrassed whisper.

Mac raised his head and regarded her suspiciously. "The *same surgery?*"

"Dane had a vasectomy after Zoe was born. He told me."

Jessica dared a look at him. He again stared at the floor, frowning eyes shifting in confusion; he absently wetted his lips. He took a deep breath and raised his eyes to face her. His look was nonjudgmental, and a certain softness had returned.

"I assumed you were taking the pill." He spoke quietly now.

"No, I...I can't take the pill. And I, I...never thought twice about it, Mac. Why should I, since you can't have children? I didn't think...it was a concern," she said, sniffing. "But I don't know how this happened." She couldn't look at him.

"Jessie," he said with a sigh, "I've had no surgery. Linda's the one who opted for sterilization, not me." He moved back before her and again held her shoulders in a gentle grip. "I thought you knew that, baby." His voice was just above a whisper and fell caressingly on her ears.

The realization of what he'd said took time to spread across her anguished mind. She lifted her face and looked tentatively into his eyes, seeking truth behind his words. He was shaking his head slowly, tenderness turning the smallest smile to his lips.

"Oh, God," she whispered, the sorrow in her eyes turning to joy as it finally struck her that the new life within her really belonged to Mac. She rushed her arms around his neck, crying openly with relief and happiness. He held her tightly, slowly rocking her as she wept, and finally she pulled away from him, self-consciously wiping her eyes.

"Well, I guess things have changed," she sniffed, "again."

"Not everything," he said solemnly. He took both of her hands in his and knelt on the restroom floor in his tuxedo. "I still want you to marry me, Jessica, and despite my deplorable temper, please know that I would have loved and married you regardless of whether the baby was mine or not."

Jessica smiled through her tears and pressed the fingers of the hand bearing his ring to her lips.

"Tell me?" His eyes were feverish with love for her.

"Oh Mac, *of course* I'll marry you."

He wrapped his arms around her legs and embraced her, then, still kneeling, he slipped his hands up under her dress until they rested on her abdomen; he first felt the softness of her tummy, then pressed his ear against her.

"Mac, what *are* you doing?" She attempted to push the dress back down, looking at him in awe, then giggled and cradled his head with her hands.

Two matronly women entered the restroom, one of them expelling a brief, sharp cry at the sight of them. Jessica blushed, but Mac turned on a beguiling smile. "We've just found out we're expecting. I was, uh, listening." He stood up then and discreetly adjusted Jessica's dress. The first woman nodded agreeably, moving aside so that the couple could exit. She stared after them, immediately turning to her companion.

"Irene! Wasn't that *Doctor Jim*?"

"Don't be silly, Francis. Did you ever see Doctor Jim wear a tuxedo?"

Grasping Mac's arm, Jessica stifled a giggle.

Back at the table, he held a compact mirror so she could repair her make-up. He shook his head again. "I can't believe this. It's incredible."

"Is it really okay?" she asked timidly.

"Okay? Jessica, I can think of nothing more wonderful. I've always wanted more children. And with you...my love, it's...it's perfect. Megan will be thrilled...Wow." He casually glanced around in excited animation. His eyes fell on his watch. "Oh, Jesus," he muttered. "We have to go."

"Go? We haven't eaten dinner yet!"

"You're not hungry anyway."

"How do you know?"

"Come on. We're late."

"Late for what?"

He took her hand and pulled her through the dining room.

"Mac, tell me where we're going."

"To a party," he told her, as they hurried down a hall and into a room filled with laughing, dancing people. People she knew and loved.

"I'm dreaming," she whispered as Mac slowed his pace and slipped an arm around her waist. Faces surrounded her, smiling, sipping drinks and...wishing her a happy birthday. In the sickness and terror of the past week, she'd dismissed all thoughts of her birthday. Roxie, Tom, Jackie, Bill...was that Peter Welles? Christine and Nick! She looked at Mac, who stood smiling smugly at her.

"Happy birthday, dear," he chided playfully.

Jessica made her way around the room greeting her friends and feeling on top of the world. "You were part of this scam," she scolded her sister and her brother-in-law. "There you were on the phone, talking like you were celebrating at the lodge!"

Christine hugged Jessica warmly. "Sharing this day is one of the best parts of being a twin. I wouldn't have missed it."

Jessica pressed her cheek to Christine's and whispered, "I have some exciting news. Talk later!" She pulled away and then spied a pair of familiar green eyes peering at her from a small table in the corner, a whimsical, appreciative smile on the lips beneath them. She carefully threaded her way through the room and sat down across from Dane.

He'd propped his foot on a chair and was casually slouched back, a drink in his hand. His hair was trimmed short and carefully groomed. He smiled lazily at her. "Didn't think I'd miss your party, did you, sweetie?"

"I'm touched. It's good to see you."

"Same." He reached for her left hand, turning the ring on her finger. "I see you accepted."

She looked at him, puzzled.

"Yeah, the bum told me. I advised him against it. Purely selfish reasons, mind you, but he wouldn't buy it. You must be stoked, huh?"

Jessica nodded slightly.

"You oughta make him buy you a bigger rock, though." He advised. "So when's the big day?"

She cleared her throat. "We haven't really talked about it yet."

"Don't ask me to give you away. I've done that already."

Jessica felt her face warm. His eyes then fixed on someone across the room, and Jessica followed his gaze to where Mac stood talking to Jackie. As if he felt their eyes, Mac put Jackie on hold and strode across to them.

"Glad you could make it, Pierce. It wouldn't have been the same without you."

"I understand congratulations are in order?"

At Mac's stunned expression, Dane pointed to Jessica's ring.

"Oh! That...Yeah, well, you didn't really think she'd turn me down, did you?"

"You can't deny me my foolish hopes, MacKendall."

"Dane, there's someone I'd like you to meet," Mac told him, motioning for Jackie to join them. As she approached, Mac grinned at Dane. "I'll let Jessie introduce you, I can't think of one damn positive thing to say."

"Thanks, MacKendall, I appreciate that."

Jessica stood up and punched Mac lightly in the shoulder. "Be nice," she scolded.

"Why? He's never nice to me," Mac complained, laughing.

"Jackie, this is Dane Pierce. Dane, Jackie Spencer. We've been friends since college. She's an actress. Please, Jackie, sit down and entertain Dane. I have to mingle."

Jackie blushed and hesitantly sat down in Jessica's chair. Dane adjusted his and moved closer to hear Jackie's voice over the music that had just started.

Mac took Jessica's hand, and as they walked away Jessica distinctly heard Dane's teasing voice: "So, Jackie, are you going to be a big star someday?" Jessica turned quickly and caught his wink at her over Jackie's shoulder.

Jessica hardly left Mac's side the entire evening. She had come so close to losing him, she clung to him devotedly. Mac found nothing wrong with her fond attention, pausing periodically to kiss her and inquire about how she was feeling. She declined several offers of champagne in favor of ginger ale, and eventually stole into the ladies lounge with Roxanne.

"Guess you and Mac worked things out?"

"Oh Roxie, you won't believe this." Jessica carefully checked all the stalls to make sure of their privacy. "Mac isn't...he can, I mean, have children. The baby is...our baby!"

Roxanne threw her arms around Jessica spontaneously.

"And Rox, that's not all." Jessica's face grew serious now, but her eyes sparkled as she held out her left hand for Roxanne's inspection.

Roxanne drew in her breath loudly. "Oh—my—God! He proposed?"

Jessica nodded happily and Roxanne hugged her again.

"You must be in heaven."

"I am beyond heaven. And this party...you did this, didn't you?"

"Well, everyone did. It was Mac's idea, and everybody just kinda helped. Dane got together your friends from the picture, and he also bought all that champagne out there. Tom arranged the entertainment, and I did the hotel and the food."

"You guys..." Jessica shook her head.

"Jess? Would you believe me if I told you something?"

"Maybe...what?"

"That I knew last Christmas that you would be with Mac?"

"Get out of here."

Much to Jessica's embarrassment, a round of toasts were raised in her honor during the evening, and she bit her lip as Dane stood from his corner table, glass in hand.

"I was going to get up and joke about having known Jess since she was a baby; but in truth, I only met her last summer on the set of *Bellerive*. Since that time, I have been lucky enough to watch her transform from a shy, naïve, idealistic girl to a talented, dedicated actress, who is *still* naïve and idealistic. Idealism and naiveté are assets in this business; without them, Jess would have never broken SAG rules by jumping into a role assigned to a friend who couldn't show up for a shoot. I remember thinking that she was a purist; she had strong convictions and good business sense. She is...not afraid of hard work, probably one of her liabilities; and she is generous to a fault."

He paused to sip his drink, then turned to Jessica, who gave him a look that pleaded with him to stop. Ignoring her discomfort, he grinned instead.

"So. What am I saying? Jessica is a special person; someone I care very much about. And tonight, besides celebrating her birthday, it is my pleasure, my utmost honor, to be able to tell you that we are also celebrating Jessica's engagement to my *good friend*, Mac MacKendall."

A roar of voices and applause filled the room. Dane at last held up his hand, obviously not finished.

"You know, I gotta say something here. It's no secret that I have looked upon this lady with affection and...admiration from the start. Hollywood is fond of saying I'm a bad loser; I don't know how they could say that, I haven't lost anything yet," he grinned, inspiring general laughter. "For those of you keeping score, I've just won a six-month court battle for the custody of my son, Alexander." More applause. He looked at Jessica and Mac again.

"But if I have to lose—some of the time, the care and attention of this delightful and lovely lady—there is no one on this earth I would rather lose to— no other I would entrust her to—than this man right here." He reached to extend his hand to Mac. They shook hands, and Dane leaned close to Mac's ear, whispering, "Now you can't say I'm never nice to you, asshole."

With new congratulations in order, the crowd converged on them, and Dane slipped away, seeking out Jackie to accompany him while he brooded.

On cue, the deejay resumed the music. Not a moment too soon for Jessica as Mac took her in his arms on the dance floor. She closed her eyes, letting the man of her dreams lead her slowly into the intimate, loving ritual of dance.

"Can we go soon?" she whispered in his ear as the song ended.

"Say the word."

"Soon," she replied. "We need to be alone."

"You're telling me." Mac smiled, planting tiny kisses on her neck. They had a great deal to talk about. "Jess? When did you find out?"

"Yesterday afternoon."

"You should have told me—"

"Last night, I know."

"You'll learn to trust me someday, I hope."

They made the rounds and said good-byes to several people, promising to meet Nick and Christine for breakfast. They were at the door when Jessica felt someone touch her arm. She turned to face Jackie at her side.

"Jess, I just wanted to thank you for..."

Jessica shook her head. "Don't thank me. I did you no favor introducing you to Dane Pierce, Jackie. *Believe me.*" She smiled knowingly and Jackie giggled.

"Do you think he'll put me in his next picture?"

Mac and Jessica exchanged comic looks and walked from the room.

"Can you believe what Dane said, Mac?" she called from the bathroom where she was washing her face.

"Quite a con, isn't he?"

"No! He was sincere, didn't you see?"

"Right. Sincerity is one of his...*finest* qualities."

"Just before we left, he told me to give you a message."

"What now?"

"He said, 'when Mac comes to his senses about what he's done, tell him I have a bottle of tequila ready with his name on it.' Now what do you suppose he meant by that? He knows you don't drink tequila."

Mac chuckled to himself. Pierce was truly a character. His head hurt just thinking about the night at the cantina.

Jessica slid between the sheets next to him, leaving the light on. Mac turned toward her and slowly pulled the sheet off of her, revealing a sexy pink lace camisole and dainty matching bottoms. His touch was light but purposeful as he slid his fingers across her abdomen and rested his hand just above the panties.

"How does it feel?" he asked softly.

"At this point, I feel the baby in my heart, not my stomach."

"You were pregnant before..." he began, somewhat hesitant. "Do you mind talking about it?"

"I don't mind, *now*. I was working on a play, at a theater in Ventura. We lived in Ventura, for a while. It was *The Crucible*. I loved it. Wesley hated my being gone so much, when his jobs were so hit and miss...I was often home late."

"You overdid it."

"No. That's what Wesley told everyone, what he *believed*."

"But?"

"I was only three months pregnant; one night a friend drove me home, a co-worker, a guy from the play. I wasn't feeling well. Wesley got furious. He took his anger out on me...and the baby." Jessica stifled a shudder. "I miscarried that night. I lied when they examined me. I was afraid they'd put Wesley in jail. I loved him then, despite his craziness. But losing the baby was more than our relationship could stand."

Mac let out a long sigh. If he had known Wesley had abused Jessica, he would have made certain that Wesley had stayed down on that convenience store floor.

"To me, he was remorseful; but to everyone else he blamed my working. I almost believed his story, and I became despondent. I finally went to stay with Christine, and Wesley headed up to Washington."

Mac moved to lay his head on her stomach. "Are you scared, Jessie?"

"No, I'm...elated." She reflected silently for a moment. "Mac, in Utah, after you flew back to L.A., and I was alone in that big room, I thought a lot about... what I *thought* I'd heard, that you couldn't have any more children. I decided right then that it didn't matter, that I would be happy to stay childless if it meant I could be with you. After all, who could want more than the beautiful daughter you already have?" She ran her fingers through his hair.

"When I first found out, yesterday afternoon, I was in such shock, I couldn't tell you. It was impossible. Later, as it sank in, I was afraid that Dane had lied to me. I was so terrified, afraid of not knowing...and I felt so, so stupid. I thought I would lose you."

"It wouldn't have mattered." Mac sighed and she felt his warm breath on her stomach. "Who knows better than I that you and Dane have had many opportunities to...become intimate. I knew that when I decided I loved you too much to stand by and let him continue toying with you. In fact, it was my fear that you were possibly pregnant when you became ill on the island. I was already living with the possibility."

"Mac, there's something else you should know."

Now he moved up, gently sliding his body onto hers, her serious tone concerning him as he looked deeply into her eyes.

"About Dane and me. It's not like you think. We were only together...on two occasions."

He frowned in disbelief.

"It's true, Mac. The first time was before you and I met. The second was...the same night you spent with Lauren."

"Really?" he whispered in clear amazement.

"I didn't know what was happening. I was bewildered, confused...no, crushed, when *she* answered your phone. I mean, you and I weren't really together, yet. I went to Dane for solace. It was wrong, I know, but I was incredibly miserable."

"I'm sure he was most sympathetic."

"Actually, he told me I was in love with you. He said that you were in love with me but wouldn't admit it. And," she smiled now, placing her hands on his cheeks affectionately, "he told me why you punched him out."

"Okay. I give up. Dane Pierce is an angel in disguise."

His lips sought hers. He kissed her with renewed passion, not unlike the first time outside on the walk.

"We haven't made love for eight days," she whispered.

"And two hours, forty-six minutes," he answered, reaching for the lamp on the nightstand. The room fell into darkness. "Still want to marry me?" he teased.

"More than ever."

He gently moved off her now and pulled her onto him, stroking her back with long, soft caresses.

"I've missed this..." he whispered. "I've missed loving you."

FOURTEEN

Lessons Learned

"Jess! The phone's ringing!" Roxanne called over the sound of Michael Bublé's voice as the girls exercised in time with the music. Jessica scurried to turn the volume down and reached for the phone.

"Hello?" she panted, brushing the hair back from her forehead.

"Hi baby, you sound out of breath."

"I am. Roxie and I are working out. I feel like I'm getting fat," she explained.

"You're supposed to be getting fat," Mac teased. "Honey, I've got bad news."

"You're going to be late again."

"Yeah, I'm sorry. You know how these things go...we've had some last-minute set changes, and I think this damned heat melted some of our equipment," he said with a chuckle. "But I should be home around...ten, I hope. I'll eat here. Maybe Roxie can keep you company for dinner?"

"Mac, I don't need a baby-sitter. I'll be fine by myself. But...I'll miss you. I'll wait up. I've got plenty to do on Meggie's room before she comes next week, so don't worry, okay?"

"Okay. I know this is the third time this week; I'll make it up to you. I love you."

"I love you, too," she said softly and hung up the phone.

She was still smiling when she returned to Roxanne, who stood waiting with her arms akimbo.

"Romeo?"

Jessica nodded.

"You two make me sick. All this mush, all the time."

"As if you didn't 'mush' over Tom, *all the time.*" Laughing, the girls resumed their workout until they were again interrupted by the phone.

"Honestly!" Jessica complained. "MacKendall-Taylor," she answered, grinning at Roxanne.

"Now that's *cute*. How ya doin', sweetcakes?"

"Hi Dane, fine, thank you," she said, trying to catch her breath. "How are you?"

"No complaints. Are you panting at the sound of my voice?"

"Sorry, darling...I'm working out my anxieties with Bublé. What's up?"

"The heat, for one thing. Hey, I have a little news to pass on, we have *Season* scheduled to premiere mid-December. So don't run off and get *married* or anything, okay?"

"Okay, I'll try to be in town."

There was a pause and Dane continued. "I was wondering if you and I could get together...for dinner maybe."

Jessica's eyes widened and she stared across the room at Roxanne, who frowned in concern.

"What for?" she managed. *Don't rock my boat, Dane. Not now.*

"I need to talk to you. It's important, Jess."

"Well, I don't know, Dane. I'm pretty busy, Mac's daughter is coming to stay with us for a couple of weeks, and I haven't finished her room, and..."

"And the air in your tires needs changing. Come on, Jess, give me a break. You can't spare a couple of hours for *me*?"

She could see his eyes before her, imploring her to give in, just a little, this once. She bit her lip. Roxanne was still frowning at her from across the room.

"I don't think it's a good idea." The sound of her own answer depressed her. He was silent, so she offered an alternative. "Maybe lunch?"

"Dinner. A quick one. I promise. Tonight, Jess, I really have to see you." She wasn't giving in, so he went for blood. "I would think after everything we've been through that you'd at least consider seeing me briefly. My future is rather... uncertain at the moment, and I just need to talk something out with someone who...really knows me. Like you do."

"Ruby? This is Jessica. Yes, that's right...he's not? Could you make sure he gets a message? Tell him I'm having dinner with...a friend...and I should still be home before him anyway...but just in case I wanted him to know I was going out. It's important, Ruby, please make sure you tell him."

"Certainly, Miss Jesseeca. I tell him. He take a break always at 6:30, only in a little while. You want him to call?"

"No, that's not necessary. Just give him the message."

Jessica sighed and pulled off the second pair of jeans that wouldn't snap around her waist. Nothing she'd worn in the Caribbean fit now that she was beginning to fill out. Even her bra was tight and uncomfortable, and she made a mental note to go shopping for new ones.

Finally finding a pair of Levis that would close, she struggled with the zipper and managed to finish dressing. She chose an airy, white cotton shirt and white sandal heels, topping her hair with a white satin ribbon.

In the garage, she paused before the Miata, choosing to drive the Lotus instead. She'd agreed to pick Dane up at his house and thought perhaps the sight of Mac's car would make a sobering impression on him. For one thing was certain: she was determined that tonight, Dane Pierce was going to get real clear about her situation.

She kicked off the pumps and drove barefoot from Laurel to Benedict Canyon, enjoying the admiring stares she got from other motorists. The Lotus was a fine car, and she'd been driving it a lot lately; Mac still preferred his old truck for driving to work and back. Parking the Lotus on the studio lot made him crazy.

At the Pierce mansion, a small boy with sandy brown hair and mischievous green eyes greeted her at the door. She squatted down on the porch and held out her hand.

"Hello Alex, I'm Jessica."

The little boy turned to flee and ran smack into his father, who'd heard the bell and was just buttoning his shirt.

"Hi Jess...I'll be just a minute." Dane called to Peter over his shoulder, then lifted his son into his arms. "Okay champ, Dad's gonna leave for a bit. You be good for Uncle Peter, you understand? Don't put any more crayons in the microwave. If you're nice, we'll go ride the horse again tomorrow. Now, when Pete says it's bedtime, it's off with you. Okay, bud?"

"Yup," Alexander nodded, shyly peeking at Jessica. Dane put him on his feet and watched with a smile as the little boy sped off. He closed the front door and joined Jessica on the porch. Spying the Lotus, he whistled. "Engagement gift?"

"No, it's Mac's. The Miata is...needs a tune-up." She walked around to the passenger side and unlocked the door for him, after which he grabbed the keys from her hand and proceeded to get behind the wheel, much to her obvious chagrin.

"Not good enough to drive your boyfriend's car?" He laughed, starting the engine.

Jessica reluctantly got in and crossed her arms. Two minutes and he already had the upper hand.

He stared at her so much as they drove that Jessica was afraid he'd plow into a parked car.

"You're different. You've...filled out nicely since Amande."

Jessica colored at his bold appraisal of her breasts.

"It's a compliment, Jessie. You're more beautiful than ever."

They ate at an out of the way diner in Hollywood, in a small, private alcove Dane had reserved. Next door, a popular dance bar prepared to open; it was still early.

He offered her wine, but to his obvious disappointment she requested sparkling water.

She was nervous, but she knew she had to get the ball rolling, tell him what she had to say, and get home. It was 7 p.m., and she had no idea how long this would take.

Jessica took a moment to appreciate him before diving into her difficult speech. He seemed himself, confident, handsome, charming...but she suspected trouble underneath. She wondered if her instincts were wrong, if he really did have something to discuss about his future, or if this really was just another ruse to get her alone with him. She gazed at his tempting features, remembering the night so long ago, in another restaurant, when she'd obsessed over his beautiful eyes. A nostalgic hand tugged at her heart.

"Dane, I need to explain why I gave you a tough time today on the phone." She took a breath. "Since the night of the party, since Mac and I are engaged, things have changed. It's...difficult...for me to see you socially. You need to understand that my relationship with Mac has changed; the last thing I want to do is create a problem. You get it, right?"

"I get it, real clearly, thank you. Shit, I'm surprised he hasn't locked you in a bell tower somewhere and thrown away the key, especially with a dangerous character like me on the loose."

"You're missing the point. It's me that feels the change. He doesn't restrict what I do. He knows that you and I are friends, and he's been awfully tolerant. But you and I, Dane, things could never be just casual again. Too much has passed between us...too much intensity."

He grabbed her roughly by the wrist and leaned closer to her face. "It's still there, isn't it, Jessica? You *do* still feel it." His grip softened a little, but his eyes were piercing and demanding. "Jess, what I said at the party, it was all bullshit. I *lied*. I want you to marry him about as much as I want to marry Rita again."

Tears welled in her shocked eyes. She couldn't believe her ears. "Don't say this, Dane, please. I love him more than anyone or anything in the world, more than anything I've ever loved in my life. And as much as I hate to admit it, you still have the power to hurt me. Please don't do it."

"So, you still care about me."

"Of course, I always will. A lot. There's no end to the effect you've had on me, on my life. I'm forever grateful for having been close to you."

"I don't want your gratitude. I want your love."

Jessica's lips parted. Silent, she stared at him with a mixture of hurt and anger, and a painful kind of love that lived in one corner of her full heart.

She took his hand and uncurled his fingers, sliding her palm across his, feeling the surface with her fingertips. She knew his hands well; they were strong, broad, and always soft, yet tonight she discovered a new row of firm, pink calluses derived from a horse's reins. Her heart ached. She lifted her eyes back to his.

"You have my love, what there is to give. I don't mean to hurt you, but there was a time, not so long ago, when I would have traded my very soul to hear the words you're saying tonight. Nothing meant more to me than you, Dane; and it seems to me we've discussed this before. You wanted my body and my soul, but not my heart. But it's a packaged deal, and you've been outbid."

"How, Jess? He's not like you. He lacks passion! He's passive, predictable. There's no challenge to him, is there? No mystery."

"If you mean he doesn't ravage my soul by dragging it on the end of a chain, you're right." Her tone turned bitter, anger at Dane welling up inside her; she would not tolerate his criticism of Mac, nor the memories of the heartless way he'd treated her before.

"There's no need to cut me down." He shook his head softly, a small smile on his lips. And, like his hands, Jessica knew those lips so well, she knew every smile in his repertoire; this one was generated by pain. It was his defense against tears.

He gently pulled her hand to his lips and kissed it slowly and with great tenderness. "I guess you've told me, huh?" he surrendered against her fingers. The warmth of his breath on her hand touched her, and she turned it to caress his face. He closed his eyes.

"I'm sorry, Dane. Mac and I, we're forever. Accept it, okay? For me? For yourself, too."

"If you'll promise to come looking for me when you finally get bored with him."

"Don't hold your breath."

He sighed and visually tried to put his feelings away, straightening up and clearing his throat. Several moments passed before he spoke again. "I don't suppose you would be interested in reading a script for me? I have a role you'd love."

"Against your lead?"

"No. It'll be hard enough to juggle the film and my...parenting duties. I'll only be directing this one. But it's a great project. You should still read it. I... wouldn't want what I said tonight to affect your interest or your decision." He paused. "I won't bother you about this again, Jessica. I had to try, and I needed to know."

"I won't be doing another film this year, Dane." She spoke quietly, looking at the table.

"Going to play the little housewife? Not your style, sweetie."

"No, you're right about that. But I'm going to be...busy, nonetheless. Talk to me next spring."

They walked to the car in silence. Jessica checked her watch: 8:55. Dane eyed the Lotus with disdain. "Too slick for me."

"You said the Porsche was back in the shop. Where's your Mercedes?"

"Toting my spoiled daughters to school and back."

"Oh..." So he had traded the Benz for Alexander. Maybe there was hope for him after all.

"Did you want to drive back?" she asked, unenthused at the prospect.

He fished her keys from his pocket and handed them to her. "Go ahead. I'm not going back."

"What do you mean? How will you get home?"

"Don't worry your pretty head about me. I'm sure I can find a ride." He grinned at her, and then regarded her thoughtfully. He shoved his hands into his pockets and took a tentative step backward, looking her up and down as she stood next to the car.

"What's different about you?" he asked suddenly.

"Nothing, of course. Why do you ask?"

"You look...radiant. Of course, my friend Mac would say you always do. But there's something new...and I don't buy into this 'true love' bullshit either. Could it be the sparkling water?" he teased, referring to her earlier refusal of the wine. Suddenly his expression changed. He stared at her for several moments, until she became uncomfortable and turned to unlock the car.

"I need to get home. I think I drank too much of that water you're talking about," she explained, absently touching her abdomen as she'd become fond of doing since she'd found out about the baby. She slid behind the wheel and closed the door.

"Yeah," he replied softly, his face momentarily reflecting the rapid thoughts passing through his mind. "Look, Jess..." He approached the car and knelt on the ground next to her door. She had never seen him on his knees, and there was a certain satisfaction in seeing him thus. "If nothing meant anything to you tonight, nothing I said or tried to say in my own asinine way, please remember one thing for me. I know you doubt my sincerity, and with reason. I've been... uncool about being honest. But believe this: I am here if you need me, anytime, anywhere. *Always*. Okay?"

She nodded, again feeling that small tug at her heart.

"Be happy, sweetie." And in his eyes, she wondered if she saw something new, some resolution not there before.

·♥·♥·♥·♥·♥·

Grimacing at the sight of Mac's Ford in the garage, Jessica parked the Lotus at 9:15. She started to walk to the house but heard activity in the pool and cut through the breezeway to the backyard.

Mac was swimming laps, his smooth stroke almost silent as his arms sliced the water. The June night was warm and still, and the garden lights cast a colorful glow on the pool deck; crickets chirped in the surrounding darkness.

She walked to the deck and dropped her purse and keys on the glass table. The sound made him turn and he swam to the pool edge near where she stood, again kicking off her shoes.

"Hi," she said softly.

"Hi." He folded his arms on the deck, staring up at her, his face unreadable and dripping.

"You're early," she said.

"You're late." Despite the implied accusation, his voice remained level and non-threatening.

She sat down at the edge of the pool, relieved to be home and away from the ordeal with Dane. She leaned forward slightly, hoping to gain a kiss from Mac. "You got my message, right?"

Instead, Mac eyed her thoughtfully, conflict evident on his face. "Yep. How *is* the captivating Dane Pierce this evening?"

The bitterness in his voice made her start. Thunderstruck, she didn't respond; she knew from his expression that her silence confirmed his assumption. She drew in her bottom lip and bit it, her mind awash with confusion over his unmistakable hostility. She watched with trepidation as he hoisted himself out of the pool, showering water onto the deck and grabbing a towel from the nearby table.

Hastily she got to her feet, her entire demeanor now altered by his disposition. He blotted his face dry then draped the towel around his neck, peered at her, searching her eyes for the answer to a question he hadn't yet posed. Jessica returned his look with artificial confidence. She cleared her throat. "The premiere is set for December."

He ignored what he must have considered to be her insignificant comment. "How long before this is over, Jessica? When can I stop wondering?"

"I don't know what you mean." She took a tiny step backward, distracted and unaware of her own movements.

"Of course, you do. Let's see, how did it go tonight? He doesn't want you to marry me, right? We're not right for each other...or maybe, the marriage doesn't even matter. Maybe it would be more interesting for *him* to be 'the other man' this time."

"No! Stop!" She shook her head in amazement, then turned to the table and picked up her keys. Her encounter with Dane had already left her weakened and grieving; she couldn't weather an argument with Mac. *I've got to get out of here; I'll talk to him when he's calm.*

She started to walk away, her head down, the keys biting into her soft palm as she gripped them in a painful retreat.

"Don't wanna fight with me, Jess? Afraid I might cuff you one on the cheek? A little unpleasantness and you turn tail. Wesley's *gone*, Jessica. It's just you and me now."

His words stopped her cold, frozen throughout. She felt him grasp her arm and turn her briskly around to face him, felt him take the keys from her hand.

"You won't be needing these," he said in a low, clear voice, tossing the keys into the bushes before her astonished eyes. A new side of Mac. The man she would marry.

Mac walked a step or two away, then turned to face her again. She knew her eyes were bright with unshed tears, but she held her gaze on his, waiting for his next words.

He extended his hands toward her, beckoning mockingly with his fingers. "Fight with me, Jess, c'mon. I'm ready. I'm as mad as hell. Don't walk away leaving me to believe you still want Pierce."

"No!"

"He snaps his fingers, and you jump in your car, no, into *my* God-damned car, and run off to be with him. He wants you now, doesn't he? More than ever. You couldn't see it, could you, his feeding you that crock of lies at the party."

"Why are you saying these things?" She finally found a voice, finally began to overcome the fear of defending herself. Mac was furious; but his hands were at his sides, not balled into fists. "It wasn't so terrible, having dinner with Dane! I called you—"

"You called when you knew I'd be out. Do you trust me so little that you were afraid to tell me yourself? Even your message smacked of misguided deceit: having dinner with 'a friend.' Now who the hell could your nameless 'friend' be? *Give me a break.*"

The night grew warmer despite the hour. Mac's eyes were dark with fury and his voice as cold and treacherous as black ice on a wintry road. Jessica struggled to put her thoughts in order, painfully piecing together what she needed to say to turn Mac around.

"Okay," she began, her voice small compared with his defiant one. "It's true. Your presumptions are correct, to a point." Jessica looked away, toward the pool. "Dane is a lonely person. He doesn't know how to be alone."

"Forgive me if I fail to lend a sympathetic ear." The sarcasm in his words burned like acid in her ears. "Jessica, tell me we have something real here; tell me you could be happy never seeing his face again. God! I want to drive over there right now and beat the hell out of him!"

Now she did see fists, tightened in rage, but with rage meant for Dane, not her.

"I can't believe you're so jealous of him!"

"I guess I forgot to put that on my resume. I have this thing about wanting to keep the woman I love to myself. Sorry."

"It's not easy to completely turn off a friendship. A...relationship. But it's over, Mac, you've got to believe it."

"Over? Again? I'm having trouble with that. Can you at least understand why this crushes me? I've been done to, before. No, I need to see him, I need to *make him understand.* I want him out of our lives."

"He considers you his friend. He saved your life, remember?"

Mac stopped and stared at her painfully. "And what good is that...without you?"

These last words, spoken softly and straight from his heart, sifted down on her like snowflakes. He lowered his eyes and turned to walk to one of two chaise lounges on the far side of the pool, where he lay down and stared up at the moonless sky, one arm across his forehead in despair.

Swallowing hard, drawing on courage born of her intense love for him, Jessica followed and sat down on the adjacent lounge. Clasping her trembling hands in her lap, she gazed at him silently, her liquid eyes cherishing their view. She cleared her throat, preparing to say something she hadn't quite formulated. He pulled his eyes away from the stars and looked at her, expectant, yet guarded with lingering skepticism. Jessica's heart ached with his pain. She extended her hand to glide over his then rested it on his chest, but Mac did not respond to her touch.

"I'm sorry I didn't trust you. You're right; I was afraid to tell you I was going to see him. I knew you wouldn't like it. I just wanted to tell him, once and for all, that there was no reason to pursue me any longer. I told him that you and I were forever, and that he was wasting his time if he thought anything different. It's the truth, Cory; I only hope you can accept the truth from me now, that you can please trust me again; I'm trying to learn, really."

Her use of his given name always touched him somehow, and he slowly brought his other hand from over his head to rest on hers. Grateful, encouraged by his gesture, her heart lifted and she continued.

"I didn't tell him about the baby. I knew he would misuse the information... and it really isn't any of his business." She blinked away the beginnings of new tears. "I won't be seeing him again." She stared at him solemnly.

Mac lifted his hand slowly to her face, sliding his fingers into the hair above her ear and around to cradle her head. Wordlessly, he pulled her toward him, maneuvering her body with his other hand to lie on top of him, his fingers slipping beneath her shirt and up her back. When her face was just before his, he spoke quietly and with conviction.

"I just love you too much, that's all. Forgive me that," he crooned, his warm breath tickling her cheek as he spoke. "I know," he continued, both of his hands now delving into the soft flesh between her shoulders, "that Dane Pierce will never totally disappear...and I didn't really mean that I wanted to do him in." He paused, recalling thoughts Jessica could only guess about. "All I really want is for us to trust each other, Jessie, that's what my kind of love is all about. It really wouldn't matter if Dane Pierce lived next door."

Overcome by his sincerity, Jessica pressed her lips forcefully to his while grasping his head firmly between her hands. He returned her kiss with renewed fervor, punctuating his declarations physically, before whispering urgently into her ear.

"There isn't anything in this world I wouldn't do for you, Jessica. Everything I have is yours to share...but don't ask me to share *you*, not with Dane or anyone else. It's something I could never do."

Jessica had lifted the hurtful veil from his eyes, now filled with devotion and promise; he was asking for her pledge of a future built on trust and fidelity.

"I am entirely and completely yours, Cory, forever...and, you might keep in mind that I feel the same, about sharing you."

Her comment had a definite effect upon him.

"I want you," he said simply, his fingers nimbly working the hooks on her too-tight bra.

"What?" Jessica looked at him in surprise. "Here?"

"Why not?" Deftly sliding her off him, he quickly dragged the two thick chaise cushions onto the plush grass alongside the pool deck, then pulled her by the wrist to stand before him while he hurriedly unbuttoned her shirt and jeans. Unzipping her pants, he slid his fingers into them and she stiffened with anticipation as he treated himself to the feel of her smooth flesh. Soon she ached for him, and she insisted he lie down with her on the cushions. They tossed aside the rest of their clothing and embraced each other fervently.

"Make love to me, *now*," she whispered, grasping at his lower back, pulling him to her, into her, until she knew he was all hers.

Nearly at the height of ecstasy, his breath burning in her ear, he withdrew ever so slightly, tormenting them both with hesitation. He demanded her promise once more.

"Tell me again that you are mine."

"Oh, Mac...yes, yes! I am yours. And...you are *mine*."

"Orion's belt," he pointed out, holding her close against the rapidly cooling air.

"Mmm..." she responded, snuggling against him underneath the beach towels that covered them.

"Fighting isn't so bad, now is it?"

"I'll never enjoy fighting with you; but I have to admit...I don't mind making up one bit."

Dane Pierce leaned lazily against the wall of the club, a cellular phone in his hand within the pocket of his rough leather jacket. Intrigued by a young girl in streetwalker attire, he shook his head at some private joke. The girl stopped and eyed him, withdrew her own phone from her bag and dialed, talking in an animated fashion while scratching the back of her thigh.

Slipping his hand into his hip pocket, Dane pulled out a torn matchbook cover. He squinted at the number printed on it, then quickly punched at the cell phone in his other hand before slumping back against the wall.

"Hey, Jackie. Dane." A sardonic smile spread on his lips. "Yeah, well, the guy I was meeting canceled...you still want to get together?" He grinned at her response. "Good, hey, I'm on my way down to the Sky bar, you know where that is? That's right...I'll meet you there in say, thirty minutes? Terrific. See you, doll."

He ended the call and walked back outside where a street vendor stood selling flowers from a cart. He pulled his wallet out and handed the man a ten-dollar bill.

"What's nice tonight, Joe? How about that...what the hell is that, anyway? An orchid?"

"Sure, man, that's an orchid. But if it's a special lady, I have some great roses here. Look at this." He fingered a perfect red rose bud.

Dane stared at the rose, then slowly shook his head. He flashed a smile at the vendor. "I'll take the orchid. You can put the roses on ice for me—for about nine months. Don't forget now, I'll be back."

The man shook his head with indifference and carefully wrapped the orchid. Dane tucked the blossom under his arm and slowly walked back to lean against the building, staring at the night sky in amused wonder. From the doorway, loud, soulful music poured into the street, seeming to swirl about him. The song was a mournful tune, recounting the pain of unrequited love; the love of a man for a woman who is, and always will be, out of reach.

"Yup," he muttered, shaking his head slightly. Reaching into the breast pocket of his jacket, Dane Pierce pulled out a cigarette and lit it.

FIFTEEN

Forever Jessica

"Forsaking all others..."

Jessica's hands shook so badly she could barely steady them long enough to slip the gold filigree band onto Mac's finger. He didn't help matters by grinning at her ineptness, making her give up a small, repressed giggle. The laugh relaxed her a little, and the ring went on easily.

"Whew! Glad we got that taken care of," Mac said to the merriment of the surrounding guests as they stood in the Great Room of the Brighton Country Chalet. "And I thought I was nervous."

Jessica giggled again, and he squeezed her hand. He hadn't taken his eyes off her since she'd appeared in the room twenty minutes earlier. Her dress was white, despite her impending motherhood, and designed with a fitted bodice ending just below the bust, giving a high-waisted appearance; but the materials were of the finest silk, lace and taffeta. A single string of white pearls adorned her neck, a balance to the sweeping neckline of the gown.

Behind them, Christine wept with joy for her twin, feeling Jessica's happiness inside her own heart. Roxanne, too, watched tearfully, remembering all that Jessica had been through during the past several months; no one deserved this rapturous day more than Jessie. A life with a man who'd flown 1,600 miles alone in a tiny plane to see to her safety; a man who'd risked it all, his very life, to protect her from harm; a man who would hold her above all others for eternity.

Tom held Roxanne tightly about the waist as they watched the couple, who'd of late become their closest friends, finally tie the knot on their fairy-tale courtship.

"I now pronounce you, husband and wife." The officiant smiled and stepped back.

Mac kissed his bride. Megan squirmed uncomfortably on the couch next to her grandmother. Reva MacKendall patted Megan's hands briskly.

"You settle down, honey. This is an important time for Daddy," she whispered, absently reaching down to touch the oxygen machine on the floor beside her feet.

"Is he ever going to stop kissing her, Grammy?"

"All too soon, dear...all too soon."

The reception was more than festive. Jessica and Mac were waited upon like royalty, Megan sitting prominently between them on the loveseat while they opened their gifts.

The Inn was closed for the July 21st weekend, and everyone stayed overnight before returning to their respective homes the following day, except for Janet Taylor. Jessica's mother planned a week's vacation with her daughter and new granddaughter, Angelica, now three months old and adorable.

"Three months old! What a big girl!" Jessica exclaimed as she held Angel on her lap.

Mac, too, was enamored and took the baby from her, kissing the infant's cheek affectionately.

"Three months. Seems a long time ago." He turned his shining eyes onto his bride, conveying what he knew was a shared thought; their own child was most certainly conceived the night of little Angel's birth.

"It's about time I got a grandchild," Jan admonished, now stealing the child from Mac's arms. "Always thought Jessica would be the first. Almost was." She turned and walked away from the couple, but her parting words were not lost on her daughter. Jessica set her jaw and got to her feet in pursuit.

Moments later, she caught up with her mother in the kitchen.

"Surely you don't still think that miscarriage was my fault?" she demanded, her face growing warm at the painful memory of the beating she had suffered. "After everything I've been through, how could you even..."

Her mother turned to face her, the infant still cradled in her arms. Jessica's building rage quickly diminished when she saw the glistening shine in her mother's eyes.

"I didn't want to believe," Janet began, her chin quivering slightly. "I only wanted the best for you. I think I knew from the start, from the time you started dating Wesley that he was wrong, that he wasn't good enough for you. But he loved you so, and I made that good enough for me. He used to ask me little things, you know, things about you, what cologne you liked, what flowers were best...and I couldn't believe anyone as sweet as he was could hurt a girl like you."

A tear escaped down her cheek and dampened the sleeping baby's forehead. Jessica took a deep breath and struggled to remain composed.

"Well, he *did*. Maybe if you had chosen to see that sooner, he wouldn't have used you to get information about me. Maybe—"

Her words had a devastating effect upon her mother. The normally bold, outspoken Janet Taylor was reduced to a trembling mass of remorse and regret, visibly shrinking before Jessica's eyes. Suddenly her mother's image changed; she was no longer the powerful, dominating parent. Instead, the older woman before her was frightened, confused and ashamed of having succumbed to Wesley's manipulation. Unable to bear her mother's grief, Jessica rushed forward and embraced her and the infant, her own tears now flowing freely down her cheeks.

"I'm sorry, Jessie. I was so blind. So stupid."

"It's okay. It's all over now. Let's just forget about it, 'kay?" Jessica kissed her mother's rouged cheek. "Come on. We've got to do this bridal garter thing."

Somehow, the simple act of forgiveness made the burden of her horrific memories just a little lighter.

Jessica and Mac spent their wedding night in the Zurich Suite. At 10 p.m., Mac finally stole his bride away and carried her over the threshold of the suite, gently landing her on the round bed where they'd spent that first amorous night together. He ceremoniously kicked the door closed behind him.

The heather gray tuxedo jacket was unceremoniously cast aside along with the rose bowtie and cummerbund. Mac fell upon the bed beside her, and they stared at the ceiling together for several moments.

"I don't believe this," he murmured.

"Neither do I," she said quietly.

"So much has happened since we were here before."

"Some of it I'd like to forget." Jessica touched his shoulder, just barely healed from where Wesley Elliot's bullet had torn across his flesh. He'd bear the scar as a lifelong reminder of the day he'd fought to save the woman he loved from her deranged ex-husband.

"God, I love you!" Mac declared passionately, grasping her chin in his fist affectionately. "Don't ever go away, okay? I don't think I could live without you, now." His voice was thick with emotion.

"I'll never go away, Cory. *Never*. You are my whole life." She touched his face, lightly dragging her fingers down his cheek and across his lips. "I can't believe we're married. We're really married!" She giggled, making his dimples appear as he looked on her adoringly.

"I missed you last night," he whispered, delicately fingering the pearls hanging from her neck. "I'm not too keen on these pre-nuptial traditions."

"It's bad luck."

"We've slept in the same bed for three months."

"I appreciate your humoring me, my husband," she chided.

His eyes became warm and seductive, his fingers leaving the pearls and dipping into the cleavage exposed by the misaligned gown as she lay on her side next to him.

"Mac..." she pouted, her expression coy and teasing.

"Jessie..." he mimicked her whining tone, moving his face close to hers. Jessica's pulse quickened as she anticipated his kiss, but he stopped just short, his lips touching hers like feathers, brushing across them slowly. He tantalized her senses, teasing her, then extended his tongue just slightly to moisten her lips.

Slowly he eased her backward until she was lying down, and he hovered over her, looking into her face before finally pressing his mouth firmly over hers. They kissed with the combined passion of all the lovers the heavens had ever blessed with true love. Jessica replayed again and again the sound of his voice saying, "I do," her ultimate dream come true.

Minutes later, Mac lifted his face for a breathless intermission. Jessica began once again working on the tuxedo studs on his shirt, and he grinned at her wickedly.

"I think I need a shower."

The "Dog Days" of August had indeed set in. The humidity magnified the L.A. smog and heated up the valleys to an unbearable degree. Even in the offices at Castle Studios, where new refrigerated air conditioners hissed from every vent, the air hung heavy and close, and Mac impatiently fussed with the button on his shirt collar in hopes of some relief. He looked up when Steve Lightner, the series producer, walked into the room.

"So. What's the bottom line, Steve? Are we out?"

"Well, Mac...we have a choice. Not a good one, mind you, but...we can bail out this season or get canceled next."

Mac unconsciously chewed on his lip. His respiration stepped up; the heat was suddenly worse.

"So, I'm out of work?"

"Mac...come on, you'll never be out of work. You're too good. What I'm saying here is, we can go out now and grab other opportunities, if we want, if *you* want, or you can ride it out. Your choice, Mac."

"*My* choice? What about all the others? There are a lot of people involved here."

"All skilled professionals. Being associated with *Doctor Jim* won't tarnish their resumes one bit. And Mac," Steve asserted, lowering his tone, "you know New Dimension still wants you for that movie deal. Maybe it's time."

"Jesus, Steve, my wife's expecting. I can't do a film *now*..."

"Just think about it, Mac. Maybe talk it over with Jessie. We'll meet again on Monday."

Mac was quiet that evening. He thought about explaining his dilemma to Jessica, but she seemed tired and away in her own thoughts. And he wanted to think it over some more first.

In bed that night, Jessica nudged him. "Cory Lee," she whispered, tugging on a strand of his hair.

"Hmmm?" he responded, his eyes staring straight up at the ceiling.

"What's on your mind?"

"Nothin' babe. It's nothing." He kissed her forehead. "Better get to sleep, Mommy."

Jessica sighed, stretching her fingers across his bare chest. She was soon asleep on his shoulder. Mac lay awake for another hour, wondering how the future would play out. He had an appointment in the morning with New Dimension Pictures.

"It's a fantastic opportunity, Mac. We're in New Zealand for, say, three months. The role was meant for you. He's an American transplant, trying to make it on a sheep ranch left him by a dead uncle. But there's a problem with water rights, squabbles from left-out relatives, you get the picture."

Mac pulled at his bottom lip in contemplation.

"Can we possibly shoot it in two?"

"Ummm...would be tight."

"I need to be here in December."

"We can make it. If you take this, we'll make it happen. What do you say?"

"Give me a day, Jack. I can't commit without talking with Jessie."

"A day. Fine. I've waited long enough to get you into this office; you take as long as you want, only you're the one with the time constraints. The sooner you say jump, the sooner we say 'how high?' Okay?"

"You got it. Call you tomorrow."

Her first maternity clothes were Mac's mostly unworn dress shirts. Jessica looked around the nursery bedroom in frustration, noting the odd angles she'd have to measure for wallpaper. Armed with a tape measure, she busily set about making notes and marking the drab, unpainted walls with her ideas. Roxanne would be picking her up in an hour.

On the ladder, a pencil clenched in her teeth, she carefully drew out where the border would be pasted. The doorbell's beckoning forced an oath from her mouth. Roxanne was early.

Jessica scrambled down the hall and threw open the front door. Stopping short, she caught her breath as she looked upon Dane Pierce standing on the porch, a bouquet of red roses in his hand.

"Hey, sweetie...how's the little mom?"

Overwhelmed, she took the roses and gave Dane a brief hug.

"They're lovely, Dane. Thanks." She took them to the kitchen and immediately put them in water. "Gosh. What a surprise. How have you been?"

"Fair to middlin,' as they say. You look good, Jess. And you should have told me you were pregnant. You never stop breaking my heart, do you?"

"Dane...you must have had some reason for coming here today."

"Alas, you're right, my pet. I'm off on a new adventure, and I couldn't go without telling my best girl good-bye."

"What kind of adventure?" Jessica walked down the hall, returning to her work in the nursery as he followed her.

"Malaysia, sweetie. Kuala Lumpur, then Cambodia."

"Whatever for?"

"A film, Jess, a major friggin' epic! The chance of a lifetime."

"Are you joking?"

"Not on your sweet life, darling. I'll be gone six months, so I came by so you can send me off in style." He reached for her, and she swiftly moved aside.

"Be serious. When do you leave?"

"Tomorrow. And I won't leave until you kiss me good-bye." His tone was now more serious, although the green eyes still danced merrily and his expression comically begged. "C'mon, Jess."

"Dane, please. You know how I feel."

"Yes, I do, and that's why I'm here. You'd hate me if I left without saying good-bye."

He had her there. She would have been hurt.

"Jessica, there's something I have to tell you. It's pretty pointless, now, and I wish I could congratulate you on your marriage, but you'd know I was lying anyway..." Dane stopped her flitting about the room by grasping her forearms tightly. "Please listen."

She stood still, peering into his face with wary anticipation.

"This film I'm doing...there's a certain amount of risk involved."

"What do you mean?"

"I can't really say. It's just that it's a political venture, there's some opposition to our being there, you understand..."

"You'll be in danger?"

"Well, probably not, but..." Dane looked down briefly. "I just want you to know...you've been the most important woman in my life for...a long time. I don't know if I'll ever get past this obsession, Jessica. I...I wish I could tell you how I feel..." He paused again, searching for words. "Look. I won't be here when, you know, the baby comes, and...well, let me know, okay? I'll be thinking of you every day."

"Of course," she said softly, her walls trembling, her defenses threatened. But before she could tear away from his gaze, before she could assert her independence from him, Dane was kissing her good-bye with the conviction of a man going off to combat.

She didn't know what made her open her eyes. Perhaps the quick return of her resolve as Dane's tongue began probing her mouth, bringing on the exhilarating, yet painful memory of their first kiss so long ago; perhaps it was the disillusion, the challenge to her belief that her mouth, her lips, all belonged to Mac, and Dane had no right to the liberties he was taking; or maybe it was just because she could feel Mac's overwhelming presence as he stood in the nursery doorway.

Jessica's eyes widened in terror, and she shoved Dane away from her. Startled, he followed her gaze and spun to face Mac, standing behind him.

Mac's shoulders dropped and he slumped against the doorjamb. His eyes were riveted to Jessica's, filled with pain and growing wrath. No one said a word until Mac himself murmured so softly she barely heard his suffering tone.

"Jessica...why?" He shook his head sadly, his defeated countenance encompassing his entire body. Then, setting his jaw, he drew in a decisive breath and walked out.

Entranced by the horror of what had transpired, both Jessica and Dane snapped from their spell and started after him, calling out for him to stop. But Mac was beyond hearing anything except whatever angry, bitter words were screaming in his own mind. He reached the gravel drive and pulled the keys to the Lotus from his pocket.

"Mac, listen, it's not like it looks, pal," Dane shouted, trotting after him. When Mac didn't stop, Dane grabbed his shoulder with the intention of turning Mac around.

Mac did turn, and in doing so wound Dane's collar tightly around his fist, bringing the paled knuckles of his right hand close to Dane's chin. His voice was cold and threatening when he spoke the acid words he'd chosen for Dane.

"No, you listen to *me, pal*," he spat, his face close to Dane's. "You know, I almost liked you Pierce, but you're bad news—and I don't *ever* want to see your face here again, you got that?"

"Go ahead, MacKendall, finish the job. Finish what you started in Amande." Dane beckoned. "Come on, if it'll make you feel better."

Mac stared at his own fist, balled in rage and poised before Dane's face. He remembered with startling clarity the night at the hospital in Amande, when he'd struck him, all because of Jessica. Jessie and Dane; would it never end?

Slowly he let go of Dane's shirt and turned toward the car.

"Really, Mac, it was my doing. I just came here to tell her good-bye. I'm leaving," Dane began, guiltily trying to rectify the situation.

"Good," Mac replied coolly, getting into the Lotus. "Then why don't you just take her with you." He glanced briefly at Jessica, standing numb with shock behind the car, one arm protectively across her slightly swelling abdomen and the other holding shaking fingers to her lips. Lips that had just been intimate with Dane Pierce. Mac again shook his head at her, then hit the throttle on the sleek, white sports car and was gone.

Dane turned to Jessica, his face awash with remorse. Wordlessly she turned and went inside, and he followed.

She sat down on the couch. He sat beside her and leaned forward on his fists. She didn't cry, despite the depth of her internal pain.

"He's gone."

"He'll be back, Jess."

"No. I promised him, and I've broken the promise."

"What promise?"

"That what just happened would never happen."

Dane cleared his throat. "It was my fault, I indulged myself...I, I'm sorry, Jess. I'm truly sorry."

"Forget it, Dane. I should have thrown you a right hook, between the legs... like he taught me." A brief, ironic smile played on her lips as she recalled the night she'd confided in Mac about her fear of Dane's power over her. Back in the old house, ages ago. He'd demonstrated with his fist how she could ward off Dane's advances. "But I didn't. I stood there and let you...I let you." Her voice faltered as she again touched her lips, despising herself for succumbing to Dane's seductive game. Again.

Dane stood and paced across the room, staring blindly out at the pool. Hot Santa Ana winds rippled its surface. "I love you, Jessica. You know that, I hope. I would never want to cause trouble for you. But I *am* trouble, Mac's right. The sooner I'm away from here, the better. I hope you understand that I couldn't go without saying good-bye."

"Of course," she said softly. "Of course."

"Look. I'll talk to him before I go. I'll make him understand you had nothing to do with what happened. I'll do this for you, Jess, I promise."

"You're not too good at promises, Dane," she reminded him. "I appreciate your concern, but it won't do any good. He's gone now."

The room fell to near darkness. Jessica sat on the floor, unaware that the sun had gone and she had not turned on a single lamp in the house. Her swollen eyes, rimmed with the red of a million tears, could tell no difference between day and night. On the table, her phone blinked incessantly with nine messages, unanswered. Oh, she'd listened to the callers as they'd left their words for her later review, but no voice had been the one she wanted to hear.

Mac had not returned. It had been four days...or was it five now? It was hard to say; after the first two lonely nights she'd become unconscious of the hour, the day, the weather.

He'd called once, the morning after the first night.

"If you need to reach me in an emergency, call Bill." His words had been crisp and impartial.

"Mac, please," she had begun tentatively.

"Not now, Jessica." He'd hung up after delivering his edict without saying good-bye.

The nine messages? Both Roxanne and Dane had called twice; Mac's boss, his accountant, his agent; some travel agency looking for Mac. And, Teddy Langley, Jessica's own agent.

She'd called Roxanne once, of course; Roxanne, her best friend and the only one she felt would truly understand. And Dane had called from the airport; Mac would not return the messages he'd left all over town.

Roxanne had finally realized that Jessica wouldn't or couldn't answer the phone and trekked across the Valley almost daily to care for her dearest friend.

She let herself in now, as Jessica sat alone in the dark.

"Jess? Where are you?"

"Here, Rox."

"It's dark in here," Roxanne mumbled, reaching for a table lamp. "How you feeling, honey?"

"Feel? I don't. My feelings are all gone."

"Okay. Get up. Let's do something. A movie?"

Jessica didn't respond.

"Anybody call?" Roxanne ventured lamely.

"Teddy." Jessica's eyes had not moved from their gaze out the back at the pool, the automatic garden lights having just come on.

"Dane's gone?"

"He called from the airport. He delayed his flight until last night...trying to reach Mac."

They did nothing the whole evening. Roxanne had brought a suitcase and temporarily moved into Jessica's old bedroom, not wanting her friend to be alone. She shared her belief that Mac would see his way clear to come home soon. Or rather, she *hoped.*

The days became a week, then nearly two; Roxanne spent half her time commuting between Mac's canyon home and her own condominium across town, and even Tom Jarrick spent time in the MacKendall household. Jessica remained despondent and communicated little with her friends. Roxanne made numerous phone calls trying to reach Mac and listened with shocked ears as someone at Castle Studios told her *Doctor Jim* was no longer in production. They hadn't seen Cory MacKendall in two weeks.

Roxanne withheld this news from Jessica, fearing it more damaging than not. Desperate, she finally dialed Bill Campbell's number, Mac's former co-star and friend. Bill answered, and Roxanne took a deep breath.

"This is Roxanne Boudreau."

"Roxie? Hi, it's Bill; we met at the wedding."

"Yes, I remember. Uh, sorry to bother you, Bill, but I need to talk to Mac. It's important."

"Unfortunately, he's out. Is there a message? Is everything okay? With Jessie, I mean?"

"No. Well, yes. She's fine. That is, she's okay, health-wise...Oh Lord, I'm not saying this right. What the hell is Mac doing, Bill?"

Quiet for a moment, Bill finally spoke with hesitation. "I'm sorry, Roxanne, I wish I could tell you. He's sleeping here, but that's about it. He's tighter than a clam. He only said that I should let him know if anyone called about his wife, in an urgent manner, you know?"

"You really don't know where he is?"

"He's working, I believe. That's all I know."

"Thanks, Bill. I really appreciate the information. Their baby is due in less than five months. If you see him, tell him...ask him to call me? I'm working at the Langley Agency."

Try as they might, her friends couldn't convince Jessica to leave the house for anything other than her monthly pre-natal exam. She was convinced that the minute she left, Mac would be there, accepting her apologies—and forgiveness —and ready to take her back. But as days passed, Roxanne lost hope that it would ever happen. He hadn't even returned her call.

She tried to get Jessica involved in various projects, encouraging her to finish decorating the baby's room; Jessica had not set foot in the nursery since the day Mac walked out. She did, however, make an effort to keep herself fit and healthy; for the sake of the baby, she offhandedly told Roxanne. Religiously taking her vitamins, walking the grounds in the morning, and watching the baby-care videos given her by Dr. Anderson, Jessica refused to let her emotional state affect the development of the tiny infant growing within her.

It was after the viewing of one such video that Jessica became mesmerized, staring spellbound at the television where her husband's adoring smile was offered to some unknown actress. The DVD had finished, and the television switched to *Doctor Jim*, already in progress on the network. She watched in hypnotic amazement as he kissed the woman with great tenderness. Jessica's heart lurched painfully in her chest and tears spring back into her eyes once again.

Only something new was happening. Her hands shot to her abdomen; what was that? A curious flutter, like the wings of butterflies brushing ever so lightly against the insides of her womb...no, no, more like a small, bubbly effervescence. It was the baby! The baby moved!

The revulsion she felt watching Mac kiss the actress subsided. Here was something new, and wonderful. She left the couch and crawled to the television screen, placing her hands lovingly against his face on the screen. "Oh, Mac..." she whispered.

In the doorway, Roxanne's eyes filled with tears watching Jessica's pathetic gesture. This could not go on much longer.

"Get up, you lazy-bones!" Roxanne called to Jessica the next morning.

Jessica only moaned softly and pulled a pillow over her head.

"Up! Now! We've got to beat the crowds!"

"What crowds..."

"Nordstrom's is having their Labor Day sale! And you, my dear, have *got* to start wearing some maternity clothes."

"No. I can't go."

"You're going if I have to get Tom over here to load you into the car. Now get up."

Somehow, Roxanne persuaded Jessica to go shopping. Removing her from "Casa MacKendall," as Roxanne called it, was good for Jessica, and her spirits lifted noticeably. They even entered a baby store and looked at layette items, Jessica eyeing tiny pink dresses with delight.

"You want a girl?" Roxanne asked, smiling.

"Oh, I don't know," Jessica said wistfully. "Either will be wonderful...right now, all I want is my husband back." Despite the sorrow in her voice, Jessica managed a small smile that was encouraging to Roxanne.

"He'll be back, Jess. Mark my words. Healing takes time."

"Healing is slow when you're alone. I know that, but he doesn't. If he'd just come home and talk to me, we could fix it."

Roxanne was impressed. This was the most Jessica had spoken about Mac since the first few days after he left.

They ate lunch at the mall.

"What do you think about writing him a letter?" Roxanne ventured.

"I did, but I tore it up. It was morose," Jessica admitted.

"It might not be a bad idea," Roxanne coaxed. "Morose or not, what's the worst that could happen? Even if he called to dispute it, at least he'd be talking, right?"

That night, Jessica sat down to write the letter. Torn between pouring her heart out and being light and newsy, like in the old days, she opted for straight forward and honest. She knew her husband well.

September 1st

My Dearest Cory,

How do I begin to tell you how I feel, how filled with pain and remorse I am in your absence? It is hard enough to deal with what has happened without the added barrier of your silence. There is no true "excuse" for what has happened, no salve to cover our wounds, but you should know the truth about that day.

Dane, as you probably already know, has gone to Southeast Asia for a six-month stay. You happened home just as he had stopped in to say good-bye. Unfortunately, it is not in Dane's nature to do things in a small way, as I am sure you are aware, and his parting display of affection was not what it seemed. You saw what you expected, what you wanted to see, not what was really happening.

Mac, my darling, I know you are hurting beyond belief or you would be here with me now. Please know that I, too, am hurting from the absence of your touch, your smile, your love; and most importantly, the loss of your trust. I know, that despite this terrible impasse in our lives, it would comfort you to know that our baby is doing fine and growing healthy. The miracle of his (or her!) stirrings within me is incredible. I want so badly to share this with you.

Please turn your eyes to your heart and soul and find me living there, waiting for you. I must confess, my first instinct was to flee to Utah, again, to hide out with Chrissie until you made a move to show that you wanted me back. But I've learned something new—I've gained a new discipline from my loving, cherished husband. I'm ready to fight, Mac. Please—come home and fight with me.

Yours, forever, Jessica

SIXTEEN

Devastation, Devotion

New Zealand was not as he expected. He had a few days to poke around before filming would begin, and he aimlessly walked the streets in Wellington, hiding behind dark glasses, hands in his jacket pockets. Small shops lined the street. Mac briefly explored these, pausing to handle various souvenirs and curios that caught his eye. The people were particularly friendly.

The street ended at the dock, and here Mac took in the sights, sounds and smells of a small part of New Zealand's fishing industry as he walked. He passed bins, crates full of live crabs, lobsters, mollusks; baskets filled with freshly caught fish.

He thought on the letter he'd hastily penned before leaving the United States.

9/02

Dear Jessica,

I regret that I cannot deliver this news in person, but I'm not yet ready to see you; my thoughts are not particularly rational and I fear I may do irreparable damage to an already bad situation.

Yes, it is me running this time, my love, I wish things were different, wish that what has happened had not. By the time you read this I will have landed in Wellington, New Zealand, to begin work on a new project. It is unfortunately without enthusiasm that I approach this unexpected windfall to my career. I am sure you know by now that "Doc Jim" has met its demise. This film is one I've wanted to do for many years, and it should do very well.

Jessica, I wish I could explain what is going on inside of me, the constant nagging, crashing around of anger and spite that won't end. I can't, won't pretend that I am anything but incensed about finding Dane in our home with you in his selfish, greedy embrace. It drives me to the point of fury every time I think about it. I'm sorry, but you know and have always known how I feel about you and Dane. I want to be different about it, but I can't. Please believe that I am trying, every minute of every day, to sort this out and make it go away.

I know this is difficult for you, too. I sometimes feel you are just an innocent in all this; you have a knack for being in the wrong place at the wrong time, especially where Dane Pierce is concerned. It's my expectation that he will not be far from you while I'm gone, and I know, realistically, there is nothing I can do to stop him from pursuing you. And I won't ask you again, Jessica. I'm on my knees only once.

I will ask you this: please take care of yourself and our child. It is the promise of this baby that keeps my heart from dying entirely within the turmoil that exists between us. I will be there to help deliver him into our world, and maybe this will be the key—?

I will be in and out of the Plaza International Hotel in Wellington. I'm told we're there for three months. I hope you will call me in any emergency that should arise. I have said a brief good-bye to Megan; she doesn't know about us. I would appreciate your discretion when you speak to her, it would be hurtful for her to know that we're having problems.

This is all I have to say. There is, of course, much, much more, if only I were not so very locked up inside. Please try to understand. I love you.

Mac

The letter was crushed painfully in Jessica's clenched, damp fist. She crumbled onto the bed, dissolving into tears. She could see Mac's face before her, the hurt in his solemn brown eyes, the accusing look as he stood in the doorway that awful day. She began whispering his name repeatedly, urgently, and incoherently. Holding her pregnant belly in her arms, she rocked softly on the bed, closed her eyes tightly, and wished him back with all her will.

Mac answered his hotel room door in irritation. He'd been trying to nap but sleep had become an elusive luxury, no longer an option. A hotel employee handed him a FedEx International envelope. He took it, fishing a bill from his pocket for the bellman.

It was from Bill Campbell. Inside, he found a note and an envelope.

Mac—this arrived the day you left. Thought it might be important. Hope all's okay. I'm going up to Tahoe for a few days but will be back Saturday. Call if you need anything. —Bill

The letter was, of course, from Jessica. Mac quickly tore it open and unfolded the pages with trembling hands.

"*My Dearest Cory...*" Tears invaded the corners of his eyes, blurring his vision as he stared at the words. "*My Dearest Cory...*" he read again, blinking.

He rubbed his eyes periodically while reading. Suddenly he froze to his spot. Dane, gone? For six months? How could he not have known that? Then he remembered the stack of messages from Dane, the day after the incident; and his angry, stubborn refusal to take Dane's calls. So that was it.

Mac fell back on the bed, his face drained of all warmth. His eyes again filled with tears. Her words burned into the insides of his eyelids. "*Come home and fight with me.*" God! He shook his head to clear it. He remembered, so clearly, the night she'd come home after dinner with Dane. When he had been so angry, tossing her car keys into the bushes so she could not run away again. He'd taunted her, baited her, harassed her until she'd raised her fists to his and finally fought for his love.

And now, here was proof that she'd learned. She wouldn't run from him again. She was ready to stand ground and make him understand. And where was he? Eight thousand miles away!

His tears darkened the sleeve of his shirt as he threw his arm across his eyes in despair. *I'm a raving, jealous fool,* he thought.

But that God-damned Dane Pierce just couldn't leave us alone.

Running his fingers over the stationery, he touched her words reverently. She'd sent this off before receiving his letter.

Standing quickly from the bed, he grabbed his hotel key and left the room. In the hotel bar, he met Sal Cicerello, the film's director, and they ordered drinks.

"So Mac, what's eating you? Something going on?"

"When do we start shooting, Sal?"

"Tomorrow. Cold feet?"

"No. Just curious."

"You just got married, didn't you?"

Mac took a long draught of the ale placed before him. He nodded.

"Got a photo?"

Reluctantly pulling out his wallet, Mac slowly flipped through the photos until he came to his favorite; a candid shot of Jessica strapping Megan to a carousel horse at the Oxnard pier. The opposing photo was of himself and Jessica dancing at her birthday party. He handed the open wallet to Sal.

"Real pics? Do guys still carry photos?"

"Why wouldn't I?"

"Well, cellphones, you know. All my family photos are on my iPhone." Sal looked from the snapshots to Mac's eyes, still too bright from his reaction to Jessica's letter. "Looks too sweet to leave at home, Mac. Why isn't she with you?"

Mac wet his lips, then cleared his throat. It did no good, his voice still cracked when he spoke. "She's...uh...pregnant."

Sal nodded but his doubt was obvious. Mac knew his excuse was lame but didn't really care to come up with anything better. Instead, he ordered another tankard of ale.

"Well. Congratulations then. When's the baby due?"

"First part of January." Mac forced a stilted smile.

September 14th was Roxanne's birthday. Jessica busied herself all day with the baking and decorating of an exquisite cake, and the wrapping of an assortment of gifts she'd purchased. Glancing at the calendar as she worked, she stared at the carefully marked off dates: it had been twenty-three days since Mac had driven away.

She no longer felt it necessary to sit by the phone. Now that she knew Mac was in New Zealand, it was unlikely that he'd be popping in for his clothes or calling to chat about the weather. The ache inside had not gone away, not by a long shot; but she'd settled into a routine, a waiting game, knowing somewhere deep inside that Mac would eventually return.

Tonight, she would make her grandest effort to be happy at Roxanne's birthday dinner. There would be only seven at the casual get-together; besides Tom and Roxanne, Tom's teenaged son and his girlfriend were coming, and another couple with whom Roxanne had made friends at work.

Everyone brought potluck. Jessica eyed the bottles of wine cooling in the refrigerator with regret. She could have used a few hundred glasses of White Zinfandel over the past two months! As if in response to her thought, the baby gave her a swift kick in the side.

Jessica almost enjoyed herself during dinner. Her cake was a masterpiece, and Roxanne embraced her warmly after they'd cut and served it together.

"I love you, Jess," she said tearfully. "I wish so bad..."

"Shhh—" Jessica warned, placing a finger to her lips. "Don't say it. I'm okay. Really." She picked up a stack of dirty dishes to move to the kitchen sink, and the phone rang. Abruptly she stopped, in the middle of the kitchen, her face suddenly ashen as she stared at Roxanne. Roxanne, too, froze in her steps.

"Probably the L.A. Times," Jessica said softly, carefully placing the dishes into the sink. "Could you grab it?"

"Sure, honey," Roxanne offered, reaching for the phone. "Hello?"

Jessica watched her from the corner of her eye as she slowly began rinsing scraps from the first plate into the disposal.

"Oh, hi...no, it's not a bad time..." Roxanne turned her back, lowering her voice, and Jessica strained to hear.

"She's...bearing up, under the circumstances. Are you...coming home?" Roxanne stole a quick look at Jessica, who had stopped and was staring at her expectantly. "I see. Of course, I'll get her." Roxanne held out the receiver to Jessica.

Their eyes communicated silently as Jessica took the phone from her with trembling hands. Swallowing hard, Jessica listened first before speaking, finally managing a rushed "Hello?"

"Hi." His one word, and Jessica's legs began to buckle. Roxanne rushed a kitchen chair under her as she slid down the wall.

"Hi, Mac," she finally responded. Roxanne hovered nearby, wanting to afford Jessica some privacy but careful not to stray too far should her friend need some support.

"Is everything okay?" he asked, his voice almost emotionless.

"Of course. I...I got your letter. I understand New Zealand is...beautiful."

"It's different." She heard him sigh, and his voice became impatient. "I just needed to make sure you're..."

"I'm fine. I'm just terrific."

"Look, Jess, I can't...can't talk about anything right now. I can't be...objective about what happened. Try to understand, okay?"

She nodded, tears stinging her tightly closed eyes.

"Okay?" he repeated.

"Sure," she whispered, then cleared her throat. "I'm sorry you feel that way."

"I probably should go."

"Yeah. It's Roxie's birthday. I have to go, too."

"Tell her...Happy Birthday."

"Good-bye, Mac."

He didn't say good-bye. Jessica hung up and curled, spineless, into the chair just as Tom entered the kitchen to find out what had happened to the girls.

Gently he knelt and lifted Jessica into his arms and carried her into the bedroom, laying her carefully down on the plaid comforter that topped Mac's bed.

"He still loves me," she murmured.

"Of course he does," Roxanne consoled her. "He wouldn't have called otherwise. This is really hard for him, too, you know."

"Is that what he said to you?"

"No. But I could tell."

September ended. The month with all the dates crossed off was gone, and a fresh page took its place. Three months to go, and she'd be a mom.

She'd finally gone ahead and continued her work on the nursery, and it was nearly decorated. She had held out, however, on buying a crib or any other furniture. She would wait on these, just as she waited on Mac.

On a whim, she called Megan to see if she'd like to shop for some of the baby necessities she had listed with her sister's help over the phone. Megan was not at home, so Jessica left a message on Linda MacKendall's voicemail. When the phone rang twenty minutes later, she jumped to answer it.

"Miss Jessica Taylor?"

"Yes." She realized belatedly that the caller did not ask for her by her new name.

"My name is Ross Mayer. I'm a doctor, with the U.S. Embassy in Phnom Pehn."

"A doctor, did you say? The connection is poor."

"Yes, Miss Taylor."

"Dane? Is this about Dane Pierce?"

"I'm sorry, Miss, there's been...an accident. I've been asked to call you."

"Oh my God...what is it? Is Dane all right?"

"He's been hospitalized. His condition is critical, Miss Taylor. Your name is listed to be notified in case of emergency."

Jessica suddenly felt dizzy and sat down. "Tell me what's happened to him, Doctor."

"He was involved in an altercation with some local people. There was apparently a dispute of some kind, Mr. Pierce had been drinking...he was assaulted and, truthfully, out-numbered."

"He's been beaten? Oh God—" Jessica bit into her fist, adrenaline rushing through her body. "He's...going to live, Doctor?"

"His chances are fifty-fifty. He's a strong man, but under the circumstances I felt it best to call."

"Can I speak to him?"

"I'm afraid not. He's still unconscious at this time."

Jessica swallowed hard and reached for a pencil. "Tell me where he is."

As the doctor rattled off the details, Jessica scratched them out onto the margin of an old newspaper lying nearby.

"Dr. Mayer, is he alone? There was a Mr. Peter Welles, and Mr. Pierce's son, Alexander, traveling with him."

"I don't recall anyone, other than some co-workers, studio people, I believe. You understand, the Embassy is making every effort to keep a tight lid on this... situation."

"Thank you for calling, Dr. Mayer. Thank you so much. And Doctor, if Dane, *when* Mr. Pierce comes around...Tell him I'm on my way."

"Roxie? It's me. Will you be here soon?"

"Yeah, Jess. You sound upset. Did Mac call?"

"No, but I need to talk to you."

"I'm leaving now."

It didn't take Jessica long to relate the brief but startling story to her friend, who looked on in amazement.

"What? No way, lady. You can't just go running off to Cambodia."

"I have to go. I have no choice. Dane may be...dying." Jessica was tossing random articles into a suitcase with determination.

"Jessie, please, listen to reason! Maybe we can have him transported home or something! You can't go there alone! Oh God, this is awful...at least wait until I can get in touch with Tom—"

"My mind is made up, Rox. I've already bought my ticket. Dane needs me. He needs someone, he's virtually all alone. I'm the closest thing he has to a relative. I called Rita, and she basically just blew me off. His parents are dead; he has no siblings."

"What about Mac?"

"Well, what about Mac? It's been six weeks, Roxie. *Six weeks.* He's forsaken me. And our child." She huffed out a sigh as she haphazardly threw the lid closed on the case. "Dane loves me. It's the least I can do. He saved my life, remember? And he put me in touch with my feelings for Mac. I owe him everything I have, including my sorry life."

"Your 'sorry' life? You even sound like Dane." Roxanne accused, leaping for the phone as it rang. "Oh, Tom, thank God you got my message. How soon can you get here?"

Tom drove onto the gravel road just as Jessica tried to force her suitcase into the trunk of the Miata. It wouldn't fit, so she grunted and hoisted it out, attempting to toss it into the bed of Mac's old Ford truck.

"You are crazy, woman. You can't drive that old heap in your condition. Have you forgotten you're six months pregnant?" Tom admonished Jessica as he yanked the suitcase away from her in irritation.

"Please, Tom, don't try to stop me. My flight leaves in three hours. I have to get to the airport!"

Tom sighed and held the suitcase out of her feeble reach.

Stomping her foot, she screamed at him. "God damn it, Tom Jarrick, put that down, now. Look, I have other friends, and I'll find someone to help if you won't."

Roxanne and Tom shared a helpless moment.

"C'mon," Tom said assertively, putting his arm around Jessica. "Come inside. We'll work something out."

Jessica stared at him suspiciously but complied.

They sat at the kitchen table, and Jessica reiterated her entire conversation with the doctor.

"Did you happen to, uh, call Mac?"

"Mac? Why would I do that? He'd probably fly into Cambodia just to watch Dane die!"

"Jessie, I think you're being unfair." Tom sighed. "Listen. You cannot go alone. I won't let you. Not to mention that most airlines won't allow a pregnant woman on board in her last trimester. But I understand how you feel; Dane Pierce is a friend of mine, too. I'm willing to escort you to Phnom Penh, on one condition. You call Mac and tell him you're going."

Jessica's face paled. Call Mac? Tell him she was flying to Cambodia to be with Dane? The realization that this news would probably finish their marriage was sobering. She sat silently considering Tom's proposition for several heart wrenching moments. Finally, she lifted her chin to speak.

"I have to do this. If Dane should die—"

"You can't prevent that, you understand."

"I'll call Mac. He's already lost faith in me; he couldn't get much angrier than he already is, but I can't let Dane die...alone." Tears streamed down her cheeks as she stood and turned away.

Roxanne rushed to her, embracing her tightly. After a few moments, Jessica pulled away. Silently she went to the phone, picking up the number of the telephone in Wellington that would ring next to Mac's bed. She'd placed a copy of the number next to every phone in the house, just in case.

The baby was kicking furiously.

She dialed the number as Tom and Roxanne exchanged grim looks.

Two rings, three, four rings.

"Hello?" He'd been sleeping, she could tell. The sound of his voice embraced her heavy heart. Jessica let out the breath she'd been holding.

"Hi," she said simply, closing her eyes tightly against the flood of tears threatening to drown her words.

"Are you okay?" he asked quickly, the sleepiness shaken from his voice at the sound of hers.

"Yes." Jessica mustered what little courage she could and ventured on. "I know you won't like hearing this, but something's happened, and I need to tell you."

"The baby?"

"No, the baby's fine. It's Dane. He's been...*had* a terrible accident. He's critical; he may not live."

"Oh Jesus..." Mac murmured something unintelligible. "Is he still in Malaysia?"

"No. He's in some hospital in Phnom Penh. He's alone, Mac. He has no next of kin."

There was silence on the line as Mac considered the meaning of her words. "You're going, then?"

Jessica bit her lip painfully, her body shuddering with barely suppressed sobs. "I think I should." Her words were barely a whisper, but he heard her clearly.

"Do you think it's wise to do that by yourself?" Mac's question was tight, guarded.

Jessica cleared her throat. "Tom's going with me."

Mac's sigh of relief was audible. "Good. Be...be careful, Jessica. Are you feeling okay?"

"Yes. I'm fine."

"Let me know how...how he ends up, okay?"

"Yeah, sure." Jessica considered Mac's response and carefully crafted her next words. "Look. I don't know why I do the things I do. There've been many times in my life when I stood silent and just let things happen, terrible things. I stayed with a man who beat me within inches of my life and killed my baby. And yeah, I've stayed blindly loyal to another man who thought nothing of putting my marriage in jeopardy. My marriage to the best man on the planet. Am I questioning my motives? I am. But there's room for forgiveness, Mac. On many levels. And this is one time when I can't just stand silent."

"I see."

"I hope you do. I really hope so."

"Good-bye, Jess. I—" Mac paused, obviously changing his mind about what he intended to say. "I've got to get some sleep."

"Sure. Good-bye."

He'd been sleeping. The phone's ringer had set his heart to pounding. Now, hanging it up, he glanced at the clock beside his bed. It was 4 a.m., and her call had wakened him from a disturbing dream, just another of many he'd had since leaving her. The sound of her voice flowed like a mountain spring over his parched soul.

Mac lowered his head and ran his hand across his face. He fought the temptation to allow anguish to consume him, but he could not escape the sickening feeling that had engulfed him at the news; his wife was traveling around the world, not to him, but to be at Dane Pierce's bedside. Nonetheless, she'd called him first and that was something. She'd also called him the best man on the planet.

He didn't bother going back to bed.

"Mac, you look like hell. I like it," Sal said to him on the set later in the day. "Now let's see some anger. Some incredible, gut-ripping hostility. These guys have just slaughtered ten of your animals. Shredded your sheep. I want you to think fury; black, thick, burning rage."

Mac touched his upper lip in thought. The new mustache was uncomfortable, but necessary. He knew rage, all right. These people had never seen the fury he'd known in the last two months. He looked at the sheep, then at Cal Trenton, his opponent: he saw Dane Pierce. Building the fury into the scene, ad-libbing the lines as he went, Mac delivered what the camera wanted to see.

Sal was elated. Cory MacKendall was a driven man.

Later, again in the hotel bar, Sal sought him out to congratulate him.

"Buy you a drink, Sal?"

"Don't mind if you do," Sal agreed happily. "What'll we have?"

"You look like a man who can handle a few shooters." Mac grinned at the Greek man with the Italian name. And this night he walked to his room on his own accord, hoping the tequila would afford him some much-needed sleep.

·♥·♥·♥·♥·♥·

The Boeing airliner belonging to Singapore Airlines touched down at Phnom Penh International Airport twenty minutes late; not bad considering the thirty-minute delay in leaving LAX. The airport was terrifyingly foreign, and Jessica felt eternally grateful for Tom's presence as he guided her through the crowds of people. She could never have done this alone. But she would have tried anyway, she thought stubbornly. Fortunately, both of their passports were in order, Tom's from a recent trip to Japan; Jessica's was still warm from the Caribbean.

They hailed a cab. Tom stowed the abbreviated luggage they had carried on in the trunk as Jessica slid into the back seat. Tom joined her and asked the English-speaking driver to take them to the hospital.

The driver stared suspiciously at Jessica's protruding stomach and hastily pulled away from the curb. Tom quickly explained that his companion was not in labor, and a gentler ride would prevent her from commencing it. Relieved, the driver slowed to a normal pace and soon deposited them at the front door of American Medical Center where Dane Pierce lay clinging to life.

After endless questioning, they were directed to Dane's room. Security had been blanketed around the American celebrity at the request of the Embassy, hoping to keep speculation about Dane's somewhat political project to a minimum. Hesitant, Jessica timidly pushed open the door and tiptoed in; Tom waited just outside.

She could not stop the gasp from escaping her throat when she saw him. Jessica stared at Dane's unrecognizable form in shock and disbelief. This could not be the tremendously attractive man she'd met a year ago.

Dane's forehead was wrapped in a bandage; below it, one eye was swollen shut and the other bore a gash from the outside corner through his eyebrow, now neatly stitched closed. His cheeks were bruised, his lips split and puffy. A large, square bandage covered some injury to his neck. His left arm was in a cast, and she could see another white dressing wrapped around the middle of his chest; his knuckles were also swollen and abraded. She could only imagine what atrocities had been committed to his lower body, covered with a clean white sheet.

Jessica nearly fainted. Hot tears filled her eyes and a lump rose in her throat that threatened to strangle her; weakly she groped for the chair next to his bed. He was still unconscious. An IV tube dripped steadily into his right arm, and an oxygen tube extended into his nose.

The slow, steady beeping of a machine monitored his heartbeat. Jessica took a ragged breath. With quivering fingers, she reached out and touched his cheek, trying to get a sense that this mess of a man was really Dane. Beloved Dane Pierce, megastar and heart-throb of ten million women worldwide.

"Oh, Dane...what have you done? You've certainly gotten yourself into trouble this time," Jessica murmured softly.

She watched him silently for ten minutes or so before Tom joined her. He grimaced at the sight of Dane's condition and pulled up a chair.

"I got the story." Tom sighed, assessing Jessica's tolerance for what he had learned. "Seems our boy was found carousing with the wrong woman."

Jessica's face fell, a sad frown distorting her features. Dane would never learn. *Never.*

"Peter took Alexander home the day before this happened. Dane decided it wasn't safe here and sent them back. Best I can tell, they don't even know about this." Tom paused, looking at Dane with regret. "He has some serious internal injuries, and his left leg is pretty messed up."

Tom left her after a time to seek a hotel room for them, and to call Roxanne as promised. Jessica remained at Dane's side throughout the night, and the following day as well. Try as he might, Tom could not persuade her to leave until the following night when she finally agreed to go to the hotel to freshen up. He promised to stay with Dane until she returned.

In the hotel room she collapsed from exhaustion.

This time she did not wake up in a hospital herself. She awoke, alone with the dawn, the child within her violently pummeling her insides. She ached from having slept awkwardly, fully clothed, on the bed, but she was rested. Finding her suitcase stowed in the closet, she quickly showered and changed, then summoned a bellman to get her transportation back to the hospital. She remembered her pre-natal vitamins and paused to gulp them down with some bottled water Tom had left her. Just before leaving the room, the phone on the nightstand purred an alien sound. She nearly ignored it, assuming the caller had misdialed; but habit prevailed and instead she reached for the receiver.

"Hello?"

"Jess?"

Jessica sat down on the bed. The last voice she'd expected to hear was Mac's, and she suddenly felt warm all over.

"Yes, it's me," she replied softly, waiting for him to speak again.

"Your cell isn't working."

"No, I...didn't have a chance to set it up for international."

"I just thought I'd check...how's Dane?"

"He's...well, there's been no change. He's in a coma." The image of Dane's pathetic figure lying in the hospital rose in her mind. "If he comes out of it, there's no telling how long...it may take months of rehabilitation. He was beaten, Mac, they beat him so badly, they ran him over with a car..."

"I'm...I'm sorry to hear it. Whatever he is, whatever he's done, I'm sure he didn't deserve that." Mac coughed, and Jessica knew it was forced. "Jessie?"

"Yes, I'm here," she managed, her voice choked with emotion.

"Are you all right?"

"Of course I am," she lied, her stamina wavering.

"You sound upset."

"I'm weary, Mac. I'm tired of...everything," she confessed, trying not to sob. "I want Dane to get well. I want to go home, and have this baby, and I want you to come back and be with me." She paused to regroup, then continued speaking before she lost her nerve; or perhaps it was just the end of her patience.

"I'm sorry I—I know you don't want to hear this, Mac, so, go back to your life, and I'll go back to mine. Only, you might as well know something else, too. I'm not leaving here until I can either take Dane home or bury him. And it better be soon because I don't want to have the baby here. I *will*, though, if I have to, so if you want to be around when your child is born, be prepared to fly into Cambodia." She hurried on before he could respond. "And Mac, I would give anything, anything if I could change what happened, I love you with all my heart, and I'm hanging up now because I am not strong enough to hear you rave at me. Goodbye."

Mac's eyebrows were high with astonishment, and he stared at the dead phone in his hand. Was that really Jessica? Gently he put the receiver down and lay back on his hotel bed. Absently he tugged at his mustache and randomly examined the various imperfections in the ceiling. Maybe things were going to be okay. Maybe...but she was still with Dane.

SEVENTEEN

Dane's Good Deed

October 15th dawned in Phnom Penh just as the 14th had and the 16th undoubtedly would. Jessica had kept her vigil at Dane's bedside for two weeks, and while his wounds seemed to be healing, he had yet to regain consciousness. The doctors explained that the nature of his head injury prevented air transport, but that the swelling was diminishing, and they expected to see some change soon.

"Soon..." Jessica muttered, playing her fingers across her bulging stomach. "Soon, Dane," she said aloud. "I've only got ten weeks left. We have to go home, dear." She stood up and leaned across him, peering into his face. The tube had been removed; he was breathing easy now. The intra-venous drip remained, and a therapist had begun exercising his muscles daily. The cuts to his face were beginning to heal, although his right eye remained swollen. She was told his internal injuries were improving.

Jessica stood and walked to the small window. The view was unremarkable, mostly of a parking lot and haphazardly parked cars. "I don't even know what I'm doing here. What are you to me, anyway? You're not my husband, although there was a time when I practiced writing your last name after my first. You're not my lover, not anymore, of course. And I wonder if you can still call yourself my friend after what you did." Was that it? Were they friends? Her secret heart said otherwise; she loved Dane in a way she could never have explained, even to herself. Fondness, affection... and some kind of misguided responsibility to care for him. Strong enough to risk her marriage to the man who was her husband. Her lover. Her *best* friend. She went back to the bedside.

"You are one big, fat, pain in the ass, Dane Pierce," she said while caressing his cheek. "You and your damned sexual appetite. Jesus! Can't keep your hands to yourself, ever! You've got a lot of nerve making me come all the way over here to tend you." On she railed, pacing the room, her voice elevating and echoing off the sterile white walls. Amidst her frustration her vocabulary became as raw as her nerves, and she surprised herself at the profanity she uttered; yet she continued to shout the words into his face. Somehow it seemed fitting to swear at Dane.

"I...love it when...you...talk...dirty."

She looked at him in shock; the whispered, dry-throated words had come from Dane's parched lips. Speechless, she leaned closer to his face in wonderment.

"If I promise...to wake up...and go home with you, will you stop shouting... and...kiss...me?" His voice was a harsh whisper.

"Oh, Dane...Dane..." Jessica rushed her arms around his neck and hugged him tightly. Tenderly she kissed his forehead, his eyes, his cheek, then gently pressed her soft, moist lips to his taut, dry, healing ones. Weakly he attempted to bring his right arm around her, and he struggled to open his eyes.

Dane squinted at her in the sunlight, and she quickly turned to draw the shade. He stared at her swollen belly.

"Holy shit—I must have taken...one helluva nap." His slow, broken speech sounded hoarse and raspy, but typically Dane.

"Oh, Dane. Thank God! I'm getting you out of here right away. I'm taking you home." Tears glistened on her pink cheeks.

"The film..."

"The film can wait, are you crazy? You almost died, you fool!" Jessica pressed the call button to summon a nurse.

With the nurse came Tom Jarrick, his eyes lighting up at the sight of Dane's lucidity.

"Tom! He's okay! We've got to make arrangements to get him home. Let's get him transferred as soon as possible!"

"Whoa, lady, settle down. We'd better talk to his doctors first, don't you think?"

Despite his improvement, Jessica refused to leave Dane, helping him to begin some solid food and painstakingly attending to his needs. The nurses weren't taking near good enough care of him, she proclaimed to Tom in the cafeteria. She learned how to change his dressings and to sponge down his battered body as he lay helpless in the bed.

"This is a switch," he teased her as she ran the cool, damp sponge down his good arm. "*You* working on *me*."

"Be quiet," she warned. "I might break it."

"Tom get off okay?"

"Yes, he left this morning. Roxie's going nuts at home alone."

"What day is it?"

"October 21st. Why do you ask?"

"My son, Alex. His birthday is the 30th. I want to be home."

"You will be, darling. I'm fighting every day to get you out of here."

Dane gently rested his hand on her tummy. "Why are you here?"

His question caught her off guard. Hadn't she repeatedly asked herself the same question? Recalling her words to Mac, wherein she'd so self-righteously claimed she needed to stop standing by while wrongs were committed? And yet, staying with Dane was wrong in itself. True, Dane was her friend. There was clearly some unshakable bond commanding her actions. But Mac was her husband. Stubborn, yes. He'd hurt her, true. But was playing nursemaid to Dane a noble gesture, or an act of revenge?

"When does this happen?" Dane asked, still caressing her baby bump.

Jessica moved his hand away. "I'm due January 7th. But babies seem impatient in my family. Could be as soon as Christmas."

"You should be home, with your husband, sweetie." The green eyes had regained their sparkle.

"You're right, Dane. I *should* be home, with Mac. But since Mac isn't there, I'd just as soon be here with you."

"What do you mean Mac isn't there? Where the hell is he?"

Jessica cleared her throat. It still hurt, badly. "New Zealand. Doing a film."

"You mean that son-of-a-bitch left you *alone*? Why didn't you tell me?"

She didn't have an answer for him, but in her heart, she knew why.

"This is still about me, isn't it?"

"I'm not sure anymore. We've been separated since...since that day. I haven't seen Mac since you have, Dane."

Dane looked away, his grief and anger evident. She could feel his pulse quicken beneath her fingers as she continued bathing him. Finally, he turned his darkened eyes back on hers. He reached up, wincing at the pain he suffered in nearly every part of his body, and touched her cheek tenderly with his aching fingers.

"Sometimes I wish I'd just left you alone." He smiled that smile, telling her that he was hurting inside. "I think I've caused you a lot of grief."

Jessica smiled back, accepting his humility with gratitude. He really had put her through hell; still, she had allowed him to do so.

"But I'm going to tell you something about that husband of yours..." he continued, slowly shaking his head. "We may both love you, honey, but that's where the similarity ends. He's a worse fool than I am."

"Dane, please—"

"Now wait, I know you hate it when I talk about Mac. But you've got to understand, for all his wonderful, straight-arrow bullshit, he doesn't know you as well as I do. If I had known about this, I would have gone to New Zealand myself and dragged him back, and he'd have been swinging his damned fists at me the whole time. I should have never left without pinning him down and making him understand."

"You tried, Dane. You even delayed your trip."

"He's a hard-headed asshole. If you were my wife, you think I'd let you go running off to Timbuktu to nurse my worst enemy back to health? Not on your life, Jessica."

"He didn't have a choice. I told him I was going. He knows he couldn't stop me."

"Oh, he *knows* that, does he? Bull. Is that what you wanted, for him to say, 'Oh, okay, honey, run along'? You know what I would have said?"

"No. What would you have said, Dane?" she humored him, knowing he was going to get this all off his chest one way or another.

"I wouldn't have been in fucking New Zealand to begin with. And I would have told you that Dane Pierce can take care of himself. And I would have tied you to the damned bedposts, if necessary. And then—"

"I get the picture."

"Do you, really? Look, I'm not saying he doesn't love you. Hell, he's been ga-ga over you since the first. He's just...screwed up. He doesn't really know how to handle you."

"And you do."

"Damned right I do," he said softly, painfully extending his hand to her head again, this time grasping her hair and pulling it, coaxing her toward his face.

She kissed him on the corner of his mouth, and then tenderly pressed her cheek against his as he whispered in her ear.

"Go get him, sweetie. Beat him up a little, like you do me. He's waiting. He doesn't know it, but he's waiting for you. He needs you, Jessica. More than I do."

Wearily she stretched out in the hotel room bed, the cool, crisp sheets soothing to her tired limbs. The baby was quiet right now, and she massaged her tummy lovingly. She thought over what had passed between her and Dane that afternoon, thought hard about her feelings and what Dane had tried to tell her.

Jessica turned to grab the small, framed photo from the nightstand. She lovingly traced the outline of Mac's face on the glass, smiling slightly to herself. Dane, in his infinite wisdom, had once again shown her the truth.

Oh, how her heart ached! She ached for Dane; would he ever find the kind of love she'd found? Sure, she loved Dane, she would always love him, for somewhere along the way their souls had meshed and had never quite divided on parting. She'd always carry part of him, and he part of her.

But her heart, her entire life, belonged to Cory Lee MacKendall.

"Why does this keep happening to me?" Mac muttered glumly, dropping the phone onto the table in frustration. "My life is a God-damned broken record."

When the Baitong Hotel in Phnom Penh told him Jessica had checked out, he couldn't believe his ears. He looked at his watch, checking the date. It was October 26th; they said she'd left the 24th, but no one answered at their house or at any other number he'd tried back home. Her cell was still going straight to voicemail. Where was she?

Wound up, he went for a walk. Dusk had fallen, and filming was over for another day. He enjoyed this film; for the first time in seven years, he played someone besides Doctor Jim, and the freedom was awesome. The professional side of his ego rose as high as his emotional side dipped low.

They were ahead of schedule, and it was hoped the filming would be wrapped up by Thanksgiving, another month away. Sal had candidly told him that an alternative plan could be worked out if Mac was unable to finish out the location shooting; a Southern California locale might be suitable for some scenes, and these were reserved for later just in case.

Ah, Jessica. Where are you? Mac stopped and stared at the sun setting on the water, breathing the salt air deeply into his lungs.

"I miss you," he said aloud. "God, I miss you."

He continued walking about the town until dark when he turned back toward the Plaza. He'd come to the realization that he'd made a bad situation worse by tearing off the way he had. He wouldn't listen to her, wouldn't give her a chance to explain...explain what? Why she was kissing another man in their own home? Not just another man; Dane Pierce. Dane was in love with Jessica, that much was evident. But Dane didn't *want* Jessica, not in a possessive sense. He just...loved her.

Mac shook his head to clear it. Nothing made sense. But one thing was for sure: he'd reacted exactly the way he'd taught her not to. The way someone else would have. "Learn to trust me," he had said, so self-righteously. And had promptly blown it.

She'd said on the phone that she was staying with Dane, and that she loved Mac with all her heart. Was it possible for her to care for Dane and still love *her husband?*

Mac entered his room more emotionally fatigued than ever. Wearily he went back to the phone and began dialing again. This time he tried the number given him for the hospital in Los Angeles where the American Medical Center in Phnom Penh had supposedly transferred Dane. He was nervous, yet relieved, when they found a room registered to Dane Pierce and rang his phone. He half expected Jessica's voice when Dane himself answered.

"So the gods saw fit to spare you, Pierce."

"Mac! Well, son of a gun. Never thought I'd hear your voice again."

"Nor I yours. How are you, Dane?"

"I'm a level three jigsaw puzzle, Mac. I think a couple of pieces got left in some alley back in Penh. And you? Down under, I hear?"

"I'm okay."

"Sorry to hear it."

Mac cleared his throat. "So, you sound pretty good. Jessie tells me you've made a great comeback."

"You and Jessie talking?"

"Of course," Mac responded, a little too quickly.

"You know, you were doing pretty good, don't start bull-shitting me now, Mac."

The phone was silent for several seconds while Mac absorbed Dane's barb. "Okay. Let me talk to her."

"To whom? Jessica?"

"My wife, of course. Is she there, or isn't she?"

"Well, let's see," Dane stalled. Mac closed his eyes in frustration. How much of Dane's inane prattle could he endure?

"She was there at the airport when they rolled me onto the plane...hmmm... you should have seen this damn thing they put me on, Mac. It was incredible."

"Dane? Please? Just tell me where she is?"

"Mac, I don't know. She didn't come back with me."

"*What?* You left her in Cambodia?"

"I didn't have a lot of choice. I'm more of a beggar than a chooser right now, you know? She insisted on taking a later flight. The one I took was specially equipped...for basket cases like me. And you know Jessie when she has her mind set."

Mac fell silent. His wife had indeed developed a stubborn streak. But where was she? "Dane. I'm asking you nice, man. Where is Jessie?"

"I guess you don't have a helluva lot of faith in me, Mac, but I'm telling you the truth. Far as I know, she was supposed to be on the ten o'clock flight Wednesday. Now you've got *me* worried."

"I can't believe you just left her there." Mac's voice was edged with contempt.

"And I can't fucking believe you left her in L.A., pal. If you'd have just pulled your cement head out of the sand for five minutes and listened for once..." Dane had apparently, finally, been provoked. He took a deep, and what Mac suspected was, painful breath. "Look, Mac, I'm sure she's fine. She'll be on the phone with...one of us soon. She's tough, you know that."

"No, I don't know that, and if you hear from her, find me." Mac sighed. "Please?"

"If you're so worried, why don't you just put your self-righteous ass on a jet and come home?"

"I'll think on that," Mac replied, rubbing his eyes. "And Dane—I'm glad you're...not dead."

Mac hung up the phone carefully. His seventh-floor hotel room faced the sea, and he could see the lights of the boats in the harbor flickering on in the darkness. Opening the patio doors, he stepped out into the cool ocean breeze and leaned on the rail.

Maybe I *should* go home, he thought. Nothing is as important as Jessica, certainly not this film. He was behaving just the way Dane had in Amande, putting a motion picture before Jessica's well-being. It didn't take long for the decision to be made. He'd call Sal, then Air New Zealand. He'd be home by tomorrow night.

While listening to Sal's phone ring unanswered in his ear, Mac started at the sound of a knock at the door.

A bellman handed him a small, pink envelope. Puzzled, he carefully pulled out a folded sheet of delicate parchment and opened it. The sight of the familiar handwriting stopped the beating of his heart momentarily.

"Join me for Cookies 'N Cream?"

One simple line. The letterhead was magenta printed in script: *"Jessica Lynne MacKendall"*

The bellman waited expectantly. Mac's face had reddened beneath his tanned skin.

"Uh...a lady gave you this? A...pregnant lady?" he stammered.

"She said to tell you she's in the dining room downstairs. And she's with child, yes."

Mac grasped the man's shoulder. "Really? She's here?"

"Yes, sir, she gave me the envelope herself."

"Right, right. Uh...I'm coming. I...need to change, comb my hair...uh, don't let her leave!" Mac hastily pressed ten dollars into the man's hand, then added another twenty. "Tie her down if she tries to go."

She'd purposely chosen a small, secluded table in the corner where she could watch the entrance undisturbed. Shifting uneasily in her chair, Jessica straightened the new pink silk dress for the third time. Her heart fluttered impatiently in her chest, her fingers nervously turning her water glass before her.

Jessica jumped a little with each entering patron. *This is silly! He's my husband. He's my lover. He's our baby's father.*

What if he didn't come? What if he was still angry? What if...what if he'd grown a mustache and was still the most gorgeous man she'd ever met?

He approached her, walking casually with his hands characteristically safe within his pockets; his crisp, black, long-sleeved shirt tucked neatly into cream-colored pleated slacks. He'd pushed the sleeves of the matching jacket up, the cuffs of the cotton shirt turned back over them. He looked more than sharp to her adoring eyes.

She was reminded of the night she'd been invited to his home after returning from Amande, when they'd reconciled their differences and had finally brought their love to the surface.

Mac stopped at the table and stared down at her. The decisive moment was upon Jessica; would he lash out, or...

"Stand up," he directed her. To support his request, he pulled his hand from his pocket and offered it to her.

Her heart thumping madly, Jessica took his hand, holding it tightly for just a moment before rising as gracefully as her unwieldy shape would allow.

Mac's eyes slowly studied the entire length of her; he tilted his head slightly in an appraising manner, his gaze finally resting upon her tummy. Letting go of her hand, he placed one of his on each side of her abdomen, as though he could almost take the sleeping child from her and hold it in his own arms.

"My, my," he said quietly, lifting his eyes to her face. "It's happening, isn't it?" She had grown only a little when he'd left her in August. It was almost November. Mac swallowed hard, his gesture telling her he'd suffered his own qualms about finally seeing her again. Suffered them and had overcome them; he was here.

At last, he allowed a small smile to form on his lips. With shaky determination, Jessica reached slowly toward him, resting her hands on his jacket lapels and then sliding them up to his shoulders. Her eyes could not get enough of his face, his soft brown eyes filled with love and forgiveness. Everything she'd carefully planned, rehearsed—all was gone now from her mind as she struggled to find words for her sky-rocketing emotions. But it was Mac who first found a voice.

"Would it be okay to save the ice cream for later?"

Dumbly, Jessica nodded, wondering what else he had in mind as he led her from the dining room and through the lobby to the front door.

On the sidewalk, he put his arm around her and walked her down the short distance to the waterfront.

"This is Oriental Bay," he told her, sweeping his arm in an encompassing gesture. "Out there, Cook's Strait. It's always windy here," he explained, stripping off his jacket and wrapping it around her shoulders protectively.

"Reminds me a little of San Francisco," she said, noticing the multitude of hills surrounding the bay, and the cable cars clinging to the apparently sheer slopes.

They walked a little farther until Mac stopped to lean against a rail bearing coin operated telescopes used by a multitude of tourists during the day; the chilly October air prevented more visitors at night, and save for a few passersby, they were alone.

He leaned casually against the rail, watching as she daintily slipped her arms into his tailored jacket and tried in vain to button it over her protruding stomach. She flashed him a look of mock-panic, and he shook his head sadly in amusement. Pulling a coin from his pocket, he slipped it into the telescope. Jessica looked through the eyepiece with delight at the romantically lit boats in the harbor.

"It's beautiful," she sighed, moving aside so he could look.

"I've seen it. I've...been here awhile."

Jessica bent to look again, absorbing the sights of this sparkling city until the shutter at last eclipsed her view. She straightened up and faced the water.

"So, I understand you want to fight with me?" he questioned to her back.

Jessica turned sharply to face him, staring at him, evaluating his meaning. His arms were crossed against his chest, his look deceivingly cool. No, she did not want to fight.

She went to him, not intending to get so close as to touch but forgot about her recent frontal extension; her abdomen brushed against his trousers and she pressed her lips together to stifle a smile. Pretending to straighten his already perfect collar, she used her false intention as a means of busying her anxious fingers as she spoke.

"Actually, fighting with you is not what I had in mind," she said softly.

"You, uh, want to dispense with the fighting and go right to the making up?" Mac queried, shuddering a little as she dug her fingers into the long hair at the back of his neck. She nodded, and he uncrossed his arms, slipping them inside the jacket and around her back, pulling her just a little closer to him. "You're *sure* now, there are a lot of terrible, mean things we could say to each other, if you want."

She stopped moving, again to check his face. Mac sat back against the rail behind him, eye level with Jessica.

"I'm sure," she managed to choke, her mind frenzied with anticipation. He was doing it again; making her wait, *again*. Was he teasing or punishing her? Abruptly she pulled away from him, walking several steps before turning to face him. "Are you going to kiss me or stand here all night discussing whether or not we should have a fight? Do *you* want to fight?"

"Only if you do, *ma petite*. Deciding whether to fight seems easy after the last few weeks, when I've been wondering if you even wanted to stay married."

"Oh, Mac..." she said softly, running to him and throwing her arms around his neck. "Staying married is the easy part."

Now he embraced her in earnest; the game was over. His lips hungrily sought hers in the kiss that had been waiting ten weeks to happen. A mutual, satisfying exhilaration filled them both to the limit; and after kissing her face and neck a thousand times over, he stopped and peered with glistening eyes into hers. He swallowed, then sniffed, turning his lips inside and biting them as he nodded slowly at some unshared thought.

Jessica's own lips quivered as she tenderly ran her thumb along his lower eyelid, solemnly wiping away an errant tear. He sniffed again.

"If you think this is bad, you should have been here when I received your letter," he confessed, chuckling in embarrassment.

Now he had her crying, too. "We really do need to talk about it, don't we?" she asked quietly.

"Yeah, we do. But not now. Right now, we need to make love."

She pressed her face against his shoulder, and he kissed her hair affectionately.

"C'mon," he coaxed, turning her back toward the hotel.

Jessica was nude except for the brief, blue panties he couldn't even see. Mac stared at her, lit by the glow of the soft city lights emanating from the picture window beside the bed.

"How...? I'm not sure how to do this..." he wondered but reached for her anyway and found a way to share his undying love with her. Despite the change in her shape, she was the same exciting, intriguing woman he'd fallen so completely in love with months before; her impending motherhood only served to enhance his devoted attentiveness to her pleasure. The weeks, no, months that had passed since they'd been together amplified their desire to share their passion with one another and no one else.

Jessica was particularly newly enamored with her husband, his physique now firmer and even more tanned than she remembered; the new mustache tickled her in an almost erotic way. Mac was more exciting than ever. She only regretted her ungainly figure; she would have liked to have been slender and svelte for this new beginning.

He was sitting lightly on top of her, knees bent, poised on her thighs as she lay back in euphoric relaxation. His hands were again resting on her stomach, his face wearing a comic, expectant grin.

"God—this is incredible..." he whispered as the baby pressed first this foot, then that, against his palms. Mac's face was alit with wonderment.

Jessica giggled up at him.

"Am I hurting you?"

"No." She laughed, placing her hands over his as he waited for the child to move again. The dim light from the lamp on the nightstand cast a warm glow on their adolescent expressions as they giggled and touched each other in comfortable intimacy.

With great care, Mac began massaging her as he remained sitting above her, his fingers sliding upward to caress first her shoulders and then her breasts, now full and firm with the promise of motherhood. His touch was not in any way erotic or sexual, only loving and comforting, and soon his hands returned to again wait for the tiny infant to squirm once more.

"I can't stop," he told her excitedly.

"Surely you experienced this before," she reminded him, "with Linda?"

Mac scoffed. "Linda was a shrew when she was pregnant. Her three favorite words were, 'Don't Touch Me.' And she hid herself. She didn't want me looking at her like that."

"How sad," Jessica murmured.

"She wasn't particularly fond of sex to begin with," he explained. "To her defense, I have to tell you she'd had a few bad experiences as a girl. I guess her past made it nearly impossible for her to...relax and enjoy making love."

"I'm sure it had nothing to do with you," she teased, running a finger down his stomach and past his navel.

"Let's just say I made a gallant effort."

Soon, he tired of sitting up and fell beside her on the bed. She turned on her side to face him.

"Do you want to talk, now?" she asked tentatively.

"I thought we *were* talking," he teased.

"You know what I mean, Mac."

"You want to talk about Dane. Okay, let's talk about Dane."

Jessica wet her lips. She could sense his impending tension and hesitated.

As if reading her thoughts, Mac reached over and grasped her jaw in his hand, the long, slender fingers caressing her cheek. "It's okay," he said, "I'm okay with this. Honest. You want me to go first? Would that be easier?"

She wasn't sure but nodded anyway.

"Okay. I blew it. I was wrong. I didn't know it then, obviously," he admitted, his face serious. "I've had a lot of time to think about it, Jess, to think about *us*. And what happened to Dane, and your going to Cambodia, all that helped me to understand. There are things we each have to accept about the other."

Jessica refrained from interrupting his train of thought, nodding softly in encouragement.

"You really impressed me by sticking with your convictions. You were up front and honest with me about your commitment to Dane. I respect that, I really do. Whether or not he *deserves* your devotion is another issue," he added wryly. "Dane has some pretty definite ideas about how I should treat you."

At this comment, Jessica frowned in concern. "What's that supposed to mean?"

"When we talked earlier, he—"

"You talked to Dane tonight? Is he okay?"

Mac rolled his eyes to the ceiling. "Yes," he answered wearily. "He's in good form. He let me know in no uncertain terms what he thought about my leaving you to come here. He had me feeling pretty guilty. Imagine that, Dane making *me* feel bad." He shook his head.

"What else did he say?"

"He's resting comfortably; he's at least well enough to be thoroughly obnoxious. And I guess we should call him back. He's worried about you."

"Worried about me? Why should he be worried about me?"

"I tracked him down when I found out you'd left Cambodia. I was frantic, babe, I didn't know where you were," he confessed.

"Well, Dane knew where I was...I told him I was flying into Wellington this morning. In fact, it was sort of his idea. He even helped arrange for my ticket."

"What? He *knew* where you were? That lying bastard told me you were supposed to have flown into L.A. Wednesday night!"

"He obviously didn't want to spoil my surprise," she said softly, running her fingers lightly over his mustache. "Don't be mad."

"More like he wanted to scare me. I was just about to call Air New Zealand when I got your note."

"What for?"

"I was going home. To you, Jessie. I'm ready to do whatever I have to, to be with you."

"God! I got here just in time!"

There is nothing better in the entire world. Being back in Mac's arms is undoubtedly the cure for all ills, Jessica thought as they lay entwined under the heavy down comforter. He slept, his slow, even breathing warm on the back of her neck; his arms encircled her, his legs tangled with hers. They had not talked about everything, nor had either of them apologized to or forgiven the other. But somehow, it no longer mattered. She knew in her heart of hearts that from this day forward, they would never be voluntarily separated again. Never.

And the next thing Jessica knew, Mac was scrambling around the hotel room, dressing hurriedly, his hair dripping wet.

"What's happening?" she asked sleepily.

"I'm late," he explained, but paused to sit at her side and look down at her lovingly. "You bewitched me, woman. I overslept."

He was dressed except for his boots, which he couldn't find. He leaned down and kissed her nose, then resumed the search.

"Where do you have to go?"

"To the prairie. It's about thirty miles north of here. I have a ranch, and a bunch of sheep, and a horse, and some nice guys that help me with the sheep, and—"

"Mac, can I come?" she asked, sitting up suddenly and smiling brightly at him.

He sat down and tugged on the rough cowhide leather boots. "Well...I don't know," he said hesitantly. "It's a long day, it's dusty, it's...hell, of course you can come. You're a seasoned pro. But you've got to hustle, babe."

Jessica jumped delightedly from the bed and, grabbing her suitcase, headed for the bathroom. She was ready to go in ten minutes flat, and they were on their way to the hotel parking lot.

"What is it?" she asked as he hopped into a large, four-wheel-drive vehicle that looked like an oversized, ungainly Jeep.

"Don't tell me you've never seen a Rover?" He held out his hand and pulled her up into the topless car. He grimaced, feigning weakness at pulling such a heavy load, then he grinned at her. "You sure look cute in that get-up."

She'd purchased blue denim maternity "jeans" and an over-sized western shirt at a duty-free shop at the airport. The temperature was perfect, she thought, the wind whipping her hair around as they rode along a dirt road north of town.

"The air is so clean here."

Her comment made his eyes leave the road and he flashed a quick smile at her. "They say it's the wind. It's Spring here, you know; Christmas in New Zealand is a summer holiday."

"You're kidding! You've learned a lot about this area, haven't you? You're going to hate going home," she lamented.

He was quiet while he considered her thoughts.

"When will you be able to go home?" she asked.

"If we finish out the film here, we'll be done by Thanksgiving."

"And why wouldn't you finish the film here?"

"I told them I might have to go home."

Jessica nodded silently. So, he'd been prepared to jump ship if she'd needed him.

"And?"

"There's a spot around Laguna Hills that we could use for the last scenes. If it's green enough. But after this summer, California is mostly brown, I'll bet."

"Well, there's no reason for you to go home. We'll just stay until you finish the film."

He turned to look at her again, this time pulling the Rover to a stop at the side of the road. "You're going to stay?"

"Why, of course I'm going to stay," she responded in surprise. "Why wouldn't I?"

"Well, I just thought you'd want to go home, you know...check things out at the house, your friends...you know," he repeated awkwardly.

Jessica stared at Mac in amused wonder.

"Bill's taking care of the house; he's staying there until we get back, I forgot to tell you." Looking down briefly, she ran the palm of her left hand down his smooth, denim-covered thigh and cupped his knee in her hand. "And as for my friends...you're the only friend I need, Cory. I'm not leaving this place until you do, so get used to having a shadow."

He shrugged, but the peace on his face told her he was thrilled that she wasn't running home to Dane. Dane had been right; Mac needed her now, more than ever, and she needed him.

"It *would* be nice to be home for Thanksgiving..." she added, after he'd turned the vehicle back onto the road.

"Yeah, it would, especially since they don't celebrate it here," he said, laughing.

EIGHTEEN

Giving Thanks and Forgiveness

"Mom, I'll get that," Jessica admonished Reva, who was feebly trying to lift a heavy tray of turkey dressing from the oven.

"You're in no better shape than I am, dear. Ask Cory to get it."

Jessica pushed a stray wisp of hair from her damp face and stubbornly lifted the casserole to a hotplate on the counter with a thud.

"I would, but your good Samaritan son has gone with Tom. You go sit down, Mom. Is it hot in here?"

"Between your pregnancy and my hot flashes..."

"It's the oven, that's what it is. That turkey is taking forever. You okay? Maybe you should go sit in with the others, Mom." Jessica began pawing through kitchen drawers in search of a basting brush.

"Jessie, I'm just fine, honey. You're the one who should be resting. Lord, I'll never forget the November when I was carrying Charlene, we had the whole family over for Thanksgiving; my sister-in-law, Cory's Aunt Jane, was supposed to bring the vegetables."

Jessica stopped looking for the brush and stared at Reva MacKendall. "Charlene?" she questioned the elderly woman.

"My daughter, Charlene. Cory's sister. Anyway, Jane was supposed to be bringing some carrots and peas, and she never showed up! How do you like that! There I was, eight months pregnant, with twenty people sitting down and all I had was turnips. And Cory cried the whole day. I'll never forget, he was teething or some such thing. And Charles, my husband, God rest him, well, men didn't do much helpin' with kids back then."

Jessica frowned in thought as she found the basting brush and hastily brushed some butter on the tops of the rolls. Mac had never mentioned a sister...but then he'd never said he didn't have one, either.

Suddenly Roxanne breezed into the kitchen carrying Megan, who was crying loudly, and sat her on the counter. "She fell," Roxanne explained breathlessly. Jessica rushed to examine the little girl's bleeding knee.

"Omigosh," Jessica breathed in a mock serious tone. "Looks pretty bad, I don't know, what do you think, Gramma?"

Reva looked over her shoulder. "Hmmm. Looks like the knee of a little girl who thinks she's a little boy."

Megan wailed. Jessica dampened a clean cloth and dabbed at the knee, prompting more screams from the little girl.

"Gosh I'm sorry, Jess, I just turned my back for a minute, and they were up in the tree."

"It's okay, Rox. She'll be fine. Where is Alex?"

Roxanne's eyes shifted to the kitchen door, where Alexander Pierce peeked around the doorjamb. Jessica rolled her eyes and smiled at Roxanne.

"I...want...my...daddy!" Megan sobbed as Jessica tenderly placed a bandage on the injured knee.

"Daddy will be back in a few minutes, Meggie. Now you just calm down. Do you want to watch your new video again?"

Megan shook her head, tears flying from her face, but she'd stopped crying now and jumped down from the counter. Spying Alexander waiting for her, she tore across the kitchen after him.

"Megan! Stay out of the tree," Jessica called after her, wearily shaking her head.

Things had roared at a furious pace since she and Mac had stepped off the airplane four days before. So much to be done, so little time...Mac had suggested they have a quiet Thanksgiving alone, but Jessica was determined to get everyone together that she'd missed; she'd been gone nearly two months.

She worried about everything. The impending birth of her baby weighed heavily on her, both emotionally and physically. Now, in the hot kitchen, she sat down and rested her hands on her still growing stomach.

"Jess, you need a break. Let me work on this," Roxanne offered, squeezing her friend's shoulders.

"I'm okay, really. Only tired. I'm not sleeping too well."

Just then, the sound of Tom's Navigator on the driveway caused them both to move toward the kitchen window. Reva remained sitting, oxygen tank nearby.

"'Bout time they got back," she muttered.

Jessica rushed to the front door, opened it, and stood watching as Mac and Tom got out of the car, both immediately opening the rear passenger doors behind them. Jessica stared in awe as Mac extended his hand into the backseat, helping Dane Pierce to exit the car. Jackie Spencer got out of the other side.

"Dane," Jessica whispered under her breath.

Mac reached back into the car and produced a cane, handing it to Dane in a comic gesture. "You okay, man?"

"I survived Jarrick's hit-and-miss driving, if that's what you mean," Dane responded cheerfully. With Jackie at his side, he walked slowly, carefully favoring his still sensitive left leg. At the edge of the porch, he paused and looked up, his eyes instantly locking on to Jessica's. A slow grin spread across his lips.

"Well, well...Jessica *MacKendall,*" he said sweetly, emphasizing her last name. "You're a sight for sore eyes."

Mac came up the steps ahead of Dane, and he embraced his wife warmly, kissing her cheek with affection.

"You all right, babe? You look tired."

Pulling her eyes away from Dane, Jessica smiled confidently at her husband. "I'm fine, darling. And where did you dig up that hot mess?" she joked, pointing to Dane.

"Valley Hospital. The nurses didn't want to let him go, but he'd worn out his welcome with the doctors."

"Actually, it was the form-pressed-imitation-open-faced turkey sandwich on today's menu that cinched it," added Tom, as the five of them moved into the house. "As rotten as you are, Pierce, we couldn't let you suffer that."

"Daddy, Daddy!"

Jessica wasn't sure who had screamed the word first, but both Megan and Alexander were racing into the kitchen with open arms. Sentiment welled in her throat as she watched Mac tenderly examine his daughter's knee; Dane painfully lift Alexander into his arms.

"This is too much," she murmured and turned her attention to Jackie, standing forlornly in the doorway. "Take your sweater, Jackie?"

"Thanks," she replied gratefully. "How are you, Jessica? You're so... big!"

"And I have another month to go, can you believe it?"

"Your home is beautiful," Jackie went on, looking around excitedly. "I really appreciate your inviting me to Thanksgiving. My folks live in Nevada, you know, and I just couldn't go home this year, what with the film and all."

"Come see the nursery." Jessica led Jackie down the hall to the baby's room. "So, what film are you doing?"

"Dane's new picture, surely you know about it? You don't have to pretend he didn't offer you the role first, Jess. I'm glad you couldn't take it," Jackie said happily, her cool gray eyes sparkling with unabashed joy.

"And how is he supposed to be doing a film when he can barely walk?" Jessica said in frustration, more to herself than to Jackie.

"Oh, Jessie, this room is gorgeous. It's perfect! You really have a flair for decorating, don't you? Whenever I try to decorate, I end up pasting the wallpaper upside down."

Somehow that doesn't surprise me, Jessica thought wryly. So, Jackie was doing Dane's new film. Why did that bother her so much?

As they returned to the kitchen, Jessica appraised Jackie's appearance critically; the waist long, shining black hair, her almost too thin waist. She was a good four or five inches taller than Jessica, giving her an advantage on the screen with tall actors...like Dane Pierce. Ruefully Jessica watched Jackie flit about, tasting the cranberries and the dressing with her fingers and stealing glances at Dane, who sat at the kitchen table with his leg propped on a chair.

Dane's eyes, however, followed Jessica as she returned to the task of finishing up the meal.

Jessica was thoughtful during dinner. One by one, she gazed at the nine other people at her table, thinking on each and giving silent thanks for their presence in her life. Strong, steady Tom Jarrick, who seemed to be on this earth to make others feel safe and secure; would he eventually ask dear Roxanne to be his wife? Reva MacKendall, her seventy-eight-year-old eyes flitting back and forth as she listened attentively to the dinner conversation of her son and his friends, her life-giving air machine at her ankle.

Bill Campbell had joined them just before dinner. Single and unattached, Bill was the type you always wanted to set up with some nice girl...and nothing ever happened. A shy man who had somehow become an actor with almost no ego, Bill could just as easily have been a high school teacher or an astronomer.

Megan and Alexander were just months apart in age, but the difference in them was as great as that of their fathers. While Dane painstakingly chopped, sliced and mashed Alex's dinner for him, occasionally coaxing the boy's mouth open for a bite, Megan was totally self-sufficient with her meal and politely asked for a second glass of milk. Both were bright, however, and played well together, sometimes out of sheer challenge. It had been Jessica's suggestion that Peter Welles join them for dinner, but after hearing the desire in Peter's voice to have some time away from the rowdy seven-year-old, she insisted that Peter take a day off and drop young Alex off at "Casa MacKendall." She'd had no inkling of Mac's plan to bring Dane home for Thanksgiving.

"If you ask me, those damned politicians have screwed up the entire thing. I remember my dad saying years ago that the whole Social Security concept would eventually collapse. We didn't agree on a lot, but I have to say he was right." Tom argued his opinion while spooning out more potatoes.

"You're right, Tom, but the new administration just might change things. Did you *really* read Senate Bill 509? Or was it 905..." Mac said.

Tom shrugged. "More thinly disguised, bureaucratic mumbo-jumbo. What do you think, Dane?"

Dane had been quieter than usual, Jessica thought, finally daring to look at him across the table from where she sat between Mac and Reva.

"I think you're both right, of course...but it's hard to put it in perspective right now, for me, that is...I've been rather removed from the news, you know?"

Of course; Dane had nearly died in Cambodia. How could he have formed an opinion of the latest ballot issue? Everyone fell silent for a moment.

"So, how are the Trojans doing?" Dane asked comically, before biting into another dinner roll. Everyone laughed at his remark except Jessica, who raised her eyes to the ceiling then smiled at Roxanne.

"Politics and football! Hasn't anyone seen any good movies lately?"

"I hear *Lost Season* is the most anticipated film of the year," Bill piped up from the end of the table. Again, they laughed, and Jessica's eyes lit up.

"Is it true, Dane?" she asked.

Dane swallowed, then cleared his throat. "It's true. The worn-out desert island plot has some sizzle left after all. The critics will be eating crow all over town. And you, my dear, are the hottest news on the block."

Jessica colored at his words. *Lost Season* seemed so remote; but the truth was, she'd already turned down three interviews since she'd returned from New Zealand.

Mac pointed his finger at Dane in jest. "Then, you haven't been totally removed from the news," he challenged.

"Well, I *have* been reading my mail. And when my investment guy wants to have lunch, I know I'm doing well." Dane told them. "You realize, the premiere is December 15th. And advance orders for the DVD are already coming in."

"Jesus, the DVD's coming out and I haven't even seen the movie!" Mac exclaimed, creating general merriment around the table.

"The fifteenth..." Jessica murmured. Unconsciously she pressed her hand against the baby within her.

"It's wonderful," Jackie offered shyly, "When we went for the pre-screening, I cried at the end."

Dane took her hand and squeezed it warmly, then looked back at Jessica. "Well, that's what we wanted, right Jess?" His green eyes seemed almost gray surrounded by his pale complexion. Little trace remained of *Lost Season's* dashing Roger Boyer on Dane's face, Jessica noted; the evidence of his nightmarish stay in Cambodia was still present. In her mind's eye, Jessica could see herself taping the small, "butterfly" bandages over his eye; sponging down his bruised and broken body; holding a cup of water to his tender, painful lips. She'd sat with him while the doctor had re-set his arm; Dane had nearly crushed her hand, gripping it for support and screaming in agony. Jessica had screamed too, screamed at the doctor to stop hurting Dane.

Jessica reached her left hand under the table and grasped Mac's thigh for support. Finished with his meal, Mac put his arm around her and leaned close to her ear.

"Maybe you should lie down, babe."

Quickly she snapped herself away from the melancholy and turned to him. "No way! And miss Mom's pumpkin pie?" she teased, giving him a quick kiss.

"Sounds good to me," Roxanne announced, standing and gathering several empty plates. Tom stood to help her, then Jackie joined in. The children scrambled out of their chairs and made for the door.

"Whoa, there, little girl," Mac hollered, and Megan stopped at the sound of his voice. "What happened to your manners?"

"May I please be excused?" she asked timidly, her brown eyes favoring her father with a most beguiling look, not unlike the one Mac often used, Jessica thought whimsically.

"Yes, you may. Take your plate to the sink, please." Mac's voice was stern but not unkind, and Megan dutifully returned to retrieve her plate. Wordlessly Alexander followed suit, and the two handed their dishes to Roxanne.

Dane raised his eyebrows. "So, Mac," he began, grinning. "Mind if Alex stays with you folks for a while? A year, maybe?"

"Who wants pie?" Roxanne asked, to which she received a unanimous cry. Jackie returned to sit with Dane and Bill. Mac rose from the table and took Jessica's hand.

"Come on," he said softly, leading her into the hallway and down to their bedroom, where he closed the door behind them. He took her into his arms and stared into her eyes for a long moment without speaking.

"Should I be worried?" he finally asked. "You seem down."

"I'm fine, Mac, honest. I really am...just...tired. I haven't slept well the last few nights—since we got back. I'm so...uncomfortable!" She uttered a short laugh, hoping to put him at ease.

"You don't mind about Dane, do you? Did I blow it by bringing him here?"

"I guess that depends on why you brought him, darling."

He didn't answer at first, apparently searching his soul for the real reason he'd invited Dane back into their home. "I wanted to share something...good with him. It's been a long, long time coming, but I think it can happen now, Jessica."

"Something other than me," she corrected him.

"No, you too. Not in the way he's accustomed to, I'm sure. But our lives... God, we've all come so far together; not just Dane, but Tom and Roxie too; I'm coming to realize that the world isn't just black and white, right and wrong, day and night...there's a lot more to it. Dane is as much a part of our lives as any of those other people out there, maybe more; and shutting him out would be like shutting out a part of us."

Jessica stared at him in awe. Was this really her stubborn, hard-headed, jealous husband talking about keeping Dane in their lives?

"Mac, do you really feel that way?"

Silently he nodded, and sensing her desire, leaned down to kiss her lovingly. "And maybe I just hated to see him spend Thanksgiving alone in the hospital with a turkey sandwich, for God's sake."

They were still kissing when the door burst open wide and Megan came tearing past them, screaming like a banshee with Alex just behind her. Like lightning, Mac's hand intercepted her petite body and scooped her up in one motion, firmly grasping her small jaw in his hand.

"Hey! What's this all about? Is that the proper way to enter a closed room?" he demanded.

Megan shook her head slowly. Alex retreated to the hall. Jessica bit her lip in sympathy for the little girl, for she'd come to discover that Mac was a father not to be reckoned with, despite Megan's childish appeal.

"How about a time out?" Mac suggested firmly.

Megan again shook her head. He put her down and sighed.

"I think that would be a good idea. Go on, ten minutes—in your room," he directed, swatting her behind lightly as she trotted from the room. He waited for Jessica in the open doorway, holding his hand out to her with the intention of escorting her back to the dining room for pie.

"Just a minute," Jessica said, pausing. Mac returned to place his hands on her shoulders.

"Yes?" He waited expectantly.

"Just—I love you, that's all."

He embraced her once more before they rejoined the others.

"Daddy, that man has my doll." Megan stood primly before Mac as he worked to build a fire in the fieldstone fireplace that evening. Mac looked to Dane who sat on the couch turning the doll in his hands, comically lifting the doll's dress and peeking underneath.

"I keep waiting for them to make Barbie anatomically correct!" Dane joked. Mac laughed aloud.

"It's okay, sugar; Uncle Dane won't keep your Barbie. Go ask him nicely, he'll give it back."

Shyly Megan approached Dane and stood silently before him.

"Hi," Dane began.

"Hello. May I please have my Barbie?"

"Of course, princess. Does your Barbie have some friends?"

"I have five Barbies and two Kens."

"Lucky Kens! My daughter has a few of these. Maybe someday you and she can play Barbies together."

"Does she have 'Bride Barbie?'"

"I don't know, cutey. Probably."

"I don't," Megan said sadly. "Why didn't your little girl come to dinner?"

Dane's smile was bittersweet as he glanced down at the sleeping boy beside him. "My little girls live with their mommy. Kinda like you, huh?"

"Did you move away from them like my daddy did?"

Dane's eyes met Mac's as the latter looked up from the fire, and the two shared silent, meaningful communication. Dane lifted Megan onto his good knee.

"Sometimes a mommy moves away, too," he began. "But you know what? I still love my daughters just as much as when we all lived together. Maybe more. Just like your daddy loves you."

Megan nodded solemnly. "But Alexander lives with you, huh?"

"That's right."

"I might come to live with my daddy, too."

"Is that right?" Dane stole another glance at Mac, reclined on the rug before the fire.

"Did Alexander's mommy marry someone else, Uncle Dane?"

"Uncle Dane..." he murmured to himself in amusement. "Well, she might, pumpkin. Why?"

"Because when my mommy marries Arthur, I want to come live with Daddy and Jessica."

Mac's mind snapped back to full consciousness, and he lifted his head to gaze at his small daughter perched on Dane's knee. Dane's own eyebrows were up, and he favored Mac with a whimsical, questioning smile.

With a groan, Mac dragged himself to his feet and lifted Megan from Dane's lap.

"Time for bed, little girl. Tell Uncle Dane goodnight."

Megan squirmed until Mac put her down, and she timidly wrapped her short arms around Dane's neck.

"Good night, Uncle Dane," she said sweetly, kissing his cheek. "I hope your leg gets better soon."

"Thanks, princess." Dane gave her a hug before turning her back toward her father. As Megan skipped ahead, Mac turned a rueful smile on Dane.

"What is it about you, anyway?"

Dane shrugged, feigning helplessness, then turned his shining eyes to the fire.

Reva retired at eight o'clock, and Roxanne pushed Tom out the door at nine; Bill followed shortly thereafter. Jessica and Jackie began making hot chocolate and exchanging details about the latest Hollywood scandals. Jessica marveled at how long she had been out of touch.

Going to the liquor cabinet, she searched in vain for the peppermint schnapps she'd picked up earlier for making the hot chocolate. Puzzled, she started to call out to Mac, but then remembered that others were sleeping. Reaching back into the cabinet, she selected a substitute. "We'll just have to use Irish cream."

Jackie smiled. "I've never heard of this...booze in hot chocolate?"

"Cocoa, *Schnapps*, Cinnamon, uh...whipped cream if you have it. We use milk, mostly." Carefully she measured a dollop of Bailey's into three of the four cups. "So, Jackie, are you staying with Dane tonight?" Too late she realized the personal way in which the question came out; she had been on an entirely different track. Sensing Jackie's immediate discomfort, she hurriedly continued. "I mean, just coming out of the hospital and all, he's probably in need of a little help, companionship...I didn't mean, well..."

"I'm no match for you in Dane's eyes, Jessie," she responded quietly, not looking at Jessica. "He hasn't asked me to go home with him."

"Match for me? You don't have to be. Hey, Jackie, don't make Dane out to be something he isn't. I know he seems...bigger than life, and sometimes he does crazy things...but really, he's just...just a guy. Inside, he has the same needs as everyone else. And just because he hasn't asked you certainly doesn't mean he wouldn't like to."

Jackie didn't answer, and Jessica suffered an awkward moment, wishing she'd kept her mouth shut. Surely Dane cared for Jackie, but...

And why had she brought it up at all?

The chaotic day settled into a cozy night. Mac sat on the floor, comfortably reclined against a hassock; joining him, Jessica sat between his legs, leaning back against him as his arms encircled her rounded abdomen. His eyes stared dreamily into the fire.

Not far away, Dane stretched out on the hearth rug, his head cradled in Jackie's lap. Absently she stroked Dane's hair; she, too, seemed mesmerized by the flames. Dane himself might have been sleeping if it were not for the slightest smile Jessica perceived as she glanced over at him.

Mac's lips found her ear and she shivered. "It was good, wasn't it?"

"What was good?"

"Our dinner party. It worked. It was fun," he whispered, kissing her ear just a little too intimately for Jessica's mood. Turning her head to avoid his advance only served to encourage his attention to her neck; his fingers slipped into the non-space between her breasts and her bulging stomach.

"Mac..." she whispered, craning her neck to look into his liquid and slightly reddened eyes; he took the opportunity to claim her mouth as she gazed at him.

The kiss made her dizzy. The scent of his cologne, the warmth of the fire... the taste of peppermint. *Peppermint?* Abruptly she pulled her lips from his and peered intently into his eyes.

"My God, Cory, you're drunk!"

"No way, sugar. You know I don't drink." Mac made a good show of false sobriety.

"He's potted, Jess, and he's one lyin' son-of-a-bitch, besides." Dane's lazy drawl piped up from where he laid, his eyes still closed and his smile broad. Above him, Jackie giggled.

"Don't be mad; it was Dane's fault. He made me do it." Mac turned on his most winsome smile.

"Right. I *made* you drink the whole damned thing. As if anyone could *make you do anything*, MacKendall, with that hard-assed attitude of yours. And by the way, thanks for sharing," Dane replied with comic sarcasm.

Jessica's eyes widened as they lit on the empty bottle on the hearth. They had put away the whole thing?

"Why should I share when you had your own?" Mac countered, pointing to another, near-empty bottle near Dane's right hand.

Jessica attempted to stand, but Mac pulled her back into his lap, this time facing him.

"And where do you think you're going?"

"To bed. If I wanted to sit around with a couple of drunks, I'd go to a bar."

Mac's expression turned to a hurtful pout as she untangled herself and crawled away from him, stopping before Jackie and Dane.

Ignoring Dane, she spoke directly to Jackie. "The guest room is at the end of the hall. If *he* can't get up, leave his drunken ass here. Help yourself to whatever you need, there's clothes, towels, whatever, in the closet in there." She leaned close and touched Jackie's shining ebony hair affectionately, and Dane chose just that moment to open his eyes and grin at her. Jessica could take no more from either Dane or Mac, and covered Dane's eyes with her hand as she continued. "Sleep as late as you like…we'll have a late brunch, how does that sound?"

Jackie nodded dreamily. *If only Dane did love her*, Jessica thought fleetingly as she lifted her hand from his face.

Before she could rise, Dane grasped her wrist.

"Thanks for dinner," he said simply.

"Thanks for polluting my husband," Jessica retorted, pulling her arm away and getting to her feet. Carefully stepping over Mac's legs she left the room.

"She's pissed, Mac," Dane warned as Mac struggled dizzily to stand.

"You think I don't know that? Thanks a lot." Despite the sarcasm, Mac bent and extended his hand to Dane. "Get up. I won't have you sleeping on the floor."

Dane nearly pulled Mac to his knees. Jackie stood by as the two men began a comic routine of each trying to steady the other, their laughter threatening to wake Alexander as he slept nearby.

"Shit, MacKendall, you're drunker than I am when I've had twice as much," Dane pointed out.

"But my liver is healthier," Mac returned, still laughing. "Or at least it used to be. Before Amande." Mac grimaced, recalling the gruesome hangover he'd suffered the morning after Dane had introduced him to tequila shooters.

"Sleep well, my friend." Dane slapped Mac on the shoulder as Mac made a crooked path from the room. Turning to Jackie, Dane put his arm around her and led her toward the hall. "Too tired to give a hurting man a massage?"

The tiny knock at the door could only be Megan, Jessica thought tiredly as she slipped out from beneath Mac's arm and tiptoed across the bedroom. Glancing at the clock, she read eight-thirty. At least it wasn't six, she thought with some comfort. Grabbing her robe, she quietly opened the door and stepped into the hall.

"Me n' Alex are hungry."

"Okay, sweetheart. Give me five minutes, okay? You go get dressed, and I'll fix you something."

"Can we go outside?"

"Sure. Stay away from the pool, and don't climb the trees. And stay out of Daddy's car, okay?"

Megan nodded and skipped off to her bedroom.

Jessica watched Mac sleeping while she hurriedly dressed in a pink T-shirt and new, blue denim maternity overalls. He was dead to the world.

"I look like a clown," she complained quietly to herself as she gazed into the wardrobe mirror. Quickly she brushed out her hair, noting that it was longer than she'd worn it since high school: almost to her waist in the back and losing the perm she'd had...when? April?

Time sure flies when you're having fun...she'd made her first major motion picture, fallen in love, become pregnant, been abducted, married, separated, had traveled around the world, and had been reconciled since January. *Yes, I've been busy.*

Slipping into her sandals, she went to the bed and leaned down to kiss Mac's cheek before leaving the room. "I love you," she whispered, noting how adorably his hair fell across his face as he slept, vaguely remembering how she'd refused to help him undress the night before. He'd managed anyway, she noticed, lifting the sheet to check, her eyes appreciating the perfection of his nude form.

Jessica prided herself on being able to cook waffles and scramble eggs at the same time without burning either. *And brew coffee, to boot.* She fed the children in record time and sent them back outside to play; now it was her time to enjoy a cup of coffee and thumb through *Variety*. Propping her feet up on an adjoining chair, she crossed her still delicate ankles and relaxed.

"I *thought* the kitchen was this way," Dane announced as he joined her moments later. "The coffee was the giveaway."

"Good morning, Mr. Pierce. Want some?"

"I'll get it...you look too perfect sitting that way."

"Well, I work hard at looking perfect."

He filled a mug and sat down across from her.

"Says here your next film is about a senator who runs amuck. I thought you'd given up acting for a while."

"Well...the part is just too good. Couldn't find anyone I like better."

"Better than yourself? How modest." Jessica smiled at Dane over her coffee cup. "I knew you couldn't stay away from the camera for long."

"Just like I can't stay away from you for long."

She stared at him intently before finally deciding to ignore his comment. "Sleep well? I take it Jackie's still asleep."

"Yes, and yes."

"She's really a sweet girl, Dane."

"She's...most attentive," Dane dodged, shifting in his chair.

"Don't break her heart." Jessica's words spilled out before she knew she'd spoken them.

"I have little control over that."

"You offer her the same money-back guarantee you offered me?"

"Cruel, Jessica. Really low."

"Sorry. I couldn't help it, darling."

"No problem." He smiled despite her rebuff. "Mac up yet?" The shine in his eyes was unmistakable.

"What do you think?"

"I think he's going to be one hurting boy when he wakes up." Again, Dane shifted his position, groaning as he tried to bend his throbbing knee.

"Sounds like *you* are one hurting boy. Can I get you something?"

"I could use a sponge bath."

Jessica stood and poured herself another cup of coffee, then sighed. "Just can't stop, can you? Let me tell you something, Dane," she said, sitting back down and lowering her voice. "There isn't much you could do to make me really angry with you. I can't forget or negate all we've been through together. But if you ever do anything again to come between Mac and me, I'll never speak to you again. I swear it. *Never*. You *do* understand that, don't you?"

Dane smiled charmingly and reached over to lightly caress the back of her hand. "Yes, I do understand." He paused and lifted his mug close to his lips. "By the way, I've decided to ask Jacqueline to marry me." His eyes captured hers; Jessica's lips parted in stunned astonishment.

They both turned as Mac appeared in the doorway.

"Jess?" His voice was soft, tentative; his right hand shaded his eyes from the light pouring through the kitchen window. Barefoot and shirtless, his button-fly jeans were mis-buttoned and his hair defied gravity.

Despite her anger of the night before, Jessica rose from her chair and rushed to him, standing on tiptoe to tenderly embrace him while pressing her cheek against his. He wobbled unsteadily and grabbed the doorjamb for support.

Dane chuckled and shook his head, struggling to his own feet to refill his mug. He then filled another mug for Mac, put it on the table and hobbled back to his seat.

"Shot of *Schnapps* in your coffee, little brother? Oh! Forgot. We're out."

Mac swallowed and wet his lips, squinting at Dane. "Don't ever leave me alone with him again," he told Jessica ruefully. "He's trying to kill me, I know it."

"He's finally caught on. Damn." Dane reached to pull Mac's chair out.

Mac and Jessica sat down at the table. After a sip of steaming coffee, Mac leaned over and kissed Jessica briefly on the lips. "Good morning, love," Mac murmured.

"Hi. You need some aspirin?"

"Already took some." He leaned his forehead into his hands.

"Share with Mac what you've just told me." Jessica smiled wickedly at Dane, hoping to get back at him for taunting her beloved, knowing he would never repeat his obvious ploy at her heart.

"About Jackie? I'm going to propose, Mac. What do you think she'll say?"

Jessica's face blushed a warm pink. He'd called her bluff. He had really repeated it! Was Dane seriously considering marriage to Jackie?

"I know what she *should* say, and if she's smart, she'll be in a dead run when she says it," Mac responded, his bloodshot eyes holding the slightest merriment for Dane's viewing.

"Okay. You two are great friends. Here I am, sharing this most serious news, and you both treat me like shit."

Mac looked at Jessica for her reaction; Jessica's eyes met his in smug skepticism, and Dane looked away.

"Hey, man, you consulted me before asking Jess."

"Yeah, and I can't repeat what you said in front of her," Mac countered in amusement. "Don't you think you ought to cool off for a while? The ink hasn't even dried on your divorce decree."

Dane only smiled.

NINETEEN

Full Circles

"I can't go."

Jessica sat on the corner of the bed, her belly filling what might have been called her lap. Silently she stared at the black velvet dress hanging in the closet.

"What's the matter, Mommy?" Mac stepped out of the bathroom, buttoning a white shirt across his chest.

Her response was a lowered chin and a pouty bottom lip. Standing before her, Mac dropped to his knees and slipped his arms around her largely non-existent waist.

"I can't go," she murmured again.

"Miss the premiere? You feel that bad?"

"I don't know." Jessica's eyes were so low they were almost closed. "I feel crummy. I look like a black barrel in that dress."

Mac pressed his cheek against hers in sympathy.

"Honey, the dress is beautiful, and you will look perfect. This is your special night. Come on," he coaxed, taking her hands and helping her to stand up. "Just put it on. You'll see."

Jessica complied, standing up and taking the dress from the closet and tossing it across the bed.

"It is pretty. Rox outdid herself this time," she agreed, but without enthusiasm. She looked at her husband, back in the bathroom and still fussing with his shirt. "You chose the Armani. It's very sexy, you know." While her eyes admired him, her voice quietly accused him.

"The Billy Martin was just...too formal." Mac came to her and held out his hand, dropping a black onyx cufflink into her hand. With a sigh, Jessica carefully threaded the link into his cuff.

"Thanks." Mac slipped on the jacket and turned to face her. Indeed, he looked better than he ever had. The collarless shirt sported a single black onyx stud at the throat; the black jacket with narrow lapels was cut stylishly short above his trouser pockets and longer in the back.

Jessica sighed again. "I guess I *have* to go to keep the women off of you."

"I'll help you. The limo will be here in thirty minutes."

Her hair was already done, worn up and in elegant curls carefully pinned all around. She had complained to the hairdresser that she could set off metal detectors with all the hidden bobby pins. Mac untied and slid off her robe, suppressing a small exclamation at the sight of her tremendous belly. Indeed, the baby wasn't due for three weeks but could come any time by the looks of her.

He helped her into the gown, carefully zipped up the back and tied the sash. Roxanne had designed the understated, charming creation, and had painstakingly adjusted it as Jessica had grown larger than expected. The dress itself was floor length, black velvet, with a round neckline trimmed with wide, ruffled, black taffeta which also dressed her cuffs. The same taffeta created the high, faux waistband that trailed to the back and tied in a bow. Simple, comfortable, tasteful.

Jessica gazed in the mirror, still pouting. Mac leaned over to kiss her neck, but she moved away.

"I look like I belong in the Macy Parade."

"You need something to cheer you up," he said, walking to his dresser and opening the top drawer. He withdrew a flat, burgundy velvet box and took it to her. "Merry Christmas."

She looked at him in surprise, intrigued. Slowly she pulled the small box open and uttered a short gasp.

"Oh my God," she whispered. Mac lifted the diamond and emerald necklace from the case and laced it around her neck, carefully clasping the back.

"You'll have to do the earrings yourself," he told her, straightening the exquisite necklace that hung almost into her cleavage. A small shiver ran through her at his touch.

"Mac, it's beautiful," she breathed, again looking into the mirror.

"Ah, it pales in the presence of your face, darling."

Jessica could not help a smile. "Did you just make that up?"

"No, I've been practicing it all day. Now get your shoes. We've gotta go."

Her depression subsiding, Jessica became increasingly nervous on the way to the theater. She'd been so preoccupied with her appearance she'd barely had time to think about the premiere itself and what it might mean to her career, her future. While she'd been to several in the past, never had she been a center attraction.

The limousine stopped behind several others ahead of them, and Jessica leaned across Mac and peered out the darkened windows in awe. Fans, hundreds of them, lined Hollywood Boulevard in front of Grauman's Chinese Theater. Somewhere, a searchlight perused the sky, advertising to the world that another blockbuster was about to begin its theatrical run. A huge banner bearing the "Lost Season" title stretched across one wall, with her and Dane's faces larger than life, cheek to cheek. A narrow red carpet extended from the theater doors to the curb, and velvet ropes held back the onlookers and paparazzi that clamored for a better view. From the car ahead of them she watched in amazement as Tom Hanks and his wife, Rita Wilson, stepped onto the red runner into a veritable storm of strobe flashes and screams.

"You ready?" Mac asked, his tone still calm, sweet, comforting.

"Absolutely not," she said, bravely putting on an almost confident smile. The limo moved briskly, stopped suddenly, and then the door opened. Mac's exit was met with a torrent of flashing cameras. The usher started forward, but Mac had already turned to help Jessica from the car.

God, help me be graceful, she prayed, taking Mac's hand.

The thunderous noise of the crowd accompanied the lightning of the flashes. Fans, women and men alike, strained against the ropes while reaching out in efforts to touch the royal couple as they made their way down the runway. Jessica grinned at the fans, waved back, and paused now and again for cameras pointed in her direction. She forgot about her protruding tummy, her pale complexion, the discomfort behind her ribs. Stealing a glance at her husband, she found him stealing one at her.

Near the entrance, radio and television entertainment reporter Jerry Dalton was waiting with a microphone.

"Well, I see Jessica Taylor, I should say Taylor-MacKendall as I understand she goes by now, approaching with her NBC doctor husband, and don't they make the handsome couple here tonight? Again, I have to say for those of you not here, this premiere rivals those of Tinseltown's hey-day, as we've seen Hollywood's brightest stars turn out for Dane Pierce's much anticipated desert island epic. Say, Jessie, Mac, I guess I don't have to ask you what you plan to do over the holidays. When's this little project going to premiere?"

"Three weeks," Jessica said, her smile so broad she felt her face would crack.

"*Maybe,*" Mac added comically, touching her belly with affection.

"And your *Night Horse* film comes out in the spring I understand?"

"That's right, Jerry."

"I would imagine the two of you will be taking a little time off now. So tell us Jess, what was it like filming in the Grenadines with Dane Pierce? We've all heard stories about rough weather, power outages, bad food, under-budgeting...was it all that bad?"

"Positively grueling," Jessica managed through her giggles. "Dane is a slave driver."

"Well, we'll see if it was worth the effort. In fact, unless I'm mistaken, your leading man may be just arriving." The reporter looked past them to where a white limo was opening to a deafening roar from the crowd. Jessica stood spellbound as Dane climbed out of the car, offering his hand to Jackie behind him.

"Should we go in?" she whispered to Mac, holding his hand tightly in hers.

"No. Let's wait for him." They stepped just inside the lobby doors and watched as Dane and Jackie made a lazy path toward them.

Dane looked nothing like the recovering, crippled man that had limped into their home for Thanksgiving dinner. His tuxedo was tailored to perfection, his face discreetly repaired by the industry's best makeup artist. And while his steps seemed casual and wandering, the MacKendalls knew it was merely a ruse to disguise the hitch in his walk. They both watched in fascination as Dane talked to Jerry, his conversation lively and, it would seem, almost joyful.

"Yes! I'm glad to be here. It's been a tough year." He squeezed Jackie close to him as he spoke. "No pain, no gain, right, Jerry?"

"If you say so, Dane. You *are* the man of the hour. The fans certainly aren't disappointed. And it looks like it's about time to go inside."

Dane's eyes lit briefly when he spied Jessica waiting. He shook Mac's hand firmly, then leaned down to kiss Jessica on the cheek.

"Well, this is it, guys. Everybody pumped?"

Mac looked at Jessica from time to time during the screening. She was clearly hypnotized, and she had not let go of his hand since they'd exited the limo. It was her first time, he reminded himself. And this film would make her career. It would forever change her life, their lives, setting forth an image for her whether she ever made another one or not.

She worried, he knew, about watching the love scenes. She'd confided as much to him earlier. So when the inevitable finally played before them, the sensual sand tumble between Mariah and Roger in the Caribbean sun, Mac leaned over and whispered into her ear, his voice low and seductive.

"Would you like...some popcorn?"

Jessica closed her eyes and sighed, a smile forming on her lips. She leaned back toward him as if to reply; instead, she grabbed his earlobe in her teeth.

"Shame on you," she whispered, but Mac was not to be bested and captured her mouth for a kiss in the darkness, both startling and delighting her.

Beside Jessica on the other side, Jackie whispered to her companion. Dane, however, might well have been alone in the theater as he watched himself embrace Jessica on the screen. Jackie was no more than a gnat buzzing about his ear.

As the credits rolled, so did the tears down Jessica's face. She had not expected the sudden rush of emotion at the film's end, and she could not explain even to herself the feelings that moved her to cry. The film was beautifully complete, the music lush and romantic. Indeed, Amande appeared all the island paradise it was meant to be. There was her name, below Dane's on the screen, and the names of the many people she knew that had performed the magic to get the story onto the film. And the *Pacifica*, majestic and strong, rocking to its own mysterious theme.

She continued to marvel as everyone else stood to applaud Dane's magnificent success. Mac held his hand out to her, and she gratefully allowed him to help her to stand. She went to Dane and hugged him.

"It was good, wasn't it?" she urged, repeatedly wiping her cheek with the back of her finger.

He didn't answer, just patted her back consolingly while smiling at Mac over her shoulder.

"It was wonderful, Jess," Jackie said, stepping between them as Dane released Jessica. "My gosh, you're so *huge!*"

Jessica's smile faded as she regarded Jackie. At 5'8", Jackie seemed to tower above her, especially since Jessica had chosen low heels in consideration of her unwieldy condition. And Jackie's dress, a short, strapless, red silk sheath, fairly glowed in the dim theater lighting. Jessica turned back to Mac and again grasped his hand.

"Drop me off," she said once the limo was underway.

"You don't want to go to Dane's party?"

"No. I just want to go home. I'm tired. The baby's been beating me to shreds all evening."

"I'll call him," he said simply, reaching for his cell phone.

"No, don't do that." Her voice was perfectly glum. "You go, Mac. Explain to him that I'm not feeling well. He'll understand, but you should go."

"And leave you home? I don't like that much."

"Just go for a while. Have a good time. I'm sure it will be fun; I hear Jackie's made him put up a Christmas tree and lights and everything." Jessica tried to sound enthused, and Mac grinned as he fussed with the button on his cuff. "Here," she beckoned, and he dutifully held out his right wrist while she carefully refastened the button.

"God, I love this shirt on you," she said quietly.

"Sure you don't—?"

"I'm sure."

"Maybe you should give Dane a call."

"No. I don't feel like arguing with him tonight. Just give him my regards."

"As long as I don't have to kiss him."

Mac wandered around the great den, admiring the collected evidence of Dane Pierce's many successes. Here were small brass soccer trophies sitting side by side with the Golden Globe he'd won for *Sioux Nation,* the Oscar for *Bellerive.* A framed letter from the president leaned in one corner beside a "People's Choice" award that acted as a bookend for several copies of the *Lost Season* script. The supporting bookend was a ceramic statue obviously constructed by a junior sculptor.

Mac paused before a shelf holding a group of randomly placed photos and snapshots. These were clearly Dane's favorites, and Mac eyed them with interest. Besides the many pictures of his children, Dane had collected some old photos that Mac presumed were images of Dane's parents; yes, the tall man did indeed possess the same glint in his eye, the same sardonic smile.

Three snapshots of Jessica completed the assortment.

Mac frowned in concern. He wasn't surprised or bothered by the inclusion of his wife's photos in Dane's home; it was the absence of Dane's fiancée's lovely face that troubled him. Well, they had not been together that long, Mac reminded himself, taking a sip from the glass of ginger ale in his hand and leaning closer to inspect a shot of Jessica posing on the deck of the "*Pacifica*" in Amande.

"She's really beautiful, isn't she?"

Jackie's voice startled Mac so that he nearly spilled his drink as he spun around. She'd crept in so silently that he'd been totally unaware of her presence, and she leaned back against the door until it snapped shut.

"Jessie? Well, I'm a bit biased," Mac responded easily, giving Jackie a warm smile. Jackie smiled back, approaching him with a glass of wine in her hand.

"Dane would appear to agree," she murmured. "He's on the phone with her now, even as we speak." Jackie made no attempt to disguise her disappointment, and now Mac noticed the tentative way she held her glass.

"Yes, I know." Mac took the glass from her and put it on the shelf. "I think you'd better go easy on that stuff."

Jackie looked at Mac solemnly and moved closer to him, reaching out to caress his forearm. "I don't know about marrying him, Mac."

"You don't know? That's a pretty serious thing to say."

Clamping his hand over hers, he subtly stopped her from stroking his arm.

"He doesn't love me."

"Jackie, he proposed to you." Mac didn't like where this was going.

"I'm not his first choice."

"I think you'd better discuss this with Dane, not me." Mac attempted to pull away from her grasp, yet she gripped his arm tighter and moved to stand just before him. Sliding her fingertips lightly up his chest, Jackie turned seductive eyes upward through her black lashes; Mac watched the vivid red nails approaching his shoulders.

"I can't talk to Dane. But I can talk to you, Mac," Jackie cooed. As she pressed closer to him, Mac could not keep his eyes from the severe cut of her neckline, her heavy breathing exposing a cleavage that seemed to be deepening by the moment.

"Jackie—"

"Must be a little lonely for you lately, what with Jessie so...you know...surely she's not up to satisfying a man like you." Sliding her arms around his neck, Jackie pressed her slender body against his, rocking her hips forward ever so slightly.

"Jackie, look—you don't know what you're doing. You need to cool off a little...then we'll talk." Mac tried unsuccessfully to untangle her arms from his neck.

"Oh, I do know what I'm doing, Mac. I've been thinking about this, about Dane and Jessie, and about you...it all makes sense. Admit it, you find me attractive, don't you?"

Mac looked at Jackie; the smoldering gray eyes, the scarlet, pouting mouth; her creamy white shoulders threatened to lift her full, erotic breasts right out of the strapless gown she wore with every breath. Her tiny waist was only slightly narrower than her trim hips.

"Well, don't you?" she repeated, her fingers delving into his hair, her chest lifting seductively. The feminine scent of her cologne compelled. Mac shook his head.

"Jackie, of course you're attractive. But—"

"Kiss me."

"No."

"Kiss me, Mac...I need it! I need *you*, now. Let him have his little princess! Just kiss me, let me show you I can be good for you, I can make it good—"

"No. Stop this, Jackie—"

She smothered his opposition with her lips, sliding her thigh between his legs and pressing it against him.

Delaying only a moment, half from the sheer surprise of her attack and half from his own unconscious involvement, Mac grasped her head firmly between his hands and pulled her away from his face. Yes, she was attractive, and yes, he hadn't approached Jessica during the last couple of weeks. Jackie was certainly a nice piece, he thought fleetingly, sensing his own arousal with a mixture of surprise and disgust.

"Jackie—" he began again as she prepared to renew her assault on his mouth. He was wondering how to separate himself from the situation without hurting her when the door opened and Dane walked in, pausing to peruse the scene before sauntering to the couch.

Dropping her arms away from Mac, Jackie cast Dane a defiant look; Mac let out a relieved sigh and raised his hands to Dane's questioning eyes.

Dane's face split into a dangerous grin and he dropped down onto the couch, spreading his arms to rest comfortably on the couch back. "Jessica sends her love, Jackie," he said, chuckling sarcastically.

"I think you two need to talk," Mac advised, walking to the door. "I need to get going anyway."

"I had your car brought up to the door. But don't go yet, man. I won't be long." Dane's eyes were on Jackie as he spoke to Mac.

After a tentative glance at Jackie, Mac left the room, closing the door behind him and feeling shaken by the whole affair.

Dane patted the couch beside him. Jackie shook her head. "Come *here*." The softness of his voice couldn't mask his anger. Jackie sat hesitantly on the couch. "What's going on?" he asked casually, too casually for the look in his deep jade eyes.

He reached to caress her cheek with the back of his hand before slipping his fingers into the ebony mane. Jackie closed her eyes, a soft smile completing the dreamy expression on her face. Tangling his fingers into her hair, Dane suddenly made a fist, winding the locks painfully. Jackie's eyes flew open, and she gasped.

"Don't screw with Mac, sweetheart."

"He wanted me, Dane."

"Don't delude yourself."

"I could have him."

"No. That's where you're wrong, Jacqueline." Dane released her and stood. "If you want to spread your legs for someone other than me, there are ten or fifteen guys waiting in line out there right now. Be my guest. *Use my bed.* But keep your talons off MacKendall. Got it?"

"Is he the only man you're jealous of?"

"Jealous? Of you and Mac? Ha! That's rare." Dane paced away, then turned, his hands on his hips. "Mac's off limits. You'll only embarrass us all if you pull that shit again. There can be only one woman for Mac. You should know that."

"Just like there can be only one woman for you. *The same woman.*" Jackie's voice was cold and hateful.

"You're drunk. Go to bed. We'll talk about this another time."

"Don't tell me what to do, Dane."

But Dane Pierce had dismissed her and left the room.

Mac thought she was asleep.

Sliding between the sheets beside her, he moved close behind, pressing his face into the coolness of her hair.

"Missed you," Jessica whispered sleepily.

"Not like I missed you," Mac responded.

"Dane called me."

"I know."

"Did you enjoy the movie, Mac? Was it really good?" With difficulty, she turned to face him.

"I almost hate to admit how good it was."

Satisfied, Jessica closed her eyes. "How was the party?"

Mac stiffened slightly at her inquiry. "Fine." He paused, running his hands around her stomach thoughtfully. "No. That's not true. Something happened, and I need to talk about it."

Jessica's eyes fluttered open. "What happened?"

"You won't believe this...Jackie tried to seduce me."

"She *what?*"

"Jess, it was unreal. She just came up and sort of...jumped on me." Sensing her shock, he hurried on. "She was drunk. She and Dane are already in trouble, I guess. I got the feeling he doesn't treat her very well."

"Dane couldn't possibly be mean to Jackie. He's going to marry her."

"I rather doubt that now. He walked in on the whole thing."

Jessica's eyes widened in amazement. "He did? What did he say? Did he think it was your idea?" Her words rushed out in an excited whisper.

"He was really pissed off, at her. He had to go outside for a while, to cool off I guess, then he apologized to me for her behavior. He seemed embarrassed. I got the feeling he didn't want me to tell you about it."

Mac could tell from her expression that Jessica could not fathom the picture he was painting. "I told him he'd better straighten things out with her. Jackie's a confused, screwed up mess. She needs someone to love...and someone to love her. And forgive me, but I just don't think he's the right person."

"So...did she...kiss you?"

Mac pulled her down to the pillow, leaning over her to peer into her fearful eyes.

"I mean...it's...okay...I wouldn't blame you if you let her...I sure haven't been much fun lately," she continued, her voice unsure and fearful.

"Yes, she did, and it's *not* okay. She kissed me like a woman starved for attention. It was incredibly sad." Mac's words wandered as he thought about Jackie's kiss. "She's a beautiful, provocative woman, and all I could think about was how much I preferred *your* lips."

"But didn't you feel just a little...aroused?"

Mac sighed softly. "Jessie, I'm not dead. But what I felt was only a reminder of how much I miss...making love to you."

Jessica considered his admission while Mac busied himself planting tiny kisses on her face. "Then why don't you?" she said at last.

Mac paused and searched her eyes. "Why don't I what?"

"Show me...how much you miss it." Slowly she slid her hands down his firm, nude form as far as they would reach. Mac frowned in concern.

"But I thought you didn't want—"

"I thought *you* didn't want. I'm not exactly what you'd call...what was it? Provocative?"

"Oh, Jessica Lynne, how could you possibly think..." His voice trailed away as he was overcome with the emotional impact of her misunderstanding.

"I just don't...want...to hurt you." His words were punctuated by kisses to her neck and shoulders while he worked the buttons on her nightgown. The thought of making love to her had suddenly filled him with an instant passion. He needed her, needed to purge the unclean feeling he'd had since Jackie had approached him. How could Jessica have thought she could *ever* be unattractive to him?

Despite the enormous satisfaction their lovemaking brought him, Mac lay awake long after Jessica had drifted off, her arms holding him possessively. Jackie's desperate, gray eyes loomed before him, alternating with Dane's cold, steel-edged gaze. Nothing good could possibly come from the situation. Someone was going to get hurt. And there was little he could do to prevent it.

He thought about Dane's reaction to finding them, Jackie with her arms around his neck, her reddened lips pressed hard to his, her knee moving between his legs...Dane had been angry, but had he shown even the smallest tinge of jealousy? No! Mac's memory traveled back to the image of the afternoon he'd returned home early, finding Dane wrapped around Jessica. He'd been consumed with jealous, raging hatred.

Dane didn't love Jackie. He was using her...and the reason was unclear.

"Mom's resting comfortably. I'm going to stay with her for a little while, but I should be leaving in about an hour. I'll call you when I leave, okay?" Mac's voice held a tinge of anxiety.

"Stay as long as you want. I'm fine, really. I built a fire, and I'm just going to watch some TV for a while. I do have a little indigestion, probably from that lasagna we had for lunch! Give Rita my love and call me back when you leave. It's raining like the dickens outside."

"You just rest. Don't go out or anything. Love you, babe."

Jessica hung up the phone slowly, then picked up the remote control. Idly she flipped through the channels, finally settling on an unfamiliar sitcom; she rarely watched television.

Her mind wandered, making it difficult to follow the plot; her first Christmas with Mac had been so wonderful, she hadn't wanted the day to be over. They had visited his mother, picked up Megan and had headed for the mountains. She could still feel the tingle of the frozen snow filtering into her collar as they threw snowballs at one another. That night they had stayed at the lodge in Big Bear, drinking hot chocolate in front of a giant, raging fire in the lounge before retiring to their suite, Megan in tow.

Now, three days later, it seemed like a dream. It would soon be New Year's Eve.

She wasn't thirty minutes into the program when the "indigestion" got worse; surely the inane comedy wasn't making her ill? No, this was more like the beginnings of cramps traveling across her abdomen. And the baby was particularly active.

On a whim, she picked up the phone and called Chrissie.

"Gosh, twice in one week! How was your Christmas, Sissy?"

"Fine, Chris. Hey, it's finally raining! Imagine that, raining in California!"

"Snowing here. We're temporarily snowed in, actually. And Angel is fussy; Nick's about to go out of his mind. How's Mac?"

"He's gone right now, his mom's not doing too well and he's out at the hospital. Chris, I'm feeling kind of weird."

"What is it, Jess? Are you in labor?" Her sister's voice sounded her alarm.

"I don't know. Sorta feels like I'm getting my period."

"Any regularity to it?"

"No, it just started. It's probably nothing."

"Start timing it. If it keeps up, say for the next fifteen minutes or so, call Mac and tell him to get his butt home."

"You think so?"

"Honey, better to be safe. He won't mind. And call me back, okay? I'll be wondering all night."

"Thanks, Sissy. It's probably nothing," Jessica repeated. "I'm not due for a couple of weeks."

She hung up feeling a mixture of relief and trepidation. Could this be labor, *really?* It was scary. She wished Mac would call again.

Five minutes later Jessica felt the first real contraction surge across her stomach. Her eyes widened in surprise, and she grasped her belly instinctively. Again, she reached for the phone and this time punched in Mac's cell number. The call went straight to his voicemail.

"Crap." Jessica blew out a breath, then dialed another number Mac had left for her.

"Westlake Hospital."

"Reva MacKendall, Room, uh...1123 please."

"Thank you, I'll connect...that line is busy, ma'am. Please try your call again later."

"Thank you," Jessica whispered, putting down the phone.

Her mind racing, she hoisted herself off the couch and went to the linen closet in the hall. Quickly she gathered some extra sheets and an old blanket, taking them to the bedroom and spreading them out. Just in case, she thought. Already she could feel the next contraction beginning to build; it had been eight minutes.

"Oh, God," she whispered, bending over as she stood beside the bed. "This is no fun." *Better call the doctor, then I'll try Mac again.*

Grabbing the phone from the nightstand, she dialed the familiar number with shaking fingers.

"Dr. Anderson's exchange."

"This is Jessica MacKendall. I think I'm in labor."

The trained receptionist asked her the usual simple questions before telling her to proceed immediately to the hospital. Dr. Anderson would be summoned. "Do you have a call-back number? Is it the number you called from?"

"Yes. I have a cell but I...I don't know where it is."

Now realizing she had little time between contractions, Jessica rushed to her closet to grab her bag, hastily throwing items into it. Suddenly she stopped, realizing she hadn't tried to call Mac again. Westlake was at least an hour's drive, possibly more in this weather. Dropping the bag, she hurried back to the phone and picked it up just as a cloud-to-ground lightning bolt struck a power pole on Laurel Canyon a quarter of a mile away.

"Casa MacKendall" fell into complete darkness, the sound of the television died away, and the phone in her hand went dead. Outside, the storm raged on, and inside, a tiny storm was building its own fury within Jessica's body.

Jessica closed her eyes. *This can't be happening.*

Mac stared at his phone in concern. *Connection failed. Again.* He didn't like it; it was eleven o'clock, and L.A. was experiencing its worst storm in seven years.

Reva MacKendall opened her faded blue eyes, her voice a soft, yet throaty whisper. "Cory," she began, her hand moving toward his. "Go home. The baby is coming."

Gently Mac took the old woman's care worn hand in his.

"Mom, the baby isn't due for two weeks," he told her, his eyes misting over as he looked upon her dear face.

"Go home," she repeated. "Jessie needs you. The baby is coming, now."

"Okay, okay," he humored her, stroking the white wisps of hair from her forehead.

"Cory, listen to me. I made a deal. He wants me to come now, but I told Him I had to see my grandson first. So He is sending the baby now. Go home, honey. I'll be fine. Jessica needs you."

Mac rubbed at his forehead. Reva had passed into a peaceful sleep amidst the monitors, tubes and machines that could keep her breathing and ticking for a few more days, hours or minutes.

Again he tried to reach Jessica, and this time the phone continued to ring in his ear. In vain he tapped in Roxanne's number, only to arrive at dead air. He decided he should go home. His mother's words haunted him; what if...no, it had been the ramblings of a dying old woman.

Mac jogged through the pelting rain to the Lotus. Starting the engine, he noticed a slip of paper on the floor and reached for it, switching on the courtesy light. Jessica had been driving the Lotus since they'd returned from New Zealand, and this was an emergency phone number list she'd placed in the car. His own name and phone number was listed first, and just below it he could make out "Dane Pierce, 555-9284." Roxanne's number followed Dane's.

His mind was a jumble of troubled thoughts as he approached the on-ramp to the Ventura Freeway. Viewing the overpass, he could see that despite the late hour, the highway was busy and the storm had created a multitude of problems. On a whim, Mac turned the car into a service station just before the on-ramp and dug into his pocket for his cell.

Jackie Spencer's hair was like black satin, lavishly spread about her like an ebony tide; a perfect contrast for the fair skin and glacial gray eyes, now closed in passion. Dane looked down at her, his emotionless face coolly appraising her features as she moaned beneath him, arching herself against him as he only halfheartedly engaged in making love to her.

Why can't I enjoy this? His eye caught the glint of the three-carat diamond on Jackie's left hand. Maybe it was best that he'd declined on setting a date, just yet.

"Dane...Dane...oh, Dane..." Jackie was a moaner, all right; he was beginning to wish his name were Fred, or anything besides Dane. Sighing, he closed his eyes and conjured the image of another woman, another time, on a tropical island five thousand miles away...and his passion renewed. Would he ever escape Jessica's spell?

His attention was fleeting, however, as the telephone rang and shattered the lovely vision in his head. Trying to ignore the insistence of the ring, Dane could sense that Jackie was oblivious to it and nearing the height of her climax. Unsuccessfully he tried to continue the momentum, only to finally pull away from her with a groan and reach for the phone. It just wasn't meant to be, he thought with despair as Jackie cried out in heated desperation.

The voice on the phone was distorted and sounded far away.

"Dane? Mac. I hope I didn't wake you."

"Wake me? Ha!" Jackie's fingernails slid painfully down Dane's back, and he swatted them away. "What's up?"

"Look, I'm in Westlake and Jessie's home alone. I'm on the road, but it's a good hour away, and she's not answering the phone. You know I'm worried or I wouldn't be calling. She wasn't feeling well earlier, and—"

"I'm on my way."

"Thank God. I'm just getting on the freeway. Oh, and Dane, there should be a key in the window box, if you can find it. *If* you need it."

"Right. I'll be there in fifteen minutes. Don't sweat it, man."

Dane bounded from the bed and began hastily dressing. Jackie fell back onto the bed in disgust.

"Don't tell me. Jessica, right?"

"Mac needs my help."

"Sure. Jessie break a nail?"

"Something's wrong. I'm just going to check it out."

"I'm coming with you."

"No. Stay here, Jackie. We'll talk later." He hoped his expression would make an impression; he was in no mood to argue.

Tears of outrage welled in her eyes as she watched him zip up his jeans and pull a sweatshirt over his head. He'd been working out every day since Thanksgiving and had regained back much of the fitness he'd lost in Cambodia. The wounds were healed, and except for the slight hitch in his walk, Dane was back in form. The left knee would take another several months to completely heal.

As he turned to go, Jackie jumped from the bed and pressed her nude body against him in one last attempt to stay him.

"Dane, don't go. Please, stay with *me*."

"I can't, baby. This is important."

"And I'm not."

"I didn't say that. Let go, Jackie." Again he gave her a steely look. Jackie retreated as he strode from the room.

The gold Porsche sped through Benedict Canyon, the raindrops creating a water show before the headlamps as Dane took the curves as fast as he dared. Mulholland Drive was practically deserted, but turning onto Laurel Canyon caused a delay, even at midnight. Impatiently he threaded his way through the canyon, passing slow vehicles on the narrow right shoulder and pushing the needle past the safe limit. Fortunately, Dane Pierce was a skillful driver, and even under enormous stress he smoothly maneuvered the car to the front porch of the MacKendall home.

The house and grounds were dark. He rushed to the front door and knocked hard against the sound of the roaring storm. Getting no response, he went to the nearest window and peered into the dark house, spying the glow of the fireplace in the family room. Again he knocked, this time on the glass.

"Jessie!" he called, the rain drenching him as he ran his hands along the inside of the flower box beneath the window. Icy wetness stiffened his fingers as they met with the jagged teeth on the key; he ran back to open the door, only to find a hinged bar lock engaged.

Cursing under his breath, he looked around for an alternate method of entry, his fear mounting that Jessica was in trouble. Stepping back from the door, he noticed that a long, narrow window bordered each side of the door, and without hesitation, Dane grabbed a large rock from the planter and slammed it into the glass. With bleeding fingers he reached inside and disengaged the bar, throwing open the door.

"Jessie?" he called out. Her response was a cry from the direction of the fireplace. Dane ran toward the glow, stopping short as he spied Jessica lying on the floor before the dwindling fire.

"Oh my God," he whispered, stunned at the scene before him.

"Dane," she murmured, her face contorted. "Is Mac here?"

"He's on his way, darlin'." He knelt beside her, his hands raised helplessly as he gazed over her. She lay back on a rolled sleeping bag, her knees bent, a sheet over her. Her face was glazed with perspiration, her eyes feverish with pain.

"How long, honey? How long has it been like this?"

"I don't know. The power's been out a while...I...I...oh, God, it hurts...so... bad..." Her contractions resumed, and Dane grasped her hand for want of anything else to do.

"Hold on, baby, hold on...Jesus...hold on, Jessie..."

As the pain subsided, she fell back against the sleeping bag.

"How long between?"

"Just a few minutes. Dane, I'm so scared...I need help...I need something for the pain...I'm dying."

"No, you're just having a baby. I won't let you die, sweetie. Come on, I'm going to put you on the bed. This isn't good, on the floor."

"No! It's dark in there!" Jessica pushed him away as he tried to lift her off the floor.

"Cut it out! I'm telling you, Mac wouldn't want his kid born on the floor, Jess." She continued to beat on him as he struggled to lift her, finally standing and turning toward the hall. "Mother of God, you must weigh three hundred pounds!"

"God damn you, put me back!" she screamed.

"No. Stop yelling at me. And stop hitting me or I'll tie you up."

"Screw you, Dane."

"Fine time to think about that. Any other time, sweetie."

She collapsed into the softness of the bed gratefully, and Dane rushed around in search of candles, finding some in a kitchen drawer. And then she was screaming again, and Dane held both of her hands tightly in his, as the contraction built and passed.

Panting, her fire subsided momentarily, and she looked up at him in appreciation. "I'm sorry—" she began, and he pressed his fingers to her lips.

"I put you through worse in Cambodia. So dish it out, Jess. You know me, I'm into abuse."

"Have you ever...delivered...a baby?"

Dane laughed out loud. "*Moi*? Surely you jest. I was a waiting room couch-potato. All three times." He stood and went to the bathroom, returning with a damp washcloth. Tenderly he wiped her face. "So...your old man better get here soon. You are in no condition to be driven—"

His words were lost as Jessica again contorted in pain.

Mac hated cell phones. And normally, he refused to use them while driving, especially under hazardous conditions. But tonight he held one in his hand, pressing the SEND button repeatedly, to no avail. Traffic in the rain proved no picnic, and as he glanced through the rain-blurred window, he noticed a red Corvette pulling alongside the Lotus. The driver beckoned to him, his meaning clear; he wanted to race.

People like that should be locked up, Mac thought in disgust as he turned away to ignore the driver. It wasn't uncommon, when driving the Lotus, to be challenged occasionally by young punks in hot cars. But in the pouring rain? On the Ventura Freeway, no less?

So it wasn't with much surprise that ten minutes later he watched as the Corvette cut off the big-rig in the lane ahead; the truck jack-knifed and slid sideways, creating a broad, steel wall before the Lotus. Furiously Mac pumped the brakes while turning the steering wheel hard to the left as he began to skid. But the brakes seemed useless, almost non-existent as the tires hydroplaned across the lane. The result was the obliteration of the entire right side of the Lotus as it slammed sideways into the truck.

"God-damned-son-of-a—BITCH!" Mac got out of the car and slammed his door. The truck driver approached him in concern.

"You all right, man?"

"Yeah, yeah, I'm fine. But I'm gonna take out that asshole up there!" Mac thrust his arm in the direction where the Corvette had come to a stop, the truck's right front wheel having clipped it. Others had stopped and gathered around the truck and the two cars. Mac strode purposefully toward the Corvette, pushing his way through the crowd to where the driver was just getting out.

Mac grabbed the youth by the shoulder, whipped him around to face him. "You idiot! What the hell did you think you were doing?"

The rain washed the tears from the boy's face before they could be detected, and Mac stared at him blindly.

"Are you high or just crazy?"

"I—I—I'm sorry..." the boy cried.

Anger and frustration consumed Mac as thoughts of Jessica's safety loomed. Despite the law preventing it, he considered leaving the scene just as a California Highway Patrol cruiser rolled to a stop behind the Lotus.

"Can we make this quick? I have to get home," Mac asked, tight-lipped.

"Sure, buddy. We all do."

"Wash your hands. Go get a baby blanket, from the nursery. And get two bath towels from the cabinet. Hurry!" Jessica snapped orders as Dane darted away in terror, praying that Mac would arrive soon.

Gingerly Jessica reached between her legs and felt the progress of the baby's head. Nothing felt familiar; in her mind, she envisioned herself splitting apart.

Dane's face blanched, nearly as white as the tiny, snowy blanket he carefully put beside her on the bed. "What do you want to do with these towels?"

"Put them under me. Now, Dane!"

Swallowing hard, he helped her spread the towels on the bed beneath her hips and thighs, and she again sat forward in intense pain.

"Oh God, oh GOD...Dane, I think...I...have to...start pushing," she panted.

"NO! Not yet?!" Dane drew in a deep breath, trying to hold his panic at bay. "I mean, okay...okay..."

Mac's voice from the kitchen was the most welcome sound either had ever heard. Bursting into the room, he rushed to Jessica as Dane stepped aside in relief.

"What's happening?" he demanded, turning to Dane while taking Jessica into his arms.

"Uh...she's uh, having the baby, Mac." Dane grinned, but anxiety accented his voice. "We're all ready, just waiting for you," he added comically.

"Okay...I'm here, baby. Everything will be fine," he told her, regretting the tears in her eyes that reflected the candlelight. "Dane! In the garage, on the shelf above the truck is a Coleman lantern. Get it!" After Dane had skipped from the room, Mac whipped the sheet off Jessica and examined her progress. "Damn," he muttered softly. The baby was crowning.

Stripping off his drenched jacket and tossing it aside, he started away and Jessica shrieked.

"Don't leave me! Mac! Don't leave!"

"I'm just getting something from the bathroom. I'm not going anywhere, sugar. Hold on."

He scrubbed his hands, then returned with a pair of scissors, a hair clasp, and a bottle of rubbing alcohol which he placed on the nightstand.

"Oh God, Oh God—I have to push..."

"Okay. Here we go."

He sat facing her at the foot of the bed. Dane had the lantern going moments later and stood expectantly at the door.

"Dane! Wash your hands and get over here to help me."

Dane looked at his hands with a frown, then hurried into the bathroom. When he rejoined them, Mac had his hands between Jessica's legs. Dane's eyes were wide as he watched, and he gripped the bedpost for support.

"Prop some pillows behind her," Mac ordered, and Dane busily began stuffing pillows behind Jessica's back as she sat up, pushing with all her strength. Furiously she clawed at the sheet, holding her breath as the most violent of her contractions shuddered across her body.

"Okay...good girl...keep pushing..." Mac's face reflected concentration as he helped the baby's head to slip away from Jessica's body, supporting it as the shoulders appeared. The contraction subsided and Jessica collapsed back into Dane's arms as he sat behind her, supporting her shoulders as she pushed. But there was no time for rest, as the spasm began again, almost immediately. "Come on, Jessie. Almost over. Just a little more, babe...God, this is incredible." Mac watched in fascination as the rest of the baby nearly rushed out into his waiting hands. A slow grin spread across his lips as he gazed down at the tiny infant whose face contorted with its first lusty cry.

Jessica had again fallen back against Dane, her eyes closed in utter exhaustion, her chest heaving in labored respiration. Tearing his eyes away from the small package he held, Mac looked to Jessica excitedly.

"Well?" she asked softly, opening her eyes expectantly.

"Well, ten little fingers, ten tiny little toes...and one little pecker," he replied happily. "A son." Carefully he looked the baby over, checking for anything that might be amiss, trying to remember the details of Megan's birth.

"Whew! Glad that's over with," Dane said with a sigh, reaching for the cloth to wipe Jessica's face and then his own. "That was tough work."

Mac flashed him a rueful smile. "Hand me the scissors, Hercules."

"Scissors?" Dane paled at the prospect of Mac's intention but handed over the shears quickly and Mac took care of cutting the umbilical cord, using the barrette as a clamp. Last, he wiped off the baby and his hands.

"Now the blanket."

"And you learned all this on a soundstage?" Dane complied, and Mac carefully wrapped the tiny boy and took him to Jessica. The flickering light of the candles and the old lantern cast a warm glow on their faces as they took turns peeking into the child's face, and Dane moved to the doorway.

"What a freaking miracle. Congratulations, you two. Wow."

"Where are you going?" Mac tore his gaze away from the fussing baby in Jessica's arms.

"I think you kids will be all right now," Dane said, shoving his hands into his pockets.

"No, go with us to the hospital. I need your help, man." Mac stood and faced Dane.

"Naw, you're under control, Doc. I, uh, have to go home and...tame a shrew."

"I'll walk you out." Mac pulled open the drawer in the nightstand and retrieved a small flashlight.

"Dane, wait." Jessica's voice interrupted them, and Dane went back to her bedside. "I want to thank you, and to say I'm sorry for being such a witch."

"The word is 'bitch,' Jessica. But no matter. I'm used to it." The laughter in his eyes warmed her.

Overcome by emotion, she touched his cheek with her free hand, and he leaned down to kiss her forehead. He then kissed the baby's tiny head before straightening up to rejoin Mac.

On the porch, Mac pulled the cell phone from his hip pocket where he had hastily stashed it. He stared at it for several seconds, then retrieved a small, crumbled paper from the other pocket, handing the flashlight to Dane. He dialed, rubbing his eyes wearily.

"Yes. This is...Cory MacKendall. I..." he paused, his mind suddenly short circuited. "My wife..." Mac stared at the charcoal sky, noticing the rain had stopped. Dane took the phone from Mac's hand.

"We've just delivered a baby. We need some transportation to the hospital. That's right, MacKendall. You got the address? Good. We'll have the kid and the mom at the curb." Dane slipped the phone back into Mac's hand. "Tough day?" he murmured, his eyes demanding Mac's attention.

Mac rubbed his face again, shaking his head to rid himself of whatever spell had befallen him. "I'm sorry," he said. "I'm toast."

"I can see that. How's your mom?"

"Not good. Any time now."

Dane nodded and looked away. "That's rough," he murmured. He kicked at the bumper of the Porsche, parked askew just inches from the front porch post.

"I guess you were in a hurry," Mac said.

"Where's *your* car?" Dane asked, looking down the long, empty driveway behind the Porsche.

"It's totaled," Mac offered simply. "I hitched a ride." Despite Dane's shocked expression, Mac did not elaborate about his accident. "Dane, I can't thank you enough for what you did tonight."

"I can't thank *you* enough for showing up when you did."

"Shit, man, you could have done it."

"No way." Dane smiled, shaking his head. "I'd better take off. Jackie's...a might peeved, shall we say?"

Mac looked at him in silent remorse. He knew it would be more than inappropriate to offer his advice about Jackie. Instead, he slapped Dane on the shoulder.

"Take care, man."

"Goodnight, Doc."

TWENTY

New Year, New Fear

"**B**ut it's supposed to be the safest car on the road."

"I don't care. I'm not driving one of those, Mac. Find something else." Jessica set her jaw as she leaned forward, facing Mac where he sat opposite her, cross-legged at the foot of the hospital bed. Defiantly she dug at the bowl of too-hard ice cream on the tray in her lap.

Mac looked up at her determined expression, sighed, and returned his gaze to the iPad on his lap. "How about a Benz? Here's that new one, nice and big, four doors..." Again he looked up, expectant.

Jessica shook her head. "Keep looking."

Mac's own jaw began to work in frustration as Dane entered the room and stood beside the bed.

"You two must work at setting up these enormously 'cute' scenes. Now, if I were sitting on the bed instead of you, they'd call me lewd. How are you doing, Doctor MacKendall?" Dane grinned and ran his hand across Mac's shoulder.

"Awfully affectionate this morning, Uncle Dane."

"Well, I just had a taco, and my fingers were greasy."

"I'm trying to find a new car for my spoiled wife. Any suggestions?"

"God! The perfect yuppie couple. Three vehicles, all two-seaters. Maybe you could install a baby seat in the back of the Ford? Good morning, sweetie." Much to Mac's chagrin, Dane sat between them on the bed, leaning forward to gain a hug from Jessica. The iPad nearly slid to the floor and Mac scrambled to catch it.

"Mornin' Dane. You look like you were up all night," Jessica teased. "You didn't really have a taco for breakfast."

"No, actually, it was two ninety-nine cent fajitas." Dane stood from the bed as Mac tried in vain to recover the site he'd been reading from. "Mac, the girls want to come in. Buy me a cup of coffee."

"How about an Acura NSX?" Jessica asked, beaming at Mac's expression of disgust. Ignoring her question, Mac followed Dane to the door.

"Sure, man. You want to drive me to the Volvo dealer?"

Choosing a corner table, both warily scanning the cafeteria for press and fans hoping to ambush them, the two men sat down with coffee.

"You won't believe this," Dane began, his face serious as he drew a folded pink paper from his breast pocket. "I had the car checked out. You've been a bit busy."

"Which car? Mine? What did they find?"

"The brake line had a hole in it."

"Why would you do that? Have the car checked?"

Dane rubbed at his chin and Mac noted an avoidance in his eyes. "I don't know." Dane shook his head slightly and looked away.

"Shit, that car was brand new. I've never heard of a defect like that." Mac scanned the service order.

"No. The hole had been *cut*." Dane's voice was low and heavy. Mac stared at him in disbelief and mounting terror as realization set in.

"Someone?"

Dane nodded slowly. "The guy said there was no mistaking the cut. It was a small hole, probably leaking slowly for a couple of days. Just enough fluid left to slow you down. Might have been okay if the pavement had been dry."

Mac pressed a hand over his mouth then leaned against his fist. "Who would do a thing like that?"

"A fan?"

"When I think of how many times Jess has driven that car during the last month...she loved that car. It could have happened when she was driving it."

"Maybe it was supposed to." Dane's eyes were sober as he stared into Mac's.

"No. No...this can't be happening."

"There should be a police investigation, you know."

"She can't go through this again. If they've released Wesley Elliot, I'll kill him. I swear it."

"They haven't." Mac again stared at Dane. "I already checked," Dane assured him, reaching across the table to grasp Mac's arm. "Hey, man. Chill. Maybe it was just vandalism. We'll just keep our eyes open." He paused while Mac took a deep breath. "Let's go buy the brat a Volvo."

"Oh, honey, he's beautiful! He's just the most precious thing." Roxanne leaned over the sleeping baby in the bassinet beside Jessica's bed.

"Thanks, Rox. He was a lot of work, he has to be worth it, right?" Jessica grimaced as she adjusted her position.

"Pretty sore, Jess?" Jackie asked, standing at the foot of the bed.

"Sore...is a euphemism. I can barely walk," she laughed, lovingly stroking the wind-up musical lamb Jackie had brought.

Jessica had not seen Jackie since Thanksgiving, and was afraid to look at her now, afraid she might reveal her knowledge of Jackie's betrayal. She did look, however, and managed a concealing smile. Jackie, she noticed, appeared uneasy and bore a bruise and a small cut beneath her eye. Jessica's own eyes widened in alarm, and she spoke before thinking.

"What happened to your eye?"

"Last night, the power went off while Dane was gone...I stumbled over Alex's fire truck and fell. Dumb me, walking around in the dark when we must have five flashlights."

Jessica nodded but felt suspicion. Roxanne noticed the interchange and jumped into the conversation.

"Tom will be by soon, Jess. He's meeting with our broker."

"Broker? As in real estate?"

"Yeah..."

"What does this mean?"

"We're thinking of buying a house! I didn't want to tell you until we were sure."

"God, how exciting!"

"I know," Roxanne paused, her face beaming. "And you've had a baby...and you're getting married. How about that? Who would've thought back in college...the three of us...by the way, how are the wedding plans coming? Set a date yet?"

Jackie adjusted the purse strap over her shoulder. "No. With the picture and all, you know, Dane's not sure when..."

Both Roxanne and Jessica nodded but regarded each other silently as Jackie took her leave moments later.

"Did I look like that when I was a baby, Daddy?"

"Yeah, sorta. Except your hair was darker."

Megan peered into Devon's tiny face again, her right arm wrapped protectively around the infant car seat as the Volvo cruised along the freeway toward Westlake.

"See, it rides really nice," Mac ventured.

"I can't see him. Is he okay?" Jessica asked, turning around and looking into the backseat. "I hate the way that car seat has to sit backwards."

"He's fine. He's still asleep," Megan answered matter-of-factly.

"Jessica?"

"The car? It's fine, darling. Really."

"I checked everything out myself. The steering, the lights, the brakes..."

"Don't you trust the dealer?"

"Sure. It's just a thing I have about cars."

Jessica ran her hand through Mac's shaggy golden locks. "I love you," she murmured.

Pushing his head back against her fingers, Mac smiled. "I thought you would hate me for buying this *conventional* car."

"I would drive the Ford if you wanted me to. And anyway, I still have my Miata." She paused, looking across the dashboard. "It's not really ugly. Just boring."

"We could use a little 'boring' for a while." Mac sighed as he spoke, glancing anxiously into the rear-view mirror.

"Mom? We're here." Mac whispered into his mother's ear, and she opened her eyes slowly, disoriented and confused.

"Cory? It's almost time."

"I know, Mom. We've brought your grandson, Devon Charles. I'm going to crank you up, Mom. Hang on." Mac pressed the button on the electric bed so that his mother could sit more upright. Carefully he took the tiny infant from Jessica's arms and cradled him for his mother's viewing.

"Charles? After your father, Cory? Oh, he'll like that. He'll be happy to hear it." Turning her tired eyes onto the baby, she lifted a shaking, withered hand to touch Devon's small chin. A weak smile tried to form on her lips.

"He's a picture of you, Cory. A picture. He'll do you proud." Her eyes wandered away from the baby. "Where is Charlene?"

"Charlene's not here, Mom."

"Yes I am."

A female voice came from the corner of the room, and they turned to see a striking strawberry-blonde, her hair piled into a messy bun on the back of her head; brown that eyes looked like they'd seen too much of the world for a woman in her early thirties. Her clothing looked expensive but garish in the solemnity of the hospital room; hastily assembled, like her coiffure.

The surprise on Mac's face reflected his astonishment as he gazed upon his sister after a ten-year estrangement. Mac hadn't expected her to show up; even though he'd called her at Thanksgiving, Charlene could not be counted on for anything except trouble. Her attitude on the phone had been one of self-servitude, asking him what was in it for her.

Mac handed Devon to Jessica and moved aside as Charlene approached the bed and peered down at Reva without emotion.

"Hello, Mother." She glanced around at Jessica, then Mac. "I see Cory's brought his nice little family here to watch you fade away."

"Cool it, Charlene. Mom's feeling good today, aren't you?"

"Charlene? Are you okay, dear? Please don't fight with your brother. They're his toys, you have toys of your own. Don't make me have to punish you."

Charlene stared levelly at Mac. Unable to stand her hateful gaze, Mac turned back to Reva and leaned to kiss her cheek.

"It's okay Mom. We won't fight. Just rest now."

"Keep an eye on your sister, Cory. She's not strong like you. I'm going to rest now."

Reva closed her eyes and drifted away from them, this time forever. As if clairvoyant, two nurses appeared and examined the old woman as Charlene stepped back into the shadows. Jessica's eyes filled with tears as Mac bowed his head to his mother's breast in sorrow. A young nurse's aide came to Jessica's side and took Devon from her arms, freeing her to comfort her grieving husband.

Gently pulling him away from Reva's still form, Jessica embraced him tightly and he pressed his face into her neck. After a time he straightened and wiped his eyes, looking around the room for his sister. Charlene was gone.

"I guess you're probably wondering about Charlene."

"No, I'm not. I'm wondering if I'll ever be able to walk again."

It was midnight, and Mac had just settled Megan into bed. Jessica sat before the fireplace, Devon asleep in her arms. Mac had barely spoken a word on the way home, and Jessica had left him to his own thoughts. She shook her head as she watched him walk about the kitchen, trying to restore order to the mess they'd left the night before.

"Come sit with me. Leave that stuff for Gretchen."

Mac paused, then wearily switched off the kitchen light. Soon he sat beside her on the couch, his eyes on his small sleeping son.

"Devon. I like that."

Jessica turned to peer into Mac's tired face. "Been a hell of a week, hasn't it?" she asked softly.

He tilted his head against hers in exhaustion. "God, I am so damned tired I can't move. There is so much I have to do."

"But not right now. Your last duty for today is to help me get into bed."

"Wouldn't consider sleeping right here, would you? No, I didn't think so," he whispered comically, slowly getting to his feet. "You need the bassinet, right?"

"It's in the nursery. If you could just roll it into our room...unless you'd rather we sleep in the other room so you can get some rest?"

Mac frowned down at her, then left to retrieve the bassinet.

Minutes later he fell into bed beside Jessica with a deep sigh, staring at the ceiling for several moments before speaking.

"I would never want you to sleep anywhere else. You are the only sure thing in my life. I need you." He turned and embraced her fiercely. "I knew she was dying, I knew it, and still I expected her to live forever. I can't believe she's really gone."

Jessica stroked his hair tenderly, as if trying to absorb his grief. So much had happened; they had much to talk about, about the funeral, Megan's future, and...Charlene. But it could wait until morning.

Ten minutes later he fell asleep, holding her tightly, his head rising with her breathing as he lay against her breast.

They buried Reva the next day, as Mac decided it would be better to put the funeral behind them before the new year commenced.

A small group of mourners, made up of mostly Mac and Jessica's closest friends, attended the short ceremony. None of Reva's nursing home acquaintances were quite travel worthy, but some sent condolences and flowers.

Roxanne made the arrangements, and hastily put together a brief reception at the MacKendall home with catered food and service.

Mac moved about in an animated fashion. Jessica, preoccupied with Devon's care, also looked after Megan, whom, like her father, behaved in a "business as usual" manner. Tom and Roxanne did what they could to lift spirits; only Dane Pierce seemed somber, pensive and watchful.

Charlene MacKendall attended the funeral but stood apart from the family. Dressed in black jeans, gray sweater, a black, wide-brimmed hat and a long, black, wool coat, she stopped traffic in the MacKendall kitchen as she walked through the front door.

The black hat and somber clothing amplified her red-blonde hair and scarlet fingernails. She looked expectantly at Mac, who touched her shoulder.

"Glad you could join us. Everybody, this is Charlene. My sister."

Charlene nodded coolly at the others and helped herself to a glass of whiskey from Dane's bottle. Dane appraised the woman through narrowed eyes from where he sat in the corner of the kitchen. Charlene returned his cold gaze and turned her back.

Drinking down her glass and pouring herself another, Charlene motioned for Mac to join her in the hall. When he did, she took out a cigarette and a match.

"Sorry." Mac took the matches from her hand. "What do you want? Surely you didn't come all the way here from Minnesota to say good-bye to Mom."

"But of course I did, Cory. And to take home what is rightfully mine." She paused to run her fingers down the expensive picture frame on the wall. "I've been here a couple of weeks, you know. I've checked around; you seem to be doing pretty damned good."

"Get to the point."

"You've been taking care of Mom, with all this dough. Surely the old bat didn't piss away *all* of Daddy's money?"

His anger flared and Mac raised his hand as if to strike her, then lowered it slowly to his side.

"Get out. Get out of my house. And make sure you never show your disgusting face here again."

"What's the matter, big brother? You gone soft? Afraid your mousy little wife might not like to see you hit a woman? Come on, surely you haven't hidden your nasty temper all this time?"

"I've dealt with my shortcomings. Apparently, you haven't. I'll walk you to the door."

"I'll go. But I'm not leaving L.A. until I get my share."

Charlene got into a waiting car, driven by an unknown companion. Mac paced on the gravel driveway, alone, breathing the chilly air deeply in hopes of cooling the heat in his gut.

Dane soon joined him, hands thrust deep into his pockets. He stared at Mac a long time.

"I always hated being an only child," he said at last. "When my parents died, I was totally alone."

"If she really needed it, I'd give her anything. But she'd just piss it away on drugs and booze."

"She's a hooker, isn't she?"

Mac looked up in surprise.

"I can see 'em comin'." Dane chuckled.

"How did your parents die?"

"They took a ride on a train. A train to hell." Dane paused with an ironic smile. "You may remember the story. About ten years, now. The engineer was loaded. Tokin' all the way from New York to Maine."

Mac frowned. "I do remember. God, that's awful. I'm sorry, Dane."

"Not as sorry as you're going to be in the morning."

"Why?"

"'Cause we're going out tonight, my friend. We have a new year to bring in, and some serious drinking to do."

"I don't know, Dane. I can't just go—"

"You sure as shit can and will. Tom's idea, and he's the good guy, so you can go. It's all arranged. The girls will be good and pissed off, and you know what? It's good for them." Clamping his arm around Mac's shoulders, they walked back to the house, Dane nodding and Mac shaking his head.

Roxanne spent the night with Jessica and the children. Jackie had declined Jessica's invitation to join them. They did not expect to see the men until morning and decided to make the best of it.

Jackie had sounded depressed on the phone, and while making popcorn, Jessica's mind flooded with memories of the past year; most especially of last New Year's Eve, and the premiere of *Bellerive*.

"God, that was an awful night," she reminisced with Roxanne later. "I was so hung up on Dane, and I had asked Mac to take me to the premiere. And Dane was there with Merrily…"

"And I was there with Zach." Roxanne's eyes looked into the past with her. "You got rather drunk, as I recall. Mac had to hold you up."

"He took me home. I was such a mess! Blubbering all over the place about Dane. And he was so disgusted with me. He put me to bed and slept on my couch."

"Why do you think Jackie didn't want to come?" Roxanne suddenly changed the subject.

Jessica shrugged. She had never shared her knowledge of Jackie's problems with Roxanne, feeling it was better left unsaid. She stubbornly hoped that Dane and Jackie would eventually work things out, although like Mac, she knew in her heart that there was nothing special between the two.

"What do you think about that bruise? Do you really think she did it by accident?" Roxanne continued.

"What are you saying? That Dane hit her?" Jessica went on the defensive but had to admit to herself that she'd been thinking the same thing.

"Not Dane, necessarily...but it does look like somebody punched her. She lives with Dane. I don't get the impression they get along all that well."

"Well I *hope* she's telling the truth. Dane couldn't possibly..." Jessica's voice trailed off as she remembered Mac's recount of his evening at Dane's party. *Dane was really pissed off.*

Jessica also remembered the night of her birthday party when she had introduced Jackie to Dane. Ruefully she recalled warning Jackie that she had done her no favor in making the introduction. How could either of them have known the irony of her words?

·♥·♥·♥·♥·♥·

This joint's jumpin,' Mac thought, as he cautiously perused the crowd spilling out on to the sidewalk.

"You should join this club," Tom suggested as he led Dane, Mac and two others to a round table in a corner. "I've been a member for ten years." The five of them together would be a coup for any paparazzo seeking candid, heart-stopping photos. Even their waiter, a too-handsome young man in his early twenties, seemed overwhelmed at the prospect of serving his famous guests.

"Man, I'm glad I don't have a face like yours," Steve Lightner commented to Tom as four girls at a nearby table spotted them and started giggling.

"Likewise," Tom replied smartly to his producer colleague.

"What will it be, gentlemen?"

"Wild Turkey. On the rocks," Dane responded without hesitation.

"Seven and seven," Tom ordered.

"How about a Rum and Coke?" Steve put in.

The waiter paused expectantly, waiting for Mac's request.

"Uh...I don't know." He looked at Dane, then turned back to the waiter. "Glass of milk?"

There was silence around the table until Dane burst out laughing; the others followed suit, and the waiter smiled in relief.

"Give me a margarita, on the rocks, no salt," Mac ordered.

"Same." Sal Cicerello echoed.

"Good to see you again, Sal."

"You, too, Mac. I've been working my ass off with postproduction. They're talking about a May premiere. Thought about what you want to do next?"

"Don't know. I'm being solicited—it's weird being off the tube. I'm not used to the time."

"That's the trick; don't get used to the time. You should keep working," Steve put in.

"What's happening with your project, Dane?" Tom asked.

Dane unwrapped a stick of gum and slipped it into his mouth. "Besides giving me an ulcer, nothing." He pulled his wallet from his hip pocket. "I'll get this round." The waiter distributed their drinks, and Dane raised his in a wordless toast.

"I hear you're casting Jackie." Mac peered at Dane from across the table, watching his reaction closely.

Eyes steady, Dane shrugged.

"Maybe."

"Who's Jackie?" Steve wanted to know.

"She's nobody. And I'm not sure she has what I'm looking for." Dane threw down the whiskey and signaled the waiter for another. Mac stirred his drink pensively, wondering about the meaning of Dane's words. But Dane was still talking.

"No, I think we just might save Jacqueline for something different. I need someone bolder...but with a touch of vulnerability."

Sounds just like Jackie to me, Mac thought.

"Against your lead?" Steve questioned.

"No. I'm not in the film."

"You were two weeks ago," Mac puzzled. "What happened?"

"Changed my mind." Dane took another draught. "I think *you'd* make a helluva senator, MacKendall...but you'd have to cut that damned mane of yours."

Mac's eyes locked onto Dane's. "What are you saying?"

"Just that I'm offering you the role, if you're interested."

"Work with you? Are you nuts, Pierce? God, I'd end up with an ulcer, too." Mac laughed and drank down his margarita. "*Cut my hair?*" Mac ran his fingers through his shaggy locks.

"You can keep the mustache, if you want."

"Gee, thanks, pal."

Dane nodded, lazily reclining in his chair, chewing the gum thoughtfully.

They were well into their third round when one of the girls at the nearby table moved in on them. Not much over twenty-one, she was rail thin and wearing a black band around her hips that doubled as a skirt; a tiny, tight, off-the-shoulder knit top barely covered her midriff, and she placed her hand on Tom's shoulder as she leaned down to speak to them.

"My friends over there sent me to ask if you boys would like some company."

Her comment sent a mild chuckle around the table. From his laid-back position behind her, Dane grabbed the girl's wrist and pulled her abruptly into his lap.

"Seeing's how all these other guys are married or spoken for, I guess I'll have to entertain all four of you. But you can be first, how about that?"

The girl wasted no time in putting her arms around his neck, and Dane flashed a rueful smile at the others. Both Mac and Tom shook their heads in mock disapproval, but Steve rose from his chair.

"Excuse me, Pierce, but I've just paid dearly to become unmarried. Give me a break." Steve sauntered over to the other table and promptly asked one of the remaining girls to dance.

"You *are* Dane Pierce! I knew it!" The girl sighed, wiggling on his lap and exposing more thigh than the others thought possible. "You know I've seen *Lost Season* three times," she said, giggling loudly over the music.

"Only three?" Dane queried silkily.

"Maybe you should buy the DVD," Mac suggested, and Dane nodded agreeably; they both laughed.

The girl turned to look at Mac, then back to Dane. Taking the drink from his hand, she finished the whiskey herself, then leaned forward conspiratorially.

"Is that Cory MacKendall?" she whispered into Dane's ear.

"Yup. That's Cory..." He watched as Mac took his turn at paying the waiter.

"Isn't he married to—"

"Come on. Let's dance." Dane stood suddenly, nearly dumping the girl onto the floor.

Fog seeped across the dance floor as colored spotlights roved crazily across the dancers. Despite his torn emotions over Dane and Jackie's doomed relationship, Mac was entertained by Dane's outrageous flirting with the young girl. Slouching back in his chair in an imitation of Dane's usual posture, he chuckled to himself.

"What's so funny?" Tom wanted to know.

"Nothing," Mac replied, pushing the hair from his eyes. "He wants me to cut my hair." A bemused smile stayed on his lips.

"Think we should call the girls?"

"The girls...yeah. Good idea, Thomas." Mac nodded and the two rose to find a quieter spot to make the call.

"What does it feel like?" Roxanne asked as Jessica put her son to her breast.

"Like nothing I have ever felt. It's very natural, and it's nice. It's the strongest feeling of being needed. It's hard to describe. Someday you'll know."

"Not sure about that. Tom's son is eighteen. If we ever did get married, I don't know that he'd want to start a new family."

The ringing phone interrupted Roxanne's thought, and Jessica answered the cordless she'd placed next to the couch.

"Hello? Hello? Is anyone there?" Quickly she replaced the receiver. "Must have been a wrong number."

"Oh...you didn't mind Tom taking the guys out tonight, did you?"

"No. Mac needed to get out. He's grieving, he's tired, and I think it was the best thing for him. Of course, Dane delights in getting Mac totally blitzed, and Mac will regret it tomorrow, but I think it's good."

The phone rang again.

"Hello?" Jessica's voice was wary this time, but the sound of Mac's voice cheered her.

"Hey, baby."

"Hey baby." Jessica smiled into the phone. "You havin' a bang-up time?"

"I'm having a time, I'm not sure if it's good or not. I guess it's fun watching Dane put the moves on someone besides you."

"What's that supposed to mean? Is he entertaining a girl?"

"Oh, is that what you call it? Entertaining? Maybe it's something he can teach me."

"On the contrary, darling. There's much you could teach him. You aren't getting polluted, are you?"

"No. I can't. A mild buzz is all I'm after tonight. Dane, on the other hand, will probably come out of here on a stretcher. I swear I've never seen him drink like tonight. Bent on destruction and no good." Mac paused, and Jessica could hear the loud music in the background. "I miss you. How's the baby? Did Jackie come?"

"No, she didn't. Roxie and I are just talking. Devon's fading in and out, and Megan's been asleep for a couple of hours. And," Jessica lowered her voice a little, "I miss you, too."

"Tom wants to talk to his old lady. You try to get some sleep, okay? Don't worry about me, I'm fine. I promise. We'll probably screw around 'til morning, but we've got a limo taking us home, so no one has to drive. I love you."

She handed the phone over to Roxanne and moved Devon to her other side. Soon, Roxanne hung up.

"Doesn't it feel weird seeing Mac and Dane hanging out together? I mean, Mac hated him so much."

"Mac never hated Dane, Roxie. He just couldn't understand him. They're so different. You've never understood him either, as I recall."

"You really fell hard for him, as *I* recall."

Jessica smiled softly. "Yes, I did."

"Ever wonder how things would have turned out if you had married Dane?"

"Dane never asked me, for one thing. But if he had, and if I had been insane enough to do it, he would have tossed me aside the minute the vows were spoken."

"You really believe that?"

"Most of what attracts Dane Pierce is the chase. The conquest is anti-climactic for him. I know that, now."

"I think he's still in love with you."

Jessica stared at Roxanne in shock. Before she could respond, Roxanne continued. "And I also think that's why he proposed to Jackie. He's gotten himself into a tough situation with her; I don't think he expected her to be the bitch you and I both know she can be. And, I think that bruise on her face came from Dane's fist."

"Roxie!" Jessica exclaimed, startling Devon from his drowsy state.

"Come on, Jess, are you blind to the way he looks at you? I wouldn't let him in this house if I were Mac."

"I can't believe you're saying these things. Dane and I are friends, good friends. And we care a lot about each other. Mac understands that now, and so should you. It hurts me that you could think that way."

But despite the strong words, Jessica's face showed doubt. Lifting Devon to her shoulder, she straightened her blouse and amended her attitude. "I'm sorry you feel like that. Does Tom feel that way, too?"

"I don't know. We don't discuss it."

"I'll bet you *do* discuss it. You two discuss everything. Does Tom think there's something going on between Dane and me?"

"He's only said he worries about Mac's tolerance of the situation. He doesn't want it to happen again."

"Mac will never leave me again if that's what you mean. He will never have reason to; and I'll stake my life on that."

"You mean you'd stake your life on trusting Dane not to do it again? Because, forgive me Jess, I'll bet he does. The 'chase' as you put it, is still on for Dane. And maybe that's why he's so buddy-buddy with your husband. He'll never marry Jackie. He never intended to." Roxanne turned her back and went to peer out the back windows before continuing. "Please don't be mad at me. It's only because I love you that I said anything. I'm sorry."

Devon had fallen asleep, and Jessica carried him to the bassinet across the room and tenderly laid him down. She crossed to Roxanne and stood beside her friend, silent tears gliding down her cheeks. Tears brimmed in Roxanne's eyes also, and she embraced Jessica tightly.

The phone rang a third time, disturbing the quiet. Jessica hastily ran the back of her hand across her eyes, glanced at Devon's sleeping form and reached for the phone.

"Hello?"

"I know you're alone, Jessica," a husky voice whispered. Instant terror coursed throughout Jessica's body as the voice went on. "He won't be back tonight. Better lock the door, Jessica." A dial tone followed.

Jessica's eyes were wide with fright.

"What is it?" Roxanne demanded.

"Oh my God," Jessica managed, slowly hanging up the phone and dropping to the couch.

"Jess?"

"He said...he knows we're alone. Said I'd better lock the door."

"Who said that? Who was it?"

"I don't know."

Jackie wore a short, sleeveless, Japanese silk dress of fuchsia. Her black hair hung nearly to her waist, gleaming, swinging as she sashayed into the room, gray eyes perusing the crowded club, seeking only one.

Tom spied her first, nudging Mac as they walked back from the lobby. "Look." Mac's eyes followed Tom's gaze, and a groan emanated from his chest.

Dane was feeling no remorse. The girl, revealed as Tina, had pushed a chair in beside him and adhered herself to his side. With one arm around her, Dane's other held a fresh glass of whiskey and a lit cigarette.

"Oh, shit," Mac muttered. "Can we rescue him?"

"We should at least try. You intercept Jackie and I'll see what I can do with Dane."

"No. *You* intercept Jackie. *I'll* warn him. Try...kissing her."

"Huh?" Tom puzzled as Mac walked away.

Mac hurried over to the table, his own head dizzy and reeling. "Dane. Get up, man."

Dane looked up at him, his eyes remarkably keen after the enormous amount of liquor he'd imbibed.

"MacKendall! I thought you'd split."

"Dane, listen, man." Mac bent to whisper into Dane's ear. "Jackie's here. Maybe you should...take a walk or something. And you can't smoke in here."

"Jackie? Here? So what?"

"Dane—"

"Fuck Jackie, Mac. Ha! She'd like that, wouldn't she?" Dane laughed out loud, then took a long drag on the cigarette.

Determined, Mac tried again. "You want to kill yourself, man? What's this shit about?" Deftly he grabbed the cigarette from Dane's fingers and dropped it into a near-empty water glass.

"Who's Jackie?" Tina purred, her lips delicately enticing Dane's ear.

The answer came as Jackie appeared at the table. Behind her, Tom shrugged regrets at his failure to detain her, and Mac sighed in despair.

Tina fell away from Dane as he stood to face his future bride; Jackie's icy gaze chilled everyone at the table.

"*I'm* Jackie," she stated clearly, her eyes scathing as she gave Tina the once over.

"My...fiancée." Dane's voice held a mock affection not lost on those who knew him. "Hello, Jacqueline."

Tension sizzled between them as they locked eyes; no one made a move. Mac's stomach churned as he stood beside Dane. He decided the picture would only be more complete if Jackie held a pearl-handled Colt pistol aimed at Dane.

Dane took a step towards her, and Mac took one back. Slipping his hands around Jackie's slender waist, Dane bent to press his lips hard against hers, kissing her lustily before the group of mesmerized onlookers until she was fighting for air and pushing him away.

"Damn it, Dane," she spat, touching her bruised lips, her face contorted in anger.

Sal stood up and walked around the table to where Tina stood, an entranced, if hurt, expression on her young face.

"Dance with me, Tina," he offered, pulling her toward the dance floor and taking the edge off the tension that had built.

"Waiter!" Steve called, beckoning to the young man who had also watched the scene unfold between Dane and Jackie. Mac sat down and finished his drink, shaking his head again at Tom who returned a defeated look.

Having lost his audience, Dane released his grip on Jackie and sat down. "Have a seat, my dear. Now that you're *here*, you might as well share yourself with us."

Steve ordered and looked expectantly at the others. "Anybody?"

"Mac needs another drink," Dane replied, "and so do I. And bring...the *lady*...a Long Island Iced Tea."

"Right, Mr. Pierce."

Jackie sat in the chair vacated by Tina. "Dane, come home with me." Jackie slid her long, hot pink nails up his arm to his shoulder. "Please?"

"Home is not where I want to be. You can go if you want."

"Dane, come on...I'll make it worth it. You don't need these cheap sluts! They're just groupies, they don't care about you the way I do." Pushing closer to him, she pressed her hand to the inside of Dane's thigh and slid it up his leg.

"Yeah, well you've got a hell of a way of showing you care, baby. You think I've forgotten your little stunt with my best friend, here? In fact, you might be able to have him now, he's almost drunk enough."

"Dane, that's enough," Mac announced. "You're crocked. Let it rest, okay? Jackie, I'll get you a cab."

"No, Mac. Thank you." Jackie's face paled. "I have my car, but I'm not leaving yet."

"It might be a good idea, Jackie," Tom put in, leaning forward across the table. "Maybe talk this out tomorrow."

"It's always tomorrow. No. Dane, come home with me now."

Dane looked at her with eyes of steel. "You don't seem to understand. I'm not going anywhere. Let's just forget this all happened, you go, I'll stay, tomorrow we'll...work things out. Okay?"

The waiter set the tall "iced tea" in front of Jackie, and without hesitation, she picked it up and sipped a third of it down, then promptly dumped the balance onto Dane's crotch and stood up.

Lightning fast, he was on his feet and had grasped her arm in a vice-like grip, his face white with rage. Simultaneously, both Mac and Tom stood, their postures defensive on Jackie's behalf.

The dangerous smile broke on Dane's face.

"This isn't 'Simon Says,' boys. I'm just going to walk the little lady to her car. And I don't need any Boy Scouts to walk me back."

Dane ushered Jackie out the front door with a firm hand. Tom sat down, but Mac remained standing, nervously wondering if he should follow them when he noticed a bouncer at the door subtly nodding at him before trailing Dane out the door.

The video monitors surrounding the bar suddenly lit with the view of Times Square in New York, and a digital clock in the corner of the screen ticked off the last remaining ten seconds of the year. Amid the din of New Year's revelers, Mac lifted his glass against Tom's and Steve's, and the three sat back to mull over the evening's events. Mac suddenly wanted to be home with Jessica, toasting with her before the fire.

The bouncer returned and nodded in Mac's direction, just before Dane re-entered the club. Wordlessly he rejoined the group and sighed.

"My apologies to everyone. We obviously have a few things to work out," he said at last, his face dark and brooding.

Relieved and feeling bold, Mac turned a critical eye on Dane, whom, he noticed, bore a fresh scratch on his cheek.

"You could save yourself a lot of grief if you just admit you made a big mistake. Break it off, man."

"Thanks, Doc, I'll remember that."

"I mean it, Dane, somebody's going to get hurt. Just tell her—"

"Save it, Mac. I already *got* hurt." Gingerly he touched his cheek. "People sure do get off on beating on me, ever notice that?"

"That's because you get off on screwing with people, my friend." Mac sipped his drink, feeling melancholy.

Dane's face took on an amused expression as he peered thoughtfully at Mac, who leaned over his fourth margarita. On a whim, Dane reached over and touched Mac's hair, tugging on one of the longer locks hanging below his jacket collar.

"We could braid it, I suppose."

"Fuck you, Pierce."

❤ · ❤ · ❤ · ❤ · ❤ ·

Jessica snapped awake from a fitful sleep and rolled quickly out of bed. The clock radio read five o'clock and she went to the bassinet to check on Devon, who hadn't awakened at three as she'd expected; her breasts were painfully full. Finding him sleeping peacefully, she tiptoed out to the hall and across to the other side of the house to peek in on Megan.

The little girl was curled into a ball, uncovered and cold. Carefully Jessica tucked the comforter around her. Going to the kitchen, she decided there would be no more sleep for her and started a pot of coffee. By the time she returned to the bedroom, Devon was fussing to be fed and she gladly spent thirty drowsy minutes nursing the infant before putting him back down to sleep again.

She assumed the men had crashed at Tom's after their night out and would probably get breakfast together at some point this morning. It had seemed like a fine idea when they left, promising that none would drive under the influence. Now she wished Mac had come home instead.

After showering and dressing, Jessica went out the front door to retrieve the newspaper and to get a breath of the new year. The terror of the crank phone call had faded, and she decided she would get their number changed. No reason to worry Mac about it.

The sun shone bright, the air smelled crisp and clean. The newspaper lay near the garage, and as she bent to pick it up, she noticed the side door to the garage stood wide open; she frowned in concern. It wasn't like Mac to miss closing the garage door. She went to peek in, only to suffer an overwhelming flashback of the night she'd found her cabin vandalized and had been abducted by her ex-husband, Wesley Elliot.

The garage appeared normal at first glance; the old Ford truck on the far end, the Miata, covered and parked in the middle, and the new silver Volvo closest to the house. Taking a closer look, she saw the glass; piles of it, all around the Volvo as every window in the car had been smashed out. All four tires had been slashed. Afraid to go farther to inspect the other vehicles, she turned and ran, heart pounding, back to the house.

Once inside, she carefully locked the front door and rushed to find her cell phone. Mac was surprised to hear her voice and began offering assurances that he'd be home soon.

"As soon as you can, please! Someone has broken into our garage."

TWENTY-ONE

Sibling

Jessica paced the family room, trying to quiet Devon while Mac sat at the kitchen table with two policemen. Mac's posture belied any semblance of confidence as he leaned against his hands, his fingers buried in his hair.

"And approximately what time did the phone call come in?"

"Jessie?" Mac hollered, his voice weary and tinged with irritation.

"Around eleven thirty, I think?" she called back over the baby's sporadic cries.

"Thanks, Mr. MacKendall. We'll be in touch. Call us if anything else... unusual occurs."

"Right. Thank you."

Mac ushered the two to the door, then leaned tiredly against it. He could hear Jessica humming softly to Devon in the back room. His mind spinning, he closed his eyes briefly.

"One thing at a time," he murmured, then took a deep breath before joining his wife.

Going to her, he encircled both Jessica and the baby in his arms, kissing her forehead gently. He couldn't shake the vision of her terror-filled eyes when he'd returned home two hours earlier. Still pale and weak from childbirth, Jessica, he knew, put up a good front; but he also knew she relied upon his strength now.

"Everything will be okay. I won't let anyone hurt you again." His voice was low but committed. Jessica flashed him a loving smile.

"I need to clean up," he said, unbuttoning his shirt and moving toward the hall.

"Bet you're hungry," she called after him, and Mac turned with a grateful smile.

"Starved. You wouldn't be thinking about throwing together some lunch, would you?"

"I might be thinking about it," she teased, settling Devon into his infant seat and carrying it with her into the kitchen.

"So Dane walked her to the car?" Jessica handed Mac a napkin and sat down across from him.

"Yeah. It was a...tense moment, at least for me. I kept having these visions that she was going to off him or something. It was like a scene from some movie, she was the scorned lover, and this other little gal he was carrying on with, she was terrified...and I kept waiting for Jackie to pull out a gun. So bizarre."

"He would have probably deserved it, flirting around like that."

"I thought so too, but the more I think about it now, Jackie's one weird chick. Maybe she brought this on herself, what do you think? You know her better than I do." Mac stuffed the last of his second sandwich into his mouth.

"She did sound a little strange when she called last night to say she wasn't coming. I just figured she was depressed about Dane leaving her home. She never mentioned she was going out."

"She wouldn't tell you, of all people. When is Roxie bringing Megan back?"

"She's keeping her all day. They went to Pasadena to look at the floats, then they're picking up Tom and going to look at homes in Malibu."

"Damn, the Rose Parade! I've already forgotten it's New Year's Day." Mac paused, then grasped Jessica's hand. "Let's go somewhere. I need to get away from here."

"What about Devon?"

"Bundle him up. He's going to be doing a lot of traveling, he might as well get used to it. We need to talk, and I can't talk here. Not today."

Ninety minutes later they were in the air and flying north. The first day of January was clear and cool, and below them the Pacific Ocean glistened like turquoise gel. Devon was wakeful but did not cry during the flight. Mac felt as though the Cessna was carrying him away from the problems he'd left at the house, and his mind seemed to clear as he put the situation into perspective.

At the small airport in Santa Barbara, Mac tied the plane down and turned to Jessica with a smile.

"Been just over a year since we did this, remember?"

"I'll never forget it."

He borrowed a car from the owner of the nearby bar and grill, for whom he'd signed autographs in the past; with Devon's car seat strapped firmly into the backseat of the convertible Mustang, they were off to the mountains of Montecito with blankets and diaper bag in tow.

As they lay together on the blanket, Mac felt temporarily at peace. Nothing could touch them here, no one could harass or molest them. Both he and Jessica desperately needed to feel safe and secure, impossible now at home. And all the while, his mind worked, planned, and filtered through the painful events of the past week. Lying on his back, eyes squinting toward the sky and Jessica snuggled against his shoulder, Mac finally spoke.

"It was one year ago today that I moved into your funky little house."

"Roxie and I were just talking about last New Year's Eve. What a disaster."

"That was a tough time for me. That night I slept on your couch, I decided I wasn't going to see you again. It was such a hard decision, and then you went and invited me to stay. I didn't want to do it because I was afraid we couldn't be just friends."

"You were wrong."

"Not entirely. We were great at being friends, but I wasn't great at *not* falling in love with you anyway." Mac chuckled. "And then, that morning I woke up in your bed, Gees! I knew how Dumbo must have felt when he woke up in that tree." He turned to peer into her eyes, still smiling. "Like, what did I do to get here? How can I get here again? Can I really fly?"

His story made her giggle with delight. After a while, Mac sighed, and his expression became serious.

"You would know I was lying if I told you I wasn't worried about what's happening. I am. But I don't think we're dealing with a real pro, here. I think it's some amateur trying to scare us for some reason. And I have a thought, but I don't think you're going to like it."

"What?"

"I want you and the kids to go up to Nick's for a while."

"Without you?"

"Without me."

She looked as if she would work up a protestation, but paused, lifting her head to check on Devon, now sleeping in his car seat nearby.

"Hear me out before you kick up a fuss. I'll fly you up there myself and deposit you with your sister. I'll come back and see if anything else happens. If it doesn't, I'll come and get you. If it does, well, I'll deal with it. But I can't function worrying about you, babe."

"What are you planning to do? Just sit and wait for someone to break in and get you?"

Mac smiled at her question. "No, I'm not painting a target on my butt. I'm going back to work. If something's going to happen, it'll happen."

"Work? You found something you want to do?"

"Well, it sort of found me."

Jessica again raised her head and he turned to face her, pulling her close against him.

"God it's been a long time since I've been able to hold you like this."

"I'm still fat."

"I still want you."

He kissed her neck and ear until she was giggling and breathless.

"Tell me about the job," Jessica asked at last.

"Would you hate it if I cut my hair?"

Jessica frowned in mock concern. "How short?"

"I'm playing a politician."

"What a coincidence. Dane's doing a film about a senator."

"No coincidence."

Jessica's eyes widened as she absorbed the news. "You're doing Dane's picture?"

"He offered it to me. What do you think?"

Jessica seemed almost more taken by this news than by the prospect of going to Utah. "It's...not up to me. But I think it's a fantastic opportunity. That's a pretty different role for you...is it a Pierce production?"

"Of course. And Dane's directing."

"You'll be playing opposite Jackie, then."

"Uh, no. Jackie's out. He's casting someone else. Hasn't found anyone yet."

"Good, because the answer would be a resounding 'no' otherwise." She ran her fingers through his hair. "Do you think you could work with him? After everything?"

"My only fear of working with Dane is that I'll be standing too close the next time someone tries to kill him."

"I'm serious, Mac. He can be difficult...he has a hellacious temper on the set."

"It's no worse than mine. And it's worth a cool million. My hair will grow back."

"So when do we leave for Utah?"

"You aren't going to fight me?"

"What good would it do? If it will give you the peace of mind you need to get going on this project, then I'll go. *If...*"

"Yes?"

"You call me every night and visit me every weekend until I come home. Deal?"

"I wouldn't have it any other way." Mac embraced her firmly. "Now," he continued. "There are a few other things we have to settle."

They discussed Megan's desire to live with them, both agreeing that it would be wonderful, if Linda were amenable. And if – *when* Jessica went back to work, they'd hire a nanny to care for both the children.

"She's already part of our family, Mac. And I'd hate her to stay with Linda if she's uncomfortable with Linda's new husband."

"Okay. That's settled." There was one more item on his agenda, but he hesitated, reflecting on just how to tell Jessica about his sister. Before Mac could begin, Devon started to fuss and Jessica tore away from him.

"He's hungry."

"How do you know?"

"Because I'm his mother." Tenderly she cradled the tiny infant, opening the snapped panel of her blouse to nurse him. Mac sat up and moved to sit close to her, watching with intrigue as the tiny mouth moved against her breast.

The moment was solemn. Magical.

It struck Mac that he had been cheated out of his son's first few days of life; the madness of the night of Devon's birth had melted into his mother's death with almost no break; the funeral, the vandalism, the long night out with his friends had all taken their toll on his fatigued mind. Now he stared down in wonder.

"Linda didn't nurse Megan," he said, caressing Devon's cheek with the back of one finger. "She was too nervous."

Jessica didn't answer. She seemed spellbound by the moment, waiting for Mac to continue.

"I really do love him, Jess. I'm sorry I haven't been with it the last few days. But things will straighten out and get back to normal. You'll see."

"Whatever that is," she murmured. "We don't really have a 'normal,' Mac."

"Maybe I shouldn't do the film."

"Maybe you just need to think about it awhile. But I'm in, for what it's worth. It would give you another opportunity to broaden your experience." She paused, not looking at him as she continued. "But it's all between you and Dane. I don't want to be involved, and I don't want to get put in the middle of anything. Okay?"

Mac didn't answer, only smiled bemusedly.

"What's so funny?"

"I can't wait to make love to you again."

Discussing Charlene would have to wait.

The second week of January brought several feet of snow to Brighton, Utah. The lodge closed as they struggled to dig themselves out, and Jessica paced across the lobby before the fire.

"You're going to wear out that rug, Jess." Christine was busy cleaning out a cabinet in the recreation area off the lobby and watched her sister thoughtfully.

"Sorry. I'm a nervous wreck," Jessica confessed.

"Miss him that much?"

"That much and more."

"He was just here four days ago."

"I know, but now he probably can't fly in this weekend. I wouldn't want him flying in this weather anyway. But—"

Christine approached her sister and touched her shoulder affectionately. "You two have something really special, don't you?"

Jessica nodded. "It's like I can't be without him now. After everything we've been through, first with what happened in Amande, then the thing with Wesley, and all that time he was in New Zealand and we weren't talking...Chris, Mac is my whole life. I need him. Need to be with him."

Just then Megan skipped into the room and rushed Jessica with a hug. Lifting the girl into her arms, Jessica embraced her tightly.

"Look at this, Aunt Chris! Look at this beautiful young lady I have here! Isn't she gorgeous? She has the loveliest brown eyes you've ever seen." Megan giggled then squirmed her way down.

"Auntie Chris? Can I have some punch?"

"In the fridge, dear. Be careful not to spill."

Megan trotted off and Christine gave Jessica a warm smile. "Cup of coffee? It doesn't seem to be getting any warmer in here."

Pierce Productions had been ready to begin filming back in December. All that had been missing was the talent, and now that Dane had cast them, "Action" was called.

In his dressing room at Paramount, Mac ran his fingers over the back of his head with trepidation, feeling the short, cropped haircut with disdain. Sighing, he leaned closer to the mirror to inspect his reflection. *Definitely conservative. Jessie will hate it.*

The charcoal pinstripe suit wasn't bad, though, and it had been ages since he'd worn a tie; a red tie, at that. Picking up the gold wire-rimmed glasses, he gingerly threaded on the earpieces and leaned back. They had styled his bangs to fall onto his forehead. Mac turned his head from side to side in surprise. *No Doctor Jim here.*

Today's scene took place in a courtroom. Mac looked around expectantly for Dane, finally spying him hard at work adjusting the lighting angles with a technician on a catwalk above. Seeing Mac below, he quickly maneuvered down a rickety scaffold and jumped to the floor.

"Jesus, MacKendall, you almost look too good for this. Maybe we should cast you as the president instead. You ready?"

"As ready as I'll get. Is she here yet?"

"Who?"

"I've forgotten her name; the actress playing the district attorney."

"Oh, Vicki? Probably. She's gorgeous, isn't she?"

"Gorgeous. Right."

The filming went okay, except that the loss of one camera slowed them down somewhat. Mac drove home, tired but satisfied with the day and happy to be working again. He couldn't wait to get Jessica on the phone, to tell her once more that nothing new had happened. He thought about flying her home in a few days when the snow melted.

He had had the Volvo taken away. *After the Lotus. After the BMW. Maybe we should try public transportation.*

The weekend after Jessica went to Utah, Mac painfully sifted through Reva's belongings, packed away some and passed the rest on to charity. He'd nearly forgotten that his mother owned a car; the small, four-door Honda had barely two thousand miles on it and would do nicely while he decided what to do about getting another vehicle for Jessica.

The following week he'd had a camera-based security system installed, including a series of lights around the outside of the property. The phone number had been changed and an intercom installed throughout the house. Tomorrow, workman would build a fence, separating the pool from the grassy side of the yard, with a locking gate in between. He called to give her an update.

"Tell me everything," she ordered with a giggle.

"It was exciting. Dane's pretty impressive, off-camera. He's awfully demanding."

"Was he on your back?"

"Not mine, but he wouldn't leave Vicki alone. I think she nearly walked off the set. And then we lost the camera, and Dane blew up, and—"

"How did you lose a camera?"

"Oh, one of those big lights, you know, up in the rafters? Came crashing down on it. Smashed it to pieces. Dane was in pieces, too. You know how much those things cost? It's outrageous."

"Mac, where were you standing when the light fell?"

"Too close for comfort, actually," he replied, then became quiet as he considered her implication. "It wasn't aimed at me, babe. It was just a fluke. Really."

"Okay." Jessica bit her lip, then took a deep breath. "So go on, what else happened?"

"Nothing, really. How are my babies?"

"Megan is eating up attention like there's no tomorrow. And Devon's sucking away."

"That's my boy. And you?"

"The truth?"

"Of course."

"I'm miserable. I need my man."

Again Mac was quiet; he didn't want her home yet. "It won't be much longer. I promise. And I'll be there this weekend, even if I have to fly commercial."

Mac hung up, deep in thought. He *had* been standing just beside the camera when the light had fallen.

Jessica's tears fell upon Devon's bare tummy as she changed his diaper. She hadn't been able to stop crying since she'd ended the call and had retreated to her room with the baby. Christine, thankfully, tucked Megan into bed, so in tune with Jessica's misery that she'd led the little girl away without a word.

"We'll be home soon, little one. Daddy will take us home." Quieting her sobs, she called the kitchen and asked Dennis to bring her a glass of red wine.

"Make it a half liter," she amended. She couldn't deal with the tension any longer.

Mac lay awake long after midnight. Jessica's absence tormented him, especially considering the reasons behind it. Was he doing the right thing? Was this terrorism aimed at her, or at him? Now he was unsure. The phone call had certainly been directed at Jess; the caller had known Mac was not home and had called her by name. The tampering with the Lotus may not have been discovered had Dane not insisted on having the car checked out; Mac would have thought the wet pavement the cause of his failure to stop. He would have also thought that the destruction of the Volvo was an act of New Year's Eve vandalism, had it been an isolated incident. But the falling spotlight troubled him. The camera had been tracking him; he'd just moved from the spot.

Filming progressed without further incident as the week wore on. Dane, however, was not himself; Mac was surprised, more than once, at Dane's subdued and distracted behavior.

"Hey, Mr. Director...how about lunch?" Mac called on Friday afternoon as the crew broke midday.

"I'm not eating," Dane commented flatly, "but I'll join you if you want some company." With a crooked, sarcastic smile he added, "for what it's worth."

They left the set and dined in an expensive, quiet restaurant in nearby Santa Monica.

"So, what gives?"

"Hmmm?" Dane responded nonchalantly.

"Something's on your mind. You've been somewhere else."

Dane didn't answer, methodically dumping two packets of sugar into his coffee and stirring it.

"You and Jackie still on?"

Now Dane looked up, keen eyes boring into Mac's inquisitive ones briefly before looking back at the coffee.

"Yeah. Still on." His words were short and stiff, and made it clear he did not intend to discuss the matter further.

Mac nodded slowly, carefully pushing aside the green onions in his salad with a fork.

"How's Jess?" Dane asked, bringing the steaming cup to his lips.

"She's fine. Getting a little wigged out, I think. She wants to come home."

"So bring her home."

"I'm afraid to."

"Then hire a damned bodyguard."

"For now, I think she's safer up there. I gotta tell you, Dane, I'm freaked out about that light."

"I know, and I'm sorry. It won't happen again."

"I'm not blaming you. It's just too coincidental. No one saw anything unusual; nobody was on the catwalk that shouldn't be, and yet—"

"I was up there myself. I went over every goddam angle with Ron. Everything was secure. No one else is even allowed up there."

"Who is this Ron? Have you worked with him before?"

"No. He's new, but his credentials are good. He worked in Vegas for several years, doing casino shows and films. Seems to know what he's doing." Dane looked weary of the conversation; he'd obviously had the accident on his mind for some time. "So, heard any more from your sister?"

"No, thankfully."

"Got a vengeance for you, doesn't she? Why is that?"

Mac pondered for a moment, reflecting on Dane's question. How could he put twenty years of sibling rivalry into one sentence?

"My dad and I were real close when I was a kid. Charlene always wanted to tag along; she wanted to be one of the guys. She wanted his love, in the worst way; it didn't happen. He had no use for little girls. She always resented my relationship with him. When she got older, he tried, but it was too late. She was gone. It hurt him, and Mom...well, she and Charlene never got along."

"And now she's after your money?"

"She thinks my dad left some money, and that it's stashed away somewhere. She doesn't know he gambled it all away before he died."

"Why didn't you tell her?"

"For one thing, it hurts me to voice the truth to her about Dad. And she wouldn't believe me anyway." Mac dabbed at his mouth with his napkin, then leaned back in his chair with a sigh. "It would be better if she just went away, back to her street life in St. Paul. I don't want her around my family. She runs with a pretty tough gang back there."

"What a waste," Dane murmured thoughtfully. "She's a pretty gal."

The fact that Dane was worried, too, didn't help.

At home, Jessica's vintage answering machine blinked with eight messages from "unknown caller," all of them blank; a dead possum floated in the pool; and Charlene MacKendall sat in the living room.

"How did you get in?" Mac demanded, his eyes narrowed in disgust.

"Old trick I learned back home. Forgot to set your alarm, big brother." Charlene lazed back on the couch. "So? The little lady coming home soon? Tell me, does she wear pearls and high heels around the kitchen to bake cookies? Or does she just wear them to bed?"

"I thought I made it clear that I don't want to see you. Why don't you just let yourself out."

"Jesus, Cory, you'd think you'd spend a little time with me, after ten years. So what happened to that cold bitch you were married to last time I saw you? Be kinda hard to get off with her, I'd think. But you must have done her once, you have a daughter, right?"

"Okay, Charlene, what do you want? What do I have to do to get rid of you?"

"Just tell me what happened to Pop's money. That's all I want, then I'll be on my way. He wrote me just before he died. He'd won a big jackpot in Reno and had put away some of it for me. *I want it.* I tried to get it out of *Mother* before she packed it in, but she was either delirious or she didn't know about it. Acted like I was a real fruitcake."

"Look. He died in debt. I paid their bills; I took care of Mom. There was no jackpot, no savings. You can have the Honda if you want it. Or I'll pay your way home."

Charlene stared at Mac, a hateful gleam in her overly made-up eyes. "I don't want her stinking, cheap car. Pop wouldn't lie to me about the money. Now where is it?"

"You're amazing. After all those years we lived with it, lived through his lying, gambling, squandering...you still believed he won the big one? All the times Mom struggled to support us, while he stubbornly insisted we'd be rich someday? You're in for a big shock, Charlene. He didn't leave a red cent. If anyone knew how to 'piss it away,' as you put it, he did." Mac turned his back on her, sauntered toward the back patio. "He never got over it, you know, you going to St. Paul. He really loved you. It wasn't until after that, when we moved to California, that he quit his job and started playing craps full time. He really mourned you."

"My heart bleeds."

"Go away. Go back to the life you've made for yourself. If you need some cash to get home, let me know. But just...go away."

"I'll be in touch. I won't be going home just yet. I'll find out the truth."

"Be my guest."

He fished the possum out of the pool. He dreaded calling Jessica, dreaded her questioning him again about coming home. But he was more certain than ever; he'd be crazy to bring her home now.

When the first week of February had passed and he had not heard another word from Charlene, Mac felt that he'd seen the last of her, at least this time around. Jessica had been gone a month. He'd made three trips to Utah to visit her and Devon, and despite his daughter's protestations, had taken Megan back to her mother.

The incident with the spotlight had been the last violence directed at him; the phone hang ups were sporadic. Dane remained distant, although his professional talent seemed to be at a high as he went about directing *The Senator*. Repeatedly he demanded retakes; his perfectionism seemed obsessive to Mac, who tirelessly complied with every change, every suggestion and nuance Dane came up with.

"I don't get it," Dane commented one night as they walked to the parking lot.

"What?"

"You haven't tried to punch me out once. I've been a real asshole."

"You're always an asshole. I've just gotten used to it."

Tonight, Dane asked Mac for a lift home, and the two tiredly climbed into the old truck.

They sat in the dark, silently enjoying the momentary solitude of the day's end, then Mac pushed the key into the ignition.

"Mac, why in hell do you still drive this old piece of shit?"

"You wouldn't understand," Mac replied, turning the key carefully to the exact spot where he knew the temperamental ignition would spark.

"You're doing an ass-kicking job."

Mac paused, gear shift lever in hand, and stared at Dane. "But?"

"But nothing. That's all, you're playing it exactly the way I thought you would. Perfect. And I hope you're paying attention to what I'm doing."

"Why should I? You're doing a damned respectable job, too."

"Just...in case. I may need some help toward the end."

"And what's that supposed to mean?"

"Nothing. Just thought you might like to learn a little about directing."

Mac dropped Dane off half an hour later, and wearily drove back toward Laurel Canyon.

"I made you a drink. How'd it go today?"

Dane glanced at Jackie and picked up the drink. "Okay. Where's my son?"

"Uh...he's at a friend's. For dinner, I think."

"You think? What friend? Where?"

"A little boy named Calvin, I think."

"What's with this 'I think' crap? Either you know where he is, or you don't. And if you don't, you'd better find out. That kid doesn't go anywhere without my permission. You're not his mother, Jackie, and don't forget it."

"He said you knew the boy. He said—"

"He's seven years old. What he says doesn't quite count, yet. Get on the horn and find him, then get him home."

"You'll embarrass him if you drag him home during dinner."

"Just...find out where he is."

They dined alone, in silence. Dane reflected on how greatly his life had changed since the day he'd left for Cambodia seven months before. Not long after his release from the hospital at Thanksgiving, Jackie had moved in without much discussion; Peter had grown tired of the tension and had moved out in early January.

"So I understand Jessie's coming home this weekend."

Her words struck him like a brick. "How do you know?" he demanded.

"I spoke with Mac last night. He's flying her home on Saturday."

Dane stared long and hard at Jackie. Saying nothing he turned back to his meal.

"I bought my dress today."

"Wonderful. What color? Red?"

"White, of course. *She* wore white, you know."

"I wouldn't know."

"I think April tenth would be nice."

"Whatever."

"You could show some enthusiasm."

"Oh, could I? The only thing that enthuses me is leaving here every morning. There is one reason, and only one stinking reason why this marriage is taking place. And so help me, if you step out of line, even one fucking inch, the deal is off. I'd rather rot in hell."

He stood up, angry eyes flashing momentarily in hostility as he strode from the room.

"I'm going after Alex," he called before treading heavily out the door, slamming it in his wake.

Jessica leaped into Mac's arms when he opened them to her, crushing her body against his and wrapping her legs around him as he spun her. The din of her screaming giggles suddenly subsided as Mac covered her mouth with his, devouring her kiss with his own.

"God, I thought you'd never get here!" she said, kissing his face excitedly as he collapsed, still holding her, onto the deep leather couch in the great room of the lodge.

"Traffic was horrible. Planes are stacked up back to Vegas." He pulled away from her, allowing his eyes to take in the length of her. "I can't believe how good you look. I guess you're ready to come home?"

Behind her, Christine stood by with a pout. "I've gotten used to her being here. I don't want her to go!"

They dined out with Christine and Nick, leaving the babies with a sitter. Afterward, back in their suite for the night, Mac stretched out on the bed while Jessica got Devon changed and into his crib.

"Nick said it was a nice change to be waited on for once."

"They work so hard, Mac. But they're so happy here. Their problems are different. They worry about the customers having a positive experience, the weather, the local politics, stuff like that."

"It's all relative. They probably see our lifestyle as glamorous."

"There's nothing glamorous about someone breaking into your garage and trashing your property."

With Devon settled and hopefully down for the night, Jessica joined Mac on the bed and invited his attention. He rolled on top of her, moving her through an amorous foreplay she had all but forgotten existed.

"Maybe we should just move in here," he whispered, delighting her ear with his lips.

"This is our third time here, huh?" she cooed back, remembering their first night of wild lovemaking. The night Devon was conceived.

"Mac?" she started suddenly. "I'm...not...protected..."

"I am," he said softly. "I didn't forget. We're not quite ready for another child right now."

She answered with a sigh and let herself drift into the delicious euphoria of his love. It was almost all new again; the tender way he caressed her body, playing her like a delicate instrument, gently urging her hips forward as he bore down upon her. And nothing had ever felt so right; no one fit Jessica like Mac, no one could bring to her the kind of sensuality, the immense pleasure he brought with each graceful movement of his being.

She remembered almost nothing from that moment until they landed the Cessna at Van Nuys late the next afternoon. The Los Angeles weather seemed tropical compared with the sub-freezing air they had left behind in Salt Lake City.

With Devon wailing loudly in the backseat of Reva's Honda, they drove home without speaking, holding hands all the way. Once there, Jessica fed Devon and chatted briefly with Roxanne on the telephone, at home in Malibu with Tom. She promised to bring Devon for a visit during the next few days.

Mac sat quietly that evening reading his script beside a single lamp in the family room. Jessica felt good to be home, and she roamed around the big house reacquainting herself with it once again.

He was gone early the next morning, leaving her a nostalgic note on the small corkboard in the kitchen.

Jess - Truck's dead. Took the "M." I'm at
Paramount all day if you need me. —Love, Mac

Jessica smiled at the memory of their past note-leaving and took comfort in returning to a routine. Maybe everything was finally going to be okay.

❤ · ❤ · ❤ · ❤ · ❤ ·

March brought winds, and commitments. The premiere of Mac's first feature, *The Night Horse*, neared, and every magazine and talk-show host in town clambered for an interview; *The Senator* had less than a month of shooting to go, but Mac's time was at a premium and Jessica felt lucky to see him briefly at breakfast. Afraid of her own shadow the first week after returning from Utah, she had finally settled into a comfort zone. No new acts of terrorism had arisen, no further calls or suspicious activity had occurred.

With Devon over two months old, Jessica had developed a routine for his care that included a daily walk, followed by his bath and nap at midday; while he slept, she completed chores and read through the scripts Teddy had collected for her. It was during just one such afternoon that Mac's sister paid her an unexpected visit.

Thinking the knock might be the mailman with a package, she threw the heavy front door open casually, only to bring herself up sharp at the sight of Charlene MacKendall striking a pose that belonged solely to that genre of women who could be called "tough." A cigarette dangled, clenched at its very edge by her reddened lips, and her eyes squinted slightly behind the smoke it emitted.

"Charlene...hello."

"Jessica. May I come in?"

"Of course."

She moved aside as Charlene threw the butt into the shrubs and showed herself to the kitchen. Glancing hastily around, she turned back to Jessica with a sort of non-expression reserved for those subjects she found most boring.

"Kid asleep?"

"Yes. Is there something I can do for you?"

"Yeah. You can give me the keys to the Honda."

"Reva's Honda? I really can't do that, Charlene."

"Oh but you can, Jess. It's mine. Your dear, sweet husband, my illustrious brother, he gave it to me, and I'm here to collect it."

"Mac didn't say you were coming by. I need the car to take Devon to the doctor later. I don't have any other vehicle I can use. Perhaps tomorrow?"

"Perhaps tomorrow my ass, sweetheart. Get the keys. And hurry."

"No. Maybe you should come back later. I'll check with Mac. If he wants you to have the car, I'm sure—"

Charlene approached Jessica, leaning close to her face.

"You might as well give me the keys. It would sure be awful if Mom's car ended up like your last two." Her lethal tone conveyed her threat.

As Charlene's implication sank in, Jessica began to tremble. Slowly she went to her purse on the counter and withdrew her key ring, wrestled the Honda key off and dropped it into Charlene's outstretched palm. Snapping her hand closed on the key, Charlene strode briskly toward the front door, turning to call over her shoulder.

"Tell my dear brother I said hello. I'm sure we'll be seeing more of each other...soon. Thanks, Jessie." Her mocking words stung Jessica in the heart.

Paralyzed, she watched as Charlene got into the Honda and drove it away. Numbly she wondered if she had left any items in the car that she would need. Finally snapping into action, she hurried to the phone and dialed Mac.

Dane watched Mac closely as he put down the phone and returned to the set. He'd seen Mac upset many times, but rarely the ashen color he now wore, the defeated slump of his shoulders and look of total dismay in his eyes.

"Ten minutes!" he called to the crew and crossed the sound stage to meet Mac halfway.

Mac's eyes seemed blind to the activity going on around him.

"Mac?"

"I have to go home."

"What's happened? Another attack of some kind?" Dane's own eyes brightened in fear as he awaited Mac's response. "Jessie's okay, right?"

"Jessie's okay. Charlene was there. She took the Honda! She apparently admitted to trashing the other cars. I've gotta get home. Jess is really upset."

"I'll come with you."

Dane delegated the balance of the day's work to his assistant director and gingerly pressed himself into the Miata beside Mac.

"Damned car was built for midgets," he complained, pushing the passenger seat back to the limit.

Mac flashed him a brief, preoccupied grin and burned rubber getting out of the parking lot.

The Miata's tires skidded a little as Mac applied the break on the gravel driveway. In the MacKendall kitchen, Jessica had made a fresh pot of coffee and was singing nursery rhymes to Devon where he reclined in his infant seat on the table. Mac rushed to embrace her, but Dane hung back at the door and shoved his hands into his hip pockets.

"Tell me exactly what she said."

"She said something about not wanting it to happen again, what happened to the other two cars. I can't repeat it exactly." Her resolve faded fast as Mac scrutinized her for more. "She said...to tell you...hello...and that you'd be seeing more of her." Unspent tears fell onto her blouse; Devon, too, began to cry, and she pulled abruptly away from Mac to pick up the child and hush him.

Mac looked to Dane, reading his reaction to the information Jessica had imparted. Dane's head tilted almost imperceptibly toward the front door, and Mac returned a slight nod.

"We'll be right back, babe. Dane's going to help me jump-start the truck, as long as he's here. We're going to need it for a couple of days. You...take care of the little slugger."

"I'm okay. I'm sorry I fell apart."

The two men walked together toward the garage. Mac shook his head. "I know what you're thinking."

"You gotta do it, man. You can't be sure she won't do something else."

"She's my *sister*."

"She's your nemesis. What if she does something to...to hurt someone? Someone you love?"

Mac stopped walking and turned to face Dane. "I used to wonder how parents could turn in their own children for doing drugs. I knew a kid in school whose folks did that. I hated them." Mac looked away to the highest treetops separating his property from the road.

"And maybe if your folks had gotten help for *her* back then, this wouldn't be happening now. And maybe if someone had gotten help for that asswipe in New York, my folks would be alive. Ever think of that? Ever think that maybe she's asking for help? She did all that shit. She has to be stopped."

"How can you be sure? How could she have dropped that light?"

"I don't know. She had a dude with her, remember? Maybe she has some help. Call that cop, Denehy. You've got to stop this nightmare." Dane turned his back. "For Jessie."

The Honda was easy to find, parked on the street in a low rent district of North Hollywood ten minutes away. Charlene was booked and jailed within hours, and the nightmare ended. With the list of "priors" faxed to LAPD by St. Paul police, Charlene didn't bear much credibility with her elaborate denial of the crimes of which she was accused. She admitted only to muscling the Honda away from Jessica, and to being born into the wrong family. Bail was set but no bond was posted.

Despondency settled over Mac for the next several days. It was inconceivable that he had turned his own sister in to the police; that Charlene had tried to kill him and then had denied it.

"You okay to go back to work?" Jessica asked later that week as she watched him put on his jacket.

"I'm okay. I've worked under stress before. I was a freakin' mess in New Zealand, and everyone kept saying, 'you're great, Mac.' I guess being happy and normal is a handicap. You...take care. I'll call you later." He gave her a brief kiss. "Love you."

He worked through his remorse, coming to terms with the impact of his sister's deeds. The film took him away from it, if temporarily, and by midday he was back on course. Dane, however, appeared worse than ever. Pale, unshaven and almost gaunt, he was jumpy and irritable, and Mac sensed it had little to do with the film, or even with the events surrounding Charlene's arrest. But Dane also seemed unapproachable, and Mac held his distance as the week wore on and eventually closed on Friday afternoon. Dane stopped for the day at one o'clock and left the studio in haste; Mac was relieved and went home.

TWENTY-TWO

War...

D ane slammed the gold Porsche to a stop inside the garage, bumping the nose just enough to jerk his neck slightly. Rushing into the house, driven by anger, he searched for Jackie, calling her name loudly as he strode briskly from room to room.

"She's not here." A small voice answered from down the hall. Dane entered Alexander's bedroom to find the young boy laying on the floor, a video game controller in his hand. His eyes were fixed on the television screen before him.

"Where is she, bud?"

"Doctor, she said. I'm sposta stay in here 'til she gets back. Is Jackie sick or somethin'?"

"Yeah...she's a little sick." Dane closed the door and sauntered back to the living room, where he poured himself a shot of tequila and waited.

She came in half an hour later, her face colored deeply from the sight of him home.

He eyed her silently, turning his drink casually on the bar before speaking. "You left him alone."

"Just a few minutes..."

"A few minutes is enough for serious shit to happen. What the hell's wrong with you?"

"Don't yell at me. I've had a traumatic day."

"Traumatic? I'd like to show you traumatic someday."

"Okay, cool it, Dane. I've still got the journal, you know. And I'll have it until the seal is on the marriage certificate. You wouldn't want it to turn up at the wrong place...at the wrong time, would you?"

Dane stared at her in open hatred. She walked casually away from him and then paused to examine her fingernails.

"I guess now that Mac's sister is locked up, you think I can't use the journal as evidence? You think it won't matter that you've been writing about your madness, your sickening obsession for Jessica MacKendall for over a year? I just wonder what she'd say if she could read it for herself, especially the part about how you wished Mac were dead."

"Enough!"

"How fast do you think Mac would change his mind about Charlene and have you locked up instead? But we both know that's not necessary, don't we darling? As soon as I am Mrs. Dane Pierce, I could care less about your crazy, black-hearted affliction. And I'll make you forget her, too. You'll see."

"You're not a quarter of the woman she is. You're not fit to wait her table. And married or not, journal or not, I won't be sharing my bed with you. Even I won't lower myself that much. You're pathetic."

Despite her callous behavior and strong words, Jackie cringed at Dane's spiteful loathing.

Dane left the house, seeking cool, fresh air to cool his burning soul. How could he have walked into Jackie's treacherous scheme of blackmail and deceit? His head ached with visions of his discovery of her malice; of finding out that Ron Jenkins was Jackie's half-brother, an ex-con just released from Nevada State Prison. It was Jackie, not Charlene, who'd wreaked havoc on the lives of his friends; who'd harassed the only woman he'd ever genuinely loved, and her husband; a man he'd come to love like the brother he'd never had.

He wasn't afraid to face jail. Jackie could be very convincing, especially since she'd made certain everyone had seen the bruise she'd gained the night he'd stumbled onto her plan. Dane Pierce had never struck a woman in his life; he could barely fathom that she would go so far as to inflict an injury upon herself to blackmail him...and yet she had. He remembered staring in horror at Jackie's smiling face, her fingers delicately touching the tiny cut beneath her eye.

"Perfect," she'd whispered illogically, madness behind her devious smile. He already suspected that he'd been silently accused of the deed. And he had been the last one seen adjusting the light over Mac's head. Had he not also been the one who'd had access to the Lotus, the night of the Christmas party, when his "fiancée" had been found in the arms of his former enemy? Jackie had stacked the evidence well, and he'd played right into her plans.

Yes, he would have gone to prison to protect Jessie and Mac; it was his fear of losing Jessica's love that had forced him to submit to Jackie's treachery. He couldn't bear for Jessica to know the secrets he'd harbored, the hurtful words he'd scribbled. Charlene's arrest had been timely and convenient, although it afforded him not relief but tremendous guilt. He'd practically dialed the police for Mac that dark afternoon. He'd put an innocent woman behind bars to serve his own purpose.

Dane sighed heavily, the freezing air turning his breath into fog.

He had been the Editor of the Sterling High Enterprise. His classmates had fully expected Dane to go into journalism as a vocation, but it was the call of the footlights he'd answered, changing his major to dramatic arts when he'd entered Cal State. Aside from trying his hand at a couple of screenplays, Dane had abandoned the literary scene, focusing all his energy upon becoming an actor.

He married Rita after a whirlwind romance, and she supported his efforts by working as a secretary for a small production company. It wasn't until the death of his parents that Dane once again put pencil to paper.

His therapist had suggested it. Dane had lost several months of his life wallowing in a black hole of depression. The loss of his beloved mother had caused a vast emptiness that nothing could fill; neither Rita nor his career could bring any kind of substance back into his world. The doctor handed him a small, leather-bound book filled with blank pages. He'd been writing in it ever since; his deepest feelings, his nightmares, his joys. And yes, his hand had formed the words that would have sent Cory MacKendall into the proverbial cornfield.

He remembered it well. He had put Jessica into the cab that morning in Amande, sending her home to Mac. He'd fought depression the entire day and had returned to the spot on the beach where she'd led him the night before; where they'd made love on the sand and had slept together until morning. And there he sat, writing in the journal, pouring his heart into the small book until he felt some solace.

Jackie discovered the journal and immediately read it, cover to cover. He wasn't sure if she hatched her scheme before or after, but she brought her threats to light the evening he suggested they call off the engagement. Life had been living hell ever since. He'd thought that Charlene's incarceration would at least deter Jackie from perpetuating her deranged pursuit of terror; would afford him some small semblance of respite from the constant fear that Jessica was in danger. But the ache only grew stronger; the gnawing in his stomach intensified until he was in unceasing agony. Could he tolerate the lie? Could he go on living with the knowledge of Charlene's innocence...and Jackie's guilt?

The air grew more frigid as the sun dipped behind the canyon hills. Searching the dusky sky for the first star, none appeared to him and he turned back toward the house.

Dane's expression turned formidable as he walked slowly back into the house. Jackie seemed to be busy in the kitchen, and he leaned against the doorframe to watch her, his eyes calm and determined.

"I've changed my mind," he stated simply.

"What do you mean?"

"I'm not going through with it. You can do what you want with the journal, I'll suffer the consequences. I won't tell them what I know about your guilt, but I won't confess to your lies either. So, it's over. I want you out by morning."

"You can't be serious."

"I am. I can't believe I let it go this far. But it's over, Jacqueline. I'll give you enough cash to keep you for a month. Better start packing."

"I don't think you'll want me to go when I tell you what I found out today."

"There's nothing you can say to change my mind."

"How about this? I'm pregnant, Dane. The baby is yours."

"That's impossible. If you've gotten yourself knocked up, you can't hang it on me."

"You're the only one, Dane. And my doctor told me that vasectomies are not always successful. Did you ever get tested after you had yours? Surely the big, brash Dane Pierce would never worry about birth control. Well, honey, get ready for number four. Or maybe, number *five*?"

Her implication was not lost on Dane. Quickly he walked to Jackie and grasped her by the hair, forcing a scream from her lips.

"You tell anyone, anyone at all about this, and I'll make you hurt. You understand? I don't want you breathing a word about it. I'll get the truth, Jacqueline. I swear it. In the meantime, you sit tight, extremely tight. You clear?"

Jackie nodded, and he released her hair. Without looking back, Dane sought out his car and left the estate.

"Does he sleep in that thing?" Roxanne asked as she watched Jessica adjust Devon's legs in the baby carrier she wore strapped to her chest.

"He loves it. Sure makes shopping a lot easier." She glanced into a shop window at an evening gown on display. "God, I need to get a dress. The Oscars are coming up, and I'm still fat. Mac thinks I've lost all the weight, but he's not the one squeezing into my clothes."

"Don't be stupid. I'll make you a dress. How's he doing, anyway? Any news on a hearing?"

"I don't know. He doesn't talk about it. He hasn't been himself since that day. He's *okay*, but not great. It's a tremendous burden for him." Jessica pushed the thought from her mind. "Let's go into Macy's. I need to find a little jacket for Dev."

After oohing and ahhing over the tiny windbreakers and car coats, Jessica selected one and the girls headed for the cashier. Jessica slowed her pace and Roxanne looked around for the cause of her hesitation.

"Here comes trouble," Jessica murmured, spying Jackie Spencer entering the baby department. "Could she have known we were in here?"

"No way! I never told her we were coming here. This is weird. What would she be doing in the children's area?"

They watched, seemingly unobserved, as Jackie lovingly examined tiny layette items. Inevitably, she spotted them and approached. She seemed friendlier than usual and invited the girls to join her for lunch. Unable to come up with a viable reason to decline, Jessica and Roxanne soon found themselves listening to Jackie's prattle over salads.

"So I want to know: why were you in the children's clothing?" Roxanne inquired, stabbing at her lettuce aggressively. "*You* having a kid now or something?"

Jackie's face froze and Roxanne choked back her surprise. It was obvious that she'd struck some chord, some element of truth, and even Jessica blushed at the overwhelming strain that passed around the table.

"I...didn't mean to pry," Roxanne murmured, looking down at her plate.

"Alexander needs some things. Dane isn't much good at looking after a kid, you know?" Jackie responded. But the words she spoke were not the words she communicated; Jessica looked at Jackie's stomach expectantly.

She's pregnant. She's cheated on Dane. Unless...

"Well, I expect you and Dane will want to have children someday, so he'd better learn, right? It's about time, he's had three already. Pass the salt, Roxie?" Jessica's voice was cool and steady. Did Jackie even *know* about Dane's sterility?

Jackie flashed a knowing smile. "Yes, we do. And the doctor thinks there's no reason why we can't."

Jessica put down her fork, and turned to Devon, asleep beside her in the booth. "Roxie, I just remembered I have to pick up Mac's tux. We have to get going."

"It was great seeing you guys! We should get together more often." Jackie beamed at Jessica, her mission so obviously accomplished, and she subtly caressed her abdomen as she spoke. Her gesture was not lost on Jessica, who watched from the corner of her eye as she packed up Devon's things and awkwardly moved from the booth.

They ducked back into Macy's and began sampling perfumes at the cosmetics counter. Jessica was counting the seconds until Roxanne made a comment, getting only to seventeen before it spilled from Roxanne's lips.

"You think she's pregnant?"

"Yes."

"You think it's Dane's?"

"Well, she sure wants me to think it is. And I can't think about it. Because if it's true..."

"You're right. Don't think about it. That's exactly what she wants."

"She doesn't know about what went on between Dane and I; she only assumes it."

"He could have told her."

"He wouldn't. Now help me find something. Something fresh and seductive."

At Paramount, filming was winding down.

Dane seemed more obsessive than ever, checking and re-checking the details, the cameras, the props. The grips and technicians made faces behind his back, angrily muttering about the tension and Dane's lack of trust. A heated argument ensued between Dane and the property master, and Dane sent the man packing mid-morning; Dane remained raw and edgy. The climax of the film's story was next to be filmed.

The "senator" is in his office, waiting for a courier to bring the computer disk containing the damning evidence. He is sitting on his desk, staring out the window, his back to the camera. A gun lies ready on the desk; it is his opponent, not his page, who enters the room and picks up the gun.

"It's over," the opponent says, aiming the gun at the back of the senator's head.

"Yes, it is," the senator responds, not turning to face the opponent.

A close up is focused on the senator's face, filling the entire screen with his expression of sadness. We hear the gun being cocked, we see the senator's expression tense in fearful anticipation as the gun clicks and doesn't fire, then clicks again with an explosion. He closes his eyes as the camera fades to black.

"Okay. That'll be a print." Dane climbed down from the camera boom and saluted Mac. "Excellent performance, Senator." He turned toward the crew. "Now let's do the dead guy. We start with a close up on the trickle of blood on the tile floor...Phil, I need more blood. This guy just blew his lousy brains out! It looks more like he cut himself shaving. Get busy!"

Mac stepped into the shadows, watching Dane's feverish energy with both respect and regret. He wondered if Dane really did have an ulcer, and if so, he decided it was warranted.

Wandering out of earshot, he called home and left a message for Jessica, then returned to watch his colleagues complete the scene with the dead congressman on the floor.

Dane beckoned to Mac to join him outside. He lit a cigarette and leaned back against the stucco building, running a shaky hand through his already disheveled hair before turning to Mac. Mac grimaced at the smoke but held his tongue.

"Look pal, I need a favor." A small paper bag had been hastily stuffed into the pocket of his jacket. Mac eyed the package curiously but turned his eyes back to Dane's.

"You've got it. Shoot."

"I've gotta leave. There's one last scene to be shot, and I want you to handle it. Then, look at the dailies for me and see what you think. I'm behind schedule or I wouldn't ask you, Mac."

"Of course, if you think I can do it."

"Shit. You could do it with your eyes closed."

"Are you okay, man?"

"No. My stomach's wasted. My head's a mess. I've got to see my doctor, or I won't live to see this God damned film on the screen."

Mac stared at him in surprise. It was unlike Dane to be so candid about his health; he sounded too serious for the smile that curled on his lips.

"You don't mind if I call you at home tonight?" Dane questioned, taking a long drag off the cigarette.

"I'll expect it." Mac's eyes again went to the small package that didn't quite fit into Dane's jacket. Dane noticed his interest and tapped the bag lightly.

"That worthless prop guy left this here. I have to drop it off on my way out." Dane started toward his car.

"You—take care." Mac shook his head, then called out to Dane. "Hey. If there's anything else I can do..."

"Forget it. I'll land on my feet. Thanks, brother."

Mac returned to the studio and put together his best efforts to direct the final scene, truly appreciating for the first time Dane's talent for making things happen. Briefly studying Dane's dog-eared copy of the script while struggling to decipher the hen-scratched margin notes, he turned to the AD with a look of concerned amusement.

"He must be kidding."

Dane hid behind dark glasses and a knit beanie as he waited for the nurse to show him into Dr. Segal's office. Despite her most beguiling smile, she was unable to coax a return grin from Dane as she led him down the hall to see the doctor.

"Sit down, Dane. Do you want the bad news or the bad news?"

"Hit me, Doc. I'm already on the floor."

"Your ulcer is worse. There is probably more tequila in your veins than blood, and your heart is working overtime. You're back with the coffin nails, too, aren't you? I might suggest an overdose of Valium. It would be faster and more painless than the way you're doing it."

"You can cut to the bad news anytime."

"Well, unless you have additional surgery, and even then it's doubtful, you couldn't possibly father a child, Dane. I'm sorry."

Dane's eyes locked onto the doctor's momentarily, seeking the truth in his eyes.

"Sorry? You're certain, Doc? I'm absolutely sterile, right?"

"Yup. Have been since I performed your vasectomy three years ago. There's been no change."

Dane nodded slowly to himself, and a bemused smile pulled at his lips. The news was met with mixed emotions; most of them joyful.

"Now. I'm going to give it one last try, Dane, because I like you. I know you've had a rotten year, and you're such a high-octane dervish you never slow down. But if you don't, if you don't give up the booze, and the smokes, and start eating some decent food, you're going to die. Do you hear me? D-I-E. You'll be dead. You've got three beautiful children, you have no business even thinking about having more, especially in the condition you're in. I suggest—"

"Thank you, Doc. Your wisdom and...compassion are greatly appreciated. And just as soon as I get through this shit I'm in, I'll turn it around. I promise."

"Don't promise me, son. Just take care of yourself."

Dane nodded and shook Dr. Segal's hand. And he was grinning, the nurse noticed, as he trotted briskly from the office.

·❤·❤·❤·❤·❤·

"Sergeant Denehy? Mac MacKendall. I need to talk to you about dropping the charges against my sister."

Jessica paused at the stove, her ears trained on Mac's voice as he spoke into the kitchen phone.

"That's right. I think I've made a mistake. No, I don't want it to go to trial... Well, I'm going to send her home. Yeah. Okay. Tomorrow morning? Fine. Thanks."

Now Jessica turned to him. "You didn't tell me you were going to do that."

"I was afraid I would change my mind again."

"You thought I would change your mind?"

"I don't know. It's done. I can't live with myself like this. She's my sister...She needs help, not prison." He paused, not looking at her. "I'm going to take her back to Minnesota and get her some help."

"She doesn't want your help."

"How do you know? If Christine needed help, you'd be there, right?"

Jessica didn't answer; instead, she turned back to the stove to stir the stew she was cooking. It's not the same, she thought with irritation. *How could he even consider comparing Chris with Charlene?*

"You're mad now?"

"No."

"Jess, try to understand how I feel! She's my *sister.*"

"You said that." Jessica began sloshing stew into their bowls.

"I really thought you'd understand."

"Mac, she terrorized us! She tried to kill you! She's not only disgraced your family, she's committed a serious crime! I'm sorry I'm not enthusiastic about putting her back on the street. She needs help, all right, but I doubt if you can help her."

Their distance from one another lasted the entire evening and was painful for them both. Mac struggled with his decision; Jessica regretted her harshness. Even in bed they lay apart, each absorbed in their disquiet.

Jessica anguished over the events of the day. The unwelcome, no, *horrifying* suggestion that Jackie might be pregnant with Dane's child overwhelmed her. That Dane might not be sterile renewed a terrible nightmare she thought long forgotten.

Thinking Mac was asleep, she slipped out of bed and quietly entered the nursery where Devon dozed peacefully on his back. Tenderly she adjusted his blanket and marveled at the perfection of his baby fists lying above his head as he slept, his tiny mouth working in a dream about nursing. She wished she could look into his eyes, to see once again that they were Mac's eyes, so brown, so open, so true. Indeed, everyone, even Dane himself, said Devon was a picture of his father. *Mac.*

"Is he okay?"

Mac's whisper made her start and she spun around. The sight of him in the doorway prompted an unwanted memory and for an instant she felt the shame and guilt return, as though she had again been found in Dane's arms rather than just thinking about him as she wondered about Devon. But Mac came to her, his loving arms wrapping around her cold shoulders in the darkness as he, too, gazed into the baby's crib.

"He's fine. He's perfect," she whispered, shaking off the memories and at least temporarily, the uncertainties.

"Come on." Gently he urged her back to their room and into bed. "I'm sorry," he murmured, holding her close.

"Me, too," she replied, closing her eyes, listening to his pain filled heart throbbing as she pressed against him.

"I'll be going down to police headquarters first thing in the morning."

It was only now, after midnight, that Mac realized Dane had not called.

·♥·♥·♥·♥·♥·

Dane Pierce sat on the upper balcony, his view of the Hollywood Hills never-ending. Sipping black coffee, he leaned comfortably back in the cushioned patio chair, squinting in the bright sunlight, the cool morning breeze just beginning to dry his freshly showered, neatly groomed hair. Overhead, a red-tailed hawk swooped low as if to check out the scene. Dane grinned, his clean-shaven face thin but relaxed, his hands steady as he held the cup, his white cotton shirtsleeves rippling in the light wind. On the glass-topped table beside him, a .38 pistol lay in plain view.

A soft smile stayed on his lips as he watched the hawk climb and then dive, enjoying a vicarious flight. Behind him, he heard the sliding patio door open.

"Good morning, Jacqueline," he said without turning.

"Good morning, darling. Enjoying the fresh air?"

"Yes, my love. I've been waiting for you to join me. Sleep well, I hope?"

Her expression suspicious, Jackie walked to the balcony wall and turned to nod at him. Wearing a striking white pantsuit, her attractiveness caught him off guard and he wished fleetingly that he could have had sex with her once more. It would have been different, now.

"You look lovely. Sit down."

Wary of his flattery, she sat, placing her oversized handbag on the chair between them, then noticed the revolver with surprise. "What's this?" she asked softly.

"A gun. It's a prop gun from the studio. Shoots blanks. I brought it home to show it to Alex."

Jackie seemed visibly shaken, staring at the gun with wide, fearful eyes.

"What's the matter? Surely you've seen them before."

"Do you think that's wise? Taking a gun around a little boy?"

"It's pretty harmless..." Dane picked up the gun as if to demonstrate, and Jackie gasped, straightening noticeably in her chair. "So where are you off to, all prettied up?" he cooed, turning the gun slowly in his hands, cocking the hammer and then uncocking it repeatedly.

"Just...shopping."

"Thought you might have a...doctor's appointment."

"N-no, not today. It's Saturday, Dane."

"So it is. By the way, I visited *my* doctor yesterday. Know what he said? Of course you do." Dane's tone was sweet and condescending. He was enjoying every moment of his performance; Jackie became more edgy by the minute.

"What are you talking about, darling? Your ulcer acting up again?"

Dane pointed the revolver skyward and aimed carefully at the hawk, slowly cocking the hammer. Jackie jumped forward.

"Don't!"

"I told you, it's harmless. We were supposed to use it yesterday when the congressman aims it at Mac, but we ran out of time. It's a great scene; it doesn't fire and he kills himself instead. At least, that's what it's supposed to do." Slowly Dane depressed the trigger, and Jackie's scream was lost in the loud report of the pistol.

The kick of the gun threw his hand backward as his wrist bent with the recoil. Dane turned to Jackie with a look of mock surprise.

"Holy shit, did you see that? I could have killed that magnificent bird. And...the congressman...could have killed...Mac..." He purposely let his words trail off. Jackie stood suddenly and backed away. "I wonder," Dane continued thoughtfully, "how this gun got loaded with real bullets? Guess there's a conspirator in our midst, princess."

"You're overworked, Dane. You're totally stressed out. You need some rest." Jackie's voice quivered, undermining her attempt to sound assertive.

"Yeah, maybe I do." He put the gun down on the table. "Now where was I? Oh, the doctor. Funny thing, Jacko, he ran this neat little test, a lot of fun for me, and it turned up the strangest thing. Seems I'm still shooting blanks, even though this gun here isn't. Imagine that."

And now he knew she saw it; the unmistakable glint in his eyes, letting her know it had all been an elaborate act, a scene played out to entrap her.

"I—I have to go," she stammered, tentatively moving toward the door. She would have to pass by Dane to make her exit, and he casually extended his leg, bracing his foot against the wall and blocking her path.

"Don't go, Jacqueline. We have a lot to talk about."

"I have nothing to say."

"I do. First, your maternity is entirely your own problem. If you are pregnant, which I don't doubt, it's some other poor slob's obligation. Your brother maybe? Hey, that would be novel. Incest is best, huh?" Dane chuckled to himself.

"Dane, stop..."

"I'm calling the police, Jackie. I'm making a statement. I'm willing to give you a head start; if you go now, you might be able to escape. Otherwise, I'm afraid everything's going on the table, and your pretty head just might end up there, too."

Jackie reached for her bag. Her eyes never leaving Dane's, she pulled out a small, black book and held it up. "What about this, Dane? What about this nasty little record? If you think I won't use it..."

"I already told you. It doesn't matter anymore. Take it. Call the God-damned *Enquirer* if you want."

Rushing forward, Jackie tossed the journal onto the table and grabbed the gun from where Dane had put it down after firing it. Training it on him, she backed toward the patio door as he jumped to his feet, clearing the way for her exit.

"You'll regret that you crossed me, Dane. Because if I can't have you, neither can she. And despite everything, I love you and could never use this against you...but I *can* make you miserable for the rest of your life. You and that choirboy husband of hers, you can both mourn her forever. It will be a pleasure to wipe that goody-good smile off her face for the last time. And I'll be laughing, Dane, because I know real life, and real love, and real passion. She couldn't begin to know life the way I do."

She turned and quickly went into the house, and Dane leaped after her. "Jackie, stop!"

He overtook her in the living room, throwing his arms around her from behind and pinning her arms tightly to her sides. Violently she struggled, the loaded .38 clenched in her fingers.

"Let—me—go!" she shrieked through her snarled mouth, turning her head brusquely to the side and biting into his muscled forearm.

Abruptly he released her and stared down as a seeping red circle began spread on his shirt sleeve. Before he could react, however, Jackie landed a debilitating kick into his left knee and was rewarded with the satisfying crunch that said she had successfully crippled him. Despite the immense pain that surged throughout his leg, Dane lunged forward, grasping her again and wrestling her to the floor.

Desperately trying to pin her arms away, Dane's entire body began to sweat from the intensity of the pain in his knee.

"You think you can stop me, but you can't. While Jessie's alive you'll never be free. You'll never love me! I can't live with that." Jackie screamed the words into Dane's face, twisting and arching as he tried to restrain her movements.

"If you lay even one finger on her—" he growled as they struggled on the floor. In response Jackie brought her knee up hard and fast against his groin; his left side already blazed with pain as he attempted to wrest the revolver from her hand. "It's over, dammit!"

"Yes, it's over." Violently wrenching her body away from him, her back to his face, Jackie seemed super-human as she freed her hands and cocked the hammer on the gun. Gritting his teeth against the agony of his throbbing knee, Dane tried to turn her around as she fumbled with the weapon, only to receive her elbow in his ribs with a new rush of agony. From behind her, he couldn't see as she turned the gun toward herself, pressing the barrel against her chest.

"Give me the gun!" Dane shouted, reaching around to try and take it from her just as she engaged the trigger.

The bullet burned through Jackie's body and into Dane's.

...and Peace

Mac had already gone when Jessica awoke. There was no coffee made, and her head ached, a hangover, no doubt, from the depression of the night before. Nibbling on an English muffin, she nursed Devon and then packed him up and strapped him into his car seat. Soon she was on Canon Road heading for Malibu.

Roxanne greeted her with surprise.

"Can I leave him for just awhile?" Jessica asked as Roxanne traded gurgles with Devon.

"Welcome to Boy's Town. We have Alex in the kitchen eating Lucky Charms."

"Alex?"

"Dane dropped him off an hour ago."

"Did he say why?"

"Nope. Just something about him and Jackie finishing up some business and Alex being bored. He said he'd be at home if we need him."

Jessica was thoughtful. "Everything he needs is in his bag. I'll be back soon, I promise. Mac's picking up Charlene, and...I just wanted Devon out of the line of fire, you know?"

Roxanne nodded and kissed Devon's head.

Jessica drove back through the canyon with the top down, something she rarely did anymore. The air was still cool, the sky clear, the foliage a rushing, watercolor palette of greens and browns. She didn't make the conscious decision to turn onto Benedict Canyon, but wasn't surprised, either, when she parked the Miata just behind the gold Porsche in the driveway. She stared up at the grand, white columned entrance for a moment, not really seeing it as Dane's house but a kind of established image for superstars living as they were expected to live. She went to the front door and knocked.

While waiting, she looked to the attached garage where all three doors remained closed. She noticed the heavy draperies that hung in the entrance were drawn. She rang the bell.

Perhaps Dane and Jackie had gone out. With a sigh, she turned and prepared to retreat when a sound from the house stopped her cold. The sound was muffled, coming from somewhere inside, but Jessica thought she recognized the unmistakable crack of a single gunshot.

Turning back, she began to knock, then pound, furiously on the front door.

"Dane! It's Jessie! Open the door!" When no answer came, she pressed her ear against the huge, solid white door and listened for any sound. She heard nothing.

Jessica paused, trying to put together her thoughts. Looking back at the windows, she knew she couldn't break the heavy, leaded glass panes. There was a door, she remembered, from the garage to the laundry room, but she didn't know the garage code to open it.

"God," she whispered, her mind racing. She looked back to her car, thinking of her cell phone and wondering if she should try to call Dane, or possibly Mac. She walked toward the car, passing Dane's, and another thought came to her.

Of course, the driver's window was down on the Porsche. She opened the door and slipped into the driver's seat, then began looking around the car. A key, maybe? Dane was careless, she reminded herself, but not that careless. Boldly she pawed through the glove box, frowning at crumbled cigarette packages. Under the seat she found an empty silver bourbon flask and two coffee cups. On the floor of the backseat, a never-used steering wheel lock, and two or three CD boxes. And on the visor was a garage door opener control. Jessica wasted no time in pressing a button.

The opening garage door revealed Jackie's convertible BMW and the door into the house. Holding her breath and saying a prayer, Jessica turned the knob. The door swung open.

Mountains of dirty laundry blocked her way, but Jessica was oblivious to the details.

"Dane! Are you here? Dane? Jackie?" she called as she made her way through the kitchen and into the dining room. "Dane! Where—"

Jessica's words were cut short by the scene waiting for her in the living room. She couldn't even scream.

Frozen to the spot for several moments, Jessica stared at the two motionless people on the floor, their bodies still bleeding onto the carpet where they lay entangled. She forced herself to move, to kneel before them, her eyes wide with shock and disbelief.

"Oh, Dane," she whispered, her fingers shaking against her lips, afraid to touch him and find out the truth. Her eyes wandered over them, seeing the gun still clutched in Jackie's still fingers, its barrel pointing toward the ceiling; Dane's arm around her, awkwardly embracing her from behind, his white cotton shirt rapidly turning a wet crimson.

A sob caught in her throat, a prelude to a whimper that grew into a cry. "No!" she shouted. "No! No, no, no! Oh God. Dane, no..." Unmindful of the blood staining the knees of her jeans, Jessica crawled around Jackie and hesitantly touched Dane's face, stroking his cheek. Doubling over, she bent to press her lips to his forehead, his eyes, his cheek. "Don't be dead. Don't be dead," she whispered, then uttered a sharp cry as Dane fell onto his back with a groan.

"Oh my God. Thank you, God." She kissed him again, then hastily got to her feet. "The phone. Where's the phone, Dane?"

Dane didn't respond, but at least he was alive.

Running into the kitchen, she found a telephone and with trembling fingers dialed "911."

Police stations never close. Inside, waiting on an old, oak chair, Mac thought of the casinos in Nevada, where you couldn't tell if it was night or day outside; the activity went on without regard.

"MacKendall?" the desk sergeant called. "She's on her way. Paperwork's all done. You can go."

Mac looked up as they brought Charlene through the door, carrying an envelope containing her personal items. She stared at Mac in silence, her face unreadable. Sergeant Denehy appeared next, speaking with Mac as Charlene waited in the hard chair.

"I hope you're up to what has to be done, Mac."

"So do I. Whether what I do is right or not, I have to believe in it; I couldn't believe it was right to leave her in jail. I'm probably a fool."

"Sergeant Denehy? There's a call coming in for you. 902-A."

"Good luck, MacKendall...I'll take that call here." Denehy reached for the desk phone.

Mac walked to where Charlene sat staring up at him with a deep hurt in her eyes. She looked younger, more vulnerable, and Mac held out his hand to her.

"Come on. We've got a lot to talk about."

"I don't need you, you know," she said, the tremor in her voice belying her bold words.

"I know that. But maybe I need my sister."

Behind him, Denehy slammed the phone down. "Mac! Wait up."

Mac turned.

"There's been a shooting. Possible attempted suicide. Two people down... Pierce's place in Benedict Canyon. It's against department policy, but I thought you'd want to know. I'm on my way."

The color drained from Mac's face as he absorbed the detective's words. "I'm right behind you."

Charlene clung to the door handle of the Ford, as if hoping it wouldn't rip off in her hand as the old truck rumbled up the canyon toward Dane's house.

"You might not want to come in. It could be bad," he said to his sister, whose face wore a cold mask.

"I've seen bad," Charlene replied, her expression cool despite the wild ride behind the police car. Mac wished he had taken the Miata that morning as he maneuvered the Ford onto the steep concrete drive leading to Dane's grand entrance. Yellow police tape already flapped in the breeze, and ambulances and squad cars were parked helter-skelter near the door. And amid those vehicles a flash of bright blue paint caught Mac's eye. The startling realization that Jessica's car was parked there momentarily ceased his heart; he couldn't get out of the truck fast enough. Running up the driveway in terror, Mac was only dimly aware of the officers impeding his path. Somewhere behind him Charlene followed.

"Whoa there." A policeman blocked their way.

"Please, let me by! I'm Cory MacKendall...My wife's in there!"

A nod from Denehy and the MacKendalls were allowed to cross the line and approach the house. At the porch they were met by two attendants rolling a gurney out the door; its passenger's face was covered and Mac held up his hand. The attendants paused as Mac pulled away the sheet covering Jackie's beautiful face.

Swallowing hard, Mac's own features contorted in pain and he re-covered her, turning away. A great swelling in his throat threatened to strangle him.

"Someone you knew?" Charlene asked quietly.

"Yeah. Someone I knew."

More policemen blocked the front door, and Mac forced his way past them.

"Jessie? Jessie!" he called, his voice laced with fear. He stopped at the sight of two large scarlet stains on the white carpeting in the living room. Several feet away, a telephone lay on the floor. Mac covered his eyes briefly with his hand and took a deep breath, then hurried on to where the activity seemed to be happening in the adjoining dining room.

He saw another gurney on the floor being readied to move, and he held his breath. Looking down, he watched as they buckled Dane's still body onto the frame, an IV bag suspended over him. A large white gauze stripe crossed his breast and shoulder, barely visible beneath the sheet.

"Oh God," Mac moaned softly, immediately dropping to his knee beside the gurney. "Dane?" he whispered. There was no response. Looking around, Mac finally saw Jessica pressed into the corner of the room, her face a silent picture of shock.

Mac let out the breath he felt he'd been holding since seeing his wife's car in the driveway. Going to her, he held her cheeks and turned her face to look at him. Neither said a word until the tears came. His voice was only a choked murmur as he whispered a simple prayer into her ear.

"Jackie's dead," she uttered between sobs.

"I know." Mac enveloped her in his arms, unable to hold her close enough or tight enough to calm himself.

Behind them, Denehy queried the paramedic tending Dane. "What have we got?"

"Single gunshot, .38 caliber. Went through the girl and lodged in his shoulder. He's critical, she's dead. He's lost a lot of blood, has moderate-to-severe trauma to the left knee. Looks like suicide, maybe attempted murder-suicide."

"Yeah?" Denehy picked up the plastic bag containing the gun from the dining table.

"The gun was in her hand."

"Hey, little brother." They all turned to look to Dane, who opened his eyes sleepily. Mac hastily wiped his own eyes and went to him. "Dane, what happened, man?"

"Guess I really pissed her off this time, huh?"

"I don't believe this...she's dead." Mac shook his head in disillusion.

"Your sister, Mac, she's innocent. Tell her...I'm sorry." Dane closed his eyes. The painkillers were sailing him away, and he fought incoherence. "It was... Jackie. But...it's over. It's really over now."

The attendants gripped the handles on the gurney, and Dane reached out to grasp Mac's arm.

"Mac...if I don't...make the cut, promise me you'll take my boy."

"You're talking crazy, Dane. Come on, you're going to be fine."

"*Promise me.*"

Mac squeezed Dane's hand in response, and the attendants rolled the gurney to the waiting ambulance.

"Mrs. MacKendall? Just a few more questions?"

Mac sat holding Jessica's hand while she painfully recounted the events of the morning. He wanted to ask her why she'd come to Dane's in the first place, but the investigators saved him the trouble.

"It was...a social call, I guess." She looked at Mac briefly before turning her eyes back to Denehy's. "I was uncomfortable about my...sister-in-law coming home. Just thought I'd hang out here for a while."

Denehy glanced to the side where Charlene stood lazily against the wall, her chin held high.

Mac let out a labored sigh, then stood. "I need some air, if you don't mind."

Denehy nodded, and Jessica looked pained. "Are we almost done?" she asked, her eyes following Mac as he went out onto the balcony.

"Almost."

Mac closed the patio door behind him and sat in one of the patio chairs. He sighed again, drawing the warmer air into his lungs, hoping to exhale some of the tension that had built into an enormous, black, shapeless mass inside him. The screaming of a hawk caught his attention, and he watched the bird circling and crying distractedly above Dane's house.

His eyes returned to the balcony and the glass table before him. He almost missed it at first, the slim, black, leather-bound book lying face down across from him. It seemed carelessly haphazard; a journal forgotten by an unknown author. Curious, Mac reached for it, and was surprised to see Dane's name embossed on the cover. He opened the book and perused the first few pages.

A diary. Written in long-hand, Dane's now familiar mish-mashed cursive filling page after page. The entries began, Mac read, several years ago, with words filled with loathing and pain:

> *There is no punishment great enough, no torture to equal the*
> *crime; the taking of my dear mother's life cannot be measured*
> *by mere mortal standards of payment. Even a life for a life*
> *cannot come close to restitution...*

Guiltily, Mac closed the book and placed it on his lap. He looked back into the house, saw Jessica still talking to detectives. He looked again for the hawk, but it had flown on. Against his will, his gaze turned back to the journal and he re-opened it, this time skipping to the middle. The date on this page was December 31st.

> *I knew it was hurting her, and still I stood there with Merrily,*
> *kissing Merrily in front her...but she was with MacKendall,*
> *and it's clear he means to have her...*

"Hey, MacKendall," Denehy called, opening the patio door. The journal snapped shut in his hands, and a blushing Mac stood while slipping the book into the inside pocket of his jacket. He turned his disoriented gaze toward the detective. "What do you suppose Pierce meant? He mentioned her name; the deceased gal, I mean."

Mac stared at Denehy, squinting his eyes in apparent confusion. "I couldn't tell you. I honestly have no idea." He followed Denehy back inside, seeking out his sister. "Can you drive a five speed?"

Mac held up the keys before Charlene's face. Taking them from his unsteady fingers, she smiled slightly, the first sincere smile she'd offered him since they were children.

"You oughta know, you taught me fourteen years ago."

"Go dig out the Mazda and we'll meet you at home."

With Jessica beside him in the truck, Mac drove slowly home and did not speak a single word.

Dinner was a dreadful event. With Charlene at their table, Jessica found herself unable to speak, to share even her grief with Mac. Mac was dealing with his own demons, the journal that did not belong to him still smoldering in the pocket of his jacket. Charlene herself watched the two of them with quiet interest, finally letting herself absorb and understand the brother and sister-in-law she had never really known.

"So. Let me get this straight. She was his lover?"

Mac grimaced and Jessica looked away.

"At first. But things just went...sideways. They had problems we didn't even know about." Mac shook his head, more to himself. "I joked about her killing him at New Year's. Remember? I *joked* about it. Man." He looked across the table at Jessica.

Jessica looked up briefly, then back to her plate. "Yes. I remember."

"Well, was he doing someone else or what?" Charlene asked boldly, looking first at Mac then at Jessica.

"Nothing like that," Mac replied, re-filling his wine glass and holding the bottle over Jessica's in question.

"Yes, please."

"She certainly was a looker, from what I saw. He must have done something pretty bad to get her to off him, Jesus!" Charlene continued.

Jessica took a deep breath and turned to Charlene, her voice cold and accusing. "It's really none of your business, and I'd appreciate it if you'd just talk about something else or...shut up."

Mac put down his fork and turned a look of surprise toward his wife, who refused to meet his eyes.

Charlene only shrugged. "Fine," she said simply, and the silence returned for a brief time, with Jessica drinking down her wine and reaching across the table for the bottle.

"Just one thing," Charlene began again, looking Jessica in the face as she spoke. "He said I was innocent. How the hell did he know that unless he was in on something?" She cut herself a bite of steak and popped it into her mouth. "Maybe *that's* why she shot him." She chewed some more, thoughtfully, then resumed her unwanted rambling. "Usually, though, it's jealousy. That's my bet. Another woman." She turned an innocent look on Jessica, who quietly put down her own fork, got up from the table and left the room.

"You really don't know when to shut up, do you?" Mac asked angrily, standing up himself.

"Ah, let her go pout."

Mac sat back down but his demeanor did not change. "You don't get it, do you? She's upset. She's *really* upset. Can't you imagine what it must feel like to walk into a house and find two of your best friends dying on the floor, blood all over the place? Is your heart so damned hard that you can't feel the pain she's feeling, or I'm feeling, for that matter! They were *my* friends too. Ah hell," he spat, standing up and wiping his mouth with a napkin, which he threw down on the table. "You don't give a good God damn about either one of us."

He found Jessica rocking in Devon's room, the baby asleep in her arms. Remembering the quantity of wine she'd had, Mac took the baby from her and laid him in the crib, then bent over her.

"I've gotta get out of here."

"Where are you going?"

"I don't know." He touched her cheek with his fingers, then stood up. "I'll be home later. It might be tomorrow, okay? So don't worry."

He didn't wait for her response, because he knew she would protest if he let her and he wouldn't go. And he needed to go.

·♥ · ♥ · ♥ · ♥ · ♥ ·

Cory MacKendall sat on the beach reading until the sun disappeared into the sea. He picked up where he left off in an all-night diner on Pacific Coast Highway, pouring coffee into himself until he thought he could just spin home. The massive guilt he'd felt at first had faded.

He started at the beginning, reading Dane's life through Dane's eyes, struggling to understand his writing and his wit and his worries. His recount of June, two years ago, was especially poignant.

She is a March breeze blowing into my oppressive August...

July:

She is perfect for the role, although that which makes her perfect also makes her deny the same...but she is, without a doubt, my Mariah... She isn't like any of the others. Making love with Jessica was like unwrapping a wonderful gift. A surprise gift, never expected, especially by the likes of me.

October:

Try as I might, I cannot seem to put her in the background. It upsets me to think that I could become so completely enticed by one woman. She is like a tattoo upon my soul. This is insane.

Later, January of last year:

...and if he's not sleeping with her, he's in love with her, and that's not good. Not good for me, anyway. And she is so sweetly naïve...

March 3rd:

It was a fantastic storm. The footage will be incredible... her bungalow was damaged and I had no place to put her except my cabin and I drank enough rum to float the Pacifica...but only because it was the only way I could stop myself... if she only knew...

March 16:

If I had any doubts about MacKendall they have been dashed, and I have the sore jaw to prove it. Too bad he is such a fool he can't see what he is doing to her, and to himself...

I drove him to the airstrip this morning, playing the role, being his "friend" when in truth I am hoping he takes a wrong turn and ends up in the Bermuda Triangle...or worse. And now she is sad. I can only hope that his abrupt departure will turn her off and buy me some time with her...

It was well past midnight, and the manager eyed him with cool indifference. Mac put the book down and rubbed his eyes, memories flooding his mind. That morning on the airstrip, Dane's smile as he said his good-byes, imparting promises to watch over Jessica's well-being. In truth, hoping Mac's plane would take a dive into the Caribbean.

Mac unconsciously began grinding his teeth. He'd known, the minute he was in the air, he shouldn't have left her there. He took another sip of very black coffee.

March 29:

I guess it was inevitable that we would be together, at least one more time. It was bittersweet. She was different this time, aggressive, hungry, and angry! Oh yes, she is mad at him, at me, at the world, for nothing is right for her; she drove me wild with her fury. Yet even though she took me there, she invited me, she consumed me, and it hurt like hell. To be so close, to have her in my hands, in my arms and yet—I didn't have her at all. She accused me of hurting her before, but that was nothing compared to the pain she is feeling now, because of him. I cannot tell her what an asshole he is, or she will hate me even more...

I put her into the cab this morning. And even though I know I will see her in a few days, nothing will ever be the same between us. For she now knows that I know her secrets. She is lost to me.

Mac took a deep breath. *Why am I doing this?* It was torture, reading Dane's most private thoughts, things he never meant anyone else to read, especially one so pivotal in his unhappiness. But he'd already read so much, he was driven to keep reading. Mac was captivated by the story, the whole story, of another man's obsessive love for his own wife.

He read for another hour or so, then stood to stretch his legs and use the restroom. He stared into the mirror, the harshness of the fluorescent lights giving him a ghostly pallor behind a day's growth on his face. His eyes were reddened, and he splashed them with cold water before returning to the empty cafe and the mesmerizing journal.

June 20:

She didn't want to come. I really had to lay it on thick, I know she was reeling with guilt the whole time we were having dinner. I know it was wrong. She's engaged now, but I had to try. It's inconceivable to me that he could make her that happy. I know her too well. But damn if she didn't slip out of my grasp again and run home to him. And if my guess is correct, she's pregnant too, which of course complicates things terribly...

August 25:

From here on, I fully deserve anything bad that happens to me, for I have caused untold damages upon the one I love more than any other. It is beyond my comprehension that I could be so despicable, and yet when I look into her eyes I lose all sense of responsibility to the outside world. She did her best to deter me, to send me packing, but insatiable ingrate that I am, I used what little magic I have left and captured her, if only for a millisecond. Unfortunately, it takes less time than that to incite an already insanely jealous husband...

...of course he has not returned my calls. I probably would feel the same way, Mac. She is worth your temper tantrums and more.

He'll be home in a day or two and they will make up and have a wonderful baby together. Maybe I will just stay in Cambodia until I can forget about Jessica. Of course, I'll be in my grave by then.

Thanksgiving Day:

I thought a lot about what I must be thankful for. I am alive, and that is right up there at number 2. Number 3 is this glorious little boy who spoils me with good-night kisses and hugs and who calls me "Daddy" right to my face. 4 would have to be the fact that I had dinner tonight with seven other people who still

profess to like me, despite my nastiness. But the fact that Jessie
and Mac will have me at their table after all that's gone down
amazes me. And for now, I am doing pretty well at ignoring the
fact that her smile still turns me inside out.

Jackie is a pleasant surprise, a delectable dish of a girl whose
adoration is almost alarming. She makes a seductive masseuse,
but I can't help but wonder what is really going on behind those
chilly gray eyes...

Indeed, a chill spread across Mac's body as he read Dane's description of
Jackie Spencer. With the vision of her covered body on the gurney, so fresh in
his mind, he was transported back to the night of Thanksgiving turkey and
peppermint schnapps. He shook his head and read on, about the premiere of
Lost Season, about how wonderful Jessica looked to Dane, how it touched him
when she cried. He read about Dane's growing fear that Jackie was not the right
woman, that there was, perhaps, something terribly wrong with her he couldn't
quite fathom. His shock and dismay the night he broke off the engagement, his
disgust and outrage at her for slamming her own face against the wall.
Apparently, it was the same night he'd helped with Devon's birth.

December 29:

Well now I have truly seen it all. Even though I have fathered
three children, I now know I was deprived of complete
fatherhood by not being present to watch them come into the
world. I can honestly say I have not been so scared in years, not
even facing those thugs in Cambodia could match the terror of
watching my darling Jessica in such pain and agony. But what a
trooper! She was far braver than I...I didn't want to see—those
places so personal to a woman. I thought this kind of pain
shouldn't happen to anyone...but the mystery of it all, the rain
outside, the candlelight flickering on her wet face...God! I shall
never forget it as long as I live. And Mac Oh, he had such
command of the situation! I must admit I am in awe of the

man, (and he's a good man, despite the fact that I wish he would fly to the moon next time.) I could not have done what he did tonight, not in this lifetime or the next for that matter. But really, it doesn't matter.

Jackie is acting very strangely. She isn't as pissed off as when I left, but I think we have to have that talk I am dreading. I know now I cannot marry her, and it is wrong to drag this out any longer. And, earlier I found her going through my desk. She knows there are items in there I consider private, including this journal, so I cannot understand why she would ignore my wishes by digging around. The more I get to know her, the more I don't want to. She scares me.

It was the last entry in the book. Thoughtful, Mac closed the journal and laid it carefully on the table. He fell back against the booth and closed his eyes.

·♥ · ♥ · ♥ · ♥ · ♥ ·

Sunday morning dawned even bleaker than Saturday as Jessica slowly sauntered into the kitchen. Her hangover was for real this time, and she stumbled blindly into the room planning to make coffee. It was already made, however, and she came to the eventual realization that the dinner dishes had been done and the entire kitchen sparkled. Quickly she looked around, thinking Mac had come home.

While walking around the corner into the laundry room, she found herself face to face with Charlene, who was loading clothes into the dryer.

"Shit you scared me!" Charlene cried, but she smiled good-naturedly and, for the first time, Jessica could see a resemblance.

"Sorry. I forgot you were here."

"Sorry you had to remember, then," Charlene quipped, tossing a dryer sheet in with the wet laundry. "These things really work?"

"I guess so. They make things smell nice. Mac says they remind him of his mother—" Jessica's words trailed off as she realized what they might mean to Charlene. But Charlene grinned at her.

"You know, I was thinking the same thing." Her smile faded a little. "Your mom still alive?"

"Yeah. She lives in Seattle." Jessica leaned back against the wall and watched as Charlene made quick work of sorting the rest of the clothes and reloading the washer. "You, uh, think you could teach your brother how to do that?"

Charlene laughed out loud. "Don't hold your breath," she advised, leading Jessica back into the kitchen. "In our house, all that shit was women's work. My dad, God love 'em, was a hard-assed Scot. Mom might as well have been an Irish washer-woman. And when I finally got it, what a slave she was, well, I just sorta got crazy mad at her. I wanted her to be strong and stand up to him." Charlene poured herself and Jessica a cup of coffee. Her voice became more serious. "I know she didn't have a choice. It was just the times. Back then, that's how you showed you loved your man. Work, work, work."

Jessica pondered her words. In a few sentences, she had explained so much.

"So, I guess what I'm saying is, don't blame Cory if he doesn't know squat about laundry and dishes."

"Oh he's great with dishes, he's a nut about keeping this kitchen clean. I'm the one who's a slob," Jessica confided suddenly.

"He didn't come home last night."

"No."

"Is that common?"

Jessica gave her a level stare. Charlene was prying again, but somehow it didn't seem so offensive today. "No, it's not."

"I'm sorry. I'm being a nosey bitch again. Just tell me to shut up, like you did last night. I'm used to it, believe me."

"He's trying to deal with what happened, Charlene. He's so sensitive. One thing I've learned about Mac, it takes him a while to process things. He needs time, and sometimes, space. It's hard for me, because I tend to be very quick to accept, to forgive, to absorb things. And," she added a second thought, "I was drunk when he left."

"Well, I gotta tell you, you sure surprised the hell outa me last night."

Jessica smiled. "I promised myself I would never get drunk again." She took a gulp of coffee, then made a face as she realized she hadn't put any milk in it. "I made such a fool out of myself once at a party...I almost lost him over it."

"Sounds like me. I promised myself...a few things...about two years ago. It was tough, man! But I'm still clean." Charlene retrieved the milk carton from the refrigerator. "Calm that down for ya?"

Jessica smiled at her sister-in-law.

"Jessie, I can call you Jessie, right? I need to tell you...I'm sorry about what happened that day I came for the car. I had no right to treat you like I did. Sometimes...sometimes I just say everything wrong. Sometimes I feel like I have to be tough, all the time, you know? Anyway, I'm sorry, and I'm sorry about your friends, too. It must have been rotten for you."

Jessica looked at Charlene, seeing the honesty in her brown eyes, the sincerity of her apology. Moving slowly at first, she put down her cup and went to embrace Charlene, once more feeling the tears sting as Charlene hugged her tightly.

Near brain-dead from exhaustion, Mac fought drowsiness and forced himself to think about what he'd read. The sun dawned as the night manager prepared to leave. He looked at Mac from time to time, undoubtedly wondering what could keep a man sitting in a diner all night long reading.

Mac pushed his fingers through his hair, still surprised at feeling most of it gone. He looked out the window to see his bike and one car in the lot, and past them to the sea and the gray horizon.

Dane was still in love with Jess.

Jackie had read the journal. The entries had ceased in December, the night Devon was born.

"It was Jackie. But it's over now," Dane had said before losing consciousness.

The journal was on the balcony, just a few yards from the bodies.

The gun in the plastic bag, Jackie's weapon...matched the one they'd used on the set the day before.

He flashed on Dane's departure from the set, the paper bag stuffed in his pocket. The gun, of course. He also recalled the fight Dane had with the prop man that morning.

He looked back at the journal; it was fascinating and yet so very hateful to him. He considered walking outside and tossing it into the sea.

Dane still wanted her! How could he not have known? All these months, working side by side, the confidences, the partying and camaraderie, and yes, brotherhood. Dane had become like a brother to him. Yet he coveted the very thing that Mac held dearest in his life. He remembered all too well the times Dane had tried—and failed—to take Jessica away.

"God," he whispered to himself. He felt as if he were being torn into pieces. Dane had saved his life. Dane had been there to help Jessica through her labor. Dane had trusted him and coached him through a difficult role, all the while struggling with Jackie's blackmail. And Dane had discovered the live ammunition in the gun—probably saving his life again. If he had genuinely wanted Mac out of the way, it would have been easy.

And still...the image of Dane kissing Jessica had been indelibly burned into his memory. So long ago, and yet, like yesterday. He remembered how close he'd come to duking it out with Dane, right there on the driveway. Indeed, Dane invited him to take the first punch.

Then there was the fact that Jessica wasted no time in getting to Cambodia when Dane got hurt. And why, what was the *real* reason she went there, yesterday, to Dane's house?

Fatigue jumbled Mac's thoughts, but the critical issue remained clear enough. Should he confront Dane with the journal or let it be?

The manager took off his apron and slid into the booth opposite Mac. He was a big man, heavy set, with a round face and, Mac noticed, kindly eyes.

"Bestseller?" he asked, gesturing toward the book on the table.

"Could be," Mac replied.

"Not many people spend the night with me unless they're lost. You lost?"

"Yeah." Mac looked back toward the ocean.

"Maybe I can give you directions. Know where you're goin'?"

"That's the thing. I don't know." Mac smiled briefly at the man, who held out his hand.

"Name's Frank. I own this poor excuse for a motel." He shook Mac's hand.

"Mac. And thanks for not booting me out of here."

"Takes a while, sometimes, to figure out which way to get somewhere," Frank said, examining his fingernails. "Me, I usually end up going the direct way. It's like there's a fire, see, and if it's a choice between sittin' by the road, choking on the smoke an' all, waitin' for it to go out, or gettin' on that bike and just screamin' through the damn thing, I'll go. With all that damn smoke, you can't ever see what's happening."

Mac tilted his head and stared at the man across from him.

"But that's just me," Frank added with a smile. He got up and went back to the cash register, watching the empty parking lot. "I hope that kid I hired to work mornings isn't stiffin' me."

Mac slipped the journal back into his pocket and stood.

"Thanks, Frank. Guess I'm goin' to a fire."

Once back on the bike, the cool ocean breeze slapping him in the face, Mac's thoughts began to clear. He suddenly realized that facing Dane with what he knew was the only way he could go home.

·♥·♥·♥·♥·♥·

The weather was warm for April, everybody said so. Jessica lounged by the pool, still fighting her headache, one ear tuned on the open door to the house where she could hear Charlene's sing-songy monologue as she stacked blocks before a wobbly Devon.

"Look at you, sittin' up so big! Oh-oh, oh-oh, I got ya!"

Jessica shook her head softly as Devon squealed with delight over his aunt's playfulness.

From the kitchen breakfast bar, Mac watched his sister adoring his young son; beyond, through the glass, Jessica lying in the sun behind dark glasses. He walked into the living room and stood behind Devon where he practiced his sitting skills.

"He'll never be happy lying down again," he murmured, and Charlene looked up in surprise. Mac squatted and brushed his fingers across Devon's silky, sparse blonde hair. "Now you can see *all* the places you can't get to, huh Slugger?"

The baby grasped the finger Mac held out to him.

"Where you been? You look like hell," Charlene commented.

"Any news?"

"She's been on the phone. She didn't tell me anything."

Mac stood and went out to join Jessica on the patio. She moved over, giving him space to sit on the chaise, then took his hand.

"Heard anything?" he asked.

"He's been in surgery all day."

"All day? For a bullet in his shoulder?"

"They took that out last night. Today they're working on his leg. His knee."

Mac was quiet while he digested this news. He squinted toward the sky, then back toward the pool.

"Thought you'd be down there."

"I didn't want to go."

"You can go now; I'll stay with Dev."

"It wasn't Dev. I—I just didn't want to go alone."

Mac met her eyes, barely visible through the sunglasses she wore. "That doesn't sound like you. Last time he got into a scrape, you traveled around the world to be with him. Seven months pregnant, besides."

"A *scrape*?" she asked, pulling the shades from her face to peer into his eyes. She sat forward, searching his face for the reason behind his tone. "What's the matter?" she finally asked.

"I'm..." Mac rubbed his eyes and pushed back his hair, as though it had fallen over his face, which of course it had not. "I'm just tired. I didn't sleep. Let me—Let me get myself together and I'll take you. If you want."

Before he could stand, Jessica leaned close to him and kissed him on the cheek. "I missed you. I'm glad you're home."

Mac nodded and left her for a shower.

Their visit with Dane was brief and strained. He was sedated and largely uncommunicative, Mac himself feeling withdrawn and separate. Jessica seemed not to notice as she struggled with her own grief. But in the days that followed, each seemed determined to create a sense of normalcy they both so desperately needed. She worked in the garden, he worked on his truck. Incognito, they left Devon with Charlene and caught a matinee in town, seeking something to laugh about together. And by Wednesday afternoon, a tentative calm had settled on the household. Charlene had taken up at least temporary residency until Mac could decide what to do with her.

"I hate April. Ever notice how nothing good ever happens in April?" Mac said as he glanced over the tax forms he'd just signed. "I'm filing for an extension. This can't be right."

"Teddy called. I invited him to stop by," Jessica told him as she stood folding baby clothes.

"Property taxes too. It was April when that lunatic Elliot showed up..."

"It was last April when we made love for the first time. It was April when I moved into this house. It was April when you told me you loved me." She continued to fold tiny shirts and miniature blue jeans, and Mac could not help a smile, despite his foul mood.

"What time is Teddy coming?" he asked, closing the file on the taxes.

"Dinner. By the way," she continued, walking back to the laundry room and calling over her shoulder, "Dane is going home tomorrow."

Mac's smile faded as he considered this news. With Dane out of the hospital, there would be no reason not to confront him. He began chewing his lip as Jessica reappeared.

"He's going to need someone to help him for a while."

"And? So?" *Don't say it, Jessie. Please.*

"I don't know what you'll think about this, but...maybe...maybe Charlene could do a few things over there until he's better able to take care of himself. He's gotta hire somebody anyway, and she's so good at that stuff..."

Mac's mouth dropped open, and his eyebrows lifted. "Char? With Dane?"

"He really wants Alex to come home, but there's no way he can manage alone."

"Char?" Mac began to laugh. "I don't know, why don't you ask her?" He continued to chuckle. "If you think they could stand each other."

"I'll talk to him about it first. I offered to take him home tomorrow."

"I can do that."

"No, it's okay. I'd rather you go out and buy me a car. I can handle Dane."

"*You're* going to carry a wheelchair up those steps. I'll handle Dane. We'll get a car this weekend. Together." He gave a "final" look, one he rarely used with Jessica, and she set her jaw but said nothing. She missed the darkness in Mac's eyes as she sailed past him on her way out.

Dane leaned his head back into the couch pillows and closed his eyes. "I can't believe this."

"Can't believe what?" Mac asked, pulling two beers out of the bar refrigerator in Dane's den. He opened them both and handed one to Dane.

"This fuckin' cast on my leg again." He groaned, leaning forward slightly to adjust his leg which was propped on an ottoman.

"How's the shoulder?"

Dane sneered in response, then took a long draught of beer.

"Forget I asked." Mac also tilted his beer, taking in about half the can before placing it on the fireplace mantel. "You going to Jackie's funeral tomorrow?"

"Wouldn't miss it for the world."

The small talk out of the way, Mac could wait no longer. Opening the zippered portfolio he had brought with him, he withdrew and tossed the journal onto the couch beside Dane, then shoved his hands into his pockets. "Thought you might be looking for that."

Dane's expression could have stopped a runaway train. Mac forced himself to take a deep breath as he paced the living room uneasily.

"And yes, I read it. Read every damned page."

"You had no right—"

"I know that, and I'm sorry. Nevertheless, I read it."

"You're *sorry*. And did you do that to punish me, or yourself?"

Mac stopped pacing briefly and stared at him.

"You're pissed off," Dane continued, his voice steady.

"Christ, Dane, you're in love with my wife! How do you expect me to feel?" Mac began pacing again, his agitation building. "I thought—I thought that was all over. I thought we were friends!"

Dane watched him cross the room in front of him. "We *are* friends. And it's a damn good thing I'm laid up here," he began.

"Why? Because otherwise I might beat the shit out of you?"

"No. Because I *would* beat the shit out of you."

"What??" Mac stared at Dane in angry disbelief.

"See this?" Dane held up his right hand, slowly curling it into a fist. "I've been saving this for you since October, and I was just beginning to think I'd never have to deliver it."

"Your arrogance is astounding!"

"I never told you about Cambodia, did I? I spared you the grisly details but you're gonna hear them now. After the baseball bats—oh, and they were nice, Mark McGwires, I think, American made—they had me down, Mac, had me spread eagle in some nasty sewer of an alley, where even the rats were afraid of them, and they were preparing to castrate me with some rusty machete or something—I couldn't see from the blood and sweat pouring into my eyes, even if I *had* been sober. That's when Cambodia's finest showed up and cracked some skulls."

Mac's face reflected his horror as he listened to Dane's story.

"The next thing I remember is Jessica—your *wife,*" he added sourly, "raving at me to wake up so she could go home."

He paused, his eyes not seeing Mac, blind to all but his memories.

"She was my angel. She took care of me. It was Jessie who changed the bandages and washed out my eyes when they got so—bad. She bathed me, she gave me injections when the nurses in that fleabag hospital wouldn't touch me. She read to me and massaged my broken body in hopes that I might someday walk again."

Mac turned his back and braced his arms upon the mantel of the fireplace while Dane continued.

"It was days before I got up the courage to ask about you. Hope against hope, Mac, that she had left you, that I might just have another chance."

"And did you try to seduce her?"

Dane grinned at Mac's question, slowly shaking his head. "Of course I did. We had the Musak, you know, piped into the room, and except for that big rip in the curtain, it was almost kinda dark. She spoon fed me caviar, sipped champagne from a Dixie cup—well, mine was in the drip bag, but still—the bed was kinda small, Mac, and she got tangled in the tube running into my nose, and then that damned bedpan kept getting in the way..."

"Sometimes you are so crude you make me sick."

"Sometimes you are so *stupid* you make *me* sick!" Dane chuckled to himself before his hostility resurfaced. "I gotta tell you pal, when I heard the truth about you and where you were, I was livid. I would have gladly turned you over to those hoodlums back in that alley." He paused, his anger growing. "How *dare* you! How dare you leave her alone like that?"

Mac spun around, his face a picture of agony.

"It was wrong! I know that! But she, she was part of it too. She should never have let you slither through the door. She could have stopped you—"

"I pushed her."

"I didn't see any pushing. Her hands were free."

"She's a sucker for a hard luck case. That heathen Elliott was a walking sob story, and she *married* him. I pulled her strings when I met her, and I did it that day, too."

"Oh, so now you're saying I'm just a sob story?"

"No." Dane looked away, filling his lungs and then exhaling slowly as if he could purge the pain from his body. "You're the exception. That's why it was so asinine of you to react the way you did."

"But you didn't see it through my eyes. You didn't see the woman I have waited for my entire life in the arms of—the man she was crazed over when I met her. You wanna talk about who hurt Jessie? Look in the mirror, Pierce. She worshipped the ground you walked on. And you turned your back." Purposefully, he grabbed the beer from the mantel and drank it down, crushing the can and propelling it into the wastebasket. "She is everything to me. Do you get that? *Everything.*"

"And you are so damned insecure, you still worry that you can't keep her. It kills me that you have so little faith in her. You don't come close to deserving the devotion she has for you. I've seen that devotion, I've seen that passion she has, and it's made me want to die. It's made me want *you* to die." Dane paused and took a ragged breath before continuing. "Yes, I love her and yes, I still want her. But in case you haven't noticed, I love her enough to step down. I made a pact with the devil himself, my life for her happiness. Because I know, Mac, I know as I know my own obsessions and fears, that if she knew about this, knew what you now know, knew about us slamming each other over her, she would die of grief."

Mac stared at him for a long moment. He was right about that; Jessica would surely suffer if she knew of the discord between them.

"Look. I won't lie. It crossed my mind, only a hundred times or so, lying in that stinking hospital over there, I could ask her to come home with me, ask her to be with me, vow to protect her, promise to give her the best damned life. But I didn't. So just stop wagging that self-righteous tongue at me. I'm the one who talked her out of going home. *I'm* the one who put her on that fuckin' plane to New Zealand."

Dane shifted his leg on the ottoman and groaned. When he spoke again, his voice was again calm and controlled.

"Anyway, it hurts to yell. Could you—could you just come over here and sit down please? You're making me nervous."

"*I'm* making *you* nervous?" But Mac complied. Something about Dane's definitive tone compelled him to sit down and listen.

Dane picked up the journal and turned it in his hands, viewing it from various angles. "These words, Mac, they weren't meant for anyone to see. Not you, not Jackie, especially not Jessica. They were for me. Some people take drugs to get them through the days and nights when there's nothing else.

"Now, I won't say I'll try to be a good boy and stop loving her. You should know, it just doesn't work that way. But she can never know about this, about today, not ever. And the only way she's gonna know is if you tell her."

Mac looked at the floor, his throat growing tighter by the minute. Dane was quiet for a time, slowly sipping his beer, mulling over his next thought.

"I meant what I said, about us being friends. I never thought it possible, to be honest. You are the last jerk on earth I wanted to get close to. You beat me hands down at my own game. And you don't play dirty. You make me sick with your morality, your reason, and you're a lousy drinker. You are forever making me look bad. But the night your son was born, it occurred to me that I didn't have to compete with you, and, I won't. You have my word, Mac."

"Why should I believe you?"

Dane peered at Mac, his eyes conveying an honesty so powerful, so bold that Mac was shaken. The machismo image, the usual cocky arrogance was, at least temporarily, stripped away, and Mac knew he needed no further assurance.

With significant effort, Dane leaned forward and extended his hand.

After a moment, Mac reached out, his own hand cautious and hesitant. "Why do I get the feeling you're going to toss me right over the back of that couch?"

Dane's serious face split into a wild grin as he grasped Mac's hand. "There's just one little word of caution," Dane added as Mac sat back down. "If you ever, *ever* take off on her again, if you leave her—for any reason—I'm only giving you twenty-four hours to get back. After that, she's fair game."

"You won't ever have to worry about that."

"I won't. It's you who should worry, pal."

TWENTY-FOUR

Lightning Strikes

Anticipation crackled throughout the theatre like unleashed electricity as the seal was broken on the final envelope. The reading of the winning film title prompted immediate, thunderous applause.

"Accepting the award for Dane Pierce is co-star and Best Actress Nominee, Jessica Taylor-MacKendall."

On stage, Kevin Costner held a gold statuette as he waited.

Best Picture. Dane's Lost Season *was the Very Best Picture of the Year!* Jessica had to remind herself to breathe as she accepted the Oscar from Costner.

At the podium, she stood before the microphone with a grin. "Mac darling, you were right, it is scarier on live TV."

When the applause and laughter had quieted to her satisfaction, her voice took on a serious tone. "I've been asked to make a brief announcement. As some of you know, a terrible...accident occurred last Saturday morning and Dane was critically injured. However," she held up her hand to quiet the murmuring crowd, "however, after several hours of surgery, Dane is doing well, is as ornery as ever, and is watching us right now, I'm told." There was an enthusiastic response from the audience, and Jessica waited patiently for it to subside.

"When Dane first told me about *Lost Season*, he said although the story had been done before, it had not been done by him. I remember thinking that if all it took was arrogance and obstinacy, *Lost Season* was sure to be a hit." The audience laughed. "But, of course, I was only partly right. Perhaps arrogance and obstinacy got the story into script form, but it was diligence, courage, determination, dedication to the art, not to mention nastiness, stubbornness, crude, despicable behavior...and lots of hard liquor that brought *Lost Season* to Oscar tonight." Again she paused for quiet. "Moreover, it took a work ethic many of you have never seen." Clearing her throat, she unfolded a white sheet of paper.

"Dane would like to thank...the Academy." To this there was an uproarious response, for it was well known among Dane's colleagues that he had clashed with the Academy on many occasions. "And...and the following." Jessica read from the list, painstakingly written out by Dane, of the many professionals who had helped bring *Lost Season* to the screen. The list was not over-long, but included both Jack Daniels and Johnnie Walker, and soon Jessica turned it over.

"Also. My dear, beloved mother and father, whom I know are here with me tonight; my wonderful children, whom, by the time they are old enough to watch *Lost Season*, will not recognize their decrepit old dad; my friends, Roxie and Tom, always there when I need them; Jessica MacKendall, a constant pain in the ass, for believing in me when no one else would, and my brother Mac MacKendall, for letting me wear the white hat once in a while."

Her cheeks rosy, her body trembling, Jessica felt Kevin return to her side and gently grasp her elbow.

"From everyone involved with *Lost Season*, thank you!"

They walked off the stage, Kevin whispering in her ear, "You should have gotten Best Actress, dammit. And what did he mean by 'a pain in the ass?'"

"I am," she said simply, reaching on tiptoes to kiss his cheek. "Thanks, Kevin." Grasping the heavy, faux Oscar, she left him to join her husband backstage.

·❤ · ❤ · ❤ · ❤ · ❤·

To some, it may seem unorthodox to picnic at the beach so soon after a funeral. But to a small group of mourners who once called Jacqueline Spencer their friend, a Sunday afternoon picnic was just the right thing to do, the Jarrick house the right place to be. Tom fired up the barbecue and Roxanne pulled out all the stops with mai tais and daiquiris sporting tiny, paper umbrellas. The large redwood deck was the perfect place to relax and watch the children running along the beach in the wind.

Jessica freed her hair from its barrette and, closing her eyes, let the breeze drag it away from her face. Despite the festive mood of the party and the afterglow of Dane's big win the night before, she couldn't help being absorbed by the earlier events of the week, the year. She still saw the faces of Jackie's parents in the chapel, their dour and accusing glances in her direction as she sat between Dane and Mac.

The family had insisted upon an open casket, but neither Jessica nor Dane approached it that grim Thursday morning. And now Mac sat beside her, painstakingly constructing a dime store kite.

"You'd think I'd remember how to do this," he murmured, carefully untangling the kite string and attempting once more to thread it.

"How did she look, Mac, when you went up there?" Jessica asked softly.

His fingers continued to work, his eyes never leaving the kite. "She looked beautiful, and peaceful."

"What was she wearing?"

"Some pink thing. Conservative. Pink lipstick. And a gold cross necklace."

"Did you touch her?"

"No."

Jessica sipped on her straw. The real question, her biggest concern, could not be answered by Mac. Jackie was the only one who knew the answer, and Jackie was dead and buried.

"There. Does this look right?"

Jessica turned to look at the kite Mac held up for inspection. "It's exquisite, darling."

"For a buck twenty-nine, it should be." He stood up and hurried down the redwood steps to the sand, calling out for Megan and Alex.

Jessica watched them for a moment, then turned her gaze back to the deck and Dane, who dozed sporadically in the chaise lounge. He wore cutoffs and sunglasses, and Jessica decided he still looked sexy despite the cast and the bandages.

Roxanne joined them from the house, tripping on the patio door track and nearly tossing a platter of hors d'oeuvres onto the deck. Dane's hand shot out to steady her, and he forced a grin to hide the pain in his shoulder.

"You okay Roxanna?"

"Just my usual, clumsy self," she said, squeezing his hand. "Thanks."

Tom appeared in the doorway behind her, wearing an enormous chef's hat the wind threatened to carry away.

"Actually, she's not her usual, clumsy self. She's a new, clumsy self," he advised them with a smile.

"Oh stop," she warned, shooing him away. "It's not for sure."

At her comment, Dane sat forward and lifted his glasses. "Oh-oh."

Jessica, too, turned questioning eyes on her friend. "Do you think?" she asked.

"Well...I was going to wait until later to tell you guys, we just used one of those drug store kits...but..."

"Oh my God! Rox!" Jessica jumped up and hugged Roxanne. "That's incredible!"

They sat down together, giggling, and Dane lay back, shaking his head. He looked up at Tom.

"You ready for this...again?"

"Oh yeah. I think I'm more ready than she is."

Roxanne's face turned more serious. "I wanted to tell you that day at Macy's. I was going to tell you at lunch, but then when *she* showed up..." She glanced hesitantly at Dane, then back to Jessica. "...all talking about babies, and acting like she was pregnant, well, I just didn't think it was the right time."

Jessica nodded, her face feeling hot despite the breeze. Roxanne kissed her on the cheek and went back into the house with Tom, leaving Jessica and Dane alone on the deck.

Dane raised his good arm and propped it behind his head, lazily regarding Jessica in her chair across from him. Jessica, however, could not seem to keep her eyes on any one thing. On the beach, Mac ran about like a mad man trying to get the kite to fly amid a waterfall of giggles from his daughter. From inside she could hear Roxanne lamenting that the potato salad was too salty. Still, Dane stared.

His voice was low but loud enough for her to hear when finally he spoke. "She wasn't, you know."

"What?"

"You heard me. Jackie. There was no baby."

Jessica's mouth suddenly became dry. She tried to swallow the lump in her throat, tried to appear calm and collected but at last gave up and went to him. She sat at the edge of the lounge and stared into his eyes. *He knew.* He knew about her fear, the terror that had been eating away at her heart for days. She took his hand.

"Thanks," she whispered.

His only answer was a subtle nod.

"So the police think she was despondent over your breaking off the engagement. You didn't tell them about all the other stuff?" Mac asked as they dined on the deck in the late afternoon.

"I just didn't think it needed to be told. She suffered. It would prove no point. But if you want the record set straight..." Dane said.

"No. That's the last thing I'd want to do. I still can't believe it. Whatever happened to Ron Jenkins?" Mac wanted to know.

"He skipped town before I could get to him. Back in Nevada, I'm sure. Please, forgive me if I seem rude, but I'm starved. I feel like I haven't eaten in six months."

"You haven't. Chow down, pal."

Dane put together a second hamburger and turned his attention to Charlene, who'd arrived late and quietly joined them.

"I didn't recognize you earlier. I apologize for ignoring you."

She eyed him coolly. In Jessica's simple, Hawaiian print dress and her rich, deep, rosy-blonde hair falling into luscious curls, she looked softer and more feminine, and for the time being, she refrained from smoking.

"'S'all right," she remarked, lowering her eyes away from his almost intimate stare.

Mac stood and took his fussing son from Jessica's arms, and soon had him back asleep on his shoulder. "The magic touch," he murmured, sliding into his chair while maintaining the rhythm of his stroke on the baby's back.

Dane gazed upon them nostalgically for a moment, then turned his attention back to Charlene. "So, what's next for you? Mac says the two of you are traveling next week."

Charlene stared at her brother briefly. "Maybe," she offered, casting her eyes down. "He thinks I need professional help. And I do, but not the kind he means." Clearing her throat, she nervously wound a paper napkin around her finger. "I owe you all an explanation. I know how I must have seemed, but...I'm not a prostitute and I don't do drugs...anymore. And Cory is not the spoiled rotten kid he was at home. We both sorta expected the wrong thing."

Mac watched his sister thoughtfully; Charlene continued.

"Our father...promised me some money. I came out to get it. I work in a halfway house in St. Paul for runaways like me. They desperately need cash to keep going...they saved my life, and I wanted to repay them. Cory's never known what it's like on the streets, and I hated him for all his luck and wealth. I realize now that luck has little to do with it."

She paused again, stealing another glance at Mac, her eyes apologetic. "So really, I can go home and take care of myself. We even have children in the house, not legally, of course, but they have no place else to go. They're like, homeless, you know? They're tough kids, but I like working with them."

"Why don't you stay here for a while?" Mac said quietly.

"In L.A.? L.A.'s a pit."

"St. Paul is a pit."

"True, but it's my pit and I have friends there."

"You have family here."

"I don't want to sponge off you, Cory. And I never told you how sorry I am for what I did. I was just so filled with hatred. Please understand."

Jessica looked at her sister-in-law with compassion.

"Look, we can put together some funds for the house. It's not a problem. Just...hang around for a while." Mac's voice was sincere.

"No. I don't want your money." Charlene's defenses went up.

Dane sighed, painfully adjusted his leg, then nonchalantly leaned forward on his fist.

"Say, Mac. Not to change the subject, but you wouldn't know of anyone looking for a job...given the circumstances, my affairs are a mess. Everything went to hell when Pete moved out."

Jessica smiled at his use of the term "affairs," and he winked in her direction.

"I need someone who can help look after Alex and manage my estate. Or maybe that's manage Alex and look after my estate. They can't be afraid to handle a tough little kid."

Mac shook his head slowly. "No, can't think of anyone off-hand."

Dane turned innocent, questioning eyes on Charlene.

"How old is your son?" she ventured, cautiously allowing their eyes to meet.

"Seven."

"He's a hellion, Char," Mac put in.

"I beg your pardon?" Dane demanded in mock irritation.

"Couldn't be any worse than my brother was," Charlene teased. "I'd like to meet him."

"He's crashed in the bedroom upstairs. Maybe you could give us a ride home later. If..." he added smoothly, "you're not busy." His voice wrapped her like fine silk.

Charlene considered his offer, squirming uneasily on the bench beside him. Dane flashed an intriguing smile, his eyes emerald and shining. She colored, turning to Jessica for support.

Jessica gave her a barely perceptible shrug and reached beneath the table to take Mac's hand. Charlene took a deep breath and turned back to Dane with a hesitant smile. "I, uh, guess I can do that."

"That would be nice. You know, I really do need to get another car. Alex is getting a little big for that backseat. I was thinking about a Jag XJ-5. What do you think, Jess? Mac?"

Before Jessica could deliver a scathing comment, Dane turned away and casually slid his arm along the top of the railing behind Charlene.

Mac and Jessica turned to one another and shared a common, unspoken, joke.

"And so it begins," Mac murmured, watching Dane's animated movements as he imparted some seductive tale to Charlene. Jessica could not hear Mac's words, but her thoughts mirrored his, adding only the word "again" to the end.

"Life's full of beginnings and endings, isn't it?" she asked as they drove away from Tom's driveway, their two sleeping children strapped into the backseat of Jessica's new Lexus.

"Yup. I never realized that more than the week Dev was born."

"Were you surprised about them?"

"What, that Dane's hitting on my sister? No. Nothing Dane does ever surprises me. Not anymore." Mac said.

"I often wonder if he'll ever be happy, you know?" Jessica said. "He didn't really love Jackie."

"No. Dane's a complex person. He makes life hard for himself. He won't be happy until he makes some changes."

"Like what, you think?"

Mac shrugged. If she didn't know, he wasn't going to tell her.

Jessica frowned at him. "Charlene's about as far from Jackie as you can get."

"She's no China doll, that's for sure. Dane's in for one hell of a surprise if he thinks he'll uncover any frailties there. She'll nail him in a minute if he tries anything she's not into."

"Oh come on, Mac. She's not that bad."

"Oh yeah? At this very moment she has a switchblade strapped to her leg."

"What?" Jessica demanded, her eyes wide.

Mac's nod was serious and foreboding. "And a grenade or two in her bag."

"She was right! You *are* a brat."

"No more so than you, *ma petite*. By the way, you still interested in that Acura NSX?"

Epilogue

AFTER ALL

"Got everything? It's a long way to come back for your toothbrush." Mac slammed the trunk on the Lexus as Charlene nodded in an exaggerated fashion.

"I have never seen anyone fuss more than you do, Cory."

"I just don't want you back too soon."

"Thanks, I appreciate your sentiment. Don't worry, Dane and I plan to enjoy this trip. We can both use the change in scenery. I still say L.A.'s a pit."

"Los Angeles may look like a garden spot after you've seen Cambodia," Jessica advised, joining them in the MacKendall driveway with Dane behind her, holding seven-month-old Devon in his arms.

"Ah, come on. It's not so bad. You were just looking at it through the harsh glare of hospital lights. It's actually quite exciting," Dane mused.

"How you can find it exciting after what happened to you..." Jessica shook her head, smiling as Dane handed the baby over to Mac.

"Charo here is going to take good care of me, aren't you, sugar?"

"Don't 'sugar' me, Dane. And don't expect me to sit by while you get your ya-yas on with some Southeast Asian honey. I'll be the first to put you back in that hospital."

Dane grinned. "Isn't she something? Jess, did you know Charlene carries a switchblade?"

"I should have had one the day I met you."

"Ooh, low." Dane feigned devastation, then his expression changed to one of discomfort. "Think I could get a couple of aspirin from you?"

"What, the mere mention of the hospital puts you in pain?" Mac teased.

Jessica gave Dane a level stare before turning toward the house. She'd clearly seen him slip his prescription bottle into his pocket after breakfast; his knee still bothered him.

"I think I have something that might help," she murmured. "Come on."

Dane followed Jessica into the house and to the guest bathroom where she retrieved a bottle of Tylenol and struggled with the child-safe cap. Glancing into the mirror, she was somehow struck by the image awaiting her; Dane stood close behind her, his chin nearly level with the top of her head. He rested his hands on her shoulders and peered solemnly into the reflection of her eyes. Quietly she studied his features, suddenly taken by subtle but significant changes she hadn't noticed before.

Mesmerized by the moment, Jessica searched Dane's face for traces of the man she'd met nearly two years ago. She felt she'd known him forever. What was different?

"Take a good look," he said softly, gently squeezing her shoulders. "Don't forget me."

Jessica didn't respond. The warmth of Dane's hands, his chest against her back was comforting; the sincerity in his eyes embraced her. *The hunger was gone.* The heated lust that had shrouded his love had been put to rest; and in its place, Dane reflected a peace that had eluded him for so long.

Jessica's vision began to blur, and she turned abruptly to face him, throwing her arms around his neck, the unopened bottle clenched in her fist.

"Oh Dane, please be careful," she whispered huskily. "I hate to see you go."

"Why the hell would I want to be careful? I wouldn't have any fun," he said with a chuckle, but the fierceness of his embrace belied his comic words.

"I mean it," she sniffed, "don't screw around. Please!"

"I don't need more screwing at this point...Charlene keeps me well sated. She's the first woman I've met that knows more about sexual gratification than I do." Dane's eyes teased hers with merriment, then softened with his smile. Sighing, he pressed his cheek against hers. Nervously Jessica glanced toward the hall, but she continued to hold Dane tightly about the neck.

"Don't worry. If he starts toward the house, she'll put him in a headlock," Dane assured her. Jessica gave him a look of surprise, and he took the opportunity to run his fingers through her hair. "Besides, he needs time to say good-bye to *his* sister, too."

The words touched her deeply and the tears returned.

"I'm your sister now? That's a new one," she said, trying to keep her tone light but failing. She brushed a tear from her cheek.

"Okay. You're right. You're no more my sister than Scarlett was Rhett's."

"You do love her, don't you Dane?"

A sad smile played upon his lips as he shook his head ever so slightly. "Ah, Jess," he began, again stroking back her hair. "Guys like me don't fall in love. That stuff's for *real* heroes. Like Mac."

"You're breaking my heart," she whispered.

"Hey, it's what I do best," he mused. "Anyway, all I ever wanted was for you to throw your panties at me."

She stared at him for an endless moment.

*God, I could just about fall into those deep green eyes of his...*Had someone said those words to her once, long ago?

They stood outside the door to Studio B. They faced the wind together on the leeward deck of the *Pacifica*. He grasped her arm from a bed in a

Cambodian hospital, his eyes bright with agonizing pain; she dug her nails into his wrist as they fearfully awaited the birth of her child. They lay together on a blanket under Caribbean stars.

Dane's lips pressed firmly against her forehead and his hands caressed her back lovingly. "You have the number where I'll be most of the time. Call me if, you know, you need anything."

"Of course," she managed hoarsely. "And you do the same."

"The last thing you want is another call from Cambodia."

"Don't be silly. You call me, you hear? Even if it's only to say hello. You can afford it," she teased, sniffing again.

"I don't know, the way Charo is spending my money."

After a lingering, affectionate gaze, Dane sighed and moved his hands to rest against her cheeks. "We'd better go. She's probably running out of endearments for dear old Mac. Although I would never run out of them for you, sweetie."

Miserable, but somehow content, Jessica hugged him once more before stepping quickly from the bathroom, only to stop and turn again to face Dane.

"I guess you didn't really need these," she said softly, extending the small bottle.

"As a matter of fact I do. This other shit puts me to sleep, which tends to rather piss off my bed partner." He grinned at her, and they walked companionably, arm in arm, back to where Charlene and Mac leaned over a map spread across the trunk of the car. Devon dozed on the backseat.

Charlene smiled a gracious welcome to Dane's wink of gratitude.

"Dane, I've decided we should go to Hawaii instead."

"Right, sugar. Just as soon as I finish the film in Cambodia."

"But Dane—" Charlene's protests were cut off by Dane's hand, pinching her lips into a pucker and kissing them briskly.

Mac secured Jessica in his arms and looked into her face, the pink nose and somber, swollen eyes evident. "Dammit Dane, I wish you'd quit making Jessie cry," he quipped.

Dane approached Mac and squeezed his shoulder. "The day I quit making women cry, I'll have to retire. Let's hit the road, shall we?"

Dear Reader

Thank you for reading STARCROSSED HEARTS, Book 1 of the StarCrossed Romance saga!

If you enjoyed this book, now would be a great time to post a review. Many thanks!

Now, turn the page for an excerpt from A HERO'S PROMISE, Book 2, where one man struggles to uphold an impossible promise to another who will never know if the promise is kept.

"Rich with intrigue and suspense, Carter's story of love and family will enthrall readers. A HEROS PROMISE weaves together threads that solve a murder and blend two families."
Four Stars!
Robin Taylor, for Romantic Times Book Club

Next Up ...

A Hero's Promise

She was moving things around inside the refrigerator, hoping to hide her embarrassment until her face recovered. Finally, returning with a can of whipped cream, she turned to him.

"Okay, so tell me why you're here. This better be good." Her serious tone matched her expression. She tilted the whipped cream can over his mug and depressed the nozzle. Whipped cream exploded from the can, over-filling the mug, spattering the table, the wall and Dane's chin.

"Holy shit, woman, I can think of better ways to get even," he said with a grin.

"Oh! Oh, I am so sorry..." Jessica grabbed a paper napkin from the counter and hastily wiped up the mess from the table. Looking back at Dane, she saw the small traces of whipped cream on his face. Without thinking, she reached across the table and wiped them away with her finger.

His eyes locked on to hers just as his fingers wrapped around her hand, pulling it slowly back toward his face. Helpless against his power, unable to deny him, Jessica sat mesmerized while Dane pulled her fingertip into his mouth and gently sucked the whipped cream from it before slowly releasing her.

"Yum," he told her, licking his lips and lifting the hot mug. "Now, you were saying? Or would you like me to spray this time?" He took a quick sip of the steaming cocoa, then picked up the whipped cream. "This could be fun."

Jessica swallowed hard, her chest rising and falling rapidly in response to his actions.

"No, I—I think maybe I'll just have marshmallows."

Buy it now - available at all the usual places. Click through BeaconStreetBooks.com for more info!

About the Series

STARCROSSED HEARTS – BOOK ONE

Silver screen heroes Dane Pierce and Cory "Mac" MacKendall are as different as cognac and Perrier, and newcomer Jessica Taylor loves them both. Despite his tantalizing green eyes and raw sexuality, Dane is not the man she thinks she needs. It is the solid and devoted - if hot-headed - Mac who wins her hand and heart, and who must endure a lifelong challenge to keep that heart safe from Dane's unending pursuit. From Hollywood soundstage to the Grenadine Islands, **StarCrossed Hearts** makes a journey around the world and through the lives of some very real characters you will not soon forget.

A HERO'S PROMISE – BOOK TWO

If you read **StarCrossed Hearts**, you know that heart-breaking, womanizing Dane Pierce will not find it easy to walk away from the one woman that sets his soul on fire. Promise or no promise, Dane will do everything he can to win back Jessica's love. Now, the heart-stopping sequel you've been waiting for: **A Hero's Promise**, a story of pain and redemption, and a love that survives the very worst of life's challenges.

THE GYPSY IN ME – BOOK THREE

Their children have grown. Some are his, some are hers; some are half-siblings, others step-brothers and sisters. Growing up the offspring of Hollywood's brightest stars, Jessie, Dane and Mac's kids are each special, each a little neurotic, and each seeking love. The MacKendall and Pierce daughters square off in this next installment to the **StarCrossed series**; who would have thought that history would repeat itself?

To Love a Vagabond - Devon's Journey - Book Four

He's the son of not two, but three Hollywood megastars. The legacy he's inherited feels more like a ball and chain than a fairytale. Devon MacKendall's life has never been easy, or simple, and when the worst possible tragedy befalls him, he heads for the road in this heart-wrenching installment of the **StarCrossed saga.** Meeting the elusive Brandy Owens is the last thing he wants, but she just might be the salvation he needs. *Coming 2023!*

Meet Anne Carter

Creating fiction gives one the power to design other lives, filled with romance and adventure, intrigue and passion. My own writing career began in middle school creative writing class, inspiring me to later major in literature. All it took was one teacher' encouragement and I was on my way.

I'm the author of nine published novels, including mystery, romance, paranormal, alternative romance and even a middle grade reader. As for the personal stuff, I'm a Virgo, a procrastinator, like warm better than cold and drink neither Coke nor Pepsi. I was born in the Midwest but migrated to California as a child. My hobbies include doll collecting, photo restoration and writing, of course. My favorite sport is ice hockey, my favorite TV shows include mysteries, romance (Duh!), cooking shows (*Great British Baking Show!*) and crime series that make you think and not count bodies. I am married to my hero of 40+ years and have 3 great kids and two--wait, THREE--delightful grands. Visit me at Beacon Street Books (where I also blog,) Facebook, and other fun cyber spots.

Also by Anne Carter

The StarCrossed Romances

StarCrossed Hearts – Book 1

A Hero's Promise – Book 2

The Gypsy in Me – Book 3

To Love a Vagabond – Book 4 (2023)

The Beacon Point Romances

Ever & Always

Point Surrender

Cape Seduction

Angel's Gate

and next up

Amoroso Pass

Paulie & Kate

Unmasking Paulie Bingham

For the Love of Katrina Bingham

Now Available from **BeaconStreetBooks.com**